NIGHT SHIFT
BROKEN HEROES

EVIE JAMES
CRAIG RICHARDS

Night Shift—a medical romance with suspense.

Broody, senior ER doc **Atticus Thorin** is about to hit 40 and facing burnout. His reputation for being an icy authoritarian doesn't faze the fiery young redhead who just started in his department. From the moment they smack into each other, he's intrigued by her admonishment to mind his manners.

Not only does **Samantha Sheridan's** sassy wit inflame the doctor's temper, but it also ignites the flames of his desire.

Atticus has spent years crafting the unbreakable walls around his scarred heart. He's built his life around control and emotional detachment, a fortress no one has ever breached.

When the one man who should have been Samantha's protector trades her to mafia drug lords, it sparks the doctor's deep-seated need to rescue those in danger and fires emotions he thought were long since buried.

Chased by the sins of her father, Samantha's past demons come to steal her away in the night, leaving her with nowhere to turn except to the man who breaks her in ways she never thought possible.

Teetering on the edge between heartbreak and healing, will he be the one to catch her, or will he let her fall?

A sizzling, workplace, age-gap romance, Night Shift is the first in a new series of standalone romances featuring a trio of brothers who each must learn to tear down their walls and find out what it's like when you allow yourself to break.

Copyright © 2024 by Evie James and Craig Richards.

All rights reserved.

No part of this book may be reproduced in any form or by any electronic or mechanical means, including information storage and retrieval systems, without written permission from the author, except for the use of brief quotations in a book review.

This is a work of fiction. Names, characters, places, and incidents are either the products of the author's imagination or are used fictitiously. Any resemblance to actual persons, living or dead, businesses, companies, events, or locales is entirely coincidental.

This book contains art, images, fonts, and other material that have been protected under copyright law. All necessary licenses have been obtained for this material and every image, font, and cover art is used with permission from the respective copyright holder. While it is acceptable to view and download this material from the book, any unauthorized reproduction or distribution of these materials is strictly prohibited and will not be tolerated. This includes, but is not limited to, sharing or selling any of the images, fonts, or cover art without the express permission of the copyright holder. Furthermore, any kind of manipulation or modification of the copyrighted material should not be carried out without the written permission of the original copyright holder. It is the responsibility of the reader to ensure that all necessary licenses have been obtained before any of the material is used in any way. Any violation of copyright law will be met with legal action.

ISBN eBook 979-8-9901969-0-2
ISBN Paperback 979-8-9901969-1-9
ISBN Audiobook 979-8-9901969-2-6

Cover and Book Design: Evie James

Publisher Contact:
Evie.James.Author@gmail.com

The desire of the man is for the woman;
the desire of the woman is for the desire of the man.

~ Madame de Staël

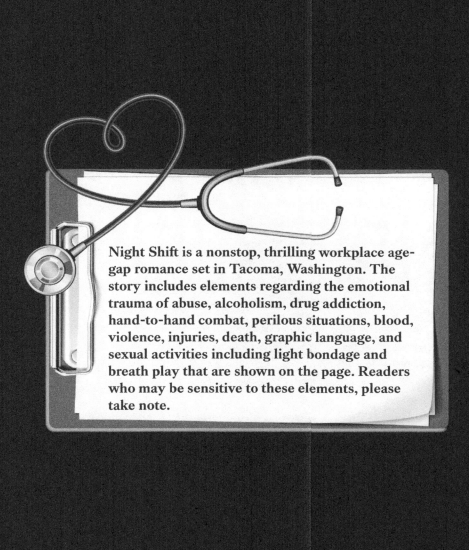

Night Shift is a nonstop, thrilling workplace age-gap romance set in Tacoma, Washington. The story includes elements regarding the emotional trauma of abuse, alcoholism, drug addiction, hand-to-hand combat, perilous situations, blood, violence, injuries, death, graphic language, and sexual activities including light bondage and breath play that are shown on the page. Readers who may be sensitive to these elements, please take note.

Chapter One

Out of nowhere, an ambulance came barreling around the corner with lights flashing and sirens blaring, just as I was about to turn into the parking lot at St. John's Medical Center. I jerked the wheel, narrowly avoiding a collision. Shaken but unscathed, I pulled into the parking lot on the corner of 19th and J, then cut the engine.

A cool rain fell relentlessly against my windshield while I sat in my car across from the entrance to the emergency department. Streetlights fought against the darkness to illuminate the area, creating halos of light in the misty air.

When I'd come here for my formal interview a few weeks ago, finding parking had been a nightmare. Thankfully, tonight, the staff lot had plenty of open spaces. As I braced myself for the night shift, the knot in my stomach tightened. I hated to admit it, but I was a bit nervous. Probably not for the reasons I should have been, but nevertheless, I was. And this wasn't the typical new-job jitters or worry about being late. No, instead, my mind fixated on something far more mundane—the vulnerability of my car in this dimly lit, unprotected parking lot.

There was no security guard in sight. This car wasn't much, but it was all I had. Dealing with a break-in or having to fix a shattered window was the last thing I needed. I'd purchased this used GTI thanks to the money I saved on tuition after receiving a scholarship for nursing school. It had taken nearly all the funds I'd saved from working at the hospital too, but I loved the little black beauty—stick shift and all. This ratty thing had given me freedom for the first time...freedom to move away from Aberdeen. Strangely enough, I was more concerned about my car getting vandalized than what awaited me across the street.

I was fifteen minutes early and had already seen three ambulances pull up to the emergency bay. It was clear that today was our turn to take on the city's worst cases. In Tacoma, St. John's and Tacoma General, both Level II Trauma Centers, alternated handling these intense days. By the look of it, my first shift was going to start off with a bang.

As I sat there in my car gathering the courage to head into the hospital, I reminded myself that the high-speed pace and medical challenges of the ED were, in fact, what had drawn me toward this choice.

I glanced down at the dashboard. The clock read 17:49. My shift would start at 18:00. A thrill of excitement surged through me while butterflies fluttered chaotically in my stomach. "You asked for this," I whispered, taking a deep breath to rally my courage as I removed my keys from the ignition. I double-checked that I had my essentials before I exited the car: stethoscope, trauma shears, at least four pens, my lunch—which hopefully

Night Shift

I would get a chance to eat—and my wit. Just as I stepped out of the car and locked it, another ambulance screamed into the bay. "Oh boy," I muttered under my breath, "this is going to be a shit show."

My fingers instinctively wrapped around the end of my braided ponytail that kept my long, curly red hair in check as I crossed the street. The style was practical, no-nonsense—much like the rest of my life.

This was it, the big leagues. A chance to prove myself as a newly minted CEN. I had always been the type to take charge, to push through hardships and challenges, and tonight would be no different. The constant whirl of activity, the sirens, the urgency—it was all here, and I was ready for it. Ready to face the chaos, ready to make a difference.

With a deep breath, I pushed open the doors to the emergency department, stepping into a world where every second counted, where my skills and my decisions could save lives.

When I badged in to the break room, a sea of unknown faces stared back at me, each displaying the weariness typical of this job. I glanced around, taking in the unfamiliar surroundings of my new workplace. The shift was just about to begin, and everyone already looked like they didn't want to be here. Welcome to the night shift.

The charge nurse entered, clipboard in hand, a clear signal that the pre-shift briefing was about to start. "Let's make this quick. We're swamped because of the wreck at 509 and Pacific," she said.

Board rounds were a familiar routine from my time in Aberdeen, but here, in this larger hospital, the stakes seemed higher. As I focused on what the charge nurse was sharing with us, nervous energy gripped me. The rapid arrival of ambulances moments earlier indicated that many daunting tasks lay ahead this evening.

After finishing her briefing, the charge nurse paused briefly and said, "Everyone, meet our new staff nurse." She gestured in my direction. "This is Samantha Sheridan, joining us from the Emergency Department at Harbor Regional Health in... Aberdeen, was it?"

"Yes, ma'am," I replied with a smile on my face, forcing myself to remember that I was the new kid on the block.

A twinge of awkwardness made my cheeks heat. The skeptical, almost pitying looks everyone now gave me were irritating. I could almost hear their thoughts: "This girl is going to be eaten alive at a hospital like this." Well, I was more than ready to prove them wrong. I couldn't wait to show them I belonged here.

The charge nurse moved on, outlining the night's current caseload and doling out our assignments. She reminded us it was trauma day. When the briefing wrapped up, a surge of adrenaline shot up my spine, and I headed toward the triage area. I remembered what Steven, the hiring manager, had warned me about night shifts at St. John's. "Expect to hit the ground running from the get-go," he had said. And boy, he hadn't been exaggerating.

When I rounded the corner, I found the scene was mostly as I'd expected. Nurses were attending to the first three ambulances, their actions routine and measured. But it was the frantic activity surrounding the last ambulance that seized my attention. As fate would have it, inside that ambulance was the very patient I had been assigned to.

The shouting seemed to be getting louder, and with each step I took, the commotion increased. I tried to spot the nurse who was supposed to give me the shift report, but wasn't sure which one she was. The charge nurse had told me to look for Bethany Raines, saying she'd have dark brown hair tied back in a ponytail and that she was a dead ringer for Alice Braga. She was probably right in the thick of things. I needed to get closer to see if I could spot her.

Before I could reach the triage area, additional medical staff flooded into the area, security officers in tow. This combination signaled trouble. One of my new coworkers was holding a little black case—that wasn't good. At my old hospital, those black cases held locking restraints for combative patients. I wasn't a fan of using them, but it beat getting punched or kicked. If they were already having to resort to restrictive measures like this, it was going to be a long, hard shift. The tension in the air was almost tangible, and my heart rate accelerated as they moved the patient into a trauma room. This was the reality of a Level II Trauma Center—unpredictable, unyielding. And this was my new normal.

I steeled myself. "All right, Sam, no backing down now," I muttered under my breath. My past, riddled with its own kind of chaos and pain, had prepared me for this moment. The hardworking, determined part of me was raring to go, even as a wave of apprehension tightened my stomach at facing this new level of encounter.

From the threshold of the doorway, I watched the rapid-fire activity unfolding. The room resonated with the sounds of shrill, rhythmic beeping from monitors and the scuffling squeaks of shoes moving across the vinyl floor. Six determined hospital staff encircled the patient, who was thrashing wildly on the gurney, his movements punctuated by violent, angry screams. One nurse pressed her hands firmly around his neck, trying to hold his cervical spine in alignment. Beside her, two techs applied pressure on his wrists and shoulders. At the same time, two security officers held down his legs, applying pressure right above the knees and feet. Another officer put locking restraints around the patient's wrists and then moved to secure his ankles.

One of the security officers hissed, "Do you want the chest strap, Doc?"

The doctor, who had just brushed past me as if I wasn't there, responded with crisp self-assurance, "Hold off on it until we can get a good look at his torso for any visible trauma."

Finally, I spotted the nurse who I would be relieving. I headed toward her. Even with her mask on, she did, indeed, resemble Alice Braga.

The patient reeked of alcohol. I stopped dead in my tracks as the smell sent a shudder through my body. The familiar scent triggered terrible memories of the only other person I had ever known to have this kind of pungency—my father. For the smell to be this strong, the man must have had a lot to drink. I shook my head, snapping myself back to the situation at hand. As soon as I stepped up next to the nurse, the doctor barked an order at me.

"We need a CT scan, stat, but there's no way this patient is going to hold still, so we'll need a sedative to knock him out." He pointed a finger at me as if I had some Ativan or propofol just sitting in my pocket.

My eyebrows shot up, and the pharmacist standing by the door said, "Don't worry about the medication. I got that. You go put the order in for the scan."

After placing the order, I returned to the nurse at the head of the bed, and she began to update me on the patient.

"This guy arrived by ambulance following reports of a collision. Evidently, he ran a red light and T-boned a minivan crossing the intersection of 509 and Pacific, which caused another car to swerve and crash into a utility pole. This was a bad one." She paused. "I'm sorry, I haven't even gotten your name yet. You walked straight into a mess." The side of her jaw clenched.

"It's Sam," I told her. "And your name is..."

"It's Bethany," she said, glancing at me. "Well, Sam, the vehicle he hit had a mother and three children in it. When police and fire arrived at the scene, they found the mother desperately clinging to her little girl, screaming for help while her other two kids were still in the van. They found the two boys deceased on the scene. When they brought her here, she was semiconscious. They took the little girl, who was in critical condition, to St. Mary's Children's Hospital just up the road. They lined this patient in the field, so we were able to draw blood right away. We're waiting to see what his blood alcohol level is, but I have no doubt that it's high."

I was trying my best to focus on her full report, but the lingering memories of that night—the one that had irrevocably changed my life—rushed to the forefront of my thoughts like a dark wraith.

"Is everything okay?" Bethany asked, concern settling in her brow. "You're turning a little pale, and the last thing we need is another patient in the department."

"I'm okay. This...is one of those cases that's hitting a little close to home." I plastered on a soft, professional smile and dug my nails into the palms of my hands to force the dark memories to recede. "Don't worry. I'm good."

While I listened to the rest of her report, I forced myself to slow my breathing. When working in the emergency department, I had one rule—not to get too invested in my patients, no matter how they affected me, good or bad. Sure, I cared about them, but if I allowed my emotions to get involved, it could be detrimental to their care. It was better to keep a professional distance. Caring for this man was going to be difficult because of the horrific pain his actions had caused innocent people. He would be a challenge, forcing me to confront my ethical boundaries.

But I was duty-bound to care for him, even if he was a piece of shit, so much like my father.

Giving Bethany a sidelong glance, I arched an eyebrow and asked, "Want to place a bet? Closest to guess his EtOH, and the loser buys coffee."

The left corner of her mouth rose. "I think you're going to fit in just fine here, and I'll take that bet. I'll go with a solid three-fifty."

The doctor rushed past me once again, this time hitting my shoulder hard enough to spin me around. In a flash, he was gone, no apologies offered.

Bethany chuckled and said under her breath, "Don't take Dr. Thorin's rudeness personally. He's like that to everyone."

Once we got Mister Charming situated and sent to CT for his brain scan, Bethany briefed me on the two other patients I'd been assigned so far tonight. Thank God they weren't in critical condition.

"I suspect that guy we just moved to CT is going to be a handful, so if he gets out of line, just remember to call security," Bethany said, then paused. "We don't need a new nurse getting assaulted by some drunk."

Looking at her with a half smile, I assured her, "Just because I'm new here doesn't mean I'm a new nurse." The last thing I wanted was for someone to get the wrong idea about me being an inexperienced "baby" nurse from a small town. I knew how to handle my own.

"Sassy and pretty... I hope you know I meant nothing by the 'new nurse' comment," Bethany said, nudging me playfully with her elbow. "And as much as I would love to stay and see what the EtOH result is for that guy, I'm fucking exhausted. It's been a long day for me. I have a hot shower, a bottle of wine, and some Outlander waiting for me when I get home."

I decided to treat our bet like they did on The Price is Right. "Sounds good, and I'll guess three hundred fifty-one for the patient's blood alcohol level." I figured this would give me a fifty-fifty chance of winning. I'd spent enough time watching that silly game show to know that this was a solid strategy.

Bethany threw me a scowl hard enough to make my cheeks heat. "You're really going to Price is Right me like that?" she asked.

"Sorry, Bethany, but I like to win."

She shook her head in disbelief, but her scowl cracked into a smile.

"All right, all right... You'd better be honest about the test result when it finally comes in. Obviously, we don't want any HIPAA violations, so don't go texting me what it came back at, but I'm going to go ahead and give you my number because... well, I guess I like you."

As Bethany walked away, a sense of relief lifted my spirits. I was pretty sure I'd just made a new friend.

It wasn't long before the patient was wheeled back from CT in a frenzied state, ruining the upbeat vibe I'd just established with Bethany. Why did my first shift have to start like this, with such a violent and out-of-control drunk? I walked into the man's room and asked the security officers if they knew what had happened during the scan. Normally, I would have received a call if something unusual was going on with a patient.

"He grabbed the CT tech and spit at her," one of the officers said.

Well, that explained why the patient was now wearing a spit hood.

That kind of behavior didn't shock me. I'd been around enough raging drunks to know they could do just about anything when inebriated. "Do we know if they completed the scan?" I asked.

The ED tech who had accompanied the man said, "He didn't even make it into the scanner before spitting at her, which forced us to pull him out of there real quick."

Moving closer to the edge of the patient's bed, I gently but firmly rested my hand on his shoulder. I might have been calm on the outside, but on the inside, turmoil raged within me like wildfire. In my most composed nurse's voice, I said, "Sir, it's very important that we complete the CT scan. You've been in a car accident, and we need to check for any brain injuries. I'll speak with the doctor about possibly giving you something more to help you relax, but I'm going to need your cooperation."

His response was a vehement "Fuck you!" followed by an attempt to spit at me. I gasped, grateful for the spit hood's protection. My hand dropped from his shoulder, and I stepped back. In an instant, despite his restraints, he managed to latch his fingers around my wrist, twisting it roughly and digging his nails into my skin. "I'll kill you, you little bitch!"

The security guard was on him in a split second, squeezing the tendons of his wrist, weakening his hold just enough for me to yank my arm from his fingers.

Turning my face from those in the room, I leaned down and grasped my knees for support. His words reverberated against my skull. Darkness fringed my vision as a memory of someone else saying those same words haunted me. I exhaled slowly, regaining a semblance of composure amid the commotion.

Night Shift

"I'll be right back," I barked at the security officers. "I need to take care of my wrist where his nails dug into my skin." Fleeing to an adjacent room, I cleaned my wrist with an antiseptic wash. Luckily, he hadn't broken the skin. I sure as hell didn't want to have to report an injury incident and deal with all the medical evaluations and follow-ups.

I took a few minutes to calm down and shove his words into the locked box within my mind where I kept so many other dark memories.

No, this definitely was not a good first day.

When I returned to the drunken man's room, we administered more medication and were finally able to subdue him enough to get him back to CT for a successful scan. This time, I accompanied the patient alongside security, carrying extra medication in case he became combative again. Some people had an extremely high tolerance for sedatives.

Once we had the monster back in his room and settled, I checked on my other patients to see how they were doing. Thankfully, their cases were less complicated. One of the patients had jammed his toe pretty badly by kicking a bedpost on his way to the bathroom. We were waiting for the X-ray results to determine if there was a fracture. The other patient had been suffering from an upset stomach since last night. We still needed to check the results of her blood work, but she would most likely receive a GI cocktail shortly. First, though, I needed to perform an oral challenge to ensure she would be able to keep it down, because she had reported three episodes of vomiting over the last twenty-four hours. Since these results were going to take some time, I notified my charge nurse that everyone was tucked in and that I would be going on break.

When I entered the break room, I was relieved to find it empty. The space was modest in size and designed for function.

The walls, painted a soothing shade of pale yellow, had an eclectic mix of motivational posters and funny hand-drawn illustrations that made me laugh despite this hellish first shift. Contributions from various staff members, I guessed. In one corner of the room stood a large whiteboard filled with shift schedules and important announcements. At the bottom was a playful doodle left by someone seeking to lighten the mood.

As I milled around the well-lived-in space, I reflexively rolled my shoulders to relieve the tension that never seemed to leave. In the middle of the room sat a long, sturdy table surrounded by mismatched chairs. Along one wall there was a small kitchenette area, equipped with a microwave that had seen better days, a coffee machine that had to be the lifeline of the department, and a refrigerator stuffed with quick meals and energy drinks.

The far end of the room housed a couple of worn but comfortable-looking couches, flanked by a small bookshelf filled with an odd assortment of medical journals, outdated magazines, and a few well-thumbed novels. Sitting on top of an issue of the Journal of Hematology & Oncology was a medical romance book with a Dr. McDreamy on the cover. Only in a hospital break room would that be normal.

The silence was a welcome change, considering how this shift had started. But just as I was grabbing my food from the fridge, I heard the door open behind me. I couldn't stop myself from letting out a soft, audible sigh. "So much for a quiet break," I mumbled.

With my lunch bag and bottle of water in hand, I turned around and smacked right into a solid figure. The impact sent the bag tumbling from my hands. Standing before me was the same doctor who had been barking orders at me earlier. His presence dominated the small room just like it had the trauma room. His air of indifference made it even more impossible not to notice him. He didn't even flinch or apologize; he merely straightened his coat as if I were the one who had intruded into his personal space.

"Hello," I managed to squeak out, mustering politeness despite his rudeness. As I bent down to retrieve my lunch, I realized my face was inches away from his crotch and jumped back into a standing position, nearly launching the bag across the room.

"You must be new here," he responded in a dismissive tone, his eyes scanning the room rather than focusing on me.

I tried my best not to be a smart-ass but couldn't resist. "And you must have forgotten what they taught you in your manners class at doctor's school. Normally, when you run into someone, you apologize, or if someone says hello, you say hi back," I said, my grin a thin veil hiding my annoyance.

He shot back, "I must have missed that class in—what did you call it—doctor's school? I think I was too busy learning lifesaving procedures to attend that one."

"Ah, so lifesaving trumps basic human interaction? I'll make a note of that in my Common Sense for Doctors handbook."

He chuckled, something I imagined he rarely did. "Common Sense for Doctors? Now, that's a book I want to read. Did you write it during your How to Survive Encounters with Arrogant Doctors nursing class?"

I laughed, raising my chin. "It's a personal project that I'm still working on. Your type is actually discussed in Chapter One: 'How to Identify a Doctor with an Overinflated Ego.'"

He smirked and eyed me curiously for a moment. "I'm honored to be your muse. But tell me, does Chapter Two cover 'How to Charm Said Doctors'?"

"Only in the appendix," I replied, spinning around in an attempt to hide my flushed face. I headed to the table. "It's a short reference."

I found a seat and plopped my lunch bag down onto the table, embarrassed yet oddly intrigued by the sharp exchange. As I sat there, trying to steady my rattled nerves, Dr. Thorin's voice lingered in my ears. Deep and resonant, the timbre had flowed down my spine and into my most intimate places. It had a panty-melting quality that was impossible to ignore. I found myself thinking absurdly that he could read the dictionary aloud, and I would be utterly enraptured, hanging on every syllable. Damn, his voice alone was auditory erotica, sending a thrill through me that was both unexpected and unsettling.

Famished and flustered, I savagely rummaged through my food.

"Did you bring anything good tonight?" he asked in a muffled voice.

When I glanced back, I gulped at the sight of his muscular ass. He was bent over, with his head stuck in the fridge. And, oh my God, what a magnificent ass it was. Nearly choking as I salivated, I coughed out, "What was that?"

With a meal-prep container in hand, he pulled his head out of the fridge and asked again, "Did you bring anything good tonight?" I hadn't noticed before, but he was tall and ruggedly handsome. When he stood upright, his head towered over the fridge, and the first thought that popped into my head was, I would climb him like a tree.

Shaking off that image, I reached into my lunch bag and pulled out an oven-roasted turkey sandwich, a bag of chips, and an apple. With a shrug, I lifted my sandwich into the air, almost as if I was offering him a bite, and said, "I have a 'sammich,' chips, and an apple."

He rolled his eyes and gave me an exasperated sigh. I immediately wondered if I had said something stupid. Did he think I was actually offering him my food? Was I offering him my food? What the hell was I doing with my hands?

"What did you call it?" he asked in a tone somewhere between sarcastic and genuinely curious.

"A sam-mitch," I pronounced, emphasizing each syllable. "It's what my mother used to call them when I was younger. It's just a stupid word that kind of stuck with me."

"And your name is Sam," he noted, more as a statement than a question.

I lifted one eyebrow. It puzzled me as to how he knew my name. I was sure I hadn't mentioned it yet.

"You have a look of confusion on your face. You're probably wondering how I know your name," he said smugly, pausing long enough to let my brain catch up. "It's on your badge."

How stupid could I look in front of this man? I snapped my head down. "Oh yeah, I forgot about that. It's actually Samantha, but I go by Sam for short."

"Looking forward to the next chapter, Sammich."

Did he just call me Sammich?

Before I could even raise my head and respond, he'd left the break room. Dumbfounded, I remembered I only had a few more minutes on break and needed to eat. There was no telling when I'd get another chance. The whole point of taking a break was to stuff food into your mouth as quickly as possible because you never knew if you'd get another opportunity during your shift. As I gobbled down my sandwich, I mulled over what had happened to me in the last few hours. My mind kept returning to the drunken patient who had unsettlingly reminded me of my asshole father and all those years I had spent living in a nightmare. And I was surprised by the unnerving feelings that had been stirred by this man, this doctor, who had gone from barking orders at me to calling me Sammich.

Despite his standoffish nature, he possessed an undeniable charm, a kind of rough, untamed allure that was hard to ignore. His scruffy salt-and-pepper beard that subtly hinted at his age was a striking contrast to his curly, dark brown hair. In the fluorescent lighting of the break room, his eyes had appeared almost gray. While his smooth bronze skin suggested he spent time outdoors, his clinical demeanor suggested otherwise. Remarkably, his face was devoid of wrinkles, likely a result of rarely smiling. I chuckled at the thought. It was as if with his aloof attitude he was challenging the world to take him as he was, without any pretense or effort to conform. Although he came off as a jerk, there was something intriguing, albeit frustrating, about him. Why were all the hot ones such arrogant assholes?

I bolted upright, my heart racing. The beats echoed in my ears, making me feel like a frantic, trapped animal, as if I were still running in my nightmare. Sweat beaded on my forehead as the remnants of the dream flickered through my mind. Reaching up, I clutched at my chest. It was the same dream that had haunted me since childhood.

It always started the same way, with the sickening stench of bourbon and the slurred shouts of my father echoing down the hallway to my room. The darkness of the night would then envelop me as I ran, driven by sheer desperation. Behind me, my father's voice would thunder, his drunken fury the driving force behind my terror. His fingers, calloused and unyielding, grazed the ends of my hair, but I was too quick, darting out of his reach and sprinting toward the safety of the woods behind our house.

Night Shift

In my dream, as in my distant reality, the night was my ally, guiding me along a moonlit path. I maneuvered through thick brambles, branches catching on my clothes as I wove in and out of the dense underbrush. I knew these woods like the back of my hand. Every root and rock was a familiar landmark in my escape. Just ahead lay my secret box, beside the gnarled, old oak tree. It was my shelter, a place where the shadows swallowed me whole, somewhere I could be away from his intoxicated rage.

My breath came in short, sharp gasps, misting in the chilly night air. Leaves crunched beneath my feet as I tried to tune out my father's distant, muffled curses.

If I just kept running, if I could reach my secret sanctuary, I would be safe. Safe until the alcohol claimed him, lulling him into such a stupor that he would forget his own daughter, forget the chase, forget the violence that lurked in his fists.

I dove into my hiding spot. My heart pounded in my ears, a relentless drumming that seemed to ricochet off the sides of the box. I pulled my knees to my chest, wrapping my arms around them and trying to make myself as small as possible. Suddenly, the forest fell silent, as if it was holding its breath. And I knew I was alone again. I had mastered the art of evasion. All I had to do was run fast and hide well, and the man who should have been my protector couldn't catch me.

But the nightmare didn't end there. Today it seemed to cling to me, the remnants of terror engulfing me like a suffocating shadow. I gasped for air, a panic attack clawing its way up my throat. My pulse raced with a wild, uncontrollable rhythm that threatened to claim my ability to breathe.

I was no longer that little girl in the woods, but the fear, the sense of helplessness, was as real as it had been back then. It was a reminder of where I'd come from, of the demons I carried within me.

Struggling for air, I stumbled out of bed, searching my small one-bedroom apartment for something, anything, to help me breathe. My bedroom offered no relief, so I staggered into the kitchen, my chest heaving. There, I found a paper bag. Clutching it around my mouth, I inhaled and exhaled, trying to steady the rapid rise and fall of my chest.

"Janie, my therapist," I muttered to myself, "focus on what she taught you, Sam." I closed my eyes, forcing myself to recall my therapist's words, the strategies she'd taught me for managing these crippling episodes. Should I call her? It had been ages since a panic attack had hit me this hard. But then, today hadn't been just any day.

If I had any hope of getting through this, I needed to use the mindfulness techniques she'd taught me.

Hurriedly, I scanned my apartment to find five things I could see. Two bananas on the counter, a stack of flattened moving boxes in the center of the living room, my favorite book sitting on the end table, my clogs by the front door, and my keys on the table. Next, four things I could touch. I found the saltshaker, the mail I'd been ignoring on the table, the fuzzy blanket crumpled on the sofa, and the lock of hair I always twisted around my finger. "Come on, focus, Sam," I murmured to myself, continuing to press the bag over my mouth and nose. Then I sought to find three things I could hear. A slow drip from the faucet, my neighbor's TV, and a dog barking in the distance. Now, two things I could smell. A lavender double-wick candle and a half-empty bag of coffee. And last, one I could taste. The box of Cap'n Crunch on the counter. I let the paper bag fall from my lips as the panic receded, then glanced around the room again.

Nestled in a rundown building in a less-than-desirable neighborhood, my apartment was a small haven I had carved out for myself. The walls, once dull and peeling, now boasted a fresh

Night Shift

coat of cheerful yellow paint. It was a color that always managed to lift my spirits. Despite the unit's modest size, I had been able to arrange the space to feel cozy and welcoming. A new sofa, adorned with bright throw pillows, occupied one corner of the living room, facing a small TV that sat on a secondhand stand. The single bedroom was cramped, but I kept it tidy. Every item in this apartment, from the thrift-store curtains to the potted plants on the windowsill, was a testament to my independence. It wasn't much, but it was mine—a small sanctuary where I was rebuilding my life, one day at a time. Soon enough, my new job, as challenging as it might be, would earn me a good living, and I'd find a better place.

Taking another shaky breath, I steadied myself against the counter as my mind, traitorous as it was, flickered back to my first day at St. John's Hospital. Over and over, it replayed the dark image of a drunk man—my patient—slamming his car into a minivan, killing two young children and seriously harming a third. Although I hadn't seen the accident, I'd witnessed the aftermath, the lives torn apart. The distraught mother had arrived at the hospital covered in a mixture of her own blood and that of her daughter. Her anguished screams as she was told about the loss of the two little boys had shattered my heart. I rubbed my wrist where phantom nails dug into my skin. The drunk man's face haunted me, conjuring up memories of my father pulling out onto the road and swerving at the last second but still slamming into the side of an SUV.

This was my reality now. Saving lives and dealing with loss was what I had chosen, what I had worked so hard for. I was determined to make my life count, particularly when things were tough, unlike the abusive father I had and unlike the kind mother I'd never truly known.

"This is your path, Sam," I whispered to myself. "You're here to make a difference, to fight for those who can't." And with that thought, I found a sliver of peace.

Throwing the paper bag in the garbage can beneath the sink, I pulled a glass from the cabinet, got a drink of water, and returned to bed. I needed to sleep and be rested for the day ahead. It was part of the job. If I made a mistake, I could kill someone. In the often chaotic turmoil of the ED, I had to be my best, stay in control, and politely manage the thousands of demands that came my way.

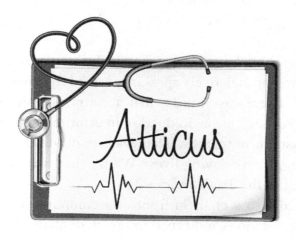

Chapter Two

As I walked into St. John's Hospital, where I'd spent more than the last decade of my life as an ED doc, a familiar sense of frustration washed over me. I was thirty-nine, teetering on the edge of forty, and the weight of my years in medicine was bearing down on me. Each step through the hospital seemed heavier than the last. Here I was, starting the second night of my monthly night shift rotation, questioning every decision that had led me to this point. Had it all been worth it? The constant grind, the never-ending stream of patients, the battles with bureaucracy—it all seemed to blend into a monotonous rhythm that left me more discouraged and exhausted with each day that passed. The prospect of turning forty only amplified my internal crisis. Was this relentless cycle of night shifts and emergency medicine all there was to my life? Had my passion for saving lives been buried under a mountain of disillusionment and fatigue? These thoughts swirled through my mind, a stormy prelude to another long night.

Another thing I was tired of was the fucking incompetence in this department. Relatively speaking, we did the same shit every single day. There was a routine to it. Routine provided structure. Structure reduced error. Reduction in error theoretically led to positive patient outcomes. That was what we were supposed to be doing, right? Saving lives? Wasn't that why we took the Hippocratic oath? To *do no harm*?

I settled into a chair in front of a computer at one of the clinical workstations and typed in my credentials. If there were ten more of me in this department, we would never have issues. But instead, I had nurses who seemed like they'd just gotten out of diapers and doctors so old I feared they might turn to dust if I breathed on them too hard.

The change to the night shift had brought me nothing but headaches, frustration, and the onset of a new twitch in the corner of my right eye. My coworkers already thought I was an asshole; adding a twitch was probably going to make me seem even more unapproachable. Not that being an unapproachable asshole was necessarily a bad thing, especially when it kept the most annoying people away. Rewind a few years, and it had been a different story. When I'd first started practicing, I'd enjoyed helping people and teaching my peers. Now, I fucking hated it when nurses asked me stupid questions. My medical degree wasn't meant to be used as their personal Google search. I even found myself scoffing at new doctors who put in every fucking order that existed because they couldn't use their brains to figure out what the problem was on their own.

I began to scroll through the current patient load, but my mind drifted. There was one upside for tonight—Bethany.

Night Shift

She worked a swing shift sometimes, so tonight I would have someone I could rely on for a few hours at least. She was one of the best nurses in the department. Although I was a little worried that she might still be upset with me for what had happened between us a year ago, she did a damn good job of keeping things professional while we worked together, and I appreciated that.

There weren't any formal policies against dating coworkers. The hospital's administration might have frowned upon workplace relationships, but I'd never let that kind of bureaucratic bullshit stop me before. Still, after Bethany, I'd sworn off going out with anyone at St. John's. I didn't need the possible hassle. At least she'd been cool about our short-lived tryst.

Leaning back and clasping my hands behind my head, I pretended to study the information on the screen while I thought about the new nurse I'd run into in the break room last night. She had entered the ED with bright-eyed enthusiasm. And while the violent drunk responsible for the horrific wreck had caused everyone in the department trouble, she'd seemed undeterred, almost energized by it all. Her eagerness to dive into the fray, as well as her curiosity about every detail of the chaotic scene, reminded me of my early days. Back then, the adrenaline rush of life-and-death situations and my raw passion for emergency medicine were what drove me. I missed the days when my career had been more than just a series of procedures and systematic decisions, when each shift had brought the thrill of the unknown.

I'd already fucked up by giving the new nurse a nickname, which told me there was something about her that I was attracted to. There was a freshness about her, a sort of vibrant energy that was hard to ignore. She had gorgeous, long, curly red hair that would stand out in any room, and her skin was pale, a milky white. There was a scattering of freckles across her nose. And those freckles, something about them was just...hot. She was definitely easy on the eyes, and I caught myself wanting to know more about her. Maybe this would be another positive thing about rotating to nights? Despite her sassy nature, it had been refreshing to have someone speak to me as if I was just another coworker and not tiptoe around because of my hardass reputation.

"Doctor Thorin, is everything okay?" a woman said from behind me. "You've been staring blankly at your computer screen for the last three minutes. If you need more time to get settled before we perform the reduction on the patient in room eighteen, let me know."

I snapped out of my reverie and looked up to find that it was her, the nurse from the break room. Dropping my hands to my lap, I spun the chair around to face her.

"Hello, *Sammich*. I wasn't aware you'd be gracing the ED with your presence tonight."

As expected, her cheeks flushed red, and her ocean-blue eyes disappeared behind a squint in reaction to my deliberately provocative tone. Her arched eyebrow and frown made it clear she wasn't amused, which provided me with a certain delight.

With a grace that belied her agitation, she straightened up, and countered icily, "So you're sticking with *Sammich*, Dr. Thorin? Is Sam really that hard to remember, or does your big doctor brain need more consonants spilling out of your mouth to always sound clever? Perhaps it's your ego needing to be propped up by reducing the nurses you work with to trivial objects?"

I couldn't suppress a grin. "Ah, Ms. Sheridan, always a delight with your sharp tongue. But of course, you misunderstand. It's merely an affectionate nickname, a bit of levity in our otherwise serious department. Surely you can appreciate a little humor, or does the nursing code forbid it?"

Night Shift

Her reply was swift and laced with equal parts sarcasm and confidence. "Humor in the ED is always welcome, Dr. Thorin, but maybe try a joke next time? I'm sure your brilliant doctor's mind can come up with something more original than a sandwich pun. Is 'Sam' too mundane for your superior tastes? Must be challenging, having to stoop to my level, what with your vast intellect constantly seeking out complexities even in the simplest of circumstances. Or, more likely, it's just another way to remind us mere mortals of our place beneath your exalted surgical hands."

This exchange, charged with a mutual snarkiness, was starting to become almost enjoyable. We were embroiled in a battle of wits that seemed to entertain us both. This was a rare kind of teasing, one that could keep the long nights in the ED lively and somewhat bearable. And as much as I was loath to admit it, it was the kind of challenge I relished—a fiery spirit that matched my own.

I raised an eyebrow, feigning surprise at her boldness. "Defensive much, *Sammich*? If you can't stand the heat, maybe the ED isn't your kitchen. We need our nurses to be as tough as they are skilled, after all. But don't worry, I'm sure you'll find your place soon enough—or find another department more suited to your delicate sensibilities."

Sam's retort came quickly. "Oh, Dr. Thorin, you thinking you're God's gift not only to medicine but to women is so *cute*. Your reputation certainly precedes you, and let's just say it's not all about your medical skills. But don't worry, I'm well equipped to handle whatever 'heat' you think you're bringing to this kitchen."

I wasn't used to being talked to like this. A part of me wanted to scold her and remind her I was a doctor and, in a sense, her superior, but I hesitated. I had just gotten on shift, and it was only the second night of my rotation. I wasn't looking to make my nights miserable by irritating this woman.

So I chose to continue the banter.

"If I told you why I call you Sammich, you'd probably vagal out right before my very eyes. The last thing I want is to lose a nurse and gain another patient. Now, don't we have a conscious sedation to perform in room eighteen?"

Sam paused for a moment. "It's no longer called conscious sedation, Dr. Thorin. The patient is not always conscious, so we now refer to it as procedural sedation. I'm sure you knew that, but maybe your age is finally catching up with you and you're forgetting the new things you learn."

Just as I was about to snap back at her, Bethany walked up and interrupted us, possibly helping me avoid an embarrassing situation, because who knew where the conversation would have gone. I stood up, shoved a pen into my breast pocket, and smiled. Bethany, not having any idea about the friendly skirmish Sam and I were having, gave me that mischievous little smile I knew all too well. It was the kind of smile that held a secret, one laced with a touch of naughtiness.

"How much longer are we planning on making this patient wait?" Bethany asked. "The pain medication given earlier is wearing off, and the sooner we get this fracture reduced and splinted, the sooner he'll feel some relief."

"That's exactly what I asked him when I found him here over five minutes ago, staring blankly at his computer screen. Followed by a diatribe about what an M. Deity he is," Sam said smugly, crossing her arms.

I took a deep breath. The exhale leaving my chest turned into a low, menacing rumble. Bethany's and Sam's pupils dilated as my growl triggered something primal within them both. For a moment, their eyes fixed on me like I was a piece of meat.

Night Shift

To redirect their focus, I asked, "Bethany, Sammich, is everything ready to perform the *procedural* sedation?" I emphasized the correct term and directed my words strictly toward Sam to ensure she knew I'd heard her correction, even though I hadn't appreciated her condescending tone when she had *informed* me of the update. She rolled her eyes.

Bethany whipped her head around, looking at Sam with suspicious awareness. "Sammich, huh? I see he's already given you a nickname. That's adorable." Then she turned back to me, her eyes blazing with resentment. Maybe she wasn't entirely over what had happened between us after all?

"The crash cart is in the procedure room," Bethany said after an awkward beat of silence. "The patient has been placed on capnography, and the cardiac leads are still intact. I have a simple face mask ready to run oxygen at two liters per minute when we're ready to sedate. The pharmacist is ready to go, and I've notified one of the techs to be ready to splint as soon as the bone is set. Is there anything else you need before we get started, *Dr. Thorin?*" She enunciated my name like she was spitting daggers. The flirty expression she'd worn just moments ago had transformed into a familiar look of indignation that I'd seen from women who knew they were no longer the queen of my court. Fuck!

"Okay, great. Then we're all set and should have everything we need. Who's going to be my primary nurse for this patient during the procedure?" I cautiously inquired.

Bethany glanced at Sam and then back at me. "I'm sure *Sammich* here will do just fine assisting you. Since I'm no longer needed, I'll be checking on other patients. Let me know if you need anything."

A look of confusion flashed across Sam's face, and her body language subtly shifted to a more closed-off posture.

I directed my attention toward Sam. "Well then, let's get this patient sedated, set, x-rayed, and out of here. It's just a broken bone, so there's no sense in keeping him here longer than necessary."

Bethany walked off with a scowl on her face that told me she'd have words for me later, but that was the least of my concerns. The last thing I wanted was the gossip train locomoting around the department. Given that Sam was new here, I was sure she had already heard plenty of stories about my difficult nature. However, based on our interaction in the break room yesterday and today's encounter, I had a gut feeling she wasn't too bothered by it. Perhaps she was accustomed to dealing with disrespectful doctors who treated her like an inexperienced "baby nurse." The words that poured out from her sexy full lips when she spoke to me suggested she could hold her own. That captured my interest. Her sass made me want to shut her pretty little mouth up with my cock.

"Dr. Thorin, you're doing it again," Sam said, once again interrupting my thoughts. Admittedly, it was necessary. The idea of me fucking her mouth was not something I needed to be distracted by before we performed this procedure. *Routine. Structure. Patient safety*, I reminded myself.

I couldn't let this firecracker sidetrack me from performing my duties. My infatuation was something I would revisit later.

I headed for the procedure room, Sam in tow.

Once we arrived, I stopped at the foot of the patient's bed and explained our plan to him. "All right, Mr. Stewart, we have our team ready." Using the chart in my hand as a reference, I pointed at each person as I introduced them. "This is your nurse, Samantha; Brian, our pharmacist; Jake, one of our ED techs who will help me stabilize your arm while I pull traction; and Kat, our respiratory therapist. We're going to be performing a procedural sedation. We'll begin by administering some propofol to relax you, allowing you to sleep. You don't have any allergies to medications, correct?"

"No, sir. Well, not that I know of," Mr. Stewart said.

"Good. We're going to monitor you as we administer the sedative, and once we see you're comfortably sedated, I'm going to apply traction to your arm, set your radial bone, and then the tech will splint your arm while you're still under. By the time you're awake, we'll have taken a subsequent X-ray to make sure everything looks good, and then we can get you discharged. Does that sound like a plan, Mr. Stewart?"

"Sounds like a plan," he echoed.

"Mr. Stewart, how much do you weigh?" the pharmacist asked.

"About one hundred seventy-five pounds."

"Perfect," the pharmacist noted. "Okay, last question. Have you ever been sedated with propofol before?"

"No, sir," Mr. Stewart said.

"Let's start him at point five milligrams per kilogram," I said, but Sam looked at me quizzically, as if I had suggested the wrong dose.

"Do you have something to say, Samantha?"

She paused, taking a deep breath in. "I think we should start Mr. Stewart on a lower dose since he's never had propofol before, maybe point two five milligrams per kilogram?"

I nearly bit into my lower lip. Sam, perhaps inadvertently, was questioning my dosage in front of everyone.

"And what exactly is your rationale for starting at a lower dose, Samantha?" I asked, my voice coming out terser than I had intended.

"Well, I'm trying to be the patient advocate that Mr. Stewart deserves. I figured if we started at a lower dose and he doesn't respond to it, we can always increase the dosage," she said, taking another deep breath to gather her thoughts. "And if we give too much propofol, Narcan or Romazicon aren't effective reversal agents, so we would have to use physostigmine, which isn't a perfect solution either."

"Well, I'm glad you know your drugs and your reversal agents, Ms. Sheridan, but I think I know what I'm doing," I said with a sharpness that cut through the tension of the room. "Now that we're done questioning the people who have actually done procedural sedations, shall we get started?"

Sam's face turned bright red as her eyes fell to study the edge of the bed. My comment had apparently struck a chord in her. Perhaps I might have been too firm with her, but I wasn't used to being questioned, especially not in front of staff and patients.

However, she had made a good point.

I looked over at Brian and glanced at Sam. "Let's start with point two five milligrams per kilogram and see how Mr. Stewart responds. If need be, we can continue with subsequent doses of point five milligrams per kilogram until he's out. Does everyone agree with this?"

"Sounds good," Sam responded immediately, her face breaking into a gratified smirk.

I turned to the patient. "Okay, Mr. Stewart, I want you to count backward from one hundred. We'll begin as soon as you're under."

"Are you sure I'm going to be okay? You guys are the medical professionals, but that whole conversation about giving me too much sedative and *reversal agents* has me a little freaked out right now," he said.

Night Shift

Sam leaned in and gently placed a hand on his shoulder. "You're going to be just fine. You have a great team at your bedside. We'll have you fixed up and out of here before you know it. Now, how about we start that countdown, Mr. Stewart?"

He took a deep breath in just as the pharmacist began pushing the propofol. After a slow exhale, there was nothing. No counting. No chest rise.

The moment I saw Mr. Stewart's chest cease its rhythmic rise and fall, my heart sank. The patient was apneic.

"Apnea," I announced sharply.

The room snapped to a heightened state of alert. Sam was right by my side, her expertise as an emergency nurse evident in her swift response.

"How much did you give him?!" I shouted at the pharmacist.

"I thought we were starting at point five milligrams per kilogram?" Brian said with uncertainty in his voice.

My frustration threatened to boil over, but Sam's calming touch on my arm refocused me.

"The patient is in respiratory arrest right now, so we need to focus up," she said with assertiveness.

Adrenaline coursed through my veins as I barked orders. "Brian, get that physostigmine ready. Kat, open that ambulatory bag and start breathing for the patient. Oxygen, now!" I demanded. Sam quickly adjusted the simple face mask, setting the oxygen flow to two liters per minute. The capnography monitor beeped ominously, indicating the absence of carbon dioxide exhalation—a clear sign of respiratory arrest.

Was this situation somehow my fault? I did not fuck up my procedures. Structure. Routine. Safe patient outcome. Maybe I'd let Sam distract me? I should have confirmed the dosage one last time before moving forward. Fuck!

Kat's hands moved deftly. "I've got the bag valve mask ready," she announced as she removed the simple face mask.

"Start bagging him, Kat," I instructed. She nodded, expertly fitting the mask over Mr. Stewart's face and beginning the manual ventilation. His chest rose and fell with each of her compressions on the bag.

I glanced at the cardiac leads. Mr. Stewart's heart rate was elevated, hovering around one hundred ten beats per minute, a natural response to the hypoxia.

Brian looked at me, awaiting instructions.

"Administer the physostigmine, twenty-eight micrograms per kilogram," I said. "We need to stabilize him." I turned to Sam. "What's his oxygen saturation?"

She swiftly checked the monitor. "Ninety-two percent and dropping."

Soon, the physostigmine started to take effect. After several more compressions of the BVM, the capnography monitor showed signs of improvement.

"Replace the BVM with the simple face mask, with oxygen flow set to two liters per minute," I instructed. "Let's see if he's able to breathe on his own and his vitals return to normal."

A few seconds later, Mr. Stewart drew in a ragged breath and then exhaled. His breathing gradually normalized.

After a few minutes, everyone's nerves settled. I needed a new plan, fast. "Brian, prepare a combination of midazolam and ketamine—point oh five milligrams per kilogram of midazolam and point two milligrams per kilogram of ketamine, max twenty milligrams," I directed.

Brian repeated the dosages back to me for confirmation and then set to work. This time, we were all on the same page.

As he administered the sedative mix, I kept my eyes glued to the monitors. Mr. Stewart's heart rate stabilized, dropping to a more normal eighty bpm. His oxygen saturation climbed back up, reaching ninety-seven percent. I let out a breath I hadn't realized I was holding.

"Respiratory rate?" I asked.

"Steady at twelve breaths per minute," Sam reported.

The new cocktail of sedatives had been effective. Mr. Stewart's body relaxed, his face losing the strained expression of unconscious distress. Now that the crisis had been averted, we were ready to proceed with the task at hand.

"Let's reduce this fracture," I said. With gentle but firm hands, Jake stabilized his arm while I applied traction and manipulated the broken bone, aligning it as precisely as I could. The tech, already prepped, began the splinting process.

"Keep monitoring his vitals," I reminded Sam and Kat. They nodded, closely watching the screens displaying Mr. Stewart's heart rate, blood pressure, and oxygen levels.

I stepped back to assess our work and Mr. Stewart's condition. His vitals had stabilized, and the reduction appeared successful.

"Let's get radiology's mobile unit in for a post-reduction X-ray," I instructed. "We need to confirm the alignment."

"Understood, Dr. Thorin," Sam replied, already in the process of meticulously documenting our intervention in the patient chart.

"And let's keep him on observation for a while," I added. "I want to be sure there are no further complications."

As the tension in the room ebbed, I took a moment to reflect. The situation had been precarious, a reminder of the thin line between life and death we trod in emergency medicine. But thanks to the quick thinking and expertise of our team, we had navigated through the crisis successfully.

Mr. Stewart would recover; I was confident about that. But this case, like so many others, would stay with me, a constant reminder of the responsibility we bore and the lives that hung in the balance.

A short time later, when Mr. Stewart came to, I leaned in and said, "You did great. In a few minutes, radiology is going to come back in with their mobile unit and take another picture of your arm. If everything looks good, we're going to get you out of here in a couple of hours. You will need to follow up with an orthopedic surgeon, so I'll get the referral set up for you. It's important that you carefully follow all the instructions they give you at discharge. Sound good?"

"Sounds good, Dr. Thorin. I'm glad nothing bad happened to me when I was out," he replied.

"Everything went just fine. However, if you ever need to be sedated in the future, make sure to let the doctors and nurses know you have a sensitivity to propofol. We've marked it in your records and will send the notes over to your primary care physician. Take care of that arm. Have a good night." With that, I headed out of the procedure room, pausing as I drew closer to Sam.

"When you take your first break, grab me. We need to talk," I said curtly.

Night Shift

Chapter Three

The dashboard clock read 17:35. Once again, I sat in my car in the staff lot at St. John's. It was the beginning of my third night shift, and I stared blankly at the hospital's imposing facade. Anxiety flooded my mind as I wondered what lay in store tonight. Drawing in a deep breath, I tried to muster the courage to step out of my car and into the tumult that awaited me inside.

Tacoma's evening chill seeped through the windows, mirroring the cold knot of unease in my stomach. My thoughts were a tangled mess. I kept replaying the events of last night's shift over and over. Bethany, the one nurse I thought I'd connected with, seemed irked at me, and I had no clue why. The atmosphere had shifted the moment Dr. Thorin called me by his absurd nickname, *Sammich*. Bethany had narrowed her eyes at me in unmistakable irritation. Now, sitting here, I dreaded facing her again. I was unsure about what I'd done to make her mad.

But it wasn't just Bethany causing my anxiety. Last night, during a reduction procedure, I'd openly questioned Dr. Thorin's propofol dosage in front of the patient and the entire medical team. There had been a brief flash of annoyance on his face before he'd reluctantly accepted my recommendation for a lower dosage. Despite this, the pharmacist had been confused about the dosage, which had led to the patient becoming apneic. Though we'd managed to stabilize the patient without any harm, Dr. Thorin had demanded we discuss the incident on my break. However, the rest of my shift had been so busy that I hadn't gotten a break. I'd ended up leaving without having that conversation with him. Now, the thought of what Dr. Thorin might say loomed large in my mind.

I had always prided myself on being a competent nurse. My grades in nursing school had been nearly perfect, and my year at Harbor Regional back in Aberdeen had allowed me to hone my skills in the ED. Not to mention I'd just earned my CEN. Yet, here I was, experiencing an emotional turmoil that had little to do with my nursing abilities and everything to do with the complexities of interpersonal relationships at St. John's—a world I was still learning to navigate.

I'd purposefully arrived early so I could find Dr. Thorin before my shift started. I refused to sit in my car any longer and stew over what he might say. With a heavy sigh, I gathered my things and reluctantly opened the car door. The brisk night air hit me like an icy slap. I stood for a moment, steeling myself before making my way toward the sliding doors of the entrance.

The ED was a flurry of activity, humming with the usual cacophony of beeps, pages, and hurried conversations. As if I was on autopilot, my feet carried me directly toward the break room.

Night Shift

At every intersection, I scanned the hallways for Dr. Thorin but didn't find him. My mind raced with potential scenarios of our impending conversation. And then, there he was, leaning into a conversation with one of the ED residents as they both scrutinized something on a tablet. They were so focused that neither of them noticed me as I slid into the break room on the other side of the hallway.

Despite my resolve to avoid romantic entanglements here at the hospital, I couldn't deny the unexpected physical attraction that simmered in my core every time I saw Dr. Thorin, which was so weird, considering how much older he was than me. No, that couldn't be right...just some mental Freudian slip.

I shoved my lunch into the fridge and then poured a cup of coffee to warm up my hands. Someone had just brewed the pot, so it was nice and hot. I added a little cream and wrapped my fingers around the steaming cup, carefully sipping as I eavesdropped on Dr. Thorin's conversation. His thick baritone was unmistakable. I shut my eyes, resting my lips against the edge of the mug and allowing his voice to resonate in my mind. It sent heat cascading to my core. His words were like molten honey dripping into my panties. The man was just discussing cardiac meds, but it was better than listening to a smutty audiobook. Jesus, had a man's voice ever affected me like this? I wondered how it would affect me if his words were naughty.

"Ahem, Ms. Sheridan. Sam!"

My name finally registering, I jumped, nearly flinging my coffee on... "Dr. Thorin, so sorry. I was lost in my thoughts and didn't see you." Shit, my face almost throbbed from the sudden burst of heat that surged into my cheeks.

"Good thing I'm quick, or else I'd have hot coffee burns on my chest." He smirked and turned back to the door, shutting it.

"Have a seat, Samantha," he said, gesturing to one of the chairs at the table. The way he said my name, so formally, sent a nervous shiver down my spine.

Gathering my things from the counter, I hesitantly walked over to the table and sat down, placing my coffee, keys, and wallet in front of me. Crossing my legs and folding my hands in my lap, I tried to appear more composed than I actually was. Dr. Thorin joined me, sitting across the table. He leaned back in his chair, his attention fixed on me. The deep furrow between his brows, along with the seriousness in his eyes, was intimidating.

"About last night's procedure," he began, his tone authoritative yet professional.

Interrupting him before he could say more, I leaned in and said, "I'm sorry I didn't stop by last night during my break. I wasn't ignoring your request, but I didn't have a chance to take a break, and my shift ended up running over with all the patients we had. I assumed you'd already left because I didn't see you anywhere in the department after the reduction procedure."

"I'm not upset that you didn't come to see me last night. And although it's rare for someone to challenge me, especially in front of others, I'm not displeased with your question regarding the propofol dosage. But I would have preferred for you to ask me to step outside the room since the procedure had yet to begin and the circumstances weren't urgent. The patient was already anxious, and our discussion didn't help."

I nodded, absorbing his words. He was right, of course. I should have considered the patient's feelings and apprehension about the procedure.

"I appreciate your advocacy for the patient," Dr. Thorin continued, "but in the future, be sensitive to the situation. It's not about questioning; it's about how and when you do it."

Both relief and embarrassment washed over me. "I understand, Dr. Thorin. I'll be more mindful in the future." My cheeks warmed again.

He leaned forward, his demeanor shifting slightly. "Now, about the other matter. I know Bethany gave you a hard look before handing off the patient. That wasn't fair to you. Hospital rumor mills are...overactive. Don't believe everything you hear, especially about me." The corner of his mouth lifted, and he stared at me as if he could read my mind.

I raised an eyebrow, unsure where this was heading. Then his grin broadened, a hint of flirtation in his eyes. "And Sammich... it's a term of endearment, you know?"

I blinked, taken aback. Was he coming onto me? My heart skipped a beat.

"You can go now," he said. "And remember, don't be afraid to question things. Just...pick your moments." His gaze slowly made its way from my eyes to my chest and back up again.

Still processing the exchange, I gathered my things and stood up. "Thank you, Dr. Thorin. I'll keep that in mind," I whispered.

"I know you will, Sammich."

As I walked out of the break room, the nickname echoed in my ears, sending a thrill through me. Was I reading too much into it? The way he said it, that slight twinkle in his eye—it was unnerving.

Shaking my head slightly, I made my way to the locker room. My thoughts were a jumble of professional concerns and personal doubts. Dr. Thorin was an enigma, and I wasn't sure what to make of him...or my reaction to him. But one thing was obvious; my time at St. John's was going to be anything but dull.

Minutes after I'd stashed my keys and wallet in my locker, a call came in via radio about a teenage gunshot victim. A jolt of adrenaline went through me. I washed my hands, slipped on a face mask, and grabbed a pair of gloves as I headed to the trauma bay.

Just as I reached the trauma bay doors, they burst open. The boy on the stretcher couldn't have been older than seventeen. His face was contorted with fear and pain, and his eyes darted around while he clutched at the edges of the gurney. The entry wound was just below his clavicle, a chilling sight.

One of the paramedics, a tall, muscular man with a relaxed ease about him, started bringing me up to speed. "Accidental shooting," he explained, his voice steady despite the gravity of the situation. "Handgun."

I blinked, taking in the paramedic's features—dark brown hair with golden highlights and deep-set dark brown eyes with a few worry lines around them. He looked strikingly familiar. Then it hit me. He was like a slightly younger version of Dr. Thorin. Only, this man's eyes were dark.

"Are you related to Dr. Thorin, by any chance?" I asked, trying to mask my surprise.

"Guilty as charged. Atticus is my big brother," he said, giving me a mischievous look. "I'm Braxton, but for heaven's sake, don't ever call me Brixxie, his ridiculous nickname for me. And you must be the new nurse, Samantha?"

It surprised me that he'd already heard of me. His easygoing manner was so different from Dr. Thorin's more intense demeanor.

"Yep, that's me. You can call me Sam. Nice to meet you, Braxton. And don't worry, I'll steer clear of the nickname. I'm all too familiar with his idiotic nicknames."

Just then, Dr. Thorin himself strode over, his presence commanding as always. He caught my eye for a brief second—a silent acknowledgment—before he turned to the boy on the stretcher. "What's his BP?" he asked without missing a beat.

Night Shift

"Ninety over sixty and dropping," I reported, checking the monitor. My eyes flicked back to Braxton, who was unloading equipment with practiced efficiency. The numbers were worrisome, and the patient was losing blood fast.

Braxton stepped toward Dr. Thorin. "We've got a bullet lodged just below the clavicle," he reported. "He's experiencing difficulty breathing, likely due to fluid accumulation in the lung. His respiration is labored, and there's reduced breath sound on the left side. Oxygen saturation was fluctuating around eighty-nine percent en route."

Dr. Thorin nodded briefly, absorbing the information with a practiced calm. "Prepare for chest X-rays," he instructed. "Notify the OR. He may need immediate surgical intervention."

I glanced back and forth between them, still taken aback by how similar they looked and sounded, yet how different they were at the same time. Braxton took one of my hands and placed it on the gauze pack the other paramedic was holding over the boy's wound.

"Nice to meet you, Sam. I'll have to make sure you meet our youngest brother, Conan, soon," Braxton said as he walked back to the ambulance. Turning to look over his shoulder, he lit me up with a winning grin, and even though he was wearing a mask, it was one of the sexiest smiles I'd ever seen.

My cheeks heated, and I let out an embarrassingly audible gasp.

Dr. Thorin noticed my reaction and raised an eyebrow but said nothing, his focus quickly returning to the patient. But in that instant, I caught a flicker of something—curiosity, perhaps—in his eyes.

"We need to stabilize him. Possible lung and vascular injury," Dr. Thorin assessed. "Get chest X-rays, type and cross for blood, and prepare for a possible thoracotomy."

While the team hustled around, I continued applying pressure on the wound to mitigate blood loss, being mindful to be gentle so as not to exacerbate the injury. Radiology techs rolled in the portable X-ray machine, and within moments, we had a clearer picture of the damage.

"He's got a hemothorax," Dr. Thorin noted, his voice steady but urgent.

The X-ray showed a collapsed lung. The bullet was perilously close to a major blood vessel.

"Chest tube insertion, now," Dr. Thorin directed, and I snapped to attention in an instant.

Handing over my hold on the gauze pack to another nurse, I quickly discarded the gloves I'd been wearing, scrubbed my hands, and suited up in my sterile gear, donning new gloves before turning back to the patient, who had been moved to one of the beds in the trauma bay.

His breathing was shallow and labored, and his fear-filled eyes flickered from me to Dr. Thorin, seeking reassurance amidst his pain.

"Hi, I'm Samantha. What's your name?" I asked him in an effort to distract him a little from the seriousness of the situation.

"Brandon," he replied softly.

"Well, Brandon, Dr. Thorin here and his team are the best. We're going to take good care of you. Soon, we'll have you feeling better. Try to take slow, deep breaths for me, okay?"

He tried to smile, but winced as pain tore through him.

Bethany swiftly entered the room with the necessary supplies—a chest tube kit, a sterile drape, and a local anesthetic. Everyone prepared for the procedure in a practiced, macabre dance. The sterile scent of the drape mingled with the sharp, antiseptic odor of the cleaning solution as we prepared the area around Brandon's wound. As we began to undertake this critical procedure, the atmosphere became somber, the quiet punctuated by the beeping of monitors and the muted shuffling of the team.

"Administering local anesthesia," Dr. Thorin announced, his voice a steady beacon in the tense atmosphere. As he injected the anesthetic around the site of the wound, Brandon winced, his muscles tensing under the sharp prick of the needle.

With precise movements, Dr. Thorin made a small incision just below Brandon's pectoral muscle. The soft, wet parting of skin was a sound I had become familiar with but never got used to hearing. "Scalpel down. Clamps," he requested calmly. I handed him the clamps, and then he carefully dissected the subcutaneous tissue, creating a pathway for the chest tube.

No one made a sound. Dr. Thorin's instruments clinked softly as we watched him work. The critical moment approached, and I braced myself. Dr. Thorin made a swift, precise insertion into the pleural space. There was a sudden, soft whooshing sound as air and blood escaped through the newly created pathway. It was both a relief and a reminder of the injury's severity.

I held the tube as Dr. Thorin secured it with sutures, his hands moving with the grace and confidence of a surgeon who had performed this lifesaving procedure countless times. The precision of each stitch was mesmerizing. The sutures were fine and delicate compared with the severity of the wound they surrounded. I shifted my focus to the chest tube itself. My job now was to ensure it remained stable and correctly positioned. I observed as Bethany connected the tube to the sealed water container. With each breath the patient took, blood and air bubbled rhythmically in the water-seal chamber.

Brandon's breathing, previously ragged and shallow, began to ease. The hissing sound of air passing through the chest tube was a sign that the pressure in his chest was being relieved, allowing his collapsed lung to re-expand.

"Tube in place. Secured," Dr. Thorin finally declared. He glanced at me and gave me a nod of appreciation for the silent coordination that had just transpired between us. It gave me a rush of professional satisfaction and relief. We had potentially saved Brandon's life with our timely intervention.

With the tube now secured, I watched intently as Brandon's labored breaths created a rhythmic dance of bubbles in the water. The sight was both fascinating and harrowing. The bubbling was not just a mechanical response but a visual cue of the air and blood being safely removed from Brandon's pleural space. Blood-tinged froth intermittently bubbled to the surface, painting a stark picture of the internal trauma. The oxygen saturation monitor beeped steadily, the numbers climbing back to safer levels.

As I cleaned the area and applied a sterile dressing over the site, Dr. Thorin's voice cut through my focus. "Samantha, I need you on the surgical team. We're going to OR three." I nodded and followed him. Around me, the team started to move on to the next steps of Brandon's care.

After I'd scrubbed in, I stepped into the operating room, where Dr. Thorin prepared for the surgery that a specialist would spearhead once he arrived. The bullet had to be carefully retrieved, avoiding further damage to the lung and nearby blood vessels.

With an unyielding focus, Dr. Thorin carefully navigated through the wound track, ensuring hemostasis and checking for any additional injuries. Dr. Sylvan, a cardiothoracic surgeon who had been called in for this complex procedure, joined us, providing additional expertise.

The removal of the bullet was precise, and the surrounding tissue was skillfully repaired. "Suturing," Dr. Sylvan finally announced. I handed him the necessary instruments and watched as he neatly closed the incisions.

After the surgery was concluded, Dr. Thorin took a moment to acknowledge the team's effort. "Good job, everyone." He peeled off his gloves, the latex snapping gently as it left his hands, and tossed them in the trash. His eyes, previously laser-focused and intense, now scanned the room. He looked at each of us in turn, giving nods of genuine appreciation. He relaxed, and a rare, small smile played at the corners of his mouth.

Post-surgery, Brandon was transferred to the PACU, where he would be closely monitored for signs of re-accumulating pneumothorax or hemothorax and for any respiratory distress. His recovery journey had just begun, but thanks to the swift action of the medical team, he'd been given the best chance for a full recovery.

As we left the OR, Dr. Thorin's eyes met mine again. This time, there was a hint of something more—something I couldn't describe. But evidently, Bethany understood. Turning to Dr. Thorin, she huffed, "Really?" and stomped down the hallway. I ducked my head and shot away to go clean up and check back in with tonight's charge nurse.

When that was accomplished, the ED was relatively quiet, giving me the opportunity to go get something to eat. I walked into the break room, finding Bethany sitting alone, eating some mixed fruit and flipping through a magazine.

"Hey, what's up?" I asked, opening the fridge and pulling out my lunch bag.

Bethany looked up, her expression tense but not unfriendly. "Hey, Sam. Mind joining me for a bit?"

I nervously chuckled, pulling out a chair. "Sure, but only if you're buying the coffee. You owe me for guessing closest to the drunk patient's EtOH level. You remember, the guy who you passed off to me the night before last? His EtOH was three fifty-eight, and now you owe me a coffee." I gestured toward the coffee machine in the corner. "And by buying, I mean getting up and making a fresh pot."

Her lips twitched into a half-smile. "Deal. And by the way..." She paused, went over to the coffeemaker, and started pouring some grounds into a fresh filter.

I held my breath. Last night, when Dr. Thorin had called me "Sammich," Bethany's reaction hadn't escaped my notice. It had been a combination of surprise and something else... jealousy, maybe?

Bethany let out a long, slow exhale, breaking the silence. "Look, Sam, about last night... I was curt with you, and I shouldn't have been. It's just...there's a bit of history between me and Dr. Thorin."

My eyebrows shot up. "History? You mean like..."

She nodded, a rueful look crossing her face. "Yeah. We had a thing. It was fun but brief, just a few hookups here and there, but I guess I'd hoped for more, even though I knew better. I suppose some part of me still has a thing for him. When I saw how much he affected you, it stirred up old feelings. But that's my problem, not yours. He made it clear he's not into relationships when I pursued him. I'd had a crush on him for years and flirted with him mercilessly. Finally, one night, it just happened. We were both stressed to the max, and one thing led to another. We were together a few more times, but then he ended things. He was apologetic. Said something about his heart not being ready for anything serious. I thought he was being dramatic, but then again, he's never let any woman get close to him, so who knows. Rumor has it that he cuts a woman loose as soon as she even *hints* at wanting a relationship." She heaved a loud sigh. "But sex with him, well, it's fabulous. Oh, my God, it's so good. Don't judge me...but fucking that man for few hours was time well spent. I'll never regret it. Every woman should have an experience like that at least once in her lifetime."

Bethany set the hot coffee, a few sweetener packets, some creamer, and a spoon in front of me. Taking my time to respond, I stirred the creamer into my coffee, trying to hide my surprise. She'd shared a lot more than I'd ever imagined she would. I realized now she was the type to overshare, but I honestly liked that. I liked that she trusted me enough to be honest and straight up about what had happened between them.

"I had no idea. I mean, with him calling me 'Sammich' and all, I just thought he was being his usual arrogant self, trying to make me feel insignificant or something. Since I started working here, we've verbally sparred a lot. I don't let anyone run roughshod over me—I like to give it back to people."

"I really am sorry," she said. "The way I spoke to you was uncalled for, and it won't happen again." Then she leaned in, her voice dropping. "Sam, he only gives nicknames to women he's... interested in, you know, in a certain way. Just be careful, okay? Well, that is, unless you do want to have the best sex of your life."

I snorted. "Trust me, Bethany, Dr. Thorin is the last man on earth I'd ever want to be with. He's such an arrogant asshole. But his brother Braxton? Holy hell girl, he's hot and so much easier-going," I said, laughing.

"Wait till you meet Conan. He works here as a nurse. If you think the older Thorin brothers are handsome, he's going to blow your mind. He's a lot younger than Atticus and wild as the day is long. He's constantly pushing every button Atticus has."

"What? All three brothers work in the medical field? And at this hospital?"

"Yes, and of course, Atticus lords over the younger two like he's some sort of Godfather. Braxton isn't too much trouble for Atticus and is only in and out as an EMT, but Conan...he lives to yank his chain. I can't tell you how many times Atticus has had to bail him out of trouble." Bethany genuinely laughed, clutching her belly. "I think it's sweet justice for all the women he's toyed with over the years."

Her expression softened, and she changed the subject. "So, speaking of men, what's your deal? Any interesting love-life tales?"

I shrugged, the question making me a bit uncomfortable. "Not much to tell, really. Just one guy in college. It was pretty...vanilla."

"Vanilla?" Bethany echoed, her curiosity piqued.

"Yeah." I didn't elaborate, and she didn't push for more.

I sipped my coffee, feeling a bit out of my depth. The world of relationships and casual sex was a far cry from what I was used to. Mostly, I'd only ever focused on school and work. I hadn't had time for much else. Bethany's frankness was refreshing, but it also highlighted how inexperienced I really was. It wasn't that I was particularly uninterested in sex, only that it hadn't been a priority for me.

I ate my food, and she returned to her magazine, but my thoughts kept drifting back to our conversation. Bethany's revelation about her history with Atticus didn't surprise me, but her advice to watch out for him did.

I didn't want a relationship with anyone, much less with someone like him. He was abrasive, and he had a reputation for being callous with everyone he worked with. No, I wanted a man who would treat me right, a man who could be both a protector and a provider. Hot as hell on the outside but a cinnamon roll on the inside—the perfect combination of sweet and spicy. But that was probably just the idealist in me. I doubted I'd ever find that kind of man in reality.

I turned to Bethany and said, "You know, you didn't need to warn me off of Dr. Thorin. I have no interest in him, or any man, right now."

"No?" Her brows rose, curiosity lighting up her eyes. "Not even for a night of fun?"

Heat crept into my cheeks. "I haven't...I mean, I'm not really interested in casual sex."

"Oh." Her eyes narrowed as understanding dawned. "You're a virgin."

"What? No!" I scoffed, glancing around uncomfortably, glad there wasn't anyone else in the break room. The last thing I needed was for the entire staff to know about my sex life, or lack thereof. "I've had sex. I'm just not a fan of meaningless hookups."

"How was it?" Bethany asked, lifting one brow inquisitively. "Your last relationship, I mean."

I busied myself with picking at my bag of chips, discomfort swirling in my chest. The truth was, I'd never enjoyed sex. I'd always been too focused on trying to please my boyfriend Benji in college to relax and enjoy anything myself. He was definitely not worth getting an IUD for; I dreaded the day I would have to get a new one.

"Well, you know...always quick, no fireworks. I never really got why people make such a big deal over sex."

Bethany's eyes widened, and she leaned back, assessing me. "Sam, are you saying you've never had...good sex? You can talk to me, you know." She touched my arm, regarding me with sincere kindness. "I won't judge you or repeat a word."

I sighed, debating how much to confess. But this was Bethany, the only friend I had in this city. At least, I hoped she was my friend. "Sex has never really been all that great for me," I admitted. "I don't know what all the fuss is about. I don't know, it's just so awkward. Oh my God, I feel like such an idiot talking about it." Leaning my elbows on the table, I covered my face.

"Oh, Sam." She pulled me into a side hug, rubbing my back. "You just haven't had it with the right person, that's all. When you meet someone you truly connect with, who takes the time to make sure you enjoy yourself...it'll be a whole different experience."

I shook my head, pulling away. "I doubt that. Besides, it's not like I have time to date. This job keeps me busy enough as it is."

"You sound like a damn nun. Trust me, good sex is worth the effort," Bethany insisted. "There's someone, or maybe *lots of someones*, out there for everyone," she said, wagging her brows. "You just have to be patient."

"Can we please change the subject?" I grabbed my trash, got up, and tossed it in the can, eager to escape this conversation.

Bethany followed, dropping her voice to a whisper. "I'm sorry. I didn't mean to embarrass you. But promise me you won't write off sex completely. When you meet the right person, it can be—"

"Evening, Dr. Thorin. What's got you so lost in thought? I noticed you've been standing out here in the hallway for a while now," said a voice I recognized as one of the night janitors.

Bethany threw her hand over her mouth, and I stumbled back with a yelp. Dr. Thorin stepped into the doorway, nodding briefly at the janitor. "Have a good shift, Harold," he said as the man walked past the doorway. His gaze flickered back and forth from Bethany to me, a muscle twitching in his jaw.

"Atticus! I mean, Dr. Thorin!" Bethany exclaimed, cheeks flaming. "What are you—we were just—"

He held up a hand, narrowing his eyes at me. My pulse hammered against my temples as a panic attack threatened to creep up from my chest and choke me. He'd been eavesdropping on our conversation. How much had he overheard? From the look on his face, it had been more than enough.

Bethany shot me an apologetic grimace and hurried off, flipping him the finger as she whipped past him. Now I was alone with Dr. Thorin, acutely aware of his formidable presence and the curiosity simmering in his gaze. My stomach knotted with nerves, though I couldn't say exactly why.

I cleared my throat, desperate to fill the tense silence. "Did you need something, Dr. Thorin?"

"No. But a word of warning." His voice was low, rough. "Bethany means well, but she has a habit of meddling where she shouldn't. Whatever she told you about me, I suggest you disregard it."

My cheeks flamed even hotter. So he had overheard enough to know that Bethany was gossiping about him. I stared determinedly at the floor, humiliated. If that was the case, he'd also heard us talking about my ridiculously pathetic sex life.

"I apologize for any inappropriate discussion," I said, the words spewing out of my mouth as if it had a mind of its own. "It won't happen again." Somewhere under the layers of embarrassment, I knew I had nothing to apologize for, but no other words would come.

He moved closer, and I caught a whiff of his clean scent—no cologne, just the man. "I might be an asshole, but don't believe her ridiculous stories. I'm not some playboy sleeping my way through the hospital staff."

"I never thought that," I said too quickly.

"No? What did you think then?"

I dared to meet his gaze—a mistake. There was a hunger in his eyes that made my pulse stutter. "Nothing. I don't have an opinion on your personal life."

He smiled slightly, but the intensity in his eyes remained, and his pupils were blown wide open. "Smart girl."

The praise shouldn't have affected me, but a flush of warmth trickled down my spine. I shifted, unsettled by his fierce perusal and the reactions of my own traitorous body. "Was there anything else?" I asked.

"Yes." He leaned in close, his breath hot against my ear. "Like Bethany said... The right man could show you things you've never even dreamed of."

I jerked away, stunned speechless. My skin was feverish, hypersensitive even, and it mortified me to realize I was so turned on. By him.

With a smug little smirk, Dr. Thorin straightened, clearly pleased by my reaction. "Just something to consider. Carry on, Sammich."

He strolled out of the doorway and down the hallway, leaving me to stare after him, equal parts bewildered and infuriated. How dare he say such things? I didn't care how skilled he was in bed—and surely that had been exaggerated anyway. And I didn't care what *things* he could show me. I wouldn't touch him with a ten-foot pole.

Even if some traitorous part of me was curious what those *things* might be.

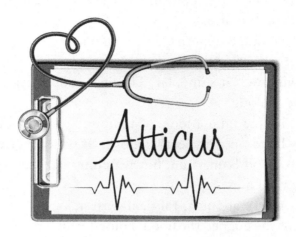

Chapter Four

Dawn was clawing its way across the sky, dragging with it a bitingly cold autumn morning. The hospital parking lot was deserted except for the last stragglers of the night shift. As I made my way to my car, pulling my coat tight against the chill, a sound caught my attention—an engine coughing, desperately trying to start.

Across the lot, Sam was struggling with her car, gripping the steering wheel of the little GTI and pleading with it to start. Each of her breaths fogged up her windshield in little white puffs of frustration.

As I approached, I noticed she was shivering. Her red curls had escaped from the confines of her braided ponytail and now framed her face in a fiery halo. Her eyes were narrowed in irritation. The bitter cold had caused her creamy, freckled cheeks to flush brightly.

"Need a hand, Samantha?" I called out.

She turned, startled, then composed herself and cracked open the window. "It's fine, Dr. Thorin. I can manage." But her hands were shaking.

"Here, let me take a look." Stepping up next to her car, I slipped my hands into my leather gloves. It wasn't normal for me to play the Good Samaritan, but watching her struggle stirred something within me.

"Don't worry about it. I'll deal with it," she said, her teeth chattering as she popped the hood. I didn't wait for her permission before raising it and peering inside. She reluctantly got out, stood beside me, and leaned over. The engine lay exposed, a mess of metal and rubber. Judging by the helpless tilt of her head, it was like an alien world to her.

"Have you checked the battery lately?" I asked, my voice taking on the clinical tone I used in the ED. "Do you know how old it is? Maybe the terminals are loose." My breath fogged up in the cold, mingling with hers in the space between us.

"Um, no, I haven't, and it's the same battery it came with four years ago," Sam admitted, her fingers fumbling with the cuffs of her jacket before she pulled her hands into her sleeves. The faint floral scent of her skin drifted from her, incongruent with the odors of grease and grit under the hood.

"Let me." I nudged her aside gently and reached in, my hands inspecting the connections. They were tight. The problem could be anything. Cars weren't my forte.

"Seems fine here," I muttered, straightening up. My gaze met hers, and I could see the strain of the night shift lingering in her tired eyes. "Might be the starter or the alternator. Who knows?"

Night Shift

"Great." She sighed, a puff of resignation crystallizing in front of her lips. "Just what I need."

"Let's try it again," I suggested, closing the hood.

Sam slid back into the driver's seat while I leaned against the open door. She turned the key, and the engine sputtered weakly before falling silent once more.

"Damn it to hell," she muttered, her knuckles white as she gripped the steering wheel.

"Seems like it's not your morning," I said, unable to suppress a twinge of something akin to empathy. This was not the kind of struggle I was accustomed to. Yet here I stood, feeling oddly helpless as I watched her battle with something as mundane as a dead car.

She tried again, but it still wouldn't start.

"It's not catching at all," I observed.

"Clearly," she huffed, then reached over and rolled up the window, her snarkiness surfacing. It was a defense mechanism, one I was beginning to recognize all too well. She stepped out of the car, one hand hanging onto the edge of the window. She shook her head grimacing at the hood. She was obviously worrying about what to do next.

"Come on, I'll give you a lift home. No sense in standing out here and turning into an icicle." I gestured toward my car—a silent command more than an offer.

"Are you sure? I don't want to impose." She hesitated, wrapping her arms around herself in a futile attempt to keep warm.

"Of course, Sammich. Let's get out of the cold." The nickname had slipped out unintentionally, a familiarity I hadn't planned. Thankfully, she didn't react but turned to grab a couple of things from the car. After she closed the door and locked it, I led the way to my car, feeling her reluctance in the slight lag of her footsteps behind me.

As we walked, an odd sensation crept along my spine—the strangeness of caring, of being drawn into someone else's orbit when I normally kept others at bay. Sam, with her fiery hair and defiant spirit, was unsettling in ways I couldn't quite articulate.

"Thank you, Dr. Thorin. Really," she said when we reached my car.

"Think nothing of it. And call me Atticus when we're not on duty. I insist."

"Atticus then," she echoed softly. Hearing my first name roll off her lips immediately sent an electric current straight to my groin.

The chill of the morning seeped into the Mercedes's plush interior despite the car's best efforts to shield us from the elements. I glanced at Sam as she slid into the passenger seat and buckled her belt with an air of discomfort that clung to her like a second skin.

"Nice car," she said, a tentative smile gracing her lips as her gaze swept over the dashboard's sleek design.

"Thank you." I started the engine, and the S-Class hummed to life beneath us. It was a machine accustomed to precision and power, much like me—or so I liked to believe.

She told me her address, and I entered it into the nav. As we pulled away from the hospital, the silence between us was charged, a live wire I was all too eager to grasp. "You know, Samantha, I couldn't help overhearing your conversation in the break room earlier," I ventured, keeping my tone casual, belying the intensity of my curiosity. "Break-room conversations can be... enlightening, don't you think?" I cast a sidelong glance at her.

Her body stiffened, her eyes widening as she froze. A flush crept up her neck, betraying her sudden discomfort.

"Can they?" Her reply was evasive. "Oh, that was just... Bethany, you know, she likes to tease."

"Does she now?" My fingers tightened on the steering wheel. "And do you always provide such...intimate fodder for her amusement?"

"Intimate isn't the word I'd use," she said, followed by a "hmph" of defiance. "Anyway, it's not like I have anything worth sharing."

"Contrary to what you might think, I find the topic quite interesting," I said pointedly, raising a brow and giving her a chuckle. "Especially your apparent lack of—shall we say—satisfactory experiences."

Her breath hitched, and she turned to stare out the window. "I don't know what you're talking about, Dr. Thorin. My experiences have been plenty satisfactory."

"Atticus," I corrected firmly, allowing my gaze to linger on the delicate profile of her face. "We're not at work now, are we?"

"Fine. Atticus," she conceded with a frosty edge. "But that doesn't mean..."

"Samantha," I said in a low voice, her name rolling off my tongue like a promise. "You've never been properly worshiped, have you? Never felt the true liberation of letting go?"

"Stop it." The words were a demand cloaked in embarrassment. "Just...stop."

"Apologies," I said, but my regret was hollow. I was intrigued by this fiery-mouthed woman wrapped in freckles and flame. She stirred something within me, a hunger for redemption—mine and perhaps even hers.

Sam shifted uncomfortably in her seat, her eyes darting to meet mine before skittering away. "None of that's any of your business, Dr. Thorin."

"Atticus," I said, correcting her again. "And perhaps not, but it intrigues me nonetheless. Besides, you're the one openly talking about it in the break room." The thought of being the one to unravel her, to guide her to unexplored heights of pleasure, sent a thrill of anticipation through me. This was more than mere attraction; it was a challenge, a puzzle begging to be solved.

"Atticus!" she hissed, saying the name like it was stuck in her throat.

Silence stretched between us once more.

When we pulled into her apartment complex, I was struck by the bleakness of the neighborhood. Her apartment building and the surrounding structures were in a sad state of disrepair. A flicker of concern ignited within me. Sam deserved better than this—a decent place to call home. Wait...why did I care where she lived? Yet, as she thanked me and stepped out of the car, a protective instinct roared to life, unbidden and fierce.

"Be careful!" I called after her, watching as she navigated the cracked pavement toward the entrance.

"Always am," she tossed back over her shoulder.

I continued to watch her as she walked away. Suddenly, a movement in the shadows caught my eye.

"Sam!" a gruff voice said, penetrating the windows of my car. A man staggered toward her, his gait unsteady and predatory. He lunged at Sam, his hand snapping out to clamp onto her arm with brutal force. The roughness of his grip was jarring. His tense muscles and bared teeth made it clear he was furious.

"Let go of me, Mac!" Sam shrieked, her breath visible in the frigid air, mingling with the fog that shrouded the scene in a ghostly veil.

"Help me, goddammit! I know you got money," Mac growled. His words were slurred, but the threat was unmistakable.

I slipped out of the car, my heart pounding at the sight of Sam's terror. Their voices grew louder as the intensity of the altercation increased, and I was able to step closer, unnoticed.

Night Shift

"Help you?" she screamed, trying to wrench her arm free. "I moved to Tacoma to *escape* you, to get as far from Aberdeen and your mess as I could!"

"Escape? You think you can just...leave, as if I never existed?" Mac hissed. "You ruined my life, girl."

"How did you even find me here?"

"Got my ways," he sneered, tightening his grip. "You owe me, you little—"

"Owe you?" Sam spat back. "I don't owe you anything. You ruined everything, not me!"

"Money, Sam! Or meds," he demanded, his words a guttural growl. The man's desperation was a raw, ugly wound for the world to see. "Grab some from the hospital. That should be easy enough for a fancy nurse like you."

Sam's response was a bitter laugh. "I don't have any money. And the hospital's meds are secured. Even if I wanted to, I couldn't!" she shouted, her defiance flaring despite her trembling. "Everything's locked up tight—just like I wish you were!"

"Give me something, or I swear..." Mac's threat hung incomplete, but the implication was clear.

The ugliness of the exchange was obviously a prelude to something darker. Mac's eyes were wild, bloodshot, and calculating—a predator pushed to the brink.

"Help me, or—"

"Or what, Dad?" she cut him off, her voice rising. "You'll beat me? Stalk me? Haunt me? You're already nothing more than a ghost of a father—a man I wish I'd never known."

I crept closer, ready to intervene, but held back, absorbing the complexity of their relationship. Sam's struggle was written in the tension of her stance, the set of her jaw. She was a warrior standing her ground.

"Don't sass me, girl," Mac hissed. "Play tough and see what happens." Then he jerked her around by the arm.

My hands clenched into fists at my sides, and my muscles were coiled, every sense on high alert.

"Get away from me!" she yelled, her voice breaking.

"Remember, I can take away everything you've built." Mac's shadow loomed over her as his hand formed a fist.

"Over my dead body," she muttered to herself, but I heard it—a promise of survival.

"Enough!" I roared, my voice steady but laced with a fury that surprised even me. "Leave her alone."

They whipped around to face me. Two pairs of eyes, wide with shock, stared at me—one pair clouded by intoxication, the other shimmering with unshed tears. Sam's gaze held a wordless plea, as though she was silently begging me not to get involved.

"Who the hell are you?" Mac snarled, sizing me up with a disdainful glance.

"None of your fucking business," I answered, stepping closer to the scumbag that was Sam's father. "I won't let you hurt her."

"Stay out of this, Dr. Thorin," Sam warned, but her voice wavered, her bravado slipping away.

"Can't do that." I shook my head and took another step toward them. "Not when someone I—"

I cut myself off before I finished that thought, aware of the line I was teetering on, the boundary between professional concern and personal involvement. But as I looked into Sam's eyes, I realized that line had been crossed, and there was no going back.

The cold had already seeped into my bones, but the chill that ran down my spine now was different—primal, defensive. Sam's breath hitched as Mac's grip tightened around her slender arm, his fingers digging in like the talons of a raptor claiming its prey. The sight triggered something in me, an instinct to protect.

"Hey! Let her go!" I yelled, my heart pounding to the rhythm of my quickening footsteps. The man swung her around, and her face paled in terror.

"Get your hands off her!" I advanced, ready to unleash the rage and fury I'd been restraining thus far. Sam deserved better than this—better than him. And whether I wanted to admit it or not, I cared about what happened to her. Damn it all, I cared.

"Unhand her," I commanded, my voice low and resonant with a menace I rarely allowed to surface. This wasn't the controlled environment of the ED; this was raw and unscripted.

Sam's face flushed with embarrassment. A muffled plea escaped her lips as she tried to wriggle free from Mac's grasp, but he only clutched her closer, his body swaying with intoxication.

"Stay outta this, buddy," Mac slurred, spittle flying from his mouth. "Family matter."

"Let! Her! Go!" I shouted. Each word punctuated the air, a clear warning shot.

But Mac was too far gone, lost in his own despair and anger. He yanked Sam against him, causing her to stumble.

I couldn't stand by any longer. In two strides, I closed the distance between us. My years of martial arts training kicked in, and my hand shot out, gripping Mac's wrist, twisting it just enough to break his hold on Sam without snapping a bone. With my other hand, I drove the heel of my palm upward into his nose.

Shrieking, he stumbled back as a string of curses flew from his mouth.

"Atti—" Sam started to protest.

"Step back, Sam," I instructed, keeping my eyes locked on Mac's, which were wild with rage.

With Mac momentarily disoriented, I shifted my stance, sliding behind him and locking my arm around his neck. The chokehold was tight but controlled—I wasn't aiming to harm, merely to incapacitate. His struggles were fierce but futile. I had the advantage of sobriety and discipline.

"If you ever touch her again," I hissed fiercely into his ear, "I will kill you."

Mac's body went limp as he realized the seriousness of my threat, the finality in my tone. For a moment, there was silence save for our ragged breathing and the distant hum of the city waking up.

"Okay, okay!" he rasped. I released my hold incrementally, ensuring Sam was well out of his reach before letting him go completely and giving him a shove.

He stumbled forward, catching himself against the grimy wall, and I put myself between him and Sam.

"Get lost, Mac," I said, leaving no room for argument. "She doesn't want you here."

"Fine," he spat, backing away but throwing a venomous look over his shoulder. "But this isn't over, Sam. Not by a long shot."

Without another word, he disappeared, melting back into the shadows he'd emerged from. For a fleeting moment, gratitude washed over Sam's features and her eyes softened, but it was swiftly replaced by a flush of embarrassment that crept up her neck and spread across her face. Her mouth opened slightly, as if to say thanks, but then closed abruptly, her lips pressing into a thin line of discomfort. I wanted to reach out and hug her, to assure her that she wasn't alone, but I hesitated, suddenly uncertain.

"Are you okay?" My question was terse. The adrenaline that still coursed through my veins was affecting even my speech.

"Y-yes, thank you," she managed, tucking a stray curl behind her ear.

"Will he come back?" I asked, though I knew the answer. Men like him always circled back to where they perceived weakness.

"Probably," she replied, her voice barely above a whisper as she attempted to regain her composure.

With a shiver, she wrapped her arms around herself, fighting off the remnants of fear or perhaps the cold—I couldn't tell. My concern for her welled up, jumbling with a frustration about my inability to immediately fix what was broken in her world.

"Thank you, Atticus," she said, lifting her eyes to meet my gaze, a silent acknowledgment of the line we'd just crossed—from professional boundaries to personal entanglements.

"Anytime." It was more than just a courteous response—it was a promise. "Let's get you inside. You're cold and shaking."

"No," she said quickly, almost reflexively. "I—I can manage."

"Are you sure?"

"Please, Atticus, just...leave it be." Her eyes pleaded with me for understanding—or perhaps for the distance she thought she needed.

"All right," I conceded, the unease settling heavier in my gut.

With that, she turned to ascend the steps to her apartment.

"Samantha, wait!" I called after her, running up to the landing halfway up the stairs. "Would you like to talk about it? That man...he's your father, isn't he? And clearly, you're terrified of him...and rightfully so."

"Terrified is a strong word. I can handle Mac Sheridan."

"Doesn't look like handling him is something you should be doing alone," I said, taking a step closer.

"Thank you...for back there," she murmured, her focus shifting to the ground. "But I don't need saving, Dr. Thorin."

"Atticus," I corrected her softly. "Call me Atticus. And it's not about saving you. It's about not letting anyone harm you again."

"Again?" She barked out a laugh, but it was hollow. "You think this was the first time?"

"Let me walk you to your door," I said, ignoring her jadedness. "It's the least I can do."

Sam hesitated, her teeth tugging at her lower lip. "You don't have to do this. You've done enough."

"Indulge me."

She gave me a small nod, and we continued up the stairs in silence.

"Nothing to say?" I prodded gently when we reached her door. Like everything else around here, it was in poor repair, its paint flaking like old scars.

"What do you want me to say, Atticus?" Sam faced me, held her palms up, and gave me a defiant scowl. "That my life's a mess? That I've got a father who's more monster than man? That I'm scared he'll come back?"

"Any of those would be a start," I said, leaning against the wall. "Talking helps."

"Maybe for some, but I've spent years trying to forget. Talking only makes it more real—makes me think about it."

"Sometimes reality needs to be faced," I said, knowing all too well the demons that could haunt those who tried to escape their past.

"Facing reality is what I do every day in the ED," she snapped. "I don't need to face more of it at home."

"Home should be your sanctuary, Samantha. Not another place filled with stress and anxiety."

"Sanctuary," she repeated bitterly. "Sounds nice. I was just beginning to feel like this place was a safe refuge...that is, until Mac showed up."

"Let's go inside," I suggested, but she shook her head.

"No... I appreciate the ride and...the rescue. But this is where you leave."

As I stood there in that shadowy corridor that reeked of mildew, an unwelcome twinge of helplessness hit me. Samantha Sheridan, with her fiery hair and battle-scarred heart, was pushing me away, and all I wanted was to pull her closer.

"All right," I conceded, careful not to let my voice betray any of my inner conflict. "But if you need anything—anything at all—you call me."

"Sure," she said with a nod, though we both knew she wouldn't.

She paused, then fogged the air with a sigh as she lifted her chin. Her eyes were a tumultuous sea, and I could see her wrestling with the storm within.

"Really, I'm fine. It's no big deal," she said too quickly. She was lying, and we both knew it. "Besides, I don't want to burden you with my problems. I don't need work to be awkward for either of us."

"Burden?" I countered softly. "Samantha, I think after what just happened, we're past professional formalities. Please, let me help."

She shook her head, and a couple of stray curls bounced along the edges of her face.

"Atticus, I appreciate what you did, but I can handle my own life," she insisted.

"Let me come in and have a cup of coffee at least?" I asked, stepping closer. The thought of leaving her alone, especially now, twisted something deep inside me.

"Thank you, but no. My place isn't... It's not somewhere I bring people," she said as a flush crept across her freckled cheeks.

"Samantha—"

"Please, Atticus." There was a finality in her tone, a plea for me to drop the subject.

"Okay," the word tasted like ash on my tongue. "But if you ever do want to talk or need anything..."

"I know where to find you," she finished for me, a faint smile touching her lips but failing to reach her eyes.

"See you at work, Samantha," I said, watching her turn away and unlock the door.

"See you later, Dr. Thorin." She slipped inside and closed the door without looking back.

As she disappeared into the relative safety of her apartment, an unfamiliar knot tightened in my gut. Who was this woman who compelled me to violence, who stirred in me the need to protect? And what would I do about it?

The chill of the autumn morning bit at my skin as I trudged down the creaking steps. The sound of her door locking behind me reverberated like a judge's gavel—final, resolute.

A siren wailed in the distance. It was a familiar sound that usually spurred me into action, but now it only deepened the furrow between my brows. Why did I even care about her? Samantha Sheridan was nothing more than a nurse I worked with—a particularly snarky one at that.

"Dammit," I hissed as I kicked at an abandoned can, sending it clattering across the parking lot. This was ridiculous. I shouldn't be worrying about a woman who was so damaged by other men that she wouldn't even consider giving me a chance to come in for a cup of coffee. I paused for a moment, leaning against the cool metal of my car. My hands found their way to my pockets while I stared up at the dilapidated building she called home.

"Get your head out of your ass, Thorin," I scolded myself. "You're not some knight in shining armor; you're a doctor—a man who's never cared enough to be caught up in this kind of mess."

Finally, I got in and slammed the door shut, then turned the key in the ignition. The engine's growl filled the silence around me. I knew I should drive away and never look back, leave her to deal with her demons on her own. It was what I was good at—detachment, disinterest. But the image of her shivering, the defiance in her voice as she'd rejected my help, gnawed at me.

"Focus, Atticus," I muttered, using the commanding tone that had always brought order to my chaotic thoughts. The car vibrated beneath me, eager to move away, but my thoughts raced. What was I doing? Why was I considering getting involved in her world?

The flash of fear on her face when he'd grabbed her had been unmistakable, and it had done something to me. And despite everything, despite my better judgment, I wanted to erase that fear and replace it with…what? Security? Comfort?

"Shit," I groaned, resting my forehead against the steering wheel. This was not about being the hero—it was about a connection that threatened to unravel the very fabric of my carefully constructed existence.

The drive home was a blur—my thoughts a maelstrom. My usual certainty had abandoned me, replaced by unfamiliar indecision. Part of me wanted to delve deeper, to solve the mystery that was Samantha Sheridan, to understand the shadows that danced behind those vivid blue eyes. Another part, the rational side that had governed my life thus far, urged caution. Involvement meant complication, and Sam's emotional baggage might end up being more than I bargained for.

By the time I reached my townhouse, the sky had brightened. A new day was dawning. I sat there in the silence of my garage, the engine idling, wrestling with emotions that were both alien and intoxicating. With a sigh, I killed the ignition and stepped out of the car.

"Damn it, Atticus!" I shouted, raking a hand through my hair. "What are you doing?"

I slammed the door and headed inside, unable to shake the disquieting sense that my life was no longer entirely my own.

Lazily, I removed my scrubs and collapsed onto my bed. The sunlight crept through the blinds, casting bars of gold across the room.

But I couldn't sleep. As I turned over for the umpteenth time, I wondered what the next shift would bring. Would Sam be there, her gaze meeting mine with the same defiance as before? Or would she fade away, just another nurse in the corridors of the ED?

Only time would tell. But one thing was certain—I was inexplicably, irrevocably drawn to the flame that was Samantha Sheridan, and whether I'd get burned remained to be seen.

I lay in bed, restless, staring at the ceiling, unable to shake the thoughts of Sam from my mind. Goddammit, I couldn't understand what it was about her that had me so wound up. My hand slid down to my cock, which was already half-hard as I thought about her. I started stroking myself slowly, hoping to relieve some of the tension that had been building within me.

It had been a long and exhausting night at the hospital, and then I'd had to deal with Sam's brute of a father. As I drifted off to sleep, my mind began to blur the lines between reality and fantasy. In the haze of my dream, I saw Samantha standing before me, completely nude. Her thick, curly red hair cascaded down over her breasts. Her creamy pale skin was dotted with freckles, and soft reddish-golden curls teased the edges of her pussy. The sight of her made my breath hitch. Her piercing blue eyes stared right at me. She reached for my dick, and suddenly, it was her hand wrapped around me instead of my own.

My pulse quickened, and the dream shifted. I found myself tied to a straight-backed chair, hands behind my back, sharp bindings biting into my ankles, wrists, and shoulders. Panic set in when I realized I'd lost all control, something I never allowed with any woman. It went against my every instinct to relinquish control. Samantha stood over me, a wicked grin on her face as she continued to stroke my now throbbing cock.

"Watch me," she commanded, her voice sultry and dominant. I tried not to show my unease, but it was hard to deny the thrill of being at her mercy. As my dick swelled under her touch, something inside me gave way. Perhaps it was exhaustion, but I allowed myself to submit to her fully. When she saw that I was surrendering, she whispered, "Good boy." The words made my cock twitch and grow even harder.

I relinquished every last shred of control. I was hers—body, mind, and soul. She had broken through my defenses and found a part of me that I'd never even known existed. And no matter how much it scared me, I realized there was no turning back. What the fuck was happening to me? Why had I given up control so easily to this woman who had invaded my thoughts? But the intensity of the moment compelled me to focus on her touch.

My chest tightened as I watched Samantha's talented hands work their magic on my dick. She cupped and teased my balls, sending shivers up my spine. The way she looked at me with those naughty blue eyes made her movements even more provocative.

"Like what you see?" she asked, her voice dripping with seduction.

I wanted nothing more than to touch her, but the restraints kept me in check. It was maddening. I was at her mercy, and yet I didn't want it any other way.

Samantha smirked and lowered her head, her long hair tumbling over my thighs like silk. Her lips hovered just above my aching cock, and then she finally went down on me, taking me into the warmth of her mouth. My breath caught in my throat when she licked the rim of my head, teasing the sensitive frenulum with each stroke.

For some time she continued licking and sucking, and soon I felt myself approaching the edge. The intensity of the moment was threatening to consume me entirely when suddenly she withdrew her lips from my cock and stood before me, a coy smile playing on her full lips.

"Are you enjoying yourself, Doctor?" she asked.

"More than you can imagine," I admitted, trying to catch my breath. "But why did you stop? I was so close…"

"Maybe I wanted to see how badly you want it," she replied, raising an eyebrow. "You've never given up control like this before, have you?"

"Never," I confessed, the admission making me feel exposed in a way I hadn't anticipated. But there was something about her that made me want to push my boundaries, to explore the unknown with her as my guide. And if that meant relinquishing control—at least for a little while—then so be it. The truth was, I had no idea how it felt. All I knew was that I had never experienced anything quite like this before, and I couldn't get enough.

Samantha straddled my lap, pressing her dripping wet folds against my aching shaft. The heady scent of her arousal turned me on even more. I tried to swallow but found it impossible because she had wrapped her hand around my throat, carefully cutting off my air supply.

I tried to protest, but my voice was choked by her grip. Sweat formed on my brow as the lack of oxygen began to overcome me.

Just when I thought I couldn't take it any longer, Samantha rose slightly. With her other hand, she guided my throbbing cock into her pussy, impaling herself on me.

All at once, I fought to breathe. I was teetering on the edge of panic when Samantha's voice brought me back: "Relax, Atticus. Just let go." And so I did.

The bliss of being inside her, coupled with the lack of air, sent my mind reeling. It was a struggle between torment and pleasure, a battle I'd never experienced before. But as my vision blurred and my lungs screamed for oxygen, a primal desire took hold—a need to claim Samantha as mine.

When she began to ride me, the room seemed to spin around us. My heart thundered in my ears, drowning out all other sounds. I was completely lost in her, in the way she moved and the pleasure she brought me.

Just as my world started to fade, I jolted awake, gasping for air. My heart was hammering away in my chest, and I realized my own hand was still wrapped around my leaking, rock-hard dick. As enthralled by the intensity of the dream as I was, it only took a couple of strokes before I came, squirting my load all over my belly. Then reality crashed down on me—it had all been a dream.

"Jesus Christ," I muttered, still trying to catch my breath. I hadn't had a wet dream since I was a teen. What the hell kind of spell did Sam have over me that she could infiltrate my dreams like this?

I couldn't believe that a nurse so much younger than me, someone with such little sexual experience, could affect me so strongly. Lying there, covered in sweat and cum, all I could think about was how badly I wanted Samantha's sassy mouth wrapped around my dick.

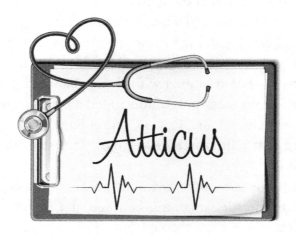

Chapter Five

Four days had passed since I'd dropped Sam off at her apartment, and during those four days my mind had been tormented. Sam had occupied my every thought. As I awaited our first shift together since the attack, I sat at a clinical workstation, staring blankly at the computer screen, the medical data in front of me barely registering. Restlessly, my leg bounced up and down, a rare sign of agitation that I usually kept under strict control. The memory of Sam's altercation with her father gnawed at me, and I needed to lay eyes on her to see firsthand how she was holding up.

"Get a grip, Atticus," I mumbled, struggling to comprehend why I was so compelled to protect this young woman. I was about to hit forty, and I was well-established in my medical career. Here at St. John's, I was both respected and feared. I was known for my emotional detachment and my clinical precision, not for allowing women to unleash emotional turmoil in my life.

But who was I kidding? From the moment I had seen Sam struggling with her car, something had shifted. The way she'd stood up to her father, a man who clearly haunted her past and threatened her present, had demonstrated a certain strength that deeply resonated with me. It was a side of Sam I hadn't expected to see, one that contradicted the snarky nurse I sparred with here in the ED.

I tried to focus on my work, but my thoughts kept drifting back to her—her defiance, her courage, her stormy blue eyes that seemed to see right through me. This was more than just a physical attraction; it was a connection I couldn't quite comprehend, one that left me feeling unbalanced.

I ran a hand over my face and sighed, slumping back into my chair. "Why am I so fucking intrigued by her?" I wondered softly out loud, my fingers drumming on the desk. She was just a nurse—a young, intelligent, quick-witted nurse who had the audacity to challenge me at every turn—and yet, there was something about her, something that made me want to break all my self-imposed rules.

Suddenly, Jack, one of our ED nurses, came to stand directly in front of me. "Dr. Thorin, can I have a word?" he asked, his brow furrowed as he leaned in.

I glanced up. "What's going on, Jack?"

He handed me a chart. "It's about Mrs. Henderson, the elderly lady who came in with back pain and nausea. She's complaining of increased discomfort, and her vitals are fluctuating. I'm concerned it might be a myocardial infarction."

I quickly reviewed her chart. "Let's get her on an ECG immediately and run a full cardiac enzyme panel. Administer aspirin and start her on nitroglycerin, stat. Also, prepare her for potential thrombolytic therapy, depending on the ECG results," I instructed, handing back the chart. "And page the cardiologist on call to come immediately. I'm pretty sure it's Dr. Patel tonight, but double-check me."

Jack nodded as he took the chart and turned to leave. "On it, Dr. Thorin. I'll make sure the cardiologist is briefed as soon as they arrive."

When I turned back to the computer to resume entering my notes, my thoughts wandered again, drifting to the memory of the fear in Sam's eyes when her father had shoved her and pulled back his fist.

Dammit, I couldn't get her out of my head.

Samantha Sheridan was going to be the death of me.

My frustration mounting, I rubbed at the crease in my forehead. She was too young. Too naive. And she was a nurse in my ED, for God's sake. After Bethany, I'd sworn I would never take a chance on another woman from this hospital.

With a snarl, I surged to my feet and began to pace. I didn't do relationships. Never had. They were too messy, too complicated. Women always wanted more from me than I was willing to give.

I'd built my life specifically to avoid the kind of intimacy Sam needed. I always kept my liaisons short and strictly physical, and women knew the score going in. It was better that way. Cleaner.

Fingers snapped in front of my face. "Did you hear me?" Bethany asked, her brown eyes wary. "We've got a multicar pileup coming in. At least six patients. ETA five minutes."

I nodded, the familiar surge of adrenaline kicking in as my mind transitioned to the trauma ahead. "Page the on-call team. And clear Trauma One through Three."

"On it," she said over her shoulder.

My gaze cut to the clock again. Time to save some lives. For now, I would shove thoughts of Sam aside.

The waiting room was utter bedlam. Police officers directed traffic while paramedics wheeled in victims on gurneys, stabilizing IV lines and clamping oxygen masks in place. Screams and sobs filled the air as loved ones tried to get information about the injured.

I spotted Sam doing triage at the admittance desk. Her expression was grim. Our eyes met over the heads of the crowd, and a quick flash of understanding passed between us. We both had a job to do.

Striding toward her, I assessed the situation. "We've got three critical coming in," I said. "One with massive internal bleeding and a possible ruptured spleen. A head trauma and a femoral break with arterial damage."

Sam nodded, already reaching for charts. "Trauma One through Three are prepped and ready."

"Perfect. Let's move them in and get to work."

The emergency department descended into controlled chaos. For the next few hours, I lost myself in the steady beeping of heart monitors and the familiar weight of medical tools in my hands.

It was nearly dawn by the time we stabilized the last victim. Exhaustion pulled at my limbs, a bone-deep ache I was long accustomed to but still dreaded.

I found Sam slumped in a chair in the break room, her eyes bleary over the rim of a coffee cup.

"Hey." I grabbed a chair and sat across the table from her. "You did good work tonight."

Her mouth curved up in a listless smile. "So did you, Dr. Thorin."

An uneasy silence fell between us. I studied the curve of her profile, the sweep of dark lashes against her skin. She was beautiful in a way that stole my breath, and it had nothing to

Night Shift

do with her physical attractiveness; it was the strength and compassion that I saw in her as she worked.

She took a long drink from her bottle of water. Watching her swallow, the memory of my dream and her naked body drifted to mind. Just as I began to imagine her lips wrapped around my cock, my thoughts were interrupted by the door to the break room opening and several people walking in. Around us, the room became a hub of activity, with fellow doctors and nurses grabbing quick coffees and sharing snippets of their night. I was half-listening, half-lost in my own world, mulling over the best approach to take with Sam after everything that had happened. As the minutes ticked by, the break room gradually emptied, the staff trickling back to their duties, leaving just Sam and me in a quiet bubble amidst the otherwise hectic night. This was the perfect chance for us to talk, without the prying eyes and ears of the hospital staff around us.

"So, Sammich," I said, trying to lighten the mood as we settled into our chairs. "Did you manage to get your car fixed?"

Sam looked up. "Yeah, one of Bethany's friends helped me. Turns out it was just a bad battery. Thankfully, it didn't cost too much to replace."

"Good to hear." I was relieved that she wouldn't have to worry about transportation.

"Thanks for asking, *Atti*," Sam said, a hint of a smile playing on her lips. The nickname caught me off guard. It was one my brothers had teased me with when we were growing up because it sounded girlie, but coming from her, I liked it.

Since I was still conflicted about my sexual attraction to Sam, I decided that the best way to get her out of my mind was to ask her on a date. Every time I'd tried taking a woman on a casual date in the past, it had always ended with me never wanting to see her again. Movie dates and picnics were not my thing.

Anything other than a casual hookup left too much time for talking, which led to me getting annoyed and my libido turning stone-cold. Meeting and fucking for hours was all I needed.

I leaned in, my mind already formulating a plan. "Say, Sam, do you like hiking?"

She eyed me curiously. "Hiking? That's random, isn't it? Since when are you interested in anything outside the ED?"

I chuckled, trying to appear nonchalant. "Believe it or not, I do occasionally enjoy the great outdoors. There are some beautiful trails around Tacoma. Ever been?"

Sam shrugged, a hint of interest flickering in her eyes. "No, I've never been hiking. Too busy studying in college and now working here. I haven't done much else."

"Well, there's a first time for everything. On my next days off, I was thinking of going and spending some time at my cabin on Tanwax Lake. You should come along. It wouldn't be a date, just some fresh air and a place to kick back for a couple of days. We could even invite some other people. My place has plenty of room."

Her brow furrowed slightly. "I don't know, Dr. Thorin. It seems kind of awkward...our age difference and all."

I nodded, understanding her hesitation. "I get it, Sam. The age difference might seem like a lot. But here's the thing—age doesn't really dictate our experiences or the connections we make. I've met lots of people my age whom I have nothing in common with, and there are plenty of people younger than me who enjoy the same things I do. It's about the person, not the number. As for the cabin, think of it as an opportunity to unwind and take a break from the stress of the ED. You've been through a lot recently—new city, new job, and...that incident with your dad. A change of scenery could do you some good." I leaned back in my seat, draping my arms over the chairs on either side. "No pressure, though. I just thought I'd ask."

Sam regarded me skeptically. "I...I don't know about it being an overnight thing either. Plus, I've never really been one for hiking. I'm not sure it's a good idea... I don't think mixing my work life and my personal life is the best thing to do. And honestly, I'm not sure I'm ready for any conversations about what happened with my father."

"If it's the outdoor activities that are worrying you, I'll make you a promise that if we encounter any bears, I'll protect you. Or at least run slower than you."

She gave me a genuine laugh. "You'd sacrifice yourself to the bears for me? How gallant."

Leaning forward and resting my elbows on the table, I gave her a mock-serious look. "Of course. It's the least I could do. And after our hike, I'll cook us dinner. My culinary skills are almost as impressive as my surgical ones."

Sam bit her lip. "You cooking? That I have to see."

"Think of it as a friendly outing then. Besides, who wouldn't want to spend a day away from this chaos?" I gestured at the hectic emergency department beyond the break room door. "And if you want me to take you home after dinner, I'll be happy to do it. No big deal."

"All right, fine. How bad can it be to go hiking and have a man make me a home-cooked meal?" she asked. "But if we run into any mountain lions, I'm shoving you at them."

Was that a trace of flirtation in her voice?

"I'll have you know I'm quite the negotiator with wildlife. They find me charming."

Sam shook her head in amusement. "Okay, I'll take you up on this little excursion. I must admit, you've piqued my curiosity in more ways than one. But remember, it's not a date."

"Absolutely, not a date," I agreed. A surprising jolt of excitement ran through me. "I'll pick you up Thursday afternoon at, let's say, one."

"Good, it's a date—uh, I mean, not a date. You know what I mean."

I chuckled, standing up as a couple of people entered the break room. "Not a date. Got it. Sounds like a plan, Sammich."

"Wow," she teased, raising an eyebrow. "Are you always this persistent, Dr. Thorin?"

"Only when it's worth it."

Just then, the intercom blared, calling for immediate assistance in the ED.

Sam stood up, slapping her professional demeanor back into place. "Looks like break time's over. Duty calls."

"Right."

As she hurried out the door, I smiled, not believing that had actually worked out. I would finally be getting to spend some time with her.

For the first time in a long while, I was excited about doing something beyond the confines of the hospital. Sam had fascinated me in an unexpected way, and the prospect of being with her outside of work gave me an adrenaline charge.

I had been with lots of women before, but they had all been casual encounters—sex for gratification and nothing more. In all honesty, that was what I'd thought I wanted with Sam too.

I threw my coffee cup in the trash and made my way out of the break room. As I replayed our conversation in my head, I wondered why I was drawn to her so strongly. Perhaps it was my protective instincts, triggered by her vulnerability in the confrontation with her father. Whatever the reason, I couldn't deny the pull I felt toward her, and it nagged at me.

"Dammit," I muttered under my breath, running a hand through my hair. Was I really interested in this girl?

The next few shifts were going to be a struggle. I wanted nothing more than to get past them and take Sam on our not-a-date hike. I was hoping that spending time together outside of the hospital would shed some light on what was going on inside my head.

While I made my way down the hallway, I weighed the possible outcomes of our outing. If we didn't feel a spark, then perhaps it would be for the best. I could move on, chalk up my infatuation to an odd fluke, and return to my solitary existence. But if we did have chemistry... I shuddered at the thought. Would I be able to keep things purely physical, as I had always done in the past?

For now, patients were waiting, and the familiar call of duty pulled me back into the fray of the ED. The hike, and whatever it might bring, would have to wait.

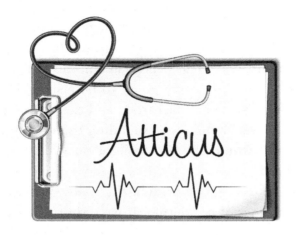

Chapter Six

It was finally our day off together.

Sliding into the Mercedes, I had to admit that the prospect of what could happen this weekend was unnerving. I often applied the same philosophies of structure and routine I used at work to my relationships with women.

Observation. Assessment. Application. Outcome. And the efficacy of my practice was solely determined by one thing: a positive outcome.

My mind, generally unplagued by worries over women, had done nothing but hassle the hell out of me over Sam.

I'd been dreaming about her. That was the first significant change I'd noticed after meeting Sam. I never dreamed...hadn't since I was fifteen. Sam had been in every single one, and these dreams had been...unusual. Unusual in the sense that I was the one who gave up control. No matter the scene, no matter the situation. Control was always…handed…over.

I pulled up to Sam's apartment, ready for our little getaway. A few minutes earlier, I'd messaged her, in hopes—or more likely expecting—that she'd be ready and waiting outside. To my irritation, she was nowhere in sight. That would be a matter for later discussion.

With a sigh, I texted her again to let her know I was out front and waiting. While my car idled in the parking lot, my gaze was drawn to the door of her apartment on the second floor, reminding me of what a fucking dump she lived in. Garbage littered the sidewalk, and a group of sorry-looking individuals, likely homeless, loitered right outside of the entrance to her apartment. It dawned on me just how desperate her situation in Aberdeen must have been for her to consider this place a refuge. And given what I knew of her father, I shuddered to think of the environment she'd escaped from. It was a good thing she'd gotten out.

My phone buzzed with her response.

On my way down.

My eyes remained fixed on the group of men that stood outside of her apartment. The protective side of me kicked in, so I decided to meet her at the entrance.

Slamming the car door shut, I shoved my keys and phone in my pocket. My long strides ate up the distance to the apartment entryway in seconds. I took the stairs two at a time, swiftly reaching her door.

"Got any spare change, fancy pants?" murmured a man who was leaning against the wall across from Sam's door.

I turned to him, my irritation flaring. "Fancy pants?" I snarled. "What if I did? What would you do with it?" I leaned toward him in a silent threat. "What if I had a bill of every single denomination, and your answer determined which one you received...if I gave you anything at all?"

The man seemed to ponder my challenge.

"For starters," he said with a crude frankness, "I wouldn't have to suck my friend's dick for my next meal."

His response left me stunned.

"You know what amazes me?" I asked in all sincerity.

"What's that?" The man coughed, hawking up phlegm and spitting it on the ground in front of me. From the sound of it, I would bet he had a bacterial infection in his lungs.

"You're out here shivering in the cold, and I can only assume that you're homeless, probably hungry, yet you've got a sense of humor." Despite the circumstances, I was genuinely intrigued.

Through a grin marred by several missing teeth, he shot back, "Who said I was kidding? Some people suck dick for drugs... others, well, for companionship and nourishment."

I almost threw up in my mouth. Why couldn't I get away from this shit? At a nonprofit hospital like St. John's, we were required to provide free or discounted care to indigent patients, so I saw lots of people similar to this guy in the ED. It never ceased to surprise me, the stories they told or the things they said.

Just as I was about to hand the man some money, Sam walked out of her apartment. "Do not encourage him!"

"Saaaaaaam...how are ya?!" the man said, greeting her with too much familiarity for my taste.

"Alex...what did I tell you about hassling everybody that walks by?" Sam said sternly.

Pointing an accusing finger at the man, wallet still in hand, I turned to Sam. "You know this guy?"

She rolled her eyes and laughed softly, treating me like a naive child she had to tolerate, which, admittedly, caused a twinge in my groin. "He's my neighbor. He hangs outside with his friends here and pretends he's homeless," she explained.

I faced Alex, tightening my grip on my wallet. "You almost had me fooled," I admitted grudgingly.

"I mean...you can still give me money if you want. I *did* make you laugh."

I shook my head but couldn't stop myself from smirking at his audacity. "I praised you for maintaining a sense of humor in what I assumed were dire circumstances. Clearly, my assessment was incorrect."

"Do you always talk like that?" he asked. "You sound like a robot."

I scoffed at him. "Yeah...you're definitely not getting any money from me."

"Okay, enough of this," Sam said, sounding almost bored with the exchange. "Alex, always nice to see you. Stop harassing people. Atti, are you ready?"

"Atti?" Alex said with a snicker.

I fixed him with a glare that could pierce steel. "It's Doctor Thorin to you."

"Ohhh...a doctor! I guess *fancy pants* was spot on. Good for you, Sam!"

Instead of responding, I took Sam's hand and grabbed her bag. Alex's laughter followed us all the way down the stairs and to the car.

Still scowling at Alex, I opened the passenger-side door for her.

"Thank you, Atti. I guess I was wrong the other day when I accused you of forgetting the manners they taught you in *doctor's school*."

I gave her ass a hard smack, and she let out a small gasp just before she slid into the passenger seat. Leaning in close to her ear, I growled, "I'm not always a gentleman."

After tossing Sam's bag in the trunk along with the supplies I'd packed, I cast one last glance at Alex, offering him a smile that quickly turned into a raised middle finger. Alex reciprocated with one of his own, as well as a loud laugh.

And with that, I slid into my seat, and we were finally en route, leaving the unruliness of her apartment complex behind us.

"So, where are we going anyway?" Sam asked.

"First, we're gonna check out Swan Creek Trail here in Tacoma, and then we'll head south to Tanwax Lake. There's a cabin my brothers and I like to use when we want to escape the city. It isn't anything fancy, but it's away from, well, everything."

Sam had a beaming smile on her face as she settled back into the soft leather seat. Today was an unusually warm day for mid-October, and she'd chosen to wear cut-off jean shorts, a light-green cardigan over a white tank top, and a pair of slip-on sneakers with a hole in one toe. I wondered if she'd ever owned a pair of hiking boots. Not that it mattered today. The trails were well-worn and not too challenging.

"Are we going to go for a swim in the lake?" Sam asked. "I didn't bring a swimsuit with me."

I glanced sideways at her, a playful grin tugging at my lips. "You know, even though this lake usually stays warm because it's small, I think swimming right now would be pretty cold. Do you think you're going to need to cool down from something?" I paused, raising one eyebrow, then dropped my voice to a conspiratorial whisper. "If you're interested in something on the more heated side, we do have a hot tub at the cabin. But there's just one rule I have for it—no swimsuits allowed." The words rolled off my tongue with a light chuckle. I'd said it more to gauge her reaction than anything else.

Her face turned beet-red. "Dr. Thorin, is this your usual tactic? Luring women to a cabin in the woods?"

"Atticus. We're not at work," I corrected gently as I thought about what she'd asked. Her question, so direct and unfiltered, had caught me slightly off guard. I turned to look at her, deciding honesty was the best approach. "This hike, the cabin...isn't my usual modus operandi for...adventures with women." My gaze hardened. "Usually, I don't invest much emotional equity into female counterparts. The women I see understand that I don't do relationships and that when we're together, it's for our mutual gratification."

Sam scrutinized me for a long time before she responded.

"So you're a 'wham, bam, thank you ma'am, now get the fuck out' kind of guy?"

I choked and then laughed, but I heard the bottom line in her question and wanted to reassure her this was different.

"Sammich, is that what you think this is?"

"Atti, at this point, I'm just along for the ride, no pun intended...or maybe pun intended. I mean, I *am* in your car with you, so..."

Swan Creek Park wasn't far from her apartment, so before we could continue the conversation, we'd arrived. I shifted the car into park and turned toward her. "Let's go for a walk."

I popped the trunk, and Sam and I got out and started unloading the things we would need. I always came prepared. Granted, I normally went hiking on my own, but today I'd made sure to bring enough hydration for the both of us.

"This hike is approximately four miles round trip and should take us a couple of hours to complete, including time to stop and explore some areas of interest. However, if you need to take a break at any point, just let me know."

Sam glanced over at me, her lips curving into a devilish smile, which meant only one thing: some smart-ass comment would follow. She didn't disappoint.

"Listen, old man, I'm worried that the Alzheimer's might be kicking in, 'cause maybe you forget that I'm young and full of stamina," she quipped, putting a stamp on her sass with a wink.

I couldn't resist reminding her, "This *old man* has done a good job of taking care of himself and is in prime condition."

Before closing the trunk of the car, I stripped off my sweatshirt, pulling it up and over my head and deliberately exposing my well-defined abs. Sam's gaze was drawn to the bare skin, and her eyes traced the contours of my torso with undisguised interest.

"Someone's in shape and has a tan," she said, eating her words with a deep gulp.

"What was that? I didn't hear you. I guess my hearing must be going with my old age as well." I said, as I pulled on a T-shirt and shut the trunk.

She laughed and turned toward the trailhead.

Rays of sunlight streamed through the canopy of leaves as we entered Swan Creek Trail. The air was fresh and filled with the scent of damp earth and the sound of small creatures skittering around in the forest. I'd always loved this hidden gem of an urban park in the middle of Tacoma, not only for its beauty but also because there weren't many people who visited it during the weekdays.

"Isn't it incredible how peaceful it is here?" I asked Sam, gesturing to the lush greenery surrounding us. "It's like we're miles away from the city."

Night Shift

"Definitely," she replied, her eyes roaming over the landscape. "I love how we're surrounded by the thick woods and it feels like we're the only ones here. You're right; it's a nice escape from the chaos of the hospital."

The damp earth squished under my hiking boots as Sam and I made our way up the narrow trail. My mind raced with questions I wanted to ask her, but I held my tongue. We walked in silence, listening to the birds chirping in the trees above us.

As we rounded a corner overlooking the stream below, I noticed how the streaks of sunlight making their way through the tree canopy lit up her beautiful auburn curls. I pulled out my phone, put my arm around her, and said, "Smile." Just as I took the picture, she poked me in the ribs, evoking a big ole grin from me while I glanced over at her. I pocketed my phone and moved on.

I noticed that Sam didn't have her phone out and wasn't snapping pictures like most people her age would be doing. Curious, I asked, "Would you like me to take some pictures of you?"

She shook her head. "No, that's okay. Whenever I'm out in nature, I try to separate myself from technology, even when it comes to taking pictures. I figure if I have a good time doing whatever it is I'm doing, the memories will be there with me forever."

Who is this girl? I wondered, surprised that she actually preferred enjoying nature rather than posting pictures about it on social media.

"Really?" I asked, genuinely curious. "You don't use your phone much, do you?"

"Actually, I didn't have a cell phone until college," she said. "I couldn't afford one, and there was no way my father would spend money on anything he didn't have to. He only gave me grocery money because he didn't want the Department of Children, Youth, and Families called, since he was given probation until I turned eighteen."

Her candidness about her past and the mention of Mac's issues with the law caught me off guard. I wanted to learn more about her story. "What happened with your father, if you don't mind me asking?"

Sam hesitated. "Promise me something first," she said, her eyes narrowing slightly. "For every question you ask about my past, you have to answer one in return."

"Fair enough," I agreed, intrigued by the prospect. My years as an emergency-room doctor had honed my ability to ask leading and fulsome questions, putting me at an advantage.

For a few strides, I mulled over how to ask Sam about her past and how to phrase my first question to get the most information from her. I decided to begin by summarizing what I knew about her so far. "From what I've gathered, your father is an alcoholic, since he reeked of it the other morning, most likely a drug addict based on the condition of his teeth, unemployed with the way he demanded money, and violent...because of the way he attacked you. And something must have happened to your mother since you've never mentioned her. I was wondering if you might want to tell me more about what's going on with your dad and what happened to your mom."

Sam's steps faltered for a moment before she righted herself. We stopped, and I turned to face her. For a minute, she remained silent, and I thought she might refuse to answer.

She bit her lip, looking down at the ground while she considered my question. Finally, she sighed, as though resigning herself to share more about her past. "My father was always a heavy drinker and sometimes became abusive to my mother when I was little, even before the wreck," she began.

Night Shift

I instantly felt a pang of regret for asking. "Shit, I'm so sorry, Sam—"

She shrugged. "It was a long time ago."

I stared at her, puzzled by her matter-of-fact tone.

"That doesn't make it any easier," I said, thinking of my own mother, who had died when I was only fifteen. The rawness of everything that had led up to it had never fully left me. "Losing a parent so young..." My voice faded. I didn't know how to comfort her, to lessen the pain of that old wound.

She shoved her hands in her pockets and started shuffling along the trail again, kicking rocks. "Mac and my mother were at a Christmas party with friends, and I was at a babysitter's house. I was eight years old. I wasn't feeling well, so the babysitter called my parents. They left the party, and of course, my dad was drunk. After picking me up at the babysitter's house, he ran a stop sign and struck another car. The wreck killed my mother and injured the people in the other car. Then my father was convicted of vehicular manslaughter but only given probation so that I wouldn't be left without a parent. His probation ended when I turned eighteen, and so did the roof over my head."

"Wow, that's...a lot to deal with," I said softly. I reached out and twined my fingers with hers, giving her a reassuring squeeze. We walked for a while without speaking.

After taking a few deep breaths, she recounted more of her tumultuous past, detailing the abuse she'd suffered under her father's drunken rages and her struggle to grow up in such a harsh environment.

"I learned early on that I couldn't depend on him, so I took care of myself. Worked my way through school and got my nursing degree. And built my own life." She lifted her chin. "I don't need anyone to take care of me. I've wrestled my demons and mostly have them pretty well caged."

I believed her. Sam was one of the most capable, levelheaded nurses I'd worked with. But I also sensed a deep vulnerability beneath her veneer of strength.

Despite everything she'd been through, she stood here, determined to build a better life for herself. And the fact that she was still willing to share some of her most painful memories with me, a man she barely knew, was both humbling and inspiring.

Before I could stop myself, I reached over and gave her shoulders a hug. She tensed but didn't pull away.

"All right," she said. "Now it's my turn to ask you a question."

"Go ahead, ask away." I braced myself for whatever probing query she might throw at me, then took her hand once again. This time, she held it firmly. We picked up the pace.

"Have you ever been married?" Sam asked simply.

"No," I said quickly, not offering anything more. She let out an exasperated huff of frustration at my lack of detail.

"Come on, Atticus. You have to give me more than that," she insisted, sticking her tongue out playfully.

"All right, all right," I conceded, allowing myself a small smile. "I've never been married because I've always been focused on my career. Relationships are just too time-consuming for me to navigate alongside the demands of being an emergency-room doctor."

That answer seemed to satisfy her, and for a few minutes we walked in a comfortable silence with the wind rustling the leaves overhead.

I really wanted to know about her past, but I didn't want to bring up any more painful memories.

"Sam, let me ask you this," I said, taking a deep breath before launching into my next question. "You mentioned that, before the wreck, your father was already a heavy drinker and could sometimes be abusive to your mother. Can you tell me more about how that affected you growing up?" I mentally rolled my eyes at the clinical way I was speaking to her. God, I could be such an uptight asshole sometimes. It was high time I learned how to approach these things with more empathy, especially with her.

Sam hesitated for a moment, and when she finally spoke, her voice was tinged with sadness. "Yeah, my father was always drunk. And when he drank, he'd get violent. My mom tried to protect me as best she could, but there's only so much you can do against someone like him."

Her steps slowed and her thumb ran over the back of my hand as she took a minute to respond. "After the car wreck, everything just spiraled out of control. With my mom gone, there was no one to shield me from his fists. I had to grow up fast, learning how to take care of myself and avoid his rages. It was...hard, to say the least."

Her words resonated within me, stirring up my own memories of loss and pain. I couldn't imagine how difficult it must have been for her to endure such hardships and violence at such a young age. At least I'd had brothers. She didn't have anyone. That deep-seated need to fix her, to protect her that lived within me, came boiling to the surface.

Sam gave me a playful nudge. "Now it's my turn to ask you a question." She leaned into my side and glanced up at me. "Why don't you build connections with women? Like, serious connections? I know I joked around earlier about the whole 'wham bam thank you ma'am' thing, but there must be a reason."

I wasn't ready for this.

As I attempted to formulate a response, I suddenly realized how tightly I was gripping her hand and tried to relax. "Let's just keep walking."

After several minutes of silence, I knew I needed to start talking, explain this to her. It was only fair, since she'd been so open with me. "Obviously, I'm a lot older than you—and I've spent a lot of years working in the emergency department. You understand how demanding it is and all the crazy hours we work, especially doing shift rotations. When I was in school and first working, there just wasn't time for relationships. After that...I guess it became a habit. And to be honest, I find women too demanding, they all want to set up house and have babies. I just don't know if I'm the commitment type, much less up for being a parent. I'm sure some psych doc would say I was fixated at some stage or another. It's just easier for me to keep things simple, you know?"

I hadn't told her the truth about the real reason I avoided relationships, because I was nowhere near dealing with all the emotional baggage I carried. She had no idea how deeply I understood her childhood trauma or that I knew how badly parents could fuck up their kids' lives.

The silence that followed my answer seemed to stretch on for an eternity. I could tell that Sam was mulling over what I'd shared and struggling with her own thoughts and questions. Finally, after a few more minutes of walking, I broke the silence.

"Sam," I began hesitantly, "I have another question for you, if it's okay."

Her crystal-blue eyes met mine, and although I sensed she was worried about what I might ask next, she gave me a small nod, signaling for me to continue.

"Based on what you've been through and the discussion I overheard between you and Bethany, do you feel your...let's just say, your less than satisfying encounters with men were a result of limited experience, or rather trust issues?" I hoped I hadn't crossed a line with my bluntness. But who was I kidding? Most of the time, I just couldn't help myself.

Night Shift

Sam's face flushed a deep crimson, and she looked away from me, focusing her attention on the trail ahead. As we approached the wooden bridge that marked the halfway point of our walk, she remained silent. The water glistened from the sunlight filtering through the trees, while a squirrel scolded us from a high branch for disturbing it. The normalcy of the scene belied the maelstrom of emotions swirling within us.

When we reached the bridge, Sam stepped up onto the first slat of the railing with her toes, leaning over the edge to watch the water below. I stood next to her, resting my elbows on the handrail, careful not to touch her as she gathered herself to speak.

"Atticus, that's...that's really personal," she choked out.

"Remember, you're the one who made the deal...a question for a question," I reminded her, my eyes searching hers to see if she was going to back out of our little deal.

I kept replaying her story in my mind, and as I did so, the pieces clicked into place. Her wariness of intimacy, her insistence on independence...it all stemmed from a childhood of neglect and abuse at the hands of the man who should have been her protector.

Rage simmered in my gut, rage at the injustice of it. If Mac Sheridan crossed my path again, I didn't know if I could restrain myself from violence. He deserved to suffer for what he'd done.

But indulging in fantasies of vengeance would serve no purpose. I was determined to prove to Sam that not all men were like her father.

"Both," she finally answered. "I've only been with one guy, in college, and he was...let's just say, young and inexperienced. He only wanted a quick fuck, and I was so afraid of making him angry or upset that I focused solely on him. Honestly, I don't understand what the big deal is with sex; it mostly just hurts or is embarrassing."

With a cynical chuckle and a shake of her head, she glanced over at me and said, "And as far as trust goes...I don't trust anyone. My father blamed me for my mother's death and his conviction. He hated me after the wreck, and when he drank, he'd beat me. I learned to run fast and hide well to get away from him."

She took a deep breath before she continued. "I guess I've become an expert at hiding—not just from my father, but from my own emotions. I think that's why I've never allowed myself to truly let go and be with a guy. I'm afraid of giving someone the power to hurt me like my father did."

Her raw honesty cut straight to my heart. At that moment, I saw Sam for who she truly was—a strong woman who'd had to deal with unimaginable pain.

"I'm guessing you think all men are bad because of your father, how you were raised, and your impoverished circumstances. Or maybe you've just never met a man who knows how to treat a woman right." I wanted her to know that not all men were like her father. I wanted her to be open to the idea that sex could be an enjoyable experience when shared with the right person. "You just need to find a man who will worship you, someone who can guide you to explore the most amazing aspects of sexuality, like building trust, experimenting safely, and discovering new pleasures together." I said this in an attempt to comfort her, but my words came out all wrong, twisted with unintentional condescension. "Just so you know, I think you're a beautiful, smart girl."

Her eyes narrowed. Hopping off the railing, she moved to stand in front of me. I leaned back, placing my elbows on the wooden plank behind me. She crossed her arms defensively over her chest and then raised her hand to chew on the tip of her thumbnail as she scrutinized me. "First of all, don't call me a girl.

Night Shift

I hate it when men call a woman *baby* or tell them they're a *good girl*, as if we're not fully formed, intelligent adults. When does someone go from girl to woman anyway? When does one earn enough respect to be considered an equal?" She paused, jutting her chin up in the air defiantly.

Damn, her eyes were as fiery as her hair. I had to run my hand over my mouth to hide what I was thinking—that her bold audacity reminded me of how she'd taken control in my dreams. In my experience, the saucier a woman's bravado, the more obedient she became upon surrender. I bet she'd love being praised as a *good girl*, knowing that she was adored—the object of my strongest desire.

Letting out a loud huff, she continued. "Look, I may be poor, but I'm not desperate. Being poor doesn't mean I'm weak or needy. I managed to get myself educated, and I have a job that pays well, has long-term security, and gives me a sense of doing something important for people who are suffering. Nursing is hard, and I've got a lot to learn, but I don't need a man to take care of me. Being independent and standing on my own two feet is all that matters to me right now." Her voice was growing more passionate while her hands gestured wildly in my face.

"Besides, in my experience—and trust me, you've made it perfectly clear that my experience in both nursing and sex is limited—most men are concrete thinkers who are self-absorbed. They only see women and, well, everything in life as transactional. It's all about what they get. It's never about an equal partnership. Maybe if I ever meet a man who's different, I'll change my mind. I get that sounds judgmental, but that's my opinion. Besides, I think sex is overrated. Maybe it's just me, and I don't have the right competence... Who knows, I'm young. Maybe I'm wrong and I'm missing out on the greatest thrill ride on earth, and a sexpert will come along and enlighten me." She threw her hands up in the air, turned, and started walking back the way we'd come.

I stood there, dumbstruck by the force of her words. A few paces away, she abruptly stopped and whirled around to throw me a defiant glare. In truth, I was completely disarmed by her candor and strength—a rarity for me. It surprised me that a woman so much younger than me was able to affect me this way.

Even though her words stung, I admired her fire. She was fiercely independent, a survivor, and she wasn't about to let anyone make her feel small or inadequate. I realized how wrong I had been to try to impose my opinions on her, to assume I knew what was best for her simply because I was older and more experienced. But then again, I did have a lot of experience pleasing women, and she barely knew how to please herself. Why was I second-guessing myself with her?

"Sam, wait." I sped up, reducing the distance between. "I'm sorry," I said, taking her by both shoulders. "You're absolutely right. I didn't mean to make such sweeping assumptions about you. It's not my place to tell you how to live your life or what to think about men and relationships."

She studied my face before nodding, accepting my apology with grace.

"Samantha," I said slowly, dropping my hands and trying to find the right words to convey what I was thinking without pissing her off further. "You've shown incredible courage in the face of adversity. I'm sorry for making stupid statements about you based on your age and background, and I apologize for being condescending or dismissive."

For a few seconds, she regarded me cautiously. "Thank you," she replied softly. "That means a lot to me."

The tension between us eased slightly.

Night Shift

For reasons I couldn't quite explain, I was compelled to share something from my past. "You know, Sam, I understand more than most how you feel. I lost my mother when I was fifteen. She passed away suddenly, and it was a devastating blow to our family. I've spent years burying the pain and focusing on my career, but seeing your resilience makes me wonder if maybe I haven't coped as well as I thought. You're handling everything with much more grace and strength than I ever have."

Sam tilted her head and knitted her brow. It seemed she was reassessing her opinion of me. She chuckled and nodded, as if she'd just had some great epiphany.

"Now I get it, Atticus. You're so painfully obvious. Simple, really...you've never gotten over the death of your mother. Whatever happened has caused you to lock away all your trust in women and throw away the key. You've developed quite the savior complex." She leaned in and placed her hand squarely on my chest and patted it. "You act like you're a connoisseur of sex, but I have to wonder just how great it is for you if you've never trusted a woman. Maybe you're not the expert you think you are."

Damn, she was blunt. I pulled back a little, stunned. Running my thumb over my lip, I studied her for a moment. "Maybe you're right. I'll give you that much," I conceded. "But at least I've gotten off with a woman. Hell, it's usually multiple times. And not to brag or anything, but I know how to make a woman come. I've never walked away from a woman without fully satisfying her. In that, I'm an expert."

Sam's mouth dropped open, but words failed her. I chuckled at her flustered expression. From the gleam in her eye, it was clear she was struggling to devise a clever retort, but it just wouldn't come.

"Come on," I said. "Let's head back to the car and go to the cabin. That is, if you're still game?"

She gave me a mischievous grin. "Absolutely, I am. You promised me a fabulous dinner, remember?"

We continued our hike in companionable silence, lost in our thoughts as we navigated the trail and reflected on the revelations we'd just shared.

Opening up to Sam had been both humbling and liberating. It made me question the emotional walls I'd built around myself over the years. In her, I'd found an unexpected source of provocation and a reminder that insight could sometimes be found in the most unlikely places.

"Sam," I said, stopping at a little bend in the path as we approached the end of the trail, "I want you to know that I truly appreciate your honesty and willingness to share very private things about yourself. I hope we can learn to trust each other."

A genuine smile spread across her face. "I'd like that, Atticus." Then she started down the trail again with a pep in her step.

"Besides, I'm guessing that you're the one who needs saving," she said, giving me a playful shove when I caught up to her. "Seeing as you're about to hit forty and have never had a loving relationship with a woman. Like you said, you've kept things simple—only sexual gratification. I bet you're now questioning if it's all been worth it. Basically, I think you pride yourself on being a transactional man, always calculating what's in it for you. But look at what it's cost you—real connections, the chance to experience love. That's more than just a trade-off, if you ask me. When was the last time you felt truly loved, not just needed for what you can provide?"

My breath caught in my throat, and I swallowed hard. She was right. But how could she know all this? It was as if she had reached into my soul and pulled out my deepest fears and insecurities. As I struggled to come up with a response, my foot snagged on a root, making me stumble like an idiot. What was going on here? How had she turned the tables on me?

"Sam, I—" My voice cracked, and I cleared my throat. "You're right. I've never allowed myself to love or be loved." I paused for a moment, gathering my thoughts. "My entire life, I've been driven to help people, fix people, to make things happen. And mostly, I've done just that. But I can never seem to fix the bigger issues that are really hurting people."

Unable to meet her gaze, I stared at the trees further up the trail. "There are always those people I see over and over again in the ED—not because I don't give them good treatment but because they don't get their underlying issues fixed, like drug or alcohol addiction, or because they can't afford the general care they need. I do the best I can, but I sometimes wonder if my life will ever be anything more than a revolving door. Just a temporary band-aid."

"Anyway," I said abruptly, forcing a smile onto my lips and changing the subject, "we should finish our walk and get to the cabin. I've got a fabulous meal planned for later: my grandmother's Swedish meatballs."

Sam laughed, and the sound was like music. "All right, Dr. Thorin. You can change the subject. But just so you know, I still think you deserve better than just going through the motions."

"Okay, Sam. I hear you," I murmured. "And maybe you should be willing to experiment and live a little before you grow old, like me."

She elbowed me in the side. "You're not that old, and I'm not some pansy."

I took Sam's hand in mine as we finished the last few yards of our hike.

"Atticus," she said, breaking through my thoughts and pulling me back to the present. "I never thought I'd get to know you like this. This entire conversation has blown my mind. I'm not sure what to think...or how I feel about it." She stopped right in front of me and turned to face me, forcing me to stop. For a moment, she chewed on her bottom lip. Then she raised her chin and rose up on her tiptoes grasping my hands for balance. We were so close that she was almost eye to eye with me. "Honestly, I'm shocked that a man so much older than me would talk to me like an equal or share his feelings, much less be so open about... well, other things."

"Yeah, well, sometimes the most meaningful connections are the ones you least expect."

Sam smiled and glanced down at our intertwined hands. "You know, your hands are so big and strong. I can only imagine how many lives you've saved with them."

"Many years of working in the ED," I said with a hint of pride. Then I added a little mischievously, "And they're also quite skilled at providing...various forms of pleasure."

"Really now?" She raised an eyebrow and flashed me a playful grin. "You've definitely sparked my interest, Dr. Thorin. Can't wait to find out if your culinary skills are as exceptional as you say—and whether your other talents live up to your claims."

Her playful sexual innuendo sent a bolt of electric current straight to my groin. Well, damn, maybe there was chemistry between us after all.

"Trust me, Sam, when it comes to making women hot, I'm as skilled in the kitchen as I am in the bedroom," I joked.

"Is that so? Well, I suppose I'll be the judge of that tonight."

I wasn't sure if she was talking only about my cooking or if she was perhaps interested in more.

Night Shift

When we arrived at the parking lot, I opened the passenger door for her. With a hint of a smile on her lips, she slid into the seat. I reached out to brush a stray curl behind her ear, letting my fingers linger on the soft skin of her neck. Her sharp intake of breath was all the invitation I needed to lean over and press a kiss to her temple.

"I'm sorry if I offended you earlier. You're right; you don't need a man to take care of you. You're perfectly capable of handling yourself."

Sam sighed, leaning closer to me she placed her hand on my chest and let it slowly trail down the plane of my abs before dropping it back to her lap. "I know you meant well. It's just... I've spent my whole life fighting for everything I've ever gotten. I won't be coddled or condescended to, even if the intention behind it is good."

"You're right," I said, running my thumb along the edge of her cheek.

A smile crept across Sam's lips. "Now you're getting it." She stretched up to kiss me, soft and sweet. "Just treat me right, and we'll be fine."

"Yes, ma'am." I grinned, capturing her mouth with mine. Fuuuck, did she taste good, and boy, was I in trouble. "So, Nurse Sheridan, what's my prognosis?"

Her eyes sparkled with mirth. "That depends, Doctor. How well do you follow orders?"

"For you?" I ran my hand up her thigh, relishing her shiver. "Implicitly."

With that, I hurriedly rounded the car, jumped into the driver's seat, and started the engine. This day had turned out completely different than I had expected. Sam beamed at me from the passenger seat, and my heart raced.

Chapter Seven

Hadn't she been bragging about being young and full of stamina earlier? It couldn't have been more than five minutes after we started driving when I glanced over and found her sound asleep with the seat partially leaning back. She looked peaceful though, relaxed. There was no hint of the high-pressure stress that seemed to cling to her at work. Her face, usually so animated and expressive, was now serene. In sleep, there was a certain beauty about her, a kind of simplicity that was rare to see. Not that I didn't find her easy on the eyes all the time. The girl could be exhausted from a hectic shift, with her hair up in a crazy bun and no makeup, and she would still make me stop in my tracks. This was the first time I'd seen her truly let her guard down, and she was—captivating. It struck me how different she appeared, almost like another person entirely, when she wasn't

Night Shift

on edge.

Traffic on I-5 was fucking terrible. All I saw was a string of red brake lights for miles ahead, but the exit to Highway 512 would come soon enough. I figured once we arrived in the Puyallup area, I could set the cruise control. From there, it would only be another thirty minutes down Meridian to the cabin.

Sam stayed asleep the whole way there. Fortunately for her, she didn't miss out on much. It was a straight shot through the towns of Puyallup and Graham, and there wasn't much to see. The radio played in the background as my thoughts wandered to how this day would end. I seldom spent time with women whose expectations for our time together didn't match mine. But Sam was different—she had no expectations at all. I was sure the only reason she'd come today was pure curiosity, especially after Bethany had given her an earful. Judging by her behavior in the ED, Sam seemed like someone who liked having all the answers. However, when it came to sexuality—particularly her own—it was clear she was aware that she was in unfamiliar territory.

If there was one thing I appreciated about having a cabin so far from the city, it was the seclusion. Yes, there were other people with homes on the lake, but not many would be there this time of year, and the woods were dense, making for a good sound buffer.

As the road changed from smooth asphalt to gravel, Sam stirred.

I turned my head toward her. "Well hello there, sleepyhead. Did someone have a good nap?"

She didn't respond. Maybe she hadn't woken up. So I attempted to rouse her through other means. I placed my hand on her thigh. Her skin was soft as silk. The moment I touched her, her leg fell to the side, almost inviting me to play. Fuck. I was tempted to slide my hand further up her leg, but I resisted.

Consent was important to me. It wasn't only a part of my practice in medicine. I wasn't the type to take advantage of a woman in any situation, especially when she was asleep. So I decided to wake her up quickly by clamping down on either side of her knee, knowing that would tickle her. She bolted upright.

"Atticus!" she squealed. "What are you doing?"

I laughed hard at her reaction. "Sammich, we're here."

She raised her seat up and ran a hand across her face to wipe off what must have been drool. "I slept the entire way?!" she exclaimed in shock.

"You did. It's no big deal. Your body was just telling you that you needed some rest. You looked so peaceful that I didn't dare wake you up. You know, Samantha, you're a beautiful woman."

"Well, look at you, being all sweet and caring. You know, I'm still trying to figure out what a dichotomy you are. Everyone at work thinks you're an asshole, and if I'm being honest, I can see why. But then, I also see this other side of you that would make those same people love you if you gave them a chance."

"I don't go to work to make friends. I don't need to be liked. You say my behavior is dichotomous, so let me present you with a scenario I face every day." I paused for a moment. "Imagine a doctor with a great bedside manner. The patients always smile when this doctor leaves the room, even if they're clueless about what he said. Ready for the twist?" I glanced at Sam before continuing. "The patients keep coming back. Not because they love their doctor, but because they don't get better. My aim in medicine is to fix people, not to keep them coming back. And that doesn't require that I'm all sunshine and roses. I am who I am...take it or leave it."

"Well, that's a shitty way to look at things," Sam said with a huff, turning to look out her window.

Night Shift

Slightly irritated, I gripped the steering wheel but then loosened my fingers. I couldn't let her know she was getting to me. "I'm just...trying to help you understand me better, that's all."

"Listen, I get it, Atticus. You compartmentalize. I do it too. I just express my frustration differently, through sarcasm. As you know." She shot me an impish grin, and a part of me wanted to kiss her right then and there. Her sarcasm and intelligence had a hold on me, and she had this way of disarming me, which wasn't something I was used to.

As we pulled up to the cabin, Sam gasped. "This place is absolutely beautiful! I mean, the cabin looks a little run-down, but look at that view."

"A little run-down?!" I said with a bit of fire in my tone. But before I could say anything else, Sam was already out of the car and running down to the dock.

Even though I wanted to unpack the car and settle into the cabin, I decided to join her.

The late afternoon air was cooler than I'd expected. The breeze off the water was sharp, probably biting at Sam's legs since she was wearing shorts. I came up behind her and wrapped my arms around her waist, and to my surprise, she relaxed into them.

"Great view, huh? I love this place even if the cabin is a little shabby," I said.

She playfully elbowed me in the ribs and laughed softly. "I was just teasing you. For Pete's sake, don't be so uptight."

"Uptight?" I asked. "You make me feel so old. But don't worry, I'll teach you the best ways for releasing tension." I gave her a little squeeze. "Let's bring our bags in and fix some dinner."

Together, we returned to the car and unloaded our things.

We both toed off our shoes at the front door, a habit from working in a hospital. "I'm going to carry our bags upstairs. Make yourself at home," I said. When I returned, I found her standing at the floor-to-ceiling back window, looking out at the lake. I'd had these windows installed because of the unbelievable view.

"Wow, this place is incredible!" she exclaimed, turning and roaming around the living room. "It's so inviting and cozy. Not what I expected of a bachelor's cabin in the woods that you and your brothers use. You've obviously spent a lot of time modernizing it. I love all the wooden details and these giant windows."

"Thanks, we've worked hard on it. It was a dump when I found it, but now, even though it's rustic, it's still cozy. I'm glad you like it." I threw her an appreciative smile before heading over to the fireplace to light the kindling under the stack of wood I'd prepared the last time I was here. I was amazed that neither of my brothers had stopped in and beaten me to it. I strode into the kitchen to start working on dinner. Sam removed her cardigan and tossed it onto the chair by the sofa. I gulped at the sight of her perfectly formed breasts and hard nipples beneath the fabric of her white tank top. I didn't want to rush dinner, but damn, was I looking forward to dessert.

Sam perched on one knee in one of the cabin's worn leather chairs, positioned near the fireplace, and leaned against its back. The fire I had just ignited crackled and popped in the stone hearth, casting an inviting glow over the room and illuminating her thoughtful gaze as she watched me. Taking a moment, I scrolled through my phone, looking for the perfect playlist to set the mood. With a few taps, I connected my device to the speaker sitting on the counter that bridged the living room and kitchen. One of my favorite features of this cabin was the open floor plan that seamlessly blended the two spaces.

From the kitchen, I watched as Sam tilted her head and listened intently to the music. "I like this song," she murmured, then began singing along with "Come Away with Me" by Norah Jones. She closed her eyes and swayed with the rhythm. I was transfixed by the rich melodic voice that came from her full lips. It took all my restraint not to pull her into my arms then and there. I wanted to caress every inch of her skin, but I reminded myself to take things slow and took a deep breath.

"This is one of my favorite playlists," I told her. "It's an eclectic mix of jazz, including classics by artists like Nat King Cole, Frank Sinatra, and Billie Holiday, as well as the more modern vibes of Norah Jones and Michael Bublé. It even has some Bossa Nova jazz of João Gilberto. Who could resist those sexy samba rhythms, hmm?"

She continued singing, lost in the music, and I simply soaked in the moment. When the song ended, I asked, "How do you feel about Swedish meatballs and cream sauce over noodles?"

Her face lit up. "Oh, yum...yes please!" she replied, her enthusiasm unmistakable.

"You're going to love it," I said as I rummaged through the fridge I'd stocked a few days ago.

After getting the things I needed, I pulled out my grandmother's old recipe from a box sitting on the counter next to the sink. The yellowed paper was brittle and stained from years of use, but it didn't matter because I'd pretty much committed the recipe to memory anyway.

"You know, my grandmother used to make these every Sunday for dinner."

"Did she?" Sam asked, her eyes lighting up with interest as she made her way over to the kitchen.

"Yes." I smiled at the memory. "And she taught me how to make them before she passed away."

She watched with keen interest as I combined the ingredients—ground pork and beef, breadcrumbs soaked in milk and egg, a blend of carefully measured spices, and onion chopped so finely it was almost invisible.

"Let's see if you can roll these meatballs properly, Sammich," I challenged her playfully, reaching out to smear a little butter onto her nose.

Swatting my hand away, she gave me a laugh before rolling a meatball with focus and precision. Then, with a triumphant grin, she neatly plopped her perfectly shaped ball onto a tray.

Pointing at it, she said teasingly, "Now that's how you roll a Swedish meatball, Atticus!"

Soon the delectable aroma of spices filled the air and the meat was sizzling in butter in the pan—just like my grandmother used to do it.

As we cooked side by side in the small kitchen, our playful flirting escalated into something more...intimate. We brushed against each other, reaching for ingredients or utensils, and exchanged cheeky glances.

Soon it was time to make the cream sauce—a combination of broth, a flour slurry, and heavy cream. This I cooked in the pan containing the remnants of the fried meatballs, and in minutes it had turned into a velvety wonder.

Then I set the noodles to boil. They were simple enough but would add a welcome contrast in texture. And of course, there was the lingonberry sauce, a sweet, tangy garnish that tied everything together. We even had an impromptu lingonberry taste test that ended in laughter and red-stained fingers.

"Okay, okay," I said, raising my hands in surrender when she pointed an accusing finger at me. She looked adorable with a dollop of the berry sauce on her nose. "You win the tasting war."

Night Shift

I couldn't help myself; I reached out and, with a gentle swipe of my thumb, removed the sauce from her nose.

"Thank you," she said softly, her laughter dying down to a low chuckle. A strange silence filled the air.

The pasta cooked to al dente perfection, and everything came together. We filled our plates in the kitchen, then moved to the wooden dining table overlooking the lake outside. After the hike, the food was a welcoming indulgence.

"God, these are delicious," Sam said between mouthfuls. She sighed appreciatively. "You're a fantastic cook."

When she licked a stray dab of cream sauce from her lips, I had to suppress a groan of pure craving. She looked so beautiful under the soft light of the pendant lamp. I flashed her a grin of appreciation that quickly melted into something more heated, and my gaze moved down to her full lips. She picked up one of the meatballs and bit off a piece, finishing by slowly sucking on the tips of her fingers.

"Thank you," I managed to utter, my voice gravelly with the need that was rising in my pants. We locked eyes for a moment, and the air between us crackled with an intensity that promised much more.

I tried to maintain some semblance of control over my libido. But Sam was making it increasingly hard, coyly licking the cream sauce from her fork while maintaining eye contact with me and peppering me with innocent yet suggestive remarks about how good the meatballs were.

After dinner, we headed over to the sink to do the dishes. While I turned on the water and squirted in some soap to fill one sink for washing, she grabbed a little red apron that was hanging on the wall. As she tied the apron strings behind her back, I imagined myself tying her wrists with them, thinking about the darker pleasures I'd like to introduce her to. But that'd have to wait. Sam would be easily spooked, and then I'd never catch her again. We bickered over who would wash and who would dry but finally settled on me washing and her drying. Soon I was scrubbing away and handing dishes off to her, pleased with how completely at ease she was in my space.

"See something you like?" she asked, noticing me staring.

I answered with a smirk before enveloping her waist with my free arm and pulling her flush against me. My heart raced when she didn't resist, but instead leaned back into me. Her body was supple against mine.

Her lips parted slightly in surprise when I bent down to lightly kiss her neck and started nibbling my way up to the corner of her jaw. "Mmm," she moaned.

The moan was like a shot of espresso—waking me right up. Words weren't necessary; our bodies were speaking plenty. I slowly pulled away from her neck, just enough to turn her toward me. Our lips met in an unhurried exploration of each other's mouths. The taste of her was intoxicating—sweet and spicy from the lingering flavors of dinner.

We stood there lost in each other's arms until suddenly she broke the silence by playfully splashing water on me from the sink.

"C'mon, you," she said with a gleam in her eye. "Let's finish these dishes so we can do something else."

Grinning, I quickly rinsed the last few dishes and handed them to her to dry. The playful tension between us grew as our bodies brushed against one another in a tantalizing dance of proximity. When the last dish was dried, I hung the towel on the hook, and she slipped off the apron.

Turning to leave the kitchen, I extended my hand to her. She took it without hesitation, the spark in her eye matching my anticipation.

Night Shift

"So, Sammich, are you up for a little experimentation on our *not-a-date* trip to my cabin? Willing to stop being...I don't know...so uptight?"

"Mm-hmm." She nodded and smiled, but the nervousness had returned. She was having to bite her lip to stop it from quivering. God, if she only knew how badly *I* wanted to bite that lip.

"You have to promise me something though," she said.

"Oh, what's that?"

"Tonight is purely an experiment. Nothing more. And under no circumstances will you tell anyone about it, especially anyone at the hospital. Tomorrow, it will be as if it never happened. You will be Dr. Thorin, and I will be Sam. No more, no less. No innuendos at work, no jokes, no nicknames, no strings, no feelings. Got it?" Her eyes were as big as saucers, her back as straight as an arrow.

"I promise it shall be done just as you have ordered. Nothing more, nothing less." I smiled and tugged her forward.

Her fingers were soft in mine, and she didn't let go of my hand as we climbed the wooden stairs to the second floor. We passed by the guest bedrooms and stopped just outside the heavy oak door of the master bedroom. She looked up at me with an impish grin, and my heartbeat quickened.

Chapter Eight

I pushed open the door to reveal my king-sized bed, which was generously layered with crisp sheets and soft blankets. A single lamp on the bedside table cast a warm glow over the spacious room. I loved the homey ambiance of this place.

I stood by the door and watched as Sam wandered around the room, gliding her fingers along the tops of the dresser and armchair on her way to stand in front of the floor-to-ceiling windows that overlooked the lake. The sun had all but set, allowing me to see her reflection in the glass. She was awestruck by the view—and so was I.

Unable to wait any longer, I walked over to stand behind her, grasping her arms in my hands. Tilting my head, I brushed her temple with a kiss.

"Samantha."

"Yes?"

"Do you trust me?"

"You know I don't trust anyone."

"Then let me help you start by showing you how to trust your own body."

Taking her hand, I guided her to the side of the bed, then dragged the covers down, allowing them to fall into folds onto the floor.

I turned and stepped toward my dresser to open one of the drawers where I kept a wide assortment of pleasure toys, and I pulled out a silky blindfold.

Sam's eyes widened, her pupils swallowing up her stunning blue irises.

I dropped my chin toward my shoulder, my smile offering her a world of unspoken promises.

With the blindfold coiling through my fingers, I moved closer to her and placed it on the nightstand next to us. Then, taking her shoulders gently, I rotated her to face the bed. Her gaze followed me in the window's reflection. I swept her auburn locks up in my hands, and I leaned in and nuzzled her neck, enjoying her light floral scent. "Mmm, you smell so good."

After letting her hair fall down her back, I carefully tucked it behind her ears, then retrieved the blindfold and stretched my arms around her. I gave her a playful wink in the reflection before I tied it snugly around her eyes.

"If you ever feel uncomfortable or want me to stop—say so." My gravelly voice betrayed my desire for her.

"Yes, sir," she sighed, wringing her hands in a display of restless anticipation.

"In return, I promise to worship your body in ways you've never dreamed possible, guiding you to heights of sexual awareness you've yet to encounter. I warn you, though, after tonight, I will have ruined it for any other man who's not worthy of you. Do you understand?"

"Yes," she whispered. Her bottom lip trembled, just like I had hoped it would. My desire tonight was to help her overcome her nervousness and fear as she sought sexual gratification.

When my lips brushed the sensitive spot on her neck behind the corner of her jaw, she instinctively responded. Her shoulder lifted slightly as her head bent gracefully toward it, embracing the tender touch.

"The blindfold will help you focus on every sensation as you experience it," I said. "Now relax and let me show you how your body was made to respond."

I slipped my hands under the edge of her tank top, allowing my fingers to graze her skin just along the waistband of her shorts. My hands glided upward, tracing the contours of her sides, and I eased her top off and over her head, revealing her breasts to my gaze.

"Mmm." An unexpected groan escaped me. No matter how much I longed to touch her, to run my tongue around her taut nipples, I resisted. Now wasn't the time. No, trust must be built one step at a time. *Observation. Assessment. Application. Outcome*, I reminded myself.

Her top dropped to the floor, forgotten, as my fingers made quick work of undoing the button and zipper of her shorts. My hands slipped beneath her panties, skimming down the smooth center of her stomach. Sliding my hands out, I caressed the curves of her hips and then guided the fabric down her legs, leaving her shorts and panties pooled at her feet.

Trailing kisses along Sam's shoulder, I savored the sight of her exposed beauty in the window's reflection. "God, you're gorgeous."

Her breath hitched, and she wrapped her arms around herself, clutching her elbows.

"Don't, Samantha. There's no need to be embarrassed when you're with me. How about you lie down on the bed and make yourself comfortable?"

Curious about how she would situate herself, I watched as she made her way to the center.

Grabbing a pillow and wrapping her arms around it, she curled up mostly on her stomach, with her right ankle crossing over her left calf. Although the position was modest, it gave me a lovely view of her ass and a peek at the dark pink lips of her pussy.

Quickly shedding my clothes, I joined her. I lay down next to her, propped up on my elbow, and then started tracing the freckles on her milky skin with my fingers. First, I glided them up her arm and over her shoulder, and then I trailed them down her spine, drawing lazy *S* curves to the seam of her ass.

As I often did with my patients to help put them at ease, I began carefully explaining every touch.

"Samantha, you've got the perfect ass—ummm—so round and firm. I'm going to outline every curve first with my fingers and then with my tongue. Is that okay?" I asked as my fingers slid down the curve of her seam.

She giggled softly. "You're the one in charge."

Taking the back of her knee in my hand, I shoved it up the mattress, giving me better access to her glistening folds. I slowly ran my fingers down the back of her leg, around her buttcheek, and then drew them across her opening to the bundle of nerves at its apex. "Goddammit, Sam, you're already soaking wet... I can't wait to slide my fingers inside of you, making you forget your own name."

She whimpered and arched her back, begging for me to penetrate her. Instead, I trailed my fingers around the edges of her pussy.

"You like that, don't you? You like the feel of my fingers sliding along your folds?"

"Mm-hmm."

I chuckled softly. This was just the beginning of me breaking her.

With a smile, I gently dipped my middle finger into her core and then back up to the apex of her folds. As I circled the swollen bundle of nerves, she gasped. *Go slow*, I reminded myself, pulling my hand away and wrapping my fingers around the cheek of her ass.

After scattering soft kisses from the center of her back to the nape of her neck, I rolled her over and drank in the sight of her. In the dim light, her fair skin seemed almost luminous. Her breathing quickened as she lay there, bared to my scrutiny.

To my amazement, situated just under her left breast was an elegantly designed tattoo of an arrow with the phrase "Unbroken, Still I Rise" flowing along its shaft. When I traced the outline of it with my fingers, a shudder ran across her body.

"You're full of surprises, Sam. Someday you'll have to tell me the meaning behind this lovely arrow. But we'll have to save that for another time," I said, placing a soft kiss on the arrowhead.

Pulling back, I took another moment to eagerly survey her body, from her toes to the top of her head, before I kissed and nibbled a line across her neck, jawline, and lips. Gritting my teeth, I fisted a handful of her hair, tilting her head back. My mouth muffled her gasp of surprise as it crushed hers.

The rough pads of my thumb caressed the line of her jaw while I explored each inch of her mouth. The taste of her was like nothing else. She was sweet and wild, a flavor that had me addicted from the first moment. This wasn't some fairytale kiss; it was raw, our tongues tangling in a battle for dominance. I reveled in it, plunging my tongue deeper into the warmth of her mouth, greedily claiming what was mine.

It was a kiss that threatened to shred any restraint I had left.

Her nails dug into my back as she whimpered against my lips.

I pulled back slightly, catching my breath. Then I bit down on her lower lip, and a groan rumbled from my chest as the metallic taste hit my tongue. I traced the seam of her lips with my thumb before diving back in with an unapologetic roughness that made her whine. Angling my head for a better taste, I pressed myself into her softness. Our noses bumped, but we were beyond caring—beyond anything except the burning need to devour each other.

Her hands went up to tangle in my hair, tugging and pulling. Every tug sent spikes of pleasure straight to my groin, turning my blood into molten fire. In that moment, I was lost to the world, lost in Sam's kisses. There was no finesse or delicacy about it, only visceral needs being met, boundaries being blurred by overwhelming desire. Just two people consumed by their craving for each other.

With each passing second, her nails dug deeper into my skin, leaving trails of fire in their wake. My own hands weren't idle; they roamed over every curve and dip of her body unabashedly.

Breaking away, I leaned back to take in the sight of her. She lay there panting beneath me—cheeks flushed, hair disheveled, face full of lust—the most beautiful mess.

I laughed. "Well, that escalated quickly."

She blushed as she ran her tongue over the slight cut I'd left on her lip.

Taking a long, deep breath, I growled, "Tonight is all about you. Your gratification. Your release. Tonight, I will break you."

The sight of her defenseless and waiting sent a surge of possessiveness through me.

I leaned down toward her neck, feeling a shudder run through her when my lips met her soft skin. Dropping lower, I traced the outline of her collarbone with my tongue as she squirmed beneath me. Her pulse hammered where my lips met her skin. The taste of salty sweat on my tongue made me hungrier for more. Muffled noises of bliss echoed in the room as I marked her with my teeth and tongue, branding every inch of her body as mine. I found satisfaction in painting her white canvas with shades of red and purple.

My hands roamed over the swell of her breasts, and I reveled in the fullness of them against my palms. Her breath hitched when I captured one nipple between my fingers, rolling it gently at first before pinching it roughly between my thumb and forefinger. Her sharp intake of breath encouraged me, and I lowered my mouth to lavish attention on the neglected one.

Her responses to me drove me to take a chance. Before I realized what I was doing, one of my hands had made it to her throat, my fingers encircling her graceful neck while my tongue swirled around her taut areola before teasing the hard nub in the center. The soft, strangled whimpers she made only drove me to want more.

Her breasts were so fucking satisfying to taste, touch, and watch—especially when they quivered under my attention. They begged for more, just like the rest of her body did.

I released her throat long enough for her to take two quick inhales before I retightened my grip and continued alternating between each peak.

Night Shift

She let out a strangled whine when my grip tightened further, her body arching in an instinctive attempt to escape the sensations I was igniting within her.

"Sam, come for me," I growled, my words vibrating against her flesh and further inflaming her need for release. "I want to own your first orgasm by a man."

Trembling, she gripped the sheets.

But I knew she could take more. This was about repressed need, about her body responding in the most primal way.

I caught her nipple between my teeth, biting down softly at first before applying just enough pressure to make her flinch in surprise.

The feel of her writhing beneath me—helpless, completely given over to me—drove me wild with desire. But I wouldn't allow myself to be consumed by it. Not yet. Tonight was about Sam's pleasure first, about bringing her past the edge of reason and straight into euphoria.

"Come for me," I commanded again, my voice rough as my hold on her throat tightened ever so slightly. My thumb brushed over her neck, pressing down on her pulse point to feel the thunderous drumming beneath.

I sucked her nipple hard to its rhythmic beat, determined to push each of her erogenous zones past their limit and prove she could come at the hands of a skilled lover without me even touching her pussy.

The urgency behind her arousal was practically a living thing between us. I could sense the tension building in her body by the way she was shaking under my touch, by the way her skin was flushed with heat.

Her body jerked beneath mine, a silent plea to let her climax.

I turned my attention to the other peak. "Shhh..." I commanded, my breath hot against her skin. "Let it go."

Her hands clenched tighter on the sheets, her body bowing with tension until suddenly she gave a desperate cry and collapsed beneath me, trembling and quaking as waves of ecstasy crashed over her.

Feeling the tension drain out of her, I released my hold on her throat. My fingers traced patterns idly on the sweat-slicked skin of her chest and belly. Her chest heaved as she struggled to catch her breath.

Slowly, her heartbeat returned to its normal rhythm. She squirmed as my hand roamed tenderly over the flesh of her breasts and stomach. The sight was enough to ignite a fresh wave of craving in me, but I knew better than to push. Not yet.

"That was just the beginning," I whispered huskily into the shell of her ear. "This night is far from over."

Lying there in the aftermath of Sam's orgasm, my cock throbbed with its own need to find gratification. I stroked it a couple of times, and a surge of satisfaction coursed through me. I'd been the first to rip an orgasm from Sam.

My gaze traveled down her body, and I took note of the way she was still shuddering from the intensity of her release and twisting her fingers in the sheets. I traced the curves of her stomach, brushing my fingers over her mound. Her hips squirmed underneath my hand, and she released a small whimper as my fingers ghosted lower. A mischievous smirk tugged at the corner of my lips when I teased the sensitive skin of her swollen cleft. In response, she inhaled sharply, her body stiffening beneath me.

Ignoring the throbbing need between my own legs, I placed a hand on her hip to steady her. Then I drew circles on her lower belly, over her mound, and along the edges of her folds. I was careful not to touch her where she craved me most. Keeping Sam on edge was all a part of the game, and I intended to play it to its extreme. Her muscles twitched in anticipation as I ran my fingers over her inner thigh, relishing the soft, silky skin under my touch.

Breathing heavily against her earlobe, I whispered, "Patience," as if saying it out loud would somehow make it easier—as if it would somehow convey how much I wanted her too.

This was a dance I was all too familiar with—an intricate balance of indulgence and restraint. It was about drawing out the tension, building up the pressure until it became too much to bear. Watching Sam writhe under my touch was the sweetest torment—the kind that left me breathless and craving more.

With each stroke of my fingers against her skin, her body reacted. I kissed her exposed hipbone, then trailed kisses across her stomach. She dug her hands into my hair, twisting it around her fingers.

She gasped when I started trailing kisses down onto her inner thighs. The small patch of hair between them glistened with wetness—a sight that strengthened my resolve to take things slowly.

"Shhh," I whispered against her skin. "Trust me." And despite the vulnerability of being blindfolded and naked under my gaze, she relaxed at my command, allowing her knees to fall open so that I could position myself between them.

My fingers skimmed along her legs as I brushed kisses over each hip bone. In response, her hips rose off the bed in a plea for contact. A needy groan escaped from between her clenched teeth.

Ignoring her wants, I moved up again, covering her body with mine and lowering my head to claim what I had left unattended for too long. Her nails dug into my shoulders as I kissed her. My lips were merciless on her mouth, robbing her of breath and sanity. It was intoxicating, like she was feeding off my roughness.

Pushing up over her, I chuckled at the sight of her swollen lips. Then I kissed my way back down through the valley of her breasts and to the center of her wet heat. I swirled my tongue around her clitoris, and she once again tangled her fingers in my hair. I couldn't help but growl at the taste of her as my tongue dove into her tightness. With a fierce grip on my head, she rode my face. I felt her climax nearing and pulled back, kissing her inner thigh.

She whimpered in frustration and tried to force my mouth back to her center. "Patience, Samantha," I reminded her. Gripping her wrists, I forced her hands from my hair and put them at her sides.

I moved up to rest an elbow to the side of her hip, placing my hand on her belly. The fingers of my other hand found their way between her legs again, stroking the damp folds of her pussy. I slipped one finger into her. The tight heat around it sent a fiery wave of desire through me.

"Fuck, you're so tight. And your juices are running down your ass," I said, a bit astonished.

I added another finger, stretching her to accommodate me while my thumb flicked against her clitoris. Her body bucked beneath me.

Sam was a beautiful sight, and her body responded to my every touch. Here she was experiencing pure bliss, and it was all because of me.

Her hips rocked against my hand, the rhythm matching the pace of my fingers. Each stroke was precise—tantalizing her until she was near the edge again. My fingers curled inside her, finding her sweet spot. I rubbed against it at a quick tempo, keeping my thumb on her clitoris while pressing down on her belly with my other hand, intensifying the sensation.

Night Shift

The room filled with whimpers and moans—an erotic symphony of her impending release—as we moved together in perfect sync.

"Come around my fingers. I want your walls to clamp down on them...now," I demanded.

Sweat ran down her temples. She panted and struggled to find her release. My fingers fucked her harder until her wetness filled the palm of my hand. "Samantha, goddammit, do as you're told," I growled.

And she complied, screaming out, "Yes! Oh, my fucking God!" as her hands slammed against the bed.

I chuckled, but the vibration in my chest reminded me of my discomfort. I was getting a serious case of blue balls and needed to step away for a second. "I'll be right back. You catch your breath. I'm not nearly finished with you. Oh, and don't touch that blindfold."

I shuffled to the kitchen and grabbed a couple of bottles of water. It was always good to stay hydrated. Tonight's pleasure was mostly for Sam, but next time...next time would be for me. She had demanded that we never speak of tonight, but I knew better. Once she got a taste of ecstasy, she'd be addicted. I had no doubt this fiery kitten would become a hellcat.

Returning to the bed, I clasped Sam's hand and pulled her up to a sitting position. "Here ya go, Sammich. Time for some hydration." I handed her the opened bottle, and she drank it greedily. "Slow down, sweetheart. You don't want to get a bellyache."

She laughed. "Oh my God, I'm a nurse. I think I can manage my water consumption. When you get old, does drinking water too fast cause you trouble?"

"No, but smart-ass comments might get you more than you bargained for," I said, snatching the bottle from her hand and dropping it onto the nightstand before I flipped her over on the bed. She landed on all fours with her ass up in the air. I gave her pale bottom a hard smack, leaving a rosy handprint. Then I had the best idea ever.

"Stay up on your hands and knees but turn in the other direction so that your head is facing toward the end of the bed." While I watched her rotate, all I could think about was the million ways I could fuck her. Damn, my balls were hurting so much I thought they'd explode.

"Raise up onto your knees and spread them apart a little more. Now put your hands on your hips," I ordered.

"What is this, some exercise program? Or are you getting your jollies by making me parade around?" she asked with her typical snark.

"You really do like baiting the lion, don't you?" I laughed.

I sat on the foot of the bed and lay back. Using my feet for leverage, I scooted up the mattress until I had the best view ever. Sam's pussy was still swollen and glistening from the two orgasms I'd given her. I needed a release, and she needed to occupy that sassy mouth.

"Sammich...you can place your hands back on the mattress. I'm ready for my midnight snack. How about you?"

She leaned over and found my knees, then glided her hands down my thighs until her hands were on either side of my ass. There, she froze, seeming to fully understand the position she was now in. I swear she stopped breathing.

"Don't you think it's my turn to receive...your attention?" I asked in a husky voice.

"Um, well...sure," she said hesitantly. "But I've never, well, you know what I mean."

"It's okay. I know you've got quite a big imagination. How about you see what you can do."

Night Shift

She swallowed hard, and it was all I could do not to laugh out loud. Tentatively, she searched for my dick. Her hands traced its perimeter where it rested on my stomach. "Whoa, okay. Big... extra-large, I'm guessing."

"Sam, use your mouth for a better purpose. How about this? A friendly wager. Whoever comes first has to spend an entire day doing exactly what the other one wants."

She was silent.

"Chicken?" I asked.

"Oh no. Just like the devil who went down to Georgia, I'll take your bet. You're gonna regret, because I'm...well, you get the point."

And with that, she went to work. What the fuck had I just done to myself? I was already desperate to get off. But I could do this. I had some tricks up my sleeve.

With one hand, she took hold of my throbbing balls and started rolling them in her fingers like a pair of fucking dice.

Using my elbows, I knocked her knees further apart, giving me full access to her pussy. Eagerly, I dug my fingers into her ass cheeks and pulled her big, juicy lips to mine. I guessed we were both competitive as hell.

Although Sam was new to this, she seemed to grasp the concept quickly. With each tentative lick she gave me, my body tensed. But I had a game to win, so I focused on sending her over the edge once more.

"Enjoying yourself?" I asked as she wrapped her lips around me and began gently sucking.

"Mm-hmm," she mumbled, the vibration of her words sending a fiery current through my cock. Her hands moved to give me a gentle stroke while at the same time she took me in deeper.

"Fuuuck," I groaned. "Good. Now it's time to up the stakes." The feeling of her hot mouth around me was so damn good.

My hands moved to her hips to pull her closer to me. She whimpered slightly as my fingers slipped inside her wetness and began stroking and teasing.

Sam threw her head back in exasperation, a fresh wave of need sweeping over her. Her grip on me tightened, and she mimicked my pace with ease. Her other hand trailed around my balls, squeezing gently in time with the movement of her mouth.

I slipped my tongue into her, lapping up the juices that were still dripping from her. The taste of her was sweet—intoxicating.

When my tongue made contact with her clitoris, she flinched, a soft gasp escaping her. She had been so focused on what she was doing that she hadn't expected me to retaliate.

I ran my tongue along her slit, finding her entrance and dipping inside. My hands moved to the insides of her thighs, and my fingers found her swollen lips. Eagerly, I pulled them apart and continued to devour her. She tasted divine—better than any woman I had ever been with before.

At the same time, Sam was working wonders on my shaft with her mouth and hand combination, sending heat running up my spine. Each stroke of her tongue against my thrumming length had me on the edge of exploding in her mouth. Fuck, I was close. Goddammit, I'd never wanted to come so badly in my fucking life.

She hummed as my cock filled her mouth and slammed against her throat. The thrumming caused me to grow harder under her touch—if that were possible. Her inexperienced mouth felt indescribably good; she was taking it slow, learning what worked and what didn't by my reactions.

It was time to end this game. Dipping my fingers deep in her pussy, I slathered them in her heavenly cream. Then I slid my hands around her ass, my fingers drifting deeper until they brushed against the tight ring of muscle hidden beneath the curve of her cheeks. I shifted my mouth, positioning it so that my lips surrounded her engorged nub, then started sucking in time to her cadence. She gasped around my dick at the unexpected pressure on her clitoris.

Sam's movements became frenzied, turning our entanglement into an erotic fury. Her mouth tightened around me once more.

With a deft push, I slipped a finger inside her puckered hole, pumping it in time to our mutual pace. "I'm going to fuck you here next time," I promised in a loud snarl. She couldn't fight it, and she came hard around my finger and mouth, her thighs quivering over my face.

When she attempted to scream, my balls drew up tight. My climax hit me with a force hard enough to shake the bed beneath us. I groaned in pure ecstasy as my cum filled her mouth. The sensation was overwhelming—so raw it was almost animalistic. She swallowed hard several times, trying to catch her breath.

After I'd emptied myself and stopped pulsing, she withdrew from me. She rolled over onto the bed, her body curling tightly into itself. A barely audible whimper betrayed her fierce battle to hold back her tears, to conceal the storm of emotions our passion had unleashed. And when she finally broke, she broke into a million pieces...each one meant for me to put back together.

Chapter Nine

Atticus spooned up against me and gently removed the blindfold. Squinting, I blinked a few times, my eyes struggling to adjust to the dimly lit bedroom. He pushed my shoulder back against the mattress, forcing me to look at him. His gaze bored into me, his brow knit in concern. "Samantha, you're okay. I promise. The orgasmic cocktail of oxytocin, endorphins, dopamine, and serotonin is just messing with your emotions." He kissed my shoulder. With a soft chuckle, and added, "I knew you just needed the right man to please you. God, you're so fucking amazing."

I squeezed my eyes shut, wishing I could be invisible. I tried to turn away from him, but he wouldn't allow it.

"Sam," he murmured, his voice a seductive haze that curled around me, "you have no idea how exquisite you are."

Night Shift

His lips, slightly swollen from ravishing me, brushed against my earlobe, and his warm breath sent shivers down my spine. "The way your body responds to mine..." he murmured, his lips briefly pulling away from my ear to press against the soft plane of my neck. "It's magical, Sam...breathtaking."

His fingers traced over my breasts, where his mouth and fingers had worked their spell just moments ago. "These," he said, a low rumble that vibrated against my skin, "the way they rose and fell under my touch, the way they succumbed to my mouth and made you come...it was divine."

His hand, a comforting warmth, slid down past my stomach to the sensitive place between my thighs. His touch was gentle, as if he were exploring sacred terrain. The memory of what he'd done there had me clenching in sweet remembrance.

"Here," he breathed, his fingers making a slow pass over the spot that harbored such power to electrify. "This...the secret sanctuary of your bliss, impossibly wet and warm—it was like burying myself in paradise. How it squeezed me, how it welcomed me...it was simply incredible."

I could hear the sincerity of his words, the simple honesty that mirrored the primal fervor in his eyes. "You are the most flawless creature I've ever seen, Samantha," Atticus murmured, his lips trailing kisses down my neck as his fingers continued to explore between my legs. "And now, you are mine."

He took a couple of cleansing breaths. "I swear, the way you moved beneath me when I touched you...when I tasted you...it was like poetry in motion. And the way you screamed when you came...God, Sam..."

His words trailed off into a groan, his fingers dipping lower to tease the sensitive flesh that still throbbed. I gasped, an involuntary reaction to the jolt of electric current that coursed through my veins.

"You're made for sex, Sam," he said. His words, like a sweet poison, seeped into my veins.

His voice resonated in the air between us, hitting me with an intensity that was both unnerving and exhilarating. It was as if every syllable he uttered was designed to unsettle me, to knock me off-kilter. His words left me both melted and aflutter, inciting a paradoxical blend of anxiety and comfort within me. Listening to his deep timbre was a guilty pleasure—a secret indulgence that made me squirm.

Overwhelmed by it all, I tried to pull away from him again. It wasn't his fault that my stupid anxiety gnawed at me. No one ever gave me anything without exacting payment. Nothing was ever free in life, and I feared I now owed him my soul. I couldn't begin to fathom why I'd agreed—no, *chosen*—to participate in this sexual experiment. Curiosity had gotten the better of me. It wasn't that I regretted what we'd done—he'd given me the best orgasms I'd ever had—it was that being with him was unthinkable, taboo even. Why had I allowed a man who was essentially my boss, sixteen years my senior, do the things he'd done? I had no answers. My carefully constructed life had been irrevocably changed. But then again, he had promised it would be as if it had never happened. Tears threatened to spill over again. Maybe he was right... All the hormones were making me crazy, and I was overanalyzing it.

"There's no reason to cry or feel ashamed, my little Sammich. Our bodies have evolved to crave sexual gratification. There's no great rule-keeper in the sky who's going to smite you down for doing what comes naturally—for finding the ecstasy we all want."

"Atticus, I'm not crying," I said defensively, wiping away a stray tear that had escaped. "I'm just catching my breath. You don't need to coddle me; I'm a grown-ass woman."

Night Shift

I got up from the bed, and the cool air rushed across my heated skin where his touch lingered. Turning away from him, I marched into the bathroom and closed the door behind me. As soon as I caught sight of my disheveled appearance in the mirror, I laughed. My lips were swollen, my cheeks were flushed, and my hair was tangled from Atticus's strong hands gripping and pulling at it. Oh my God, how many marks had he left on me? Taking a deep breath, I steadied myself against the marble countertop. Wow, I looked like I'd been ridden hard and put up wet, and we hadn't even had actual sex. My heart hammered in my chest. I was still reeling from the amazing orgasms I'd just experienced. It was the first time a man had ever made me come.

I turned on the faucet, letting the cold water run over my hands before splashing it onto my face. The water provided a momentary respite from the emotional whirlwind inside me. This was my attempt to regain some semblance of control and release some of the heat still pulsing through my veins.

"Get it together, Sam," I muttered under my breath, staring at my reflection. I couldn't let this newfound vulnerability consume me. I was stronger than that. I had faced far worse than this in my life, and I would not be undone by a man's touch, no matter how intoxicating it might have been.

"Sam, are you okay in there?" Atticus called out softly.

"Yeah," I replied, trying to keep my tone steady. "I just need a minute."

With one final breath, I straightened my shoulders and stepped back into the bedroom, ready to face whatever came next. Of course, I found Atticus leaning back against the headboard with his legs sprawled out and his cock standing at attention. I froze, my heart pounding in my chest, and my thoughts raced as if they were trying to outrun the reality of what we had done. What could possibly be driving my attraction to this man? Was it his authority, his experience, or the simple thrill of doing something forbidden? "Psychology 101," I muttered to myself. "You want what you can't have." But deep down, I knew there was more to it than that. There was something about Atticus—his intelligence, his confidence, his raw sexuality—that made it impossible for me to look away. I was like a moth drawn to a flame, even knowing that getting too close could kill me. Whatever it was, I had to sort through these feelings before I lost myself completely.

"Atticus," I said, clearing my throat and trying to sound composed, "I need a few minutes alone to think. I'm going to soak in the hot tub for a little while."

"Of course," he replied, his eyes softening with understanding. "I'll make us some coffee and bring it out in a few minutes."

"Thanks," I whispered, then darted back into the bathroom to find a towel. Pulling one out from under the sink, I wrapped it around my body. The fabric was rough against my sensitive skin, but it provided a sense of protection, shielding me from the intensity of Atticus's gaze.

The hot tub was nestled on the back side of the cabin, in a corner overlooking the lake. When I stepped outside onto the deck, the cool October air hit my skin, causing goose bumps to form. The sky was clear tonight, providing a breathtaking view of the stars.

After easing myself into the warm water, I allowed the soothing jets to massage away the tension in my muscles. The battle raged in my mind, my thoughts shifting between the whirlwind of wanton desire I had for Atticus and the fear of the potential consequences I might unleash if I tried to pursue this relationship beyond tonight. I took a deep breath and released it slowly, letting the steam envelop me as I gazed at the stars above.

Night Shift

After a few minutes, I closed my eyes, allowing the steam and the gentle hum of the jets to cocoon me in a world of my own.

"Here you go," Atticus said, his voice breaking my reverie. He approached, carrying two steaming mugs of coffee. "Pumpkin spice latte. It's that time of the year, you know."

"Thank you," I said, taking the steaming mug from him and cradling it between my hands. The familiar aroma of pumpkin spice filled the air.

"Sam," he began, hesitating for a moment before continuing. "I want you to know that whatever you're feeling right now, it's okay. I won't push you into anything you're not ready for."

"Atticus, I—" Unsure of how to articulate the mess of emotions swirling within me, I took a deep breath. "I'm grateful, really. But I need to sort through this on my own before I can even begin to talk about it."

"Take all the time you need," he said gently, giving my shoulder a reassuring squeeze before retreating back inside the house, leaving me alone with my thoughts once more.

I leaned my head back against the edge of the tub. The crisp air kissed my face as the heated water cradled my body. I allowed my mind to wander, focusing on the delicious thought of joining the multiple-orgasm club. It was both thrilling and terrifying, knowing that I'd experienced such pleasure with a man I'd never imagined I could be intimate with. I wondered if I'd ever be able to go back to the way things had been before. In truth, I had believed multiple orgasms were an urban legend, fabricated by women who wanted to make others feel inadequate. Now I knew better. I'd thought I was tough, that I could handle whatever sexual adventures life threw at me, but I'd been so wrong. With Atticus...who knew where the limits were? I'd barely had a taste and had practically lost my mind.

I wanted to be the strong woman who could walk away from him tomorrow, keeping our tryst a secret between us and never mentioning it again. After all, I was the one who had made him promise that tonight was purely an experiment and nothing more. I'd intended for us to return to work as if nothing happened, for him to go on treating me like just any other ED nurse in his department. But now, after experiencing such intense sexual indulgence, I wasn't sure I could do that. Just as he'd predicted, my body felt ruined for future men, spoiled by the touch of the sexy doctor.

"Beautiful view, huh?" A little while later, Atticus's voice startled me out of my thoughts again. He stepped onto the porch, carrying two fluffy white towels.

He paused at the edge of the hot tub, taking in the sight of me. "You're even more beautiful in the moonlight, Sam," he said, setting the towels on the edge of the hot tub next to me. "May I join you?"

"Yes," I replied softly, the heat of my desire becoming hotter than the water surrounding me.

Atticus shrugged off his robe, leaving it draped over a nearby chair before easing himself into the hot tub across from me, giving me space but remaining close enough for conversation. "Sam, I just want you to know that you're incredible. And whether or not you want to hear it, you should know how amazing you are sexually. Damn, I just have to tell you that your pussy tastes divine, and I'm serious when I say that I would love to fuck all of you."

I laughed nervously, flattered by his compliments yet feeling vulnerable. "You're incorrigible, you know that?"

"Guilty as charged." He grinned. "But remember our promise? Tonight's an experiment, nothing more. We won't tell anyone at the hospital, and tomorrow we'll go back to being Dr.

Thorin and Sam, the ED nurse. No innuendoes, no jokes, no nicknames, no strings, no feelings."

"Got it," I replied, holding his gaze. And in that moment, I wished it was that simple, that I could forget everything and move forward without any lingering feelings. But deep down, I knew that wasn't going to happen.

Atticus shifted closer to me. The steam from the water danced around us, creating a surreal veil that seemed to encase us in a private world. He leaned in and kissed me. As his lips brushed against mine, an electric current shot through me, awakening every nerve ending in my body. His kiss was a perfect balance of tenderness and desire, as if he knew exactly what I needed. Without pulling his lips away from mine, he picked me up and set me on his lap, positioning me so that my legs straddled his hips.

"Sam..." He groaned between kisses. "God, I want to fuck you." His mouth trailed down my neck, causing shivers to run down my spine. He continued down over my collarbone. Finally, at the water's edge, he reached my breasts, where he took one nipple into his mouth, sucking and playing with it. My breath caught in my throat, the sight of him setting my body aflame.

"Atticus," I whispered, tangling my fingers in his dark brown hair. "Take all of me." His hands roamed over my body, leaving goose bumps in their wake. Finally, they found my pussy, and he slid two fingers inside me, curling them expertly, making me moan.

"God, you're so beautiful," he said, his voice husky with lust. He continued to finger-fuck me while his thumb rubbed my clitoris in slow, teasing strokes. My hips bucked against his hand. I was desperate for more.

"I want more," I begged, reaching down to wrap my hand around his hard cock. We shared a rough, passionate kiss while he positioned me over him. His shaft pressed against my entrance, and I couldn't suppress a gasp at the size of it.

"Slowly," Atticus instructed, lifting me up just enough before guiding me onto his thick cock. My tightness made progress slow, but with each incremental movement, I stretched to accommodate him. I leaned back, allowing him better access to my nipples, and he took full advantage, sucking and nibbling on them as I whimpered with need.

"Atticus," I moaned, the pressure inside me building. He gripped my hips and set a steady pace, guiding my body up and down his shaft, the water swirling and sloshing around us. With each stroke, the tension within me grew more and more unbearable until, finally, we both reached our peak, and our cries of rapture intertwined in the cool night air.

"God, Atticus!" I gasped, my body still trembling from the intensity of our lovemaking. "That was...incredible."

"Damn right it was." He grinned, pressing a soft kiss to my forehead.

The sound of laughter and footsteps approaching pierced our haze of pleasure. My eyes snapped open. Atticus's brothers, Braxton and Conan, appeared on the porch. Their jaws dropped, and they stared at us with wide eyes.

"Holy fuck!" Braxton exclaimed. "I didn't know we were walking up on a porn set!"

"Get it, brother," Conan said, grinning like a madman. "Those tits look mighty fine! Maybe we should join?"

Mortification surged through my veins like a tidal wave, drowning any remnants of happiness I had just experienced.

"Get the hell out!" Atticus shouted at them, shielding me protectively.

I couldn't bear their gazes any longer. Unsheathing Atticus's cock in one fell swoop, I leaped up from the water. With my hands, I covered myself as best I could and quickly snatched a nearby towel. Holding it tightly against my body, I sprinted for the bedroom. My heart pounded in my chest as I slammed the door shut, trying to catch my breath. But it wasn't enough; I needed more distance between myself and the humiliating scene outside. So I darted into the bathroom, locked the door behind me, and turned on the shower.

"Shit, shit, shit," I muttered under my breath, berating myself for letting my guard down, for allowing this disastrous situation to unfold. The warm water cascaded over my body, and I tried to wash away the embarrassment. What would Braxton and Conan think of me now? Would they tell everyone at work about what they'd seen?

"Pull it together, Sam," I whispered to myself, forcing the tears back. This was not the time for self-pity or regret. I couldn't change what had happened, but I could control how I reacted to it.

My insecurity threatened to overwhelm me as I stood there beneath the hot spray of water. Steamy tendrils filled the shower stall, clouding my vision and making it difficult to see anything beyond my own body. As I watched droplets of water run down my trembling form, all I could think was that I had made a colossal mistake.

"God, what was I thinking?" I asked myself, my voice barely audible amidst the relentless torrent of water. My thoughts raced back to Atticus, his brothers, and the horror of being caught in such a compromising situation. Would they keep their mouths shut? Or would my one night of reckless abandon become fodder for gossip and ridicule at work?

Anger bubbled up inside me, directed at both myself and Atticus for getting me into this mess. I had been so curious about sex, so desperate to experience the sensuality I'd heard others speak of. But now, all I felt was shame and regret.

With my body still trembling from the emotional turmoil, I stepped out of the shower. As I wrapped a towel around myself and began to dry my hair, my thoughts drifted to Bethany. She had raved about Atticus's sexual prowess, practically swooning while recounting their encounters. If she found out about us... I didn't even want to think about the fallout. A pang of guilt hit me when I realized she might be hurt if she found out what had transpired today. She had harbored hopes for a relationship with Atticus, even though he'd made it clear that he wasn't interested in anything serious.

"Stupid, stupid, stupid," I said, chastising myself and gripping my hair tightly in frustration. While what had happened was undeniably life-altering—an experience unlike any I had ever known—I still wished that things could have been different. That maybe, just maybe, fate would have dealt me a different hand and I could end up with someone who truly cared for me, rather than a man whose only interest lay in sexual pleasure.

"Life would be so much easier if we could just be with the people who liked us back," I whispered to myself, staring at my reflection in the foggy mirror. "Why did it have to be him? Get it together, Sam," I ordered myself as I finished drying my hair. "You knew what you were getting into. You can't let this... whatever it was...change things."

I slipped into a pair of big gray sweatpants and an extra-large T-shirt, the soft fabric caressing my skin as I desperately tried to gather some semblance of dignity. The events that had unfolded between Atticus and me would remain locked away in my mind, never to be spoken of again. After all, what choice did I have but to suck it up and pretend that it meant nothing to me?

Night Shift

"Time to move on," I murmured, steeling myself for the challenges that surely awaited me outside that door.

Taking a deep breath, I returned to the bedroom.

There he was, lying on the bed in all his naked glory, a hard-on standing proudly between his legs. My heart stuttered in my chest, and I couldn't help but stare for a moment before snapping back to reality.

"Atticus," I said, trying to sound calm, "do you ever get enough sex?"

He chuckled, and the sound was somehow both inappropriate and endearing at the same time. "No, Sam, I don't think I ever do."

"Good for you," I snapped, my cheeks burning with embarrassment. "But our little experiment is over, and I want to leave."

His laughter faded, and his face shifted into a serious expression. "Sam, about Braxton and Conan—"

"God, I can't believe they saw me like that," I said, my voice shaking. "I'm so humiliated."

"Sam, I'm so sorry about—"

"Save it. What's done is done. Let's just...move on."

"Are you okay?" he asked, his eyes searching my face.

"I will be." I forced a half-hearted smile onto my face. "Let's just make sure this stays between us, okay?"

Atticus laughed, but there was an edge to it, a hint of something bitter beneath the surface. "Sam, my brothers don't think anything of it. They know I have casual sex all the time." He paused, then added softly, "I made them promise not to say anything about us to people at work."

"Great," I muttered, crossing my arms over my chest. "So they won't tell anyone that I let you fuck me like some cheap whore."

"Hey," Atticus said sharply, his eyes narrowing. "Don't talk like that."

"Whatever!" I shouted, turning away from him. I wasn't sure if I was relieved or even more hurt by his insensitive approach. It was just a one-night experiment; I had no right to be upset. But I couldn't help it—I felt ashamed and cheap. "Take me home, Atticus," I demanded. "Right now, or I'll call an Uber."

"An Uber? This far from the city?" He raised an eyebrow, clearly amused.

"Then you'll just have to drive me," I shot back, shaking with anger.

Without a word, Atticus pulled on his clothes and grabbed his keys. He passed me as he went out the door, his expression unreadable. "Let's go."

As we made our way downstairs, my emotions swirled chaotically. I was infuriated at myself for letting things go so far with him, mortified by the whole situation, and hurt by his cavalier attitude toward our night together. My chest tightened, and my breaths came in short gasps. Atticus noticed my distress and took my hand, squeezing it gently.

"Are you okay?"

"Fine," I lied, my vision starting to swim as I struggled to draw air into my lungs. "Just get me home."

"Sam, try to breathe," he told me, his voice softer than I'd ever heard it before. "I've got you."

Despite his assurances, my panic continued to rise, threatening to consume me completely. All I could think about was how everything had changed in one night and how desperately I wished that things could have been different.

The panic clawed its way up my throat, clenching it like a vise. Soon I was gasping for air, each breath more labored than the last. Alarm surged through me as I realized I was having a full-blown panic attack.

"Atticus!" I barely managed to choke out.

He wrapped his arm around my waist. His earlier laughter was gone, replaced by concern. "Sam, sit down on the edge of the sofa," he instructed, guiding me gently. "Hang your head between your knees. Just breathe."

My body trembled as I followed his instructions, but the panic continued to build. Atticus walked into the kitchen and returned with a paper bag.

"Here, breathe into this," he said, placing the bag over my mouth and nose. While I tried to steady my breathing, the world seemed to close in around me. The room spun, and tears began to stream down my face.

"Shh, it's okay, Sam," Atticus whispered, sitting beside me. He rubbed soothing circles on my back, trying to ground me and ease my fear.

When the worst of it had subsided, the sobs broke free.

"I've had panic attacks since my mom was killed," I confessed, my voice wavering as I clung to the last shreds of my composure. "I thought I had them under control, but..."

"Shh," he soothed, pulling me close. "You don't have to explain. I understand." He hesitated before continuing. "I'm sorry if I somehow hurt or damaged you. I never meant to."

He leaned back, and guilt flickered across his face as he studied me. Did he blame himself for this? I didn't blame him. I just didn't have the emotional capacity to deal with all of this right now.

He helped me gather my things, handling me gently and carefully as if I were made of glass. The silence between us was heavy while we made our way to the car. All the passion and playfulness from earlier was now only a distant memory.

We remained quiet on the drive back to Tacoma, the soft strains of jazz music filling the car. A few times, Atticus broke the silence and tried to comfort me, but I didn't have the energy to respond.

When we pulled up outside my apartment building, I finally turned to him and spoke. "Tonight never happened," I said bluntly. "Our not-a-date was just a walk in the park, nothing more."

The finality of my words hung in the air between us as I climbed out of the car. "Good night, Dr. Thorin."

I slammed the door behind me, leaving Atticus and our one-night experiment in the past where they belonged.

Night Shift

Chapter Ten

When I entered the ED for my shift, a headache was throbbing against my skull and nervous dread was eating at me. It was my first shift since I'd gone with Atticus to his cabin three days ago, and the memory of our sexual encounter was still vivid in my mind. A knot of anxiety twisted my stomach, and my hands were clammy. I wasn't eager to see him again or for my coworkers to find out what we'd done. But I soon learned that Atticus had finished his night rotation and I wouldn't be seeing him anytime soon. He was back on day shifts, a fact that brought me both relief and an unexpected pang of disappointment.

As I walked through the ED, I kept scanning for his familiar, commanding presence out of habit, only to remember he wasn't on shift. It was weird to not hear his deep voice in the hallways. I missed it more than I'd thought I would. To make matters worse,

Bethany wasn't here tonight either. Working with the other doctors and nurses was fine—we were all professionals—but I didn't have the same vibe with them as I did with Atticus and Bethany. At least with them not around, I didn't have to worry about slipping up and mentioning something about what had happened between Atticus and me.

Trauma cases came in waves, keeping us busy. We handled a teenager who had a broken leg from a motorcycle accident, then an elderly woman with chest pains. Each case was a diversion from my tumultuous thoughts. I moved from patient to patient, administering medication and offering words of comfort, but my mind kept drifting back to Atticus. In particular, I wondered why he hadn't texted me. The emotional whiplash of everything was throwing me totally off-kilter. For a while there, I'd been seeing him so much at work. Then we'd had mad, crazy sex, and now there was radio silence. I didn't know how to process all of it.

The intensity of what we had shared was overwhelming. For the first time in my life, I'd experienced true sexual pleasure, and it was all thanks to him and his wicked ways. But it wasn't just the physical connection that haunted me. Atticus had listened to my stories about my father and had seen me for the strong, independent woman I truly was. It was new to me for a man to treat me with such understanding and respect. He never looked at me with pity or acted as if I was beneath him, despite knowing about my mother's fate and my father's actions, because he, too, had endured similar trauma.

Yet the reality of our agreement—to not go beyond a one-night stand—hung over me, a persistent shadow clouding my thoughts. It was as if Atticus had vanished, leaving no trace behind except the memories that were etched into my mind. The idea that he could so easily adhere to our agreement, that he could detach so completely, left me with an odd sense of loneliness.

A part of me regretted making him agree to utterly deny the attraction between us. Perhaps his interest lay only in the thrill of the chase, and now that he'd conquered me, I would become just a forgotten memory. The idea that he might still want me, that he might reach out, was a fantasy. But I was torn between the professional boundaries we had set and my undeniable longing for his touch.

The shift dragged on, each hour a reminder of Atticus's absence. I missed not only the physical intimacy we had shared, but also the emotional bond we had unexpectedly forged. The snarky banter, the shared understanding of loss, the way he had treated me as an equal—it had been a rare thing in my life. Dammit, couldn't he have texted me? It was impossible to understand how he could bury his face in my most intimate places and then, in an instant, act like it was nothing more than licking a lollipop. Maybe I wasn't merely naive but just plain stupid.

"Come on, Sam. Stop obsessing over some heartless old doctor," I muttered as I sat at the nurses' station trying to chart some notes about my latest patient.

When I clocked out at the end of my shift, the hospital corridors seemed cold and impersonal. In moments like these, when the few people I'd begun to connect with weren't around, the reality that I was still an outsider here hit home. It was like the hospital was just a place to work, nothing more—with no friendly chats or familiar faces to break up the routine.

In the locker room, I shoved my arms into my coat and gathered my things. Then I headed out to my car. I had nothing to do except go home alone. It seemed Atticus had kept his promise perfectly—our night together had become a fleeting moment, and he'd already forgotten about it.

The weeks flew by, each day blurring into the next as I adjusted to working at St. John's emergency department. The leaves outside shifted from vibrant shades of red and gold to a dull brown, a reminder that Thanksgiving was just around the corner. Since my night with Atticus, I hadn't heard so much as a word from him. I had to assume that our passionate encounter had been nothing more than a one-night stand in his eyes, so I did my best to push it out of my mind.

My new job helped keep me focused on the present. Every day I grew more confident, and the feverish pace helped to keep me focused on the present. The feverish pace of the ED became my solace, drowning out any lingering thoughts about Atticus. I'd found my place among the night-shift team. They were a cool group of people, and their camaraderie and support were amazing.

There was Bethany, of course, who was unfailingly armed with snappy, sarcastic one-liners. I had also made friends with Jack, a fellow nurse with a wicked sense of humor, and Marissa, an experienced charge nurse who took me under her wing, patiently answering my questions and offering guidance.

"Sam!" Bethany called out to me one day as I came on shift. "A bunch of us are getting together for Friendsgiving this Thursday. You should come!"

"Friendsgiving?" I asked, my curiosity piqued.

"Yeah!" She grinned. "It's like Thanksgiving, but with friends instead of family. Since most of us don't have family nearby, we figured we'd celebrate together. What do you say?"

"That sounds really nice, actually. I'd love to come."

Night Shift

"Yay, I'm so glad!" Bethany smacked her hands together excitedly. "Jack, Marissa, and Caleb—he's a firefighter we're friends with—are all coming too. It'll be a blast."

"Can't wait," I said. I was grateful to be included.

"Okay, I'll add you to the group text," she said as she left.

As Thanksgiving approached, I was riding a wave of optimism. My job was going well, I was making friends, and I was slowly learning to navigate life without letting the trauma of my past define me. Even the nightmares that had so often tormented my dreams had given way to a new form of torture—smutty wet dreams. I'd take those over the memories of my father's fists any day. Although the memory of that night with Atticus still haunted me, I was determined not to let it overshadow the good things happening in my new life in Tacoma.

The night of Friendsgiving arrived. The restaurant we'd agreed to meet at was bustling with activity. "Sam! I'm so glad you could make it," Bethany said, pulling me into a tight hug. "This is going to be such a blast!"

Marissa and a guy I didn't know walked in, and Bethany threw her arms around each one of them in turn.

"Caleb, this is Sam. Sam, this is Caleb, one of my firefighter buddies," Marissa quickly said in introduction. Before we could say more, a hostess directed us to follow her, and we were taken to a table near the bar.

Warm lights flickered above us, casting a cozy glow over our group. Caleb slid into the booth next to me while Bethany and Marissa, who were already deep in conversation, took seats across from us. Our server delivered glasses of water and special Friendsgiving menus. Tonight's theme was a Mexican fiesta. I couldn't think of a better way to celebrate Thanksgiving than with tacos and enchiladas.

Just as we settled in, the sound of hurried footsteps approached, and Jack finally made his appearance, sliding into the seat next to Caleb with a sheepish grin. "Sorry I'm late, guys. Time just got away from me."

Marissa waved off his apology with a smile. Jack's gaze shifted around the table, and he asked, "Where's Kristen tonight, Marissa?"

Marissa took a deep breath, her smile fading a bit. "Oh, Kristen and I...we decided to go our separate ways," she announced, a touch of relief in her voice. "Turns out, she was more into staying home and binge-watching reality TV than actually living life."

Bethany quickly chimed in. "Speaking of living life, guess who's got a new boy toy? Oh my God, Brad was so incredible in bed. I swear he has the biggest dick I've ever seen." She winked dramatically, causing a ripple of laughter around the table.

"And he's absolutely hot," she continued, leaning forward with a conspiratorial grin. "Like, could-be-a-model hot."

Caleb raised an eyebrow and smirked at Bethany. "So, what you're saying is, he's almost as hot as me?"

Jack rolled his eyes and snorted, taking a sip of his water before saying, "Yeah, but does he know how to navigate a conversation without mentioning his abs every five minutes and grabbing his crotch?"

The table erupted in laughter.

Bethany pretended to ponder Jack's question, tapping her chin. "Hmm, I'll have to conduct a thorough investigation and report back."

Marissa laughed, shaking her head. "Please, Beth, spare us the details."

Night Shift

The conversation flowed seamlessly from one topic to the next. The Friendsgiving dinner was a lively affair, the kind of gathering I hadn't realized I'd been missing out on until I was right in the middle of it. The restaurant buzzed with an inviting energy, and our table was in the perfect spot for both people-watching and intimate conversation. Soon, the server took our orders and delivered our drinks. The girls all got margaritas while the guys had Dos Equis.

Lost in my thoughts, I didn't register that Marissa was making some sort of toast until she shouted, "Cheers!" We all clinked our glasses together before taking sips of our drinks. The atmosphere was light and fun, and I was grateful for these newfound friends who had made me feel so welcome.

Bethany, always the life of the party, was in her element, bouncing between stories about some of our more eccentric patients and teasing Marissa about her new profile on Hinge. With her quick wit and infectious laugh, Marissa volleyed back with her own playful jabs. Their banter was a highlight of the evening.

Caleb was charming as well. He had a natural storytelling ability that had us all laughing. His tales from the fire station, which ranged from heartwarming to downright hilarious, added a different flavor to the conversation than our medical-centric stories.

Jack was more reserved tonight but had a dry sense of humor that always caught me off guard in the best way. At one point, he shared a story about a particularly bizarre ED incident that had us all in stitches.

The conversation soon shifted to plans for the upcoming holiday season. We shared stories about our traditions, or, in most cases, the lack thereof. It was comforting to know I wasn't the only one without family nearby.

The food was delicious. We'd ordered an array of appetizers and main dishes that were a mix of your typical Mexican fare and some more adventurous choices. We all shared, passing plates, each of us trying a bit of everything.

Throughout the evening, I found myself opening up more than I had in a long time. There was something about the combination of good food, great company, and lots of laughter that made it easy to forget my usual insecurities. We talked about everything from our favorite TV shows to our aspirations both within and outside of our careers.

When dessert arrived, Bethany brought up the topic of dating. The conversation quickly turned into a hilarious exchange of dating-app disasters and blind-date blunders. Even I chimed in with a story about the guy I'd dated in college, though I carefully steered clear of mentioning anything about Atticus.

"Hey, Sam," Bethany said suddenly, leaning across the table and waving a forkful of cake for emphasis. "Have you thought about who you're taking as your date to the hospital's annual holiday party next week? It's a fancy-schmancy gala they throw every year to say thank you for all our hard work."

The question caught me off guard. "Uh, honestly, I hadn't really considered it," I said, my cheeks heating up. "I mean, I saw the announcement about the gala, and I have that night off, but I didn't think I'd go."

"Are you kidding?" Marissa asked, her dark curls bouncing as she shook her head. "Girl, you need a night out to let loose and have some fun! Plus, it's a great opportunity to mingle with the higher-ups."

"Exactly," Jack added, propping his elbows on the table and clasping his hands together. I couldn't help but notice how his tight T-shirt showcased his muscular arms. "You never know who you might meet, or what doors this event could open for you."

"All right, all right," I conceded, smiling at their enthusiasm. "I'll think about going to the gala, but I don't even have a date."

"Who needs a date?" Bethany said, smiling. "Just come and enjoy yourself!"

"Yeah, don't worry about it," Jack reassured me, glancing around Caleb to see me better. "We've got your back. We'll help you find someone awesome to go with."

"Speaking of dates," I ventured hesitantly, "do any of you know who Dr. Thorin is taking?"

"Dr. Thorin?" Bethany asked, her brow furrowing. "Yeah, I heard he's taking Dr. Vanessa Sinclair. She's an OB-GYN who works in the office building next to the hospital. She's drop-dead gorgeous too. Why do you want to know?"

My stomach churned at the mention of Atticus's beautiful date. I shouldn't care, but my heart ached at the thought of seeing him with someone else. "No reason really. It's just that... you know, he's got a certain reputation, and after what you told me a while back, I was just curious."

But I was a terrible liar and couldn't hide the fact that the news had bothered me.

"Hey," Marissa said, turning her head to the side and giving me a concerned look. "You okay?"

"Uh, yeah," I stammered, trying to shake off my feelings. "I'm fine. Just tired from work, I guess."

"Let's change the subject then," Bethany suggested. "What do you think you might wear to the gala?"

"Oh God, I have no idea. I don't own any party dresses," I said, cringing inwardly as I pictured the price tag of a fancy dress.

Marissa took a sip of her margarita and said, "Then tomorrow you're coming over to my place, and I'll fix you up. I was in a big sorority in college and have a ton of dresses I only wore once." After taking a big bite of her tres leches cake, she turned toward Bethany. "Hey, I've got a great idea. How about the three of us plan on getting ready together before the gala and then all ride together to the hotel? We can have a blast getting all glammed up and pregaming."

As we finished up dessert, Bethany glanced toward the dance floor with a mischievous grin. "Okay, guys, dinner's over, but the night's just getting started! Who's up for dancing?" She stood up with a flourish and headed that way.

Caleb chuckled and rose from his seat. "You don't have to ask me twice," he said, offering his hand to Marissa. "Let me show you how it's done?"

Marissa laughed, taking his hand. "Lead the way, fireman." They both headed toward the dance floor.

Jack, who seemed a bit more hesitant but also intrigued, nudged me. "You dance, Sam?" he asked, giving me a half-smile.

I shrugged, smiling back. "I can hold my own. You coming?"

Together, we joined the others. The music was some upbeat, old-school disco tune. The atmosphere was electric, filled with the buzz of laughter and the rhythm of the music.

Bethany, ever the social butterfly, was soon chatting up a storm with a group of people we didn't know. Her laughter was boisterous, drawing us all into the conversation.

"You're from the hospital, right?" one of the guys in the group, who introduced himself as Mike, asked. "I've heard crazy stories about emergency room nights there."

"Oh, you have no idea—especially during full moons," Bethany replied with a wink. "But what happens in the ED stays in the ED, right Sam?"

"Exactly, patient confidentiality and all that."

Night Shift

As the night wore on, we danced, laughed, and mingled with different people. I stayed on the sober side, enjoying the company and the music. The energy on the dance floor was contagious, and soon I was letting loose, feeling free and happy.

At one point, a tall, charming guy approached me.

"Hey, I couldn't help but notice your dance moves," he said, smiling. "I'm Derek."

There was something about him that caught my attention. Tall and undeniably handsome, he had an attractive confidence. On his face was a great lopsided grin, and I found myself smiling back almost instantly.

"Hey, I'm Sam," I said, still moving to the rhythm of the music. He joined in, and we danced together, everything around us fading into the background.

Derek leaned in closer, a playful glint in his eyes. He gently ran his fingers through a lock of my hair that was lying on my chest, moving it over my shoulder and stroking my collarbone with his thumb. "You know," he said, his voice low and slightly teasing, "your hair really is something else. It's like flames in this dim light."

He paused, lifting his gaze to mine, and my stomach fluttered. "And those eyes, damn, they're like the clearest blue sky," he said, placing his hands on my hips and pulling me closer.

With a soft smile, he nuzzled my nose with his, moving to whisper in my ear. "But these freckles," he said, his voice dropping to a growl, "they're absolutely enchanting." With that, he eased away, planted a gentle kiss on my cheek, and chuckled.

Heat rushed down my spine, and my pulse quickened. His flirty remark, coupled with the kiss, sent a cascade of tingles across my skin.

"Thank you," I said. A laugh bubbled up, surprising me, and I tucked a loose strand of hair behind my ear in a futile attempt to hide my embarrassment. "You're not so bad yourself."

He laughed, and we continued dancing, eventually drifting toward the bar. "Can I buy you a drink?" he asked.

"Sure," I agreed, deciding to go for something non-alcoholic, since I was the designated driver tonight.

While we were sipping our drinks, the DJ switched to a slower song. Derek held out his hand. "Care for a slow dance?"

I nodded. This time, we ended up in a more intimate position on the dance floor, with my hands wrapped around his neck and his hands hovering over my lower back, the edges of his fingertips grazing my bottom. Derek was a wonderful dancer, his movements smooth and in perfect sync with mine. We swayed to the music for several blissful minutes. The chemistry between us was undeniable.

Toward the end of the song, Derek leaned in and kissed me. It was a passionate kiss, one that caught me off guard but wasn't unwelcome. Just as our lips parted, I heard a familiar voice.

"Get it, girl!" Bethany cheered from a short distance away, winking at me and giving me a playful grin.

I laughed, a little embarrassed but also enjoying the moment. Derek smiled, his eyes twinkling with mischief.

When the bar announced last call a few minutes later, he gently pulled me away from the dance floor. "Sam, would you like to go to dinner sometime?"

I hesitated for a moment, then nodded. "That sounds nice."

He took my phone and, with a sly grin, typed in his information.

Before leaving, he kissed me one last time—a sweet and lingering kiss. It was nice, really nice, but when he walked away, my mind drifted back to Atticus. Derek was charming and handsome, but Atticus's kisses had been something else, something I wasn't sure could be matched.

I drove everyone home, replaying the night in my mind. Derek was great, but Atticus was in a class of his own.

Friendsgiving had been a blast, a perfect mix of good company and great fun. I made sure everyone got home safely, then finally headed back to my own place. I was content, and a little tired, but mostly grateful for having something to do on Thanksgiving other than sit home alone. It was a night I wouldn't forget, a reminder of the good things in life outside the walls of the hospital.

Later that evening, I stood in front of my bedroom mirror and tried to picture myself at the holiday gala. Although I didn't know what Dr. Sinclair looked like, I imagined her as annoyingly beautiful, and the image of her and Atticus together ate at me. I could picture them turning heads at the gala while I stood on the sidelines, feeling insignificant. As I changed into my pajamas, I wondered if I would ever be able to move on from the man who had turned my world upside down in just one night.

When I finally fell asleep, my dreams betrayed me, filling my mind with images of Atticus and me tangled together, our bodies glistening with sweat as we fucked on every surface of the cabin. I woke up feeling pathetic and frustrated. I needed to find a way to put him out of my mind once and for all. Although I wasn't sure how exactly I was going to do that yet, I resolved to go to the hospital's holiday gala and prove to myself—and to him—that I could move on without a second thought.

Chapter Eleven

The chill seeped through my clothes as I fought to clear my mind. Returning to consciousness was like surfacing from deep water, only to find I had been dragged into a nightmare. My body was lying prone on some kind of cold, hard surface—concrete maybe? I realized I was in the heart of a warehouse, a grim arena set for my day of reckoning. I'd been drugged, snatched, and unceremoniously dumped here, and I now lay broken before the leaders of Volkovi Nochi, the reality of my situation unfolding in cruel clarity.

Shadows flickered across the grungy walls, offering no solace from what was to come. Viktor Volkov, the feared Pakhan of the Volkovi Nochi, towered over me, a specter of vengeance, his silhouette a portent of the storm to come.

Night Shift

"You've been a bad investment, Mac Sheridan," he said, his words cutting through the silence, emotionless and cold as ice. "Stealing from us, selling our product as if it was your own? Did you think we wouldn't find out?"

My throat raw, I struggled to rasp out a response. "I didn't... I swear, Viktor. You've got it all wrong."

His humorless laugh chilled me to the bone. "You insult my intelligence. We have proof."

Before I could protest, his fist smashed into my face with brutal force. Pain exploded across my skull, disorienting me and blurring the grimy walls that boxed us in. Blood filled my mouth, its iron taste a reminder of my defenselessness.

One of his thugs, Ivan Krovopuskov, a mountain of a man with a gruesome scar running along his left cheek, stepped forward. "This is for your lies," he snarled, delivering a crushing blow to my ribs. The *crack* that followed was unmistakable—a sharp, agonizing break of bone that echoed off the warehouse walls.

I gasped for air, each breath a razor slicing through my lungs. "I'm not lying," I managed to choke out, the words barely audible over the ringing in my ears.

Viktor leaned in close, putting his face inches from mine. His breath was foul with the stench of vodka and cigars. "You are a cockroach, Mac. And what do we do with cockroaches?" He gestured, and another torrent of blows rained down on me. "We crush them under our boot."

In a feeble attempt to protect myself, I raised my arms, but it was useless. Mercilessly, his goons rained down punches and kicks. Each blow was a hammer driving nails of agony through my flesh.

"Please," I choked out, "you have to believe me. I wouldn't... wouldn't betray you."

Viktor's boot connected with my stomach, and I curled into a ball, fighting the darkness that threatened to engulf me. "Believe you?" he spat. "You are nothing but a thief, a liability we can no longer afford."

His words blurred into a discordant noise of hatred. My heartbeat thundered in my ears. I was overwrought with pain, each new wave of punches crashing over me with unyielding force.

As I teetered on the brink of unconsciousness, Viktor's voice cut through the haze. "This is what happens to those who dare to double-cross us."

Each breath was now a battle, and while I lay there on that unforgiving floor, my mind slipped into the past. It was strange how, in moments of sheer agony, memories long buried resurfaced with vivid clarity.

I was back in my childhood home—a cramped, dingy apartment that always smelled faintly of mildew and cigarettes. My father, a man consumed by his own demons, mostly found at the bottom of a bottle, was a mere shadowy figure. There was a vague image of my mother, a tired, worn-out soul. She'd left me as a boy, leaving me with nothing but a faded photograph and a heart full of questions.

School had been a battleground, a place where I'd learned to fend for myself. I hadn't been the smartest kid, nor the strongest, but I'd been quick—quick to learn the ways of the street, quick to understand that in this world, you either took what you wanted or you got taken.

By my late teens, I had fallen in with a local gang. They were my family, the brothers I'd never had. We'd started small—petty thefts and minor drug deals—but it had given me a sense of belonging, a purpose. The rush of adrenaline, the quick cash, it was intoxicating.

Night Shift

Then came the night that changed everything. We had planned a simple job, a smash-and-grab at a local store. But things went sideways fast. Alarms blared, police sirens wailed in the distance, and in the chaos, I'd made a decision that would haunt me forever. I left one of my own behind, a kid who was barely sixteen, to take the fall. While I hid in the shadows, I saw the betrayal in his eyes as the cops cuffed him. It was a look I would never forget.

That had been the turning point for me. From there, I'd only descended into deeper darkness. The jobs had gotten bigger, the stakes higher. Eventually, my reputation had caught the attention of the Russian Bratva. They'd been expanding their operations and were looking for someone with my particular set of skills. The money was good, too good to pass up. So, I'd stepped into their world, a world of drugs and violence, a world where life was cheap and loyalty was just another word for fear.

As I lay here now, broken and bleeding, a pawn in their brutal game, I realized how far I had strayed from the scared little boy in that dingy apartment. I had become a man I didn't recognize, a man my mother wouldn't have recognized. The irony wasn't lost on me. In trying to escape the life I'd been given, I had sprinted headlong into a nightmare of my own making.

There had been this brief, shining time when I'd tricked myself into believing I had everything figured out. I'd had cash flowing in like water, a cozy spot in the suburbs, Jennifer by my side, and Samantha, our kid, rounding out the picture of domestic bliss. The front I'd put up as a successful software consultant while I'd been dabbling in high-stakes trading on the side, had lent me the veneer of a respectable, well-off community member. Everything had been smooth sailing until that godforsaken wreck had torn it all down.

That night, if Jennifer had not insisted on leaving the party early to tend to Samantha's complaints of a stomachache, we'd never have been on that road. The crash that followed sealed my fate in the most twisted of ironies—killing Jennifer and leaving Samantha motherless. And me? I was shackled not by bars but by the relentless focus of the law breathing down my neck and a conviction of vehicular manslaughter that clung to me like a second skin.

That fucking judge, with his sanctimonious smirk, had thought he was handing me mercy on a platter by tying my probation to Sam's coming of age. As if living every day with the ghost of my past mistakes hovering over me was some kind of blessing. Prison, with its routine, three square meals a day, and the Volkovi Nochi's network weaving through its underbelly, would have been a damn sight better than the purgatory I found myself in now. At least behind bars, I could've leaned into the system, kept my head down, and emerged with a semblance of life waiting for me. Instead, I was trapped in limbo. Every day was a reminder of the life I could've had if not for the whimper of a child's complaint that night.

And now, as the darkness threatened to claim me, the faces of my past flashed before my eyes—mocking what little existence I had left. Each was a reminder of the choices I'd made, the paths I'd taken. And I wondered, had it all been worth it? The money, the power, the fear I'd instilled in others—had it brought me anything but this moment of reckoning?

The past was a ghost, untouchable and unchangeable. All I had now was the present, a present filled with pain and regret.

The relentless pain continued to wash over me. All of a sudden, a desperate, despicable idea took root in my mind. Gasping for air, I managed to raise my head.

Night Shift

The hammer of a gun cocked. The cold steel pressed firmly into the back of my head. Words were difficult to formulate. Thunder. That was the sound I heard as my heartbeat boomed in my ears.

"Good night, Mr. Sheridan."

"Wait...wait," I choked out, struggling to form the words. "I have...something...you want."

Before the trigger could be pulled, one word managed to escape my bleeding lips...

"Samantha."

Viktor, who had been standing back, observing the spectacle with a detached air, leaned in, his interest piqued. "What could you possibly have that I'd want, Mac?" he asked, his tone laced with skepticism.

I swallowed hard, tasting blood and bile in my mouth. "My daughter," I said, the words like poison on my lips. "Samantha."

A murmur went through the crew of thugs. Viktor's eyes narrowed. "Go on," he prompted, a cruel curiosity in his voice.

"She's...beautiful," I stammered. "Intelligent, healthy, and naive. A perfect...untouched...commodity."

I could see the wheels turning in Viktor's head as he calculated the potential of my offer. "And?" he prodded, his interest growing.

"She's an emergency department nurse," I said, then coughed. The pain from my injuries shot through my veins like an electric shock. "She can...help you. Help treat your wounded. She's valuable." Each word was sputtered out with blood.

The room fell silent. Outside, a car horn blared. I remained immobile, drawing in ragged, labored breaths while I waited for his response. Viktor stared at me, his expression unreadable. Then, slowly, he began to nod.

"It's an interesting proposition, Mac," he said, his voice smooth as silk yet dangerous. "But why would you offer your daughter? What does that say about you?"

I had no answer. The truth was too appalling. I had crossed a line, a line no father should ever cross. In my desperation to save my own skin, I had betrayed the one person who should have meant everything to me.

Viktor turned to his men. "Get him up," he ordered. "I want to find out more about this girl."

They roughly hauled me to my feet, causing the pain in my ribs to flare anew. All at once, the significance of what I'd just done sank in. I had sold my daughter's life, her safety, for a few more breaths in this wretched world.

As I stumbled out of the room, supported by the very men who had just beaten me, I knew there was no going back.

They shoved me into a chair in a dimly lit back office, forcing me to face a massive mahogany desk. Viktor sank into a black leather chair behind it, his presence dominating the shadowed space. Resting his elbows on the polished surface, he clasped his hands together and glared at me, his eyes radiating contempt. The room seemed to shrink under his scrutiny.

He motioned to one of his men, who promptly pulled out my phone from his pocket and pitched it at me. "Show me this daughter of yours."

A few years ago, I'd befriended Sam using one of my fake Instagram accounts. Quickly, I tapped the screen and pulled up her profile. Images of Sam filled the screen, displaying her vibrant life and innocence. I handed the phone to Viktor, and a twisted smile crept across his face.

"She's a pretty one, isn't she?" he mused, his gaze lingering on a photo of her in her nurse's scrubs, smiling, the caption proudly announcing her first night shift at St. John's ED.

Night Shift

His next words sent a chill down my spine. "Redheads aren't usually my type, but for this girl, I'd make an exception. I'd love to see my handprint on her fair, freckled ass." He chuckled.

One of his thugs, a brute with eyes as cold as Viktor's, leaned over the desk to see her pictures as he scrolled through. "Looks like she'd be a pretty little fuck, boss."

Viktor's attention snapped back to me, sharp and calculating. "An ED nurse, you said, huh?" he asked rhetorically. Then he continued to scroll through Samantha's account. "She could be very useful. I have men who sometimes need...special attention. Your Samantha could tend to them at my compound in Russia."

My head spun—not from the beating but from the sheer terror Viktor's words elicited. The thought of Sam caught in the web of this monster made bile rise in my throat.

Viktor tossed the phone back to me. "I think we might have a deal, Mac. But remember, if you're lying about her skills or her... compliance...it'll be you who pays the price."

He stood and headed for the door. "Let's make arrangements," he said, signaling for his men to bring me along. "We'll need to verify her credentials and...persuade her to join our family. As for you"—he pointed at my face—"you get to live another day. I can't trust you to deal the dope, so I'm assigning you to one of my brigadiers, Maksim Chernov. You'll be his *shestyorka*. He says jump, you ask how high. He runs a tight ship. You mess up and he'll slit your throat."

I had sealed my fate, and worse, I'd sealed Sam's. The road ahead was one of darkness, a path paved with betrayal and regret. In that moment, I understood the true nature of hell—it wasn't a place but a realization of one's own monstrous actions, with no redemption in sight.

My mind spun as I thought about what I had doomed Sam to. What kind of father traded his own daughter's life for his own?

I was half-dragged out of the room, my battered body aching with each step.

Viktor led us into another room, this one starkly furnished with a long table and several chairs. He motioned for his men to set me down on one of the chairs. Despite the throbbing pain, I forced myself to focus, to understand their plan, to find some way to regain their trust.

Viktor began outlining their strategy with clinical precision. "We need to do this quietly, no mess no fuss. We can't afford to draw attention." He scanned the room, ensuring everyone understood the gravity of the situation.

One of his men, a burly figure with a nose that had been broken too many times to count, spoke up. "We'll need to watch her, learn her routines. The best time would be when she's alone, vulnerable."

It made me sick to my stomach to hear them talk about Sam like she was just another target. My bruised and swollen hands clenched into fists under the table.

Another one of Viktor's goons, a lean and wiry man with cold, calculating eyes, suggested, "What about when she's leaving the hospital? Late shifts, fewer people around. We can grab her, sedate her, and get out before anyone notices."

Viktor nodded. "Good. We'll need a clean vehicle, untraceable. And arrange for immediate transport out of the country. We can't keep her here long."

The conversation turned to logistics, and they meticulously planned the kidnapping. Routes, timing, contingencies—they discussed it all as if they were planning a business meeting, not the abduction of an innocent woman.

Viktor turned to me, his gaze icy. "You'll stay out of sight, Mac. If you try anything, if you warn her or the police, you both die. Understand?"

Night Shift

I nodded. There was nothing I could say; I was hollow and empty inside. I had become the architect of my own daughter's destruction.

Soon the meeting concluded, and some of the men dispersed to set their plan in motion. The pain of my beating was nothing compared to the agony of my betrayal. I had sentenced Sam—my bright, beautiful daughter—to a fate worse than death. What kind of monster had I become? Or perhaps I'd always been this way...

The conversation among the remaining men shifted from the kidnapping to broader Volkovi Nochi operations. In a relaxed manner, they began discussing drug trafficking routes.

Viktor leaned back in his chair and regarded the men across from him with sharp and calculating eyes. "We need to ensure the new shipment moves smoothly. The ports are getting more scrutiny lately."

One of his lieutenants, a tall, burly man with a thick beard, nodded and said in a thick Russian accent, "Aberdeen and Tacoma are still our best bets. Aberdeen's smaller, less attention. But Tacoma has better infrastructure for larger shipments."

Another thug added, "We've got contacts in both ports. But we should consider diversifying the entry points. Maybe smaller, more frequent shipments through Aberdeen to avoid drawing too much attention."

Viktor stroked his chin thoughtfully. "True. Aberdeen's lesser security makes it ideal for the more...delicate parts of our operation. But Tacoma's capacity is invaluable. We'll need a good mix of both to keep the supply chain flowing without hiccups."

"The key is in the timing and the routes within the States," said the burly man, unfolding a map on the table. He pointed at several highways and back roads that connected the ports to major cities. "We've got to avoid the major checkpoints. I-5 is always crawling with patrols, but if we take the longer routes through the back roads, we can minimize the risk."

Viktor nodded in agreement. "Good. Keep the shipments smaller, and vary the schedules. We can't afford a pattern. And ensure the local operations are ready to receive and distribute quickly."

A sense of dread was building within me. This wasn't just about Sam anymore. I was entangled in a web that spanned far beyond anything I had imagined. The scale of their operation was staggering, and the casual way they spoke of smuggling drugs through these ports was disturbing.

Viktor's scrutiny fell on me then, sharp and assessing. "Remember, Mac, you're part of this broader operation now. Your...contribution has bought you some time. But we're watching you. One wrong move, and it's not just you who pays the price."

I was in too deep, a pawn in a game where human lives were played with as if they were mere commodities. And now, with Sam's life in the balance, the stakes were higher than ever.

The beating had taken its toll on me. I slumped forward onto the table as the lights faded. I had one final thought before seeing darkness...

What have I done?

Chapter Twelve

A couple of days after Friendsgiving, I was leaving the hospital tired. It had been a particularly grueling shift, and my feet ached. I trudged through the dim parking lot, lost in thought. The chilly November air nipped at my exposed skin, and I pulled my coat tighter around me. The parking lot was still and calm, the gravel crunching loudly under my boots. As I was fumbling with my keys, a powerful hand clamped over my mouth.

"Make a sound and you're dead," a gruff voice hissed menacingly in my ear. Panic surged through me when another figure, brandishing a knife, appeared in front of me. My heart raced as I realized there were two beefy men, both wearing black ski masks, assailing me.

I squirmed and tried to scream, but the man's grip only tightened around my face. When I twisted my body and managed to land a knee to his groin, he momentarily loosened his hold. Seizing the opportunity, I bit down hard on his hand, tasting blood.

He recoiled in pain. "Stupid bitch!" he growled, releasing my mouth. I screamed, fighting back with all my strength, adrenaline coursing through my veins.

"Leave me alone!" I shouted, trying to sound confident. The man with the knife lunged at me. Without thinking, I jerked my arm up, trying to protect my face. The knife sliced into the underside of my forearm. Instinctively, I dodged and tried to fight back, but they were too strong and well-coordinated. Dealing blow after blow, they beat me down. My vision began to blur, and I struggled to stay conscious.

"Get her in the car!" one of them barked as the other lifted me by an arm and dragged me toward a black SUV. I fought against his grip and managed to fall to the ground.

Suddenly, like a whirlwind of fury and power, Atticus's youngest brother Conan appeared.

"Let her go!" he shouted, his voice ringing out through the parking lot as he charged toward us. With lightning reflexes, he tackled the guy I'd just kneed, throwing powerful punches that drove the man's head into the ground. Conan wasted no time in engaging the other man, demonstrating his martial arts expertise with his swift, precise movements.

"Conan, he's got a knife!" I cried out between labored breaths. Relief washed over me when I saw he was having no trouble holding his own.

"Stay back!" Conan warned me, his eyes filled with concern as he continued to battle the assailants.

The fight continued, with Conan at the center, a storm of fists and kicks. He moved with an almost superhuman speed, forcing the two men to stay on defense. One attacker finally lunged at him, swinging wildly, but Conan deftly sidestepped and delivered a sharp jab to the man's ribs, followed by an uppercut that snapped the man's head back.

The first assailant joined in, trying to flank Conan. But Conan was like a wild animal, cornered, dangerous, and unpredictable. He spun around, his leg sweeping out in a powerful hook kick. His foot connected with the guy's jaw, catching him off guard and sending him crashing to the ground.

The other attacker, undeterred, rushed at Conan with the knife, slashing in a desperate frenzy. But Conan, with the agility of a seasoned fighter, caught the man's wrist, twisting it until the knife clattered to the ground. Swiftly, he kneed the man in the gut, then delivered a crushing elbow strike to the back of his neck, sending him sprawling. With a kick to the face, the man was left unmoving.

Before I realized what was happening, the first man ran at me, grabbed me by my ponytail, and jerked my head back.

"Get in the car!" he snarled, punching me in the ribs. Before I could react, Conan had him in a chokehold. As they thrashed about, I stumbled and hit the ground hard, the asphalt biting into my knees. The attacker struggled for a few moments, then went limp as he lost consciousness. Conan threw him on the ground like a sack of garbage.

For a moment, everything was still. Conan stood over the two men, his chest heaving with exertion, his eyes scanning the parking lot for any further threat.

I stood there, dazed and bleeding, my mind racing to process what had just happened. Conan had been a maelstrom of protective energy, his every move calculated to incapacitate without causing fatal harm. In that chaotic moment, he was not just Atticus's brother, but a hero who had emerged from the shadows to save me.

"Are you okay?" he asked, panting heavily as he helped me to my feet.

"Y-yeah," I stammered, wincing at the pain from the cuts on my arm and the various punches I'd received. I was shaking and dizzy, and the fingers on my left hand were tingling as they grew numb. Bright red blood dripped from my hand onto the ground. My eyes snapped up at Conan as I smashed my other hand over the wound. Conan scooped me up in his powerful arms and carried me back into the ED, shouting for security to go after the men who had attacked me.

As soon as we'd entered the hospital through the trauma bay doors, a flurry of people rushed to help us. Conan bolted into a room and gently laid me on a bed. He grabbed a pair of scissors and sliced through the sleeves of my coat and shirt, his eyes filled with worry.

"Go get my brother," he bellowed at the nurse who'd followed us in.

Conan swiftly assessed the wound on my inner forearm. His hands, although large, moved with surprising gentleness. He quickly grabbed a gauze pad from a nearby tray and pressed it firmly against the cut, attempting to stem the flow of blood as he applied pressure to the wound.

"Keep your hand elevated," he instructed in a calm but authoritative tone. I nodded, raising my arm. He wrapped the gauze tightly around it, securing it with medical tape. The pressure was firm and slightly uncomfortable, but I knew this was the best way to slow the bleeding.

Conan turned his attention to the rest of my body, running his hands lightly over me to search for other injuries.

"Conan, thank you…for saving me," I whispered, my voice trembling. The terror of the attack still coursed through my veins, but his presence provided me with a sense of safety.

"Sam, I'm just glad I was there in time," he said, his green eyes darkened by his wide pupils. Pain throbbed beneath my battered skin, but his touch remained tender and careful.

"Are you okay?" I asked.

"Don't you worry about me. It's what I've trained for years to do. Whooping bad guy ass is my jam," he said with a big grin on his face.

His words brought me comfort amidst the chaos that had just unfolded. Though I still couldn't completely shake the fear and confusion of the attack, I knew I was going to be okay, at least for now.

"Sam, do you have any idea who those guys were?" Conan asked as he started cleaning the cut on my cheek. His worried eyes met mine.

"No. I have no idea. Do you think they were after me specifically, or was it just random?" I asked.

"Those guys looked like professionals. Their Denali had to have cost a mint."

I shuddered at the thought of being targeted. No, that wasn't possible. I was a nobody. I didn't have anything anybody would want.

As I lay on the hospital bed, vulnerable and unnerved, I wondered what might have happened if Conan hadn't been there. It was a bit surreal to be experiencing this side of the ED—to be the victim in need of care.

"I...I don't know—" My voice hitched as I choked back tears.

"Shh, it'll be okay. They probably thought you were someone else. A case of mistaken identity," he whispered.

With a Steri-Strip in hand, he leaned in close to the cut on my cheek. And it was then, in this hazy, probably shock-induced moment, that I realized just how drop-dead gorgeous he was. While Braxton looked a lot like Atticus, Conan was so different.

He was tall, and his body was unmistakably muscular, a clear testament to his dedication to working out. His build was thick yet defined, and his muscles rippled under his skin in a way that was hard to miss.

The auburn beard on his face was wild and untamed, perfectly suiting his other rugged features. His dirty-blond hair, tied up in a bun, gave him an intensely masculine appeal. But it was his eyes that truly captured my attention; they were a brilliant emerald green, sparkling with confidence, drawing me in.

His skin was fair and dotted with freckles like mine, which added a boyish charm to his face. His lips, full and inviting, had more than their fair share of freckles, especially around the left lower side. It was a unique feature that only added to his charm. The crow's feet around his eyes were more pronounced when he smiled, and a mischievous smirk seemed to be his signature expression, making it look like he was always on the brink of a playful joke.

His arms were covered in full-sleeve tattoos, intricate designs that hinted at the passions and experiences of his life.

At that moment, as I took in Conan's striking appearance, I found myself momentarily breathless, suddenly and acutely aware of his raw, almost intimidating, appeal.

Just then, the door to the room swung open, and Atticus appeared, finding Conan tenderly holding my cheek, his lips a mere couple of inches from mine. Conan stepped back, and heat flared in my cheeks.

Atticus's gaze moved back and forth between his younger brother and me, an odd look of confusion crossing his face. Shaking it off, he asked in a tight, clipped voice, "Samantha, are you all right?"

"Atticus, yes, I'm okay. Conan saved me."

Night Shift

Atticus rushed over to me, and his expression changed. Our eyes locked for a moment, and I noticed an intense fear in his winter-gray gaze, but there was something else too—a possessiveness that caught me off guard.

"Sam, what happened?" he demanded.

"Someone tried to kidnap her," Conan said, slipping into a protective stance beside me. "I managed to stop the thugs, but she got hurt."

Atticus's eyes narrowed as he took in my injuries. A jealous energy now seemed to be radiating off him. It was as if he couldn't bear the thought of anyone else taking care of me. He quickly grabbed some gloves and supplies from a nearby cart.

"Let me see your arm," Atticus said in a clinical tone, extending his hand to me. I hesitated for a moment before lowering my injured arm. He removed the gauze, revealing the deep cut and a couple of smaller ones on my inner forearm.

His eyes widened and his breath hitched while he examined the wounds. For an instant, I saw a haunted look in his eyes, as if he were reliving a terrible memory. He took a step back, visibly shaken, before regaining his composure.

"Let's move the head of your bed up so that you can be more comfortable while I work on your arm." He pressed his lips in a tight line. "Conan, can you bring me a suture kit, please?" I noticed a slight tremor in his voice.

Conan nodded and quickly retrieved the necessary supplies.

The atmosphere in the room grew tenser. Atticus's usually steady hands were trembling slightly, a sign of the emotional turmoil beneath his professional exterior. He began by cleaning the deep cut carefully, his touch gentle yet focused. The antiseptic stung a bit, but it was a necessary discomfort.

"Is everything okay, Dr. Thorin?" I asked, trying to understand the agony I saw in his eyes.

"Everything's fine," he grunted, clearly struggling to maintain his composure.

"Atticus," Conan said softly, placing a hand on his brother's shoulder. They exchanged a brief, intense look that spoke volumes about some secret they shared.

Atticus turned away to prepare a local anesthetic to numb the area. "You'll feel a small pinch," he warned, and true to his word, there was a brief, sharp sensation as the needle pierced my skin. Gradually, the area around the cut began to feel numb, the pain subsiding as the anesthetic took effect.

With that, Atticus started the suturing process. He threaded the needle with a steady hand and got to work. Each stitch was deliberately and carefully placed. His skill impressed me. I could barely feel the sutures being placed, just a slight tugging sensation. His breathing grew more labored with each stitch, a sign of how personally he was taking the situation. It was as if each suture was a mark of his own failure to protect me and he was determined not to leave any more scars than he had to.

Conan was also observing Atticus closely, his head tilted in contemplation. His eyes softened with admiration, yet there was a line of concern etched onto his forehead. It was obvious that Conan understood his brother's emotional conflict.

Atticus finished the suturing with a last knot, then carefully bandaged the wound, ensuring it was secure and protected.

He took a step back, his gaze lingering on my arm before meeting my eyes. There was a vulnerability there that I had never seen before. He was no longer just my doctor, but someone deeply affected by my injury.

"Are you sure you're okay, Dr. Thorin?" I asked.

"Yes. I'm good, Samantha," he said, having regained his usual clinical composure.

"Thank you," I whispered, touched by the care he had shown me despite his unease. But he just nodded curtly.

"Rest now," he said, his voice soft but distant. "I'll check on you later." And with that, he turned and left the room.

I wondered what had caused him to have such an intense reaction to my injuries. Conan met my questioning gaze but said nothing, leaving me to ponder the mystery of Atticus Thorin's past and the emotional scars that haunted him.

Conan busied himself cleaning up. After a few minutes, I couldn't resist asking, "What was that all about? Why did he react that way to my cut?"

"Don't worry about it, Sam. It's his cross to bear. He's spent most of his life dealing with our mother's shit. You're not going to get through that wall any better than the rest of us. He's built it to be impenetrable, like everything else about his heart. He's ruthlessly unemotional. Don't take it personally."

I bit my lip as I thought about his words. "I don't know. At the cabin, he seemed—"

"Don't, Sam," Conan said. "Don't get your hopes up with him. I know y'all...well, had a good time, but that's all it was. Atticus doesn't do relationships. I'd hate to see a smart, pretty girl like you get hurt. He is who he is."

The memory of Conan and Braxton walking in on us while we were in the hot tub had my face getting hot. "Oh, about that night...you haven't told anyone, have you?" I had to ask. I needed the closure.

"Hell no. I'd never do that. I'm not some gossip. Don't worry, your secret is safe with me."

Although his answer gave me a sense of relief, the tension in the room remained thick. Conan, sensing my unease, shifted the conversation by changing the topic.

"Hey, Sam, are you going to the hospital's holiday party this weekend?" He gave me a crooked smile.

"Um, I don't know." I hesitated, glancing toward the door where Atticus had disappeared. "Bethany and Marissa have tried to convince me I should go, even though I don't have a date. But I haven't decided yet." I couldn't look him in the eye, so instead I picked at the bandage on my arm, embarrassed at the admission.

"Ah, well, that's easily solved!" Conan exclaimed, turning to face his older brother, who had just reentered the room. "How about it, Sam? Would you like to go to the gala with me?"

Atticus visibly stiffened at Conan's proposition. He tried to hide his reaction by looking down at the clipboard in his hand, but the jealousy that flickered across his features was unmistakable. The sight gave me a strange satisfaction and sent an amused thrill skittering across my skin. After all, he'd ignored me for weeks after we'd visited his cabin, leaving me feeling used and discarded.

"Sure, Conan," I said, smiling brightly. "Since you gallantly saved the princess"—I playfully winked at him—"it's only fitting that my knight in shining armor should take me to the gala. I'd love to go with you." Shit, had the shock from the attack brought out some cocky inner bitch I didn't know about?

Atticus's jaw tightened, and he looked away from us, clearly bothered by my decision. I wanted him to know that I was genuinely interested in getting to know his brother and was not just trying to make him jealous. But deep down, a part of me also wanted to see if it would affect him.

"Great!" Conan grinned broadly.

Night Shift

Atticus made a derisive noise, unable to stop himself. "Ah," he muttered, his tone dripping with sarcasm. "How...nice for you both."

"Come on, Atti," Conan chided, rolling his eyes. "You've already got your hotshot OB-GYN doc as your date, remember? No need to be so grumpy about it."

The mention of Atticus's date sent a pang of jealousy through me, though I tried to suppress it. Atticus's eyes flashed with anger, and for a moment, I worried the brothers would come to blows right there in the sterile hospital room.

Instead, Atticus crossed his arms, held the clipboard over his chest, and leaned against the wall, avoiding eye contact with Conan and me as he scrutinized his fingernails. "Fine," he ground out through clenched teeth, then glanced at his watch. "Do whatever you want."

"Great!" Conan beamed, seemingly unfazed by the tension between him and his brother. He turned to me, his green eyes sparkling with excitement. "It's a date then, Sam," he said, giving me a sweet little kiss on the cheek.

"Fine," Atticus grumbled. "Enjoy your little party."

"You bet we will," Conan shot back, still smirking. "Now, if you'll excuse us, I need to make sure Sam is doing okay after that ordeal."

"Whatever, just make sure you get some rest and keep those sutures clean, Sheridan," Atticus muttered, pushing himself off the wall.

"Was there some reason you came back to my room?" I asked.

Flustered, Atticus walked over to me. "Yes...well, I wanted to check you for a concussion. Let's do that, shall we?" He turned to Conan with a glare, set his shoulders stiffly, and clenched his jaw. "All right, Samantha, I'm going to check your pupils first," he said then, his voice all business. He shone a small light into my eyes. I tried not to blink too much. With his face this close to mine, I could see that the usual warmth in his eyes had been replaced with something else, something I couldn't quite decipher.

Conan, who was standing a little too close for comfort, watched the procedure intently. "She took quite a hit, Atticus. I think she should stay and be monitored for a while."

Atticus didn't respond immediately, focusing instead on his examination. Finally, he stepped back and sighed. "Your pupils are reacting normally, but I want to do a few more tests. And yes, she should definitely not drive home," he said stiffly. "Can you follow my finger without moving your head?"

I nodded and did as he instructed.

As he continued with the examination, asking me to recall simple facts and testing my coordination, he avoided looking at Conan. Although he was behaving as professionally as ever, it did seem that he was struggling to keep his emotions in check.

When the exam was over, he spoke without making eye contact. "You seem to be okay for now, but I want you to let us monitor you for any changes for a couple of hours."

"Thanks, Atticus," Conan said, clapping a hand on his brother's shoulder. Atticus just nodded formally. His eyes finally met mine for a fleeting moment before he turned and left the room.

Once he was gone, the tension in the air evaporated, but the confusion and unspoken words lingered. There was a lot hiding beneath Dr. Thorin's cool exterior, but I had no way to understand what it was.

I was thrilled at the thought of going to the gala with Conan, especially given Atticus's jealous reaction. But I also wanted to figure out what exactly was going on between the brothers.

Night Shift

"He seemed totally annoyed," I said, chewing on my thumbnail, a nervous habit I'd had since I could remember.

"Who knows? Hey, don't worry about Atticus," Conan said gently. "He'll get over it—eventually. Besides, you deserve someone who treats you right."

I nodded, appreciating his reassurance. "Thanks, Conan. I'm looking forward to getting to know you better."

"Sorry about ruining your coat. You know we're taught not to disturb the site of an injury any more than necessary. Let's get what's left of it off you. I've got a sweatshirt in my locker that you can have." Conan helped me lean forward, then slid the remains of my coat off.

Moments later, two police officers entered the room. "Ms. Sheridan, we'd like to take your statement regarding the attack," one of them said, pulling out a notepad.

"Uh, sure," I mumbled, suddenly feeling very exposed. The worry of why two men in ski masks would have tried to kidnap me came rushing to the forefront of my thoughts. "Did you capture them?"

"No, sadly they got away before we arrived," the officer said.

"Is there anyone who might want to harm you?" the other asked, studying me intently.

My mind raced to the one person who might have something to do with it—my father. The thought made my chest tighten, and I struggled to find the words to explain. The situation was embarrassing enough without having to talk about it in front of Conan.

"I-I don't know," I stammered. My breath started coming in quick gasps as panic threatened to overwhelm me.

"Hey, maybe give her a moment to calm down?" Conan suggested gently, placing a supportive hand on my shoulder.

"Of course," the officer agreed, taking a step back. "Take your time."

I closed my eyes, focusing on my breathing and trying to slow down my racing thoughts. Conan's hand remained on my shoulder, a soothing presence amid my internal chaos.

After a few minutes, I took a deep breath, opened my eyes, and looked at the police officers, ready to tell them what little I knew about my father's possible involvement in the attack.

"The only person who's ever given me any trouble is...well, my father. A while back, just after I started working here, he—"

My breath hitched, and my throat closed up. Suddenly, the panic attack swelled, and I became dizzy. My body trembled as the blood rushed out of my head.

Conan's eyes filled with concern. "Hang on, Sam. I'll be right back," he said gently before rushing out of the room.

"Please, just breathe," I whispered to myself, trying to regain some control over the situation. But my chest tightened, and my vision blurred as fear and anxiety started to consume me.

Moments later, Conan returned. "I asked a nurse to go find Atticus. He'll help take care of your breathing."

I tried to focus on the steady rise and fall of Conan's chest as he stood beside me, holding my hand. Soon, Atticus burst into the room, his face tight with concern. He quickly assessed the situation. "Samantha, I'm going to give you a fast-acting medication to help calm you down." Nodding, I watched as he prepared a syringe with lorazepam, a sedative known for its efficacy in treating acute anxiety. "It should help relax you and help with any pain you're experiencing."

"Thank you," I managed to whisper.

"Small pinch," he warned gently before administering the injection in my arm. The medication worked swiftly, and within minutes, the crushing weight of the panic attack began to lift. To aid my breathing, Atticus placed an oxygen mask over my nose and mouth, then instructed me to take slow, deep breaths.

"Better?" he asked. This was the side of him I liked so much, and it tugged at my heartstrings. I wished he would acknowledge what had happened between us, but that seemed unlikely now.

"Y-yes." The medicine and oxygen were working their magic. My heart rate slowed, and the fog of panic lifted.

Atticus gave me a small, reassuring smile before stepping back. "All right, how about you give the police your statement now?" He gestured for the officers to reenter the room, and they approached cautiously.

Feeling more in control, I pulled the oxygen mask away from my face.

"Are you all right now?" one officer asked, genuine concern in her eyes.

"Yes," I replied, trying to sound confident even though I was anything but. "I'm ready to continue."

"Good," the other officer said, nodding. "Now, tell us everything you can about your father's possible involvement in the attack."

With a deep breath, I began to explain about my dark relationship with my father. I recounted the terrifying morning when he had attacked me outside my apartment, desperate for money and drugs. Atticus listened intently, his face betraying no emotion as I spilled the details of my humiliating past.

Conan had moved to the other side of the bed and was listening closely as well.

"Like I said, it was early in the morning when I got home from work," I continued, my hands trembling slightly. "He was waiting for me, demanding money and drugs."

"Did he say why he needed them?" one officer asked.

"Probably to feed his addiction," I snapped, bitterness seeping into my tone. "It wasn't the first time he had demanded something like that."

"Has he ever been violent toward you before?"

"Yes," I admitted quietly, swallowing hard. "But not since I moved away."

"Dr. Thorin, you mentioned earlier that you witnessed the altercation that morning?" the other officer asked, turning his attention to Atticus.

Conan's eyes shot to Atticus, his mouth dropping open.

Atticus nodded, his jaw set. "I did. Everything Sam has told you is accurate. I got to her just as her father was becoming more aggressive." He paused, and his eyes locked onto mine.

"Did you intervene?" the officer inquired.

"I did. After a physical altercation where I subdued him, he left, but not after throwing a threat out at Sam, telling her he wasn't done."

"Did you report the matter to the police, Dr. Thorin?"

"No, the man was drunk out of his mind, so I assumed it was just an idle threat. Sam didn't seem to think his behavior was out of the ordinary for him, and she told me not to worry about it. So I let it go."

"Thank you, Dr. Thorin," the officer said before shifting his focus back to me. "Ms. Sheridan, do you have any reason to believe your father could have been involved in the recent attack?"

My pulse thrummed at a frenzied pace as I contemplated the possibility. Was my father capable of hiring people to hurt me? I didn't want to believe it, but deep down, I worried he'd had something to do with what happened. "I...I don't know," I confessed. "I haven't seen him since that morning, but it's possible. He was always unpredictable. But he's broke. I don't see how he could hire those types of men to come after me."

"Thank you for your cooperation," the first officer said, closing her notebook. "Once we identify the attackers, we'll look into any connections they might have to your father. The hospital chief administrator is getting us the security camera footage. Maybe we'll be able to trace their vehicle. In the meantime, please don't hesitate to contact us if you remember anything else or have any concerns about your safety."

"Of course," I replied, trying to sound more composed.

After the officers left the room, Atticus and Conan lingered in an awkward silence. I wanted to talk to Atticus alone because he knew the full story of my past, but I didn't want to hurt Conan's feelings by making him leave. Conan already looked pissed, and I couldn't risk making things worse between him and Atticus.

Conan moved to stand nose-to-nose with Atticus. "Brother, are you telling me you knew about Sam's past and still brought her up to the cabin? What the fuck were you thinking? I know you're a goddamn womanizer, but I never thought you'd take advantage of a girl like Sam. What the fuck?"

Atticus shoved Conan. "You, little brother, don't know shit. Now shut the fuck up and get out of my face before I knock you on your ass."

My anger rising, I jumped off the bed and hurtled myself between the two big oafs. "Stop it. Both of you. This is all so fucked up!" I yelled. "Conan, I know you mean well, but what you don't know is that Atticus and I had...an arrangement. The cabin was no big deal. Honestly, it meant nothing. Nothing at all."

Atticus grimaced.

Conan spun around, shaking his head. "So you say. But I was there. I know what I saw in your face, Sam. Try to deny it all you want, but you can't cover for my narcissistic brother like all the others. Don't think for a minute I don't know the truth. You're different, Sam, young and sweet. You deserve better—you deserve a man who has a beating heart, not a stone-cold rock," Conan spat out.

"Please, Conan," I begged. "Don't say those things. I'm so sorry. It's all my fault. I don't want to come between you and your brother. And I'm not some little girl, I'm a goddamn woman capable of making my own mistakes...I mean *choices*. Just pretend none of this ever happened."

Conan's face fell. Atticus didn't speak but just stood there stoically.

Walking up to me, Conan took my hand. "Sam, I'm sorry I lost my temper. I tend to have a short fuse. It's one of my shortcomings. I just think you're a nice girl and don't want to see you hurt. Are we still on for the holiday gala?" he asked sweetly.

How could I say no? Conan was so sincere, just a big teddy bear really. God, could this scene be any more awkward? Why couldn't I have met Conan before Atticus? Life was so unfair.

"Of course, Conan. Let's just go as friends and call it good. None of us need any more drama, since we have to get along to work together."

"Sure thing, Sam. Here, give me your phone and I'll put my number in."

I fished my phone out of my coat pocket, pleasantly surprised it hadn't been broken in the scuffle, and handed it to Conan. Seconds later, he returned it and left, shouldering Atticus on the way out of the room.

Atticus didn't move, didn't even make eye contact with me, but finally said, "Sam, you can't drive. I'll give you a ride home."

"No, Atticus. I'll order an Uber. I'd hate for anyone to get the wrong idea, especially since you've done such a good job of honoring our agreement."

Night Shift

He took a long, deep breath and turned to me. "Sam, this is what you said you wanted." He stepped toward me and gently wrapped his arms around me. "God, I was so scared when I heard what happened. You shouldn't return to your apartment. It's not safe. I think—"

Pushing away from his grasp, I said, "Dr. Thorin, just stop... I'm not your responsibility. You can't fix what's broken in my life. I'll be fine. Always have been."

Just then, Conan pushed open the door. "Here's the sweatshirt, Sam. If you need anything else, let me know."

With a grateful smile, I took the sweatshirt and pulled it over my head, groaning from the pain that suddenly seemed to be everywhere. Now I fully understood the expression: *I feel like I've been beaten*—because I had been. "I'm going to go to HR and see what all they need for me to do. There's bound to be a boatload of paperwork to fill out." And with that, I gathered my things and walked away from the Thorin brothers.

Just as I made it to the door, Atticus called my name, then said, "If there's anything I can do to help, please let me know."

Turning back and glancing over my shoulder, I whispered, "Thank you, Atticus. I appreciate it." And then I walked away.

I wondered if we would ever be able to face the truth about what had happened between us or if the tension would only continue to grow.

Chapter Thirteen

I dialed Bethany's number, and my hands shook slightly as I held the phone up to my ear. The ringtone reverberated through my aching head before she picked up.

"Sam? What's up? It's early," she said, her voice raspy from still being half-asleep.

"I...I was attacked, Bethany. Right after my shift, in the parking lot. These guys, they beat me up and tried to kidnap me." I stumbled over my words in the rush to get them out.

"What? Oh my God, Sam, are you okay? Where are you?" she asked in panic. Her sleepiness had instantly been replaced by alarm.

"I'm at the hospital. They're gone now, but it was close, really close."

"Hold on, I'm coming to you. Don't move, okay? Stay where you are." In the background, her sheets rustled, and her feet hit the floor. "I'll be there in fifteen minutes."

"Thank you, Beth. You're the only person I'm close to here in Tacoma."

"Of course, honey. You sit tight. See you in a hot minute."

I hung up, leaning against the wall outside HR as I waited for them to see me. The events of the attack replayed in my head like a nightmare I couldn't wake up from.

After what seemed like an eternity, Lucy, one of the HR managers, invited me into her office to deal with the necessary paperwork. The sedative Dr. Thorin had given me earlier dulled the edges of my panic but not all the pain from my injuries.

Once I'd finished my meeting in HR, I wandered through their office area, still feeling freaked out about everything that had happened. I spotted Bethany waiting for me in the hallway, her eyes wide with worry. As soon as she saw me, she ran to me, enveloping me in a bear hug.

"Ow! Beth, careful!" I cried out, wincing as pain shot through my battered body. Quickly, she pulled away.

"Oh shit, I'm so sorry, Sam. I just…I was so worried." She looked me up and down, assessing me, her eyes swimming with concern.

"It's okay. I'm riding high at the moment on whatever magic meds Dr. Thorin gave me, I lied so she wouldn't worry."

"How can you be this calm? I'd be a blubbering idiot."

I chuckled, but decided against telling her about the multiple bouts of panic I'd suffered from the ordeal. "Calm? Ha! It's been more like getting strapped into the front seat of an emotional roller coaster, hands in the air, screaming at the top of my lungs kind of morning. But really, it's okay, I'm just a little sore. No big deal. Honestly. Let's just get out of here."

Bethany's worry shifted to surprise, and then she laughed. "Only you could still find humor in this, Sam."

Her laughter was contagious, and despite everything, I found myself chuckling too.

"Come on, you're staying with me. No arguments," Bethany insisted, her tone brooking no disagreement.

"Bethany, I can't impose on you like that. I'll be fine at my place," I tried to argue, though the thought of being alone in my apartment gave me the creeps.

"No way, Sam. Not with those guys out there. You're staying with me, end of discussion. It could be days, even weeks, before the police find them."

I hesitated, torn between not wanting to be a burden and being afraid of facing the night alone. "I...I don't know what to do, Beth. I really don't want to be alone today."

Bethany reached out, taking my hand in hers. "You won't be alone. I've got you. Let's get your stuff and head to my place."

Gratitude filled me, and I nodded, finally relenting. "Thank you, Beth. Really, I don't know what I'd do without you."

She was offering me more than just a place to stay. This would be a safe haven, and she was giving me the support and I care I desperately needed right now.

Bethany and I made our way through the hospital and out the sliding doors of the ED. As we stepped outside, the sunlight warmed my face, making me squint.

"You know, the HR department was actually really nice about everything," I said as we walked toward Bethany's car. "They were super apologetic about the attack."

"Really?" Bethany glanced at me, her eyebrows raised in surprise.

"Yeah. I even told them this might not have happened if they'd had a guard for the employee parking lot." I couldn't help

Night Shift

but chuckle. "You should have seen Lucy's face. She looked like she was about to have a heart attack right there."

Bethany snorted. "Yeah, they don't want you to sue them. Can you imagine the headlines? 'Hospital Nurse Attacked Due to Lack of Security.'"

I laughed, the sound mingling with the morning chirps of nearby birds. "They were super understanding though. Told me to take the next two weeks off and it wouldn't count as vacation or sick leave—just extra time, at the hospital's expense."

We were both laughing at that when we reached her car, a sleek Volvo XC60 that gleamed under the sun's rays. "Wow, they really don't want you to sue them," she said, unlocking the car with a push on her key fob.

I paused, admiring the vehicle's elegant lines. "Maybe I should sue them. Could end up with a nice car like this," I joked, a smile tugging at the corners of my mouth.

Bethany rolled her eyes, but her smile was indulgent. "Get in, troublemaker. Let's get you settled, and then we can plot your grand lawsuit over lunch."

I slid into the passenger seat of her car, sighing as I sat back in the leather seat. Having a friend like Bethany made this whole ordeal bearable.

As Bethany navigated the streets, the smooth purr of the engine filled the cabin, blending with the low hum of the radio, which was playing a soft country tune. The leather seat cradled me gently, feeling so good after all that had happened. I glanced out the window, watching the city pass by in a blur.

"Tell me everything," Bethany said. Though her eyes were fixed on the road ahead, her attention was fully on me. "How did it happen?"

I took a deep breath and began to recount the attack. I described the brutal force with which they'd beaten me, how each punch and kick had landed on my body, and the sharp pain that had accompanied the nasty cut on my inner forearm. As I spoke, Bethany's grip tightened on the steering wheel, her knuckles turning white.

"It was all so terrifying," I said quietly, tracing the bandage on my inner forearm. "And then Conan showed up. You should have seen him, Beth. He was like something out of a movie, with all his martial arts skills and raw power. He beat the crap out of both attackers."

"Oh my gosh, that's so wild. Unbelievable."

"Conan was incredible. And afterward, he was so sweet and caring. It's hard to believe he's Atticus's younger brother. They're so different."

"Yeah, that's for sure. Who stitched you up?"

"Atticus was on duty," I said, glancing down at my bandage. "He sutured the cut on my arm and was surprisingly kind during my panic attack. But he's just so...odd. I can't figure him out. He was tender, attentive even, one minute and stone cold the next. It's so confusing."

"Mmm, Conan's a great guy; that's for sure. And well, I told you about Atticus. Those two are as different as night and day. Not sure Atticus is the tender filet mignon type—more like the overcooked shoe leather kind of steak you can never quite swallow," Bethany teased.

My chuckle turned into a sigh, and I relaxed again into the soft leather seat. Bethany reached over, giving my hand a gentle squeeze. "It sounds like a lot to process, Sam. Both Conan and Atticus took care of you in their own ways. It's understandable to be confused about Atticus. People are complex, you know?"

I nodded, grateful for her understanding. "Yeah, I guess you're right. It's just been so much to take in."

Minutes later, we were pulling into the parking lot of my apartment complex. Bethany parked the Volvo, and we both got out. She accompanied me up the stairs, hovering like a mother hen.

As she stepped into my apartment, she beamed with appreciation. "This place is so cute, Sam! I love the yellow paint; it's so bright and cheerful."

She moved closer to the main wall in the living room, where I'd hung my collection of Ansel Adams black and white prints. "And these pictures are amazing. You have great taste."

I smiled, following her gaze. "Thanks, Bethany. Ansel Adams's work has always fascinated me. It's my goal to one day visit all the national parks." I paused, scrunching up my face a bit sheepishly. "Actually, so far, I've never even traveled outside of Washington state."

Bethany turned to me, her mouth falling open in surprise. "Really? Well, we need to change that. How about we make a pact to take a girls' trip to Hawaii one day?"

The idea sent a thrill through me. I'd never thought about the prospect of exploring somewhere so cool with my best friend. "That sounds amazing," I said, excitement bubbling up despite the fact that I would have to hide at her place for who knew how long.

As I gathered my things, Bethany reminded me, "Don't forget all your hair and makeup stuff, and pack for several days. Remember, the gala is only four days away, and you and Marissa were planning on getting ready at my place. I'm guessing you'll be staying with me at least through the weekend."

I nodded, mentally checking off what I needed to bring, and in a few minutes, we were leaving my apartment with bags in tow. In the hallway, we passed by Alex, my neighbor. He flashed me a cheeky grin. "Hey, Samantha, what happened to Mr. Fancy Pants Doctor who picked you up a while back? You two still dating?"

My cheeks heated up. Caught off guard, I stammered out a denial. "No, I... We're not seeing each other. That wasn't a date. He was just helping me out when my car wouldn't start."

Alex raised an eyebrow, his smirk widening. "Sure looked like a date to me, the way he was holding your hand."

I mumbled a quick goodbye and practically bolted to Bethany's car, my heart racing. Once safely inside, I blurted out, "Alex is just a nutty neighbor. Says all sorts of crazy stuff."

Bethany glanced at me, a hint of curiosity in her eyes. "Remind me, when did Atticus drive you home? Was that when your car battery died?"

"Yeah, exactly," I said smoothly, feeling a twinge of guilt. "Just a friendly, albeit awkward, gesture."

Bethany seemed to accept my explanation, and so the subject was dropped, but while we drove, I sat there, stewing in my thoughts. I hated to lie, especially to her. I hoped she'd never find out the truth about what had happened with Atticus. The last thing I wanted was for the situation with him to put a strain on our friendship.

When we arrived at Bethany's condo, she parked the Volvo and immediately jumped out, moving around to the trunk before I could even unbuckle my seatbelt. "Let me get those," she insisted, reaching for the heavy bags I'd packed.

"Thanks, Beth. I really appreciate it."

"Welcome to my humble abode!" she announced when we entered her cozy one-bedroom condo.

Bethany's place was flawlessly styled and welcoming, a testament to her impeccable taste. I admired her attention to detail. Every corner of the room looked like it came out of a showroom. She led me through the compact space, pointing out where everything was. "You'll crash on the pull-out sofa. I know it's not a five-star hotel, but it'll do," she said with a smile. "And hey, the bathroom's huge, perfect for all us girls to get ready for the gala. Oh, and Marissa and I decided to get ready at my place instead of hers because I have a little more room."

"Your place is perfect for a girls' night," I agreed.

Once settled, we decided to order Chinese food and distract ourselves by bingeing episodes of *The Witcher*. Damn, Henry Cavill was fine. With a pleasant sigh, I sank into the cushions, the day's earlier events receding into the background. For the first time since the attack, the tight knot of tension in my chest began to loosen, allowing me to breathe a bit easier.

"I needed this, Beth. Thanks for taking me in," I said.

Bethany smiled, her eyes soft. "That's what friends are for, Sam. I'm your girl."

In the safety of her condo, with the night stretching quietly before us, I allowed myself to believe that maybe everything would eventually be okay.

Bethany and I were halfway through the second season when my phone buzzed. Glancing at the screen, I saw Atticus's name. Puzzled, I answered as Bethany paused the show.

"Hello?"

"Sam, it's Atticus. I just wanted to check in. Have you cleaned the suture site?" His voice was clinical, all business.

"Yes, I cleaned it," I replied, shifting to find a more comfortable position on the sofa.

"And are you experiencing any headaches? Symptoms of a concussion?" he continued, ticking off a list of concerns.

"No headaches, Atticus. I'm monitoring for symptoms," I said, trying to be patient.

He didn't pause. "What about your ribs and the other areas where you were punched, any signs of a hematoma?"

I sighed, rubbing my forehead. "They're bruised but manageable. Atticus, I'm an ED nurse. I know how to take care of myself."

There was a brief silence on his end. "Of course. I just wanted to make sure."

I couldn't hold back any longer. "You know, Atticus, it's not my physical condition you should be worrying about. You owe me—and Conan—an apology for how rude you were."

Bethany's eyes snapped to me, but I barreled on.

"And you can't just coldheartedly ignore me for weeks and then act all concerned because you had to do your job as the attending ED doctor. I'm not going to be all Suzy Sunshine just because you decide to check in now."

Bethany's eyebrows shot up.

Realizing I'd let slip more than I'd intended, I quickly wrapped up the call. "Good night, Dr. Thorin. Thanks for the medical advice," I said, laying the sarcasm on thick before ending the call.

Without missing a beat, she crossed her arms and turned to me, a smirk playing on her lips. "Suzy Sunshine, huh? That's a new one."

I groaned, covering my face with my hands. "Please don't ask, Beth. It's complicated."

She laughed, shaking her head. "Your secret's safe with me. But seriously, if you need to talk…"

"I know," I said, and although I was grateful for her friendship, I didn't want to get into it all right now. "Let's just get back to the show, okay? Henry Cavill needs to make an appearance in my dreams tonight."

Bethany giggled before pressing play, but the curious side-eye she gave me said this conversation was far from over.

The days that followed blended together, marked by my recovery and Bethany's unwavering support. My bruises slowly began to change from angry purples and blues to sickly greens and yellows. Even though this was a sign of healing, every time I caught a glimpse of myself in the mirror, it disheartened me. By Saturday morning, the reality of the holiday gala loomed over me like a dark cloud.

My dread of the upcoming evening pressed down on me as I sat at Bethany's kitchen table, nursing a cup of coffee and nibbling on toast. "Beth, I'm not sure if I should go tonight," I finally admitted, breaking the silence.

Bethany placed her mug of coffee down mid-sip and gave me a puzzled look. "Why on earth not?"

I gestured to myself, pointing out the bruises covering my arms and then the stitches, which stood out starkly against my fair skin. "Look at me. I'm a mess. And this"—I touched the bandaged cut on my arm gingerly—"is far from pretty."

Bethany stood up, walked over, and took a friendly hold of my shoulders, turning me to face her directly. "Sam, you're going to be fine. Marissa and I have already scoped out the perfect dress for you. She's bringing over some options with long sleeves—perfect for hiding those bruises and keeping you warm. It's the end of November, after all."

I smiled a little at her enthusiasm. "And the cut on my cheek?" I asked skeptically.

"With a bit of makeup magic, we'll have it looking like nothing more than a shadow. You'll see; you're going to look fabulous," she said, reassuring me with a confidence I wished I could feel.

"Okay...but what about Conan? I don't want to ruin his night by showing up looking like I just crawled out of a dumpster."

"Conan? What's there to worry about?" A grin spread across her face. "He's not only drop-dead gorgeous, but also one of the most relaxed, laid-back guys I know. Honestly, if I hadn't...you know, fucked his brother, I'd be all over that."

My cheeks heated up, and I quickly took a sip of coffee to hide my embarrassment.

"Don't leave Conan hanging, especially after he's been so great. Plus, it's a chance for you to get out and forget about everything for a little while," Bethany nudged, her tone turning serious.

Her encouragement, coupled with the reminder of Conan's kindness, solidified my resolve. "Okay, okay, I'll go," I conceded, setting down my mug with a sigh.

Bethany clapped her hands together and beamed. "That's the spirit! Tonight is about us having fun and showing the world that nothing's going to keep Samantha Sheridan down. Besides, just wait until you see the dresses Marissa's bringing over—you're going to love them."

A short while later, Marissa arrived, lugging what seemed like an entire closet's worth of dresses, shoes, and makeup. She grinned at me as she set down her haul on Bethany's living room floor, exclaiming, "Behold, your fairy godmother has arrived!"

"Wow, you weren't kidding," I said, eyeing the assortment of gala-worthy attire she'd brought. "Did you leave anything in your closet?"

Marissa chuckled, shaking her head. "For you? I'd bring the whole thing if I could."

We sifted through the dresses, the room filling with the sound of hangers clinking and fabric rustling. Marissa and Bethany shared the latest hospital gossip, recounting stories and updates

Night Shift

I'd missed during my days away. Their tales, a mix of the absurd and the endearing, reminded me of the camaraderie I'd been starting to truly enjoy.

"Okay, ladies, snack time?" Bethany suggested after a while, moving toward the kitchen. Shortly, she returned carrying a tray laden with cheese, crackers, and grapes. She carefully set it down among the scattered makeup items.

Marissa popped open a bottle of prosecco and poured each of us a glass. "To Samantha's gala debut," she toasted, raising her glass.

We clinked glasses, and the lighthearted banter continued as we indulged in the sparkling wine and snacks. The atmosphere was a perfect blend of anticipation and relaxation, a good distraction after worrying so much over who'd attacked me.

Eventually, the preparation for the evening began in earnest. "Shower time! Let's get all dolled up," Bethany announced, leading the charge. We each took a long, luxurious shower, carefully cleaning and shaving our girly parts in an effort to be perfect for our dates that night.

The ritual of getting ready—from the careful selection of dresses to the meticulous application of makeup—transformed the condo into a bustling hub of activity. Marissa's earlier joke about being a fairy godmother didn't seem so far-fetched now as she started to work her magic on us.

As I stepped out of the shower, wrapped in a towel and feeling the warmth of the water still clinging to my skin, I caught a glimpse of myself in the mirror. The bruises were there, a reminder of the ordeal I'd endured, but for the first time in days, I saw past them. Tonight, with my girls by my side, I was ready to face the world again.

"Here's to looking fabulous and kicking ass tonight," Marissa declared, lifting her wineglass in the air. "Let the transformation begin!"

Bethany and I raised our glasses and then each took a nice long draw of the sweet wine.

"Ready for the magic touch?" Marissa asked, brandishing a makeup brush like a wand.

I nodded, a smile spreading across my face. "Let's do this."

"Okay, ladies, let's get glammed up," Marissa announced, her focus turning first to Bethany. As she applied foundation and blended eyeshadow, the conversation flowed effortlessly. The laughter and chatter continued while we primped and preened, each of us transforming under the skilled hands of our self-appointed fairy godmother.

While she worked on Bethany, I admired the array of dresses laid out for us. Each one was stunning, chosen to suit our individual styles.

Bethany's dress caught my eye first—a deep-red, strapless number that would fall just above her knees, perfectly complementing her figure and her vibrant personality. Marissa had selected a shimmering silver dress for herself. It had a daring backless design that spoke volumes about her fearless nature.

"I can't wait to show off in these dresses," Bethany gushed. "We're going to turn heads for sure!"

"Definitely," I agreed, admiring the long-sleeved, emerald-green dress Marissa had picked out for me. The fabric would perfectly hide the stitches on my arm. "Thank you again for bringing so many options, Marissa. These dresses are incredible," I said, unable to keep the awe out of my voice.

Marissa, who was just finishing applying a smoky eye on Bethany, beamed and nodded in thanks.

"Wait till you see yourself in that green, Samantha. It's going to be showstopping," Bethany chimed in, standing to admire her makeup in the mirror.

Marissa moved on to me, steadily applying makeup with an artist's touch. "Can't wait to see everyone's faces when we walk in. I bet there will be some interesting plus-ones at this gala," she mused, blending eyeshadow on my lids.

"Yeah, the hospital gala won't know what hit it," I joked, my nervousness about the evening ebbing amidst the cheerful banter.

"Speaking of interesting dates, what do you think about Dr. Thorin's latest arm candy, Dr. Sinclair?" Marissa asked, a hint of mischief in her tone as she stepped back to assess her work.

Bethany snorted. "Oh, please, like it matters. Everyone knows she won't be around after tonight. Atticus doesn't do repeats."

"Exactly," Marissa agreed, laughing. "Dr. Sinclair is this month's flavor. I swear, that man goes through women like I go through coffee."

Their blunt comments should have stung, but the truth in their words was undeniable. Atticus's reputation was well-known, and I had no illusions about where I stood—or didn't stand—in that equation.

"All right, let's get dressed," Bethany said, glancing at the clock. "We're running behind." Panic set in as we realized how late it had gotten.

In a flurry of activity, we slipped into our dresses, adjusted our hair, and grabbed our purses. We raced out the door and piled into the waiting Uber, our excitement bubbling over into animated conversation.

"I just want to dance and forget about work for a few hours," Marissa said, leaning back in her seat.

As the city lights passed by, I had a surge of gratitude for these women by my side. Despite the undercurrent of drama with Atticus and the lingering effects of the attack, my heart was happy. Tonight was about celebration, friendship, and maybe just a little bit of healing.

Night Shift

Chapter Fourteen

My heart raced as we got out of the Uber and headed for the revolving doors, our heels clicking on the pavement. Bethany, Marissa, and I had barely made it a few steps when I caught sight of Atticus and Dr. Sinclair.

They stood just ahead of us, engaged in what seemed like a casual yet intimate conversation. Vanessa was breathtaking in a floor-length red gown that complemented her tan skin flawlessly. Her thick, dark brown hair fell in perfect waves down her back. She was the ideal image of refined beauty. Atticus was beyond dashing in his dark bespoke suit that was obviously crafted to fit him perfectly. Every stitch, every seam, was tailored for his frame. The fabric, a deep shade of midnight blue, caught the light with his every movement, enhancing his already commanding presence. It was complemented by a crisp, white shirt and a tie that subtly echoed the darker hues of his suit, striking a balance between elegance and authority. His hair, usually a tangle of rebellious curls, had been styled to a neat, understated elegance, framing his face and drawing attention to the sharp angles of his jaw and intense winter-gray eyes. There was an air of effortless grace about him tonight, a natural charm as he stood at Vanessa's side. Together, they resembled Hollywood movie stars who had stepped straight out of a glamorous red carpet event.

"Wow," I muttered under my breath, unable to tear my eyes away from them. Jealousy seared through me, and I suddenly felt awkward, painfully aware of my short, borrowed party dress. I wasn't even in their league.

Atticus caught me staring, dropped his chin toward his shoulder, and smiled at me with that *game on* look as he grazed his thumb over his bottom lip. His gaze drifted down to the tips of my shoes before quickly returning to my eyes. I was paralyzed. His scrutiny sent my anxiety spiraling as my bottom lip quivered. How could I have ever imagined he'd be interested in more with me? No, *more* had never been an option.

"Sam, don't worry about them," Bethany whispered, and I broke my fixated stare away from the man who'd forever changed me.

Marissa, noticing my discomfort as well, joined Bethany. They quickly closed ranks around me, their voices a steady stream of chatter designed to distract. "Come on, Sam, let's check in," Marissa said, stepping up beside me and guiding me forward.

Bethany leaned in. "Ignore them. Tonight is about having fun, remember?"

Despite their efforts, my gaze inadvertently met Atticus's as we passed by. The glance we exchanged was charged. In his eyes was a mix of emotions I couldn't quite decipher. It was heated,

Night Shift

intense, and for a brief moment, the world around us seemed to blur into the background.

Biting hard on my lip to break away from his spell, I hastened my steps and focused on moving through the door as it revolved, not wanting to get run over. I was determined not to let the momentary connection with him disrupt the evening.

Bethany and Marissa chatted animatedly, pulling me along with them, their words a comforting buzz that helped me regain my balance.

When we entered the lobby, Conan bounded up to us with his signature grin on his face. "Samantha!" he exclaimed, enveloping me in a gentle, playful hug. "You look absolutely stunning!"

Despite everything, I couldn't help but compare his appearance to that of his older brother. Conan's choice of attire for the evening was a stylish suit that complemented his build perfectly. Unlike his brother, who had a meticulously polished look, he'd opted for a more relaxed vibe, skipping the tie and leaving the top button of his shirt undone. This small act of defiance against formality lent him an air of approachability that was all Conan.

His normally unruly auburn hair, which often seemed to have a life of its own, was tied up into a knot. This choice tamed his wild locks while accentuating the sharp angles of his jawline and cheekbones, framing his face in a ruggedly handsome way. It was a look that suited him exceptionally well, walking the line between carefree and deliberate.

But what truly set him apart this evening were his eyes. Conan's emerald green eyes always had a hint of mischief lurking within them, but tonight, they seemed to sparkle with an extra dose of it. Perhaps it was the festive atmosphere of the gala or just his natural exuberance shining through, but his gaze held a promise of laughter and lighthearted fun.

In truth, Conan was always the embodiment of relaxed confidence. He didn't need the trappings of traditional formality to make an impression; his charm and warmth did that effortlessly. He was indeed the antithesis of Atticus, not just in appearance but in demeanor as well. While Atticus carried an aura of untouchable perfection, Conan exuded a warmth that drew people in, making him attractive in his own unique way. His more casual look perfectly captured the essence of who he was—someone who valued comfort and connection over conformity and prestige.

His compliment, simple and sincere, grounded me, reminding me that tonight was not about Atticus or Vanessa but about enjoying the company of friends. Shaking my head to clear my musings, I leaned into him and whispered, "Thank you." Then I slipped my hand into his, and he gave me a playful wink before pulling me forward through the lobby.

Soon after, Bethany's date, Brad, approached us with a friendly wave. "Hey, everyone. Wow, you all look fantastic," he said, his gaze sweeping over our group. Bethany beamed up at him as she introduced everyone.

Marissa, who had chosen to come solo following her recent breakup, shrugged off any suggestion of needing a date. "Who needs a date when you've got killer company like this?" she quipped with her usual bravado, her smile bright but carrying a hint of her recent heartbreak.

Together, we made our way through the hotel lobby, the noise and warmth enveloping us like a welcome embrace. Conan stayed close to me. His casual ease made me feel more comfortable in my own skin, and as we moved further into the heart of the hotel, the earlier encounter with Atticus and Vanessa began to fade into the background of my mind.

When we neared the grand ballroom, my heart raced in anticipation of the night ahead. The heavy double doors swung open to reveal a breathtaking scene that left us all speechless.

"Wow," Marissa finally murmured, her eyes wide with wonder. "I didn't expect it to be this beautiful."

Before we could step inside, a familiar face appeared. It was Kristen, Marissa's former girlfriend, clutching a bouquet of roses that spoke louder than words. She nervously bit her lip before making her move, planting a sweet kiss on Marissa's cheek.

"Hey," Kristen said softly, her voice full of vulnerability. "Can we talk for a minute?"

Marissa's face flushed with excitement, her body language betraying her happiness at seeing Kristen. A smile took over her face, and she nodded, unable to contain her joy. "Of course," she replied quietly. Then she turned to us and managed to ask, in a voice full of disbelief, "Give us a sec?"

Kristen's arm found its way around Marissa's waist, pulling her close. "We'll be right back," she promised, locking her gaze on Marissa with an intensity that left no room for doubt. As Kristen led her away, Marissa inhaled the scent of the roses and leaned into Kristen's embrace.

"Think we'll see those two again tonight?" Conan joked, a mischievous grin on his face. "Or will they just find a room and have makeup sex all night?"

Bethany laughed, shaking her head. "Knowing Marissa, it's anyone's guess. But hey, love—or lust—conquers all, right?"

Brad chimed in, "Well, I guess the gala just got a bit more interesting."

All of us laughed, our spirits lifted by the unexpected reunion.

We stepped into the ballroom, awestruck by the exquisite decorations. The transformation of the space into a holiday wonderland was nothing short of breathtaking. Silver tablecloths shimmered under the soft glow of overhead lights, and each table had been adorned with large flower arrangements that added bursts of color to the elegant decor. A bar spanned one wall, offering an array of tempting concoctions. Tables laden with delectable hors d'oeuvres lined another wall, their enticing aromas wafting through the air.

"Wow, they really went all out," Bethany said, her eyes wide as she scanned the room.

Conan nodded in agreement. "This is incredible. Feels like we've stepped into a movie scene."

Brad, ever the observer, pointed toward the wall to our left. "Check out the bar setup. Looks like they're fully stocked." His comment drew everyone's eyes to the extensive array of bottles and glasses that promised a night of festivity.

"I hope everyone's hungry," I said, noting the variety of bite-sized delicacies.

The live band, positioned at the far end of the ballroom, filled the air with music that was both lively and sophisticated, setting the perfect backdrop for an evening of celebration. The dance floor, large and inviting, already pulsed with the movements of enthusiastic partygoers swaying to the rhythm.

Bethany chuckled. "Looks like the dance floor is the place to be tonight."

Conan clapped his hands together and rubbed them back and forth, a smile playing on his lips. "I say we grab a drink, sample some of the food, and then see where the night takes us."

The four of us moved further into the room, mingling and chitchatting with coworkers and some of the upper echelon of the hospital's management.

Conan, who was already in a buoyant mood, made a beeline for the bar. "First round's on me!" he declared, returning moments later with a drink for each of us on a server's tray.

Eagerly, I took one of the pretty little martinis and thanked him. Soon we were all laughing as the buzz started to go to our heads. At one point, Conan playfully spun me around. "You look so beautiful tonight, Samantha. How are you feeling?"

I chuckled, the compliment catching me off guard but warming me all the same. "Thanks, Conan. I'm feeling mostly better, but I still look a bit Frankensteinish with all these bruises and the cut." I gestured toward my arm. "Hence, the long sleeves."

Conan smirked, his eyes twinkling with amusement. "Well, I think Frankenstein's monster never looked so good."

He bolted over to the hors d'oeuvres table and returned grinning. "You have to try all this," he said, offering me a bite from his plate. His boyish excitement was charming, and I found myself enjoying his insistence that I try a bite of everything as he fed it to me like I was a little bird.

Our conversation flowed effortlessly, the topics ranging from the trivial to the deeply personal. With Conan, it was easy to laugh.

He dashed over to the dessert table and returned before I even realized he'd left. "So, now you have to try the chocolate eclairs. They're to die for," he said as he popped the entire chocolate-covered confection into his mouth.

"With a recommendation like that, how can I refuse?" I asked, accepting the treat he offered. We continued with our light and easy banter, enjoying being in each other's company.

It was only when I glanced around, looking for Bethany and Brad, that I realized they had slipped away to the dance floor, leaving Conan and me absorbed in our own world. "Looks like we've been abandoned," I noted, a smile playing on my lips.

Conan followed my gaze to where our friends danced near the band. "Seems like it. But hey, more eclairs for us, right?" he joked, his laughter mingling with the music.

The ease of his company, the shared jokes, and the gentle way he made sure I was having a good time made the evening unexpectedly delightful.

As the evening progressed, Conan's flirty demeanor became more pronounced. His hand lingered on my arm a little longer, and his glances got more cheeky. The band shifted gears, and a moment later, the opening chords of John Legend's "All of Me" filled the ballroom with a romantic melody that seemed to slow time itself.

Conan leaned in. "May I have this dance, milady?" he asked, his voice soft yet holding a hint of mischief. He offered his hand with a theatrical flourish that drew a laugh from me.

"Of course, kind sir," I said, playing along and accepting his hand. With one graceful motion, he led me onto the dance floor and twirled me into his arms in a move that was straight out of a fairy tale.

I was immediately taken aback by his skill as a dancer. Despite his muscular frame, he moved with a gentleness and precision that made it easy to follow his lead. He masterfully guided me through the dance, tucking his thigh subtly between my legs in a way that was both respectful and sensually charged.

Being so close to him while we moved in perfect harmony with the music was intoxicating. I became lost in the moment, the rest of the world fading away as if we were the only two people in the room. Conan kept his eyes fixed on me, and his look of genuine infatuation made my heart flutter.

Around us, people seemed to take notice. Our fellow partygoers were starting to stare, but I didn't care. In that moment, Conan made me feel like a princess, cherished and adored.

As the second slow dance began, he pulled me closer to him, wrapping me in his muscular arms. My entire body pressed against his, and I couldn't deny the heat that radiated between us. He leaned down, his breath warm on my ear as he whispered wickedly, "You have no idea how much I want to take you back to my hotel room right now, Sam."

A deep blush bloomed across my cheeks, and my heart raced in my chest. Conan's lips brushed the hollow of my neck, nibbling gently and sending shivers down my spine.

Slowly, with an almost unbearable sensuality, Conan kissed me—long, hard, and deep. His hands cradled my face tenderly. When he finally pulled back, it was as if a haze had descended over me. I was lost in lustful longing—eyelids heavy and lips slightly parted.

"Ahem." The sound of someone clearing their throat loudly next to us broke through the spell that had been cast. Startled, I looked up to find Atticus standing beside us, Vanessa at his side. He was close enough for me to see the anger that burned in his usually unemotional eyes. His jaw was clenched tightly, his hands curled into fists at his sides.

Conan's response to the interruption was a low, almost imperceptible growl. Caught between the two, I found myself at a loss. The kiss lingered on my lips like a promise, but it was now overshadowed by the shift in the atmosphere brought on by Atticus's appearance.

"Really, Atticus?" Vanessa scoffed in annoyance, her gaze darting between the two of us. "Your obsession with this girl is so obvious. You've barely taken your eyes off her all night. Watching her with Conan like some sort of voyeur..." She sneered at me and then turned her icy gaze to Conan. "You'd better watch out. He might just steal your date."

With a huff, she turned on her heel and strode away from us, her red gown billowing behind her like a flag of war. Atticus watched her leave but remained where he was. His eyes met mine once more, a storm of emotions crossing his face before he turned and hurried after Vanessa, leaving a slew of whispers and speculative glances in his wake.

"Wow," Conan chuckled as his brother disappeared from sight. "Guess we really got under their skin, huh?"

Stunned, I stood there trying to process the whirlwind of emotions that had just played out before us. But I couldn't shake off the feeling of shame that had settled over me, nor could I ignore the lingering confusion in my heart. I was torn between the tender passion I'd experienced with Conan and the memories of the dark hunger Atticus had awakened within me. No matter how hard I tried, it seemed I couldn't escape the tangled web of my own emotions.

Conan gently placed a hand on my shoulder. "Are you okay?" he asked.

"Yes, of course, I'm fine."

Giving me a brilliant smile, Conan leaned in. "Who do you think has him more worked up, me or you?"

"Conan, please," I muttered, nervously swiping my hands down the front of my dress. His question had put me on the spot and made me flustered, but the truth was that I'd been comparing the two of them all night. They were so different, but they both had a powerful hold on me.

"Sorry, Samantha," Conan said. "I didn't mean to upset you."

"It's not your fault," I assured him, forcing a smile. "I'm just... Hell, I don't know."

Night Shift

The night had taken a turn I never could have expected, leaving me to wonder what the fallout of those few charged moments would be.

As we started working our way back toward our friends, Conan, ever the source of light in any situation, burst into laughter, seemingly amused by the drama. "Well, I'd say that went rather well, wouldn't you?" he joked, his arm guiding me gently toward the table.

I was anything but amused.

"Sure, if you find—"

Before I could finish, Marissa and Kristen appeared at our side, their hands entwined, faces glowing with happiness.

"Guess what?" Marissa couldn't contain her excitement. "Kristen and I are giving it another shot!"

"That's wonderful," I said, genuinely pleased for them.

Conan echoed my sentiment. "Congratulations!" he exclaimed, pulling Marissa into a friendly hug. Other coworkers nearby offered their own well-wishes.

"Cheers to second chances," Conan said, grabbing his glass from the table and raising it, prompting a chorus of agreement from the group.

For a while, Conan and I ate, drank, and mingled with our colleagues. Eventually, we found ourselves back on the dance floor with Bethany and Brad, laughing when "Electric Slide" started playing and we joined in a group dance.

The band transitioned smoothly into Ed Sheeran's "Perfect," and Conan, with a playful tug, drew me into his arms. Despite the lingering soreness from my injuries, the thrill of dancing, of moving in sync with Conan, made the pain and discomfort all but disappear.

I caught glimpses of Atticus through the crowd, and each time, his gaze was fixed on me with an intensity that stole my breath away. But when the song neared its end and Conan dipped me, wrapping his powerful arms around my back and pressing a tender, romantic kiss to my lips, the drama of the evening seemed suddenly unimportant.

When he lifted me back up, the spot where Atticus had been standing was conspicuously empty. A fleeting sense of disappointment washed over me, but it was quickly overshadowed by the warmth of Conan's embrace.

As the last chords of "Perfect" faded away, Conan leaned in and whispered seductively into my ear, "I've booked a hotel suite for tonight. Let's sneak away and make this night unforgettable." The revelation sent a ripple of surprise through me, and deep inside, a knot of anxiety formed.

"Really?" I asked, trying to sound as excited as he did. "That's...that's sweet of you."

"Come on," he said, taking my hand and leading me away from the dance floor. We half-danced and half-walked down the hallway, laughing as we made our way toward the elevator.

"Are you ready for a little nightcap?" he asked with a smile as he ran his hand down my back and leaned in to kiss my neck.

"Of course," I replied, forcing a grin.

My palms were growing clammy. When the elevator doors opened, we stepped inside, and I leaned against the back wall, my heart racing.

The truth was, I didn't know why I was so nervous. Conan had been nothing but kind, attentive, and fun. And yet, I couldn't shake the image of Atticus watching me with such possessiveness.

As we entered the suite, I took a deep breath, trying to steady myself. The room was elegant and sophisticated, decorated in soothing shades of cream and gold. Conan took off his jacket, tossed it onto a nearby chair, and turned to face me, his

Night Shift

expression hungry with desire. I stood there, suddenly unsure. My earlier confidence had vanished.

He tilted his head and squinched his eyebrows, silently inquiring about my hesitation.

"Hey, are you okay?" he asked, closing the distance between us in a few steps.

"Y-yes, I'm fine," I stammered, forcing another smile. "Yeah, I just... I didn't expect this, I guess. Sorry... I was just thinking I should text Bethany and Marissa where I am so they don't worry."

I quickly sent the girls a text and laid my phone on the table by the TV.

Turning, I walked over to the large windows overlooking the bay. The view of all the boats lined up along the docks was beautiful. I lost myself in the lights reflecting off the gently lapping water. It was then that Conan approached me from behind, encircling my waist with his arms.

Our reflection in the glass stirred a memory, unbidden yet vivid. The cabin. Atticus. He'd held me this way in front of the window right before blindfolding me. The memory was so clear, so evocative, it was as if I could feel his presence here with us.

I was still processing my thoughts when Conan gently turned me around to face him. He pressed his lips against mine and kissed me passionately. His tongue explored my mouth. That reminded me of Atticus too, and I couldn't help but respond to him. As the heat between us intensified, his hands traced the curves of my waist and lingered over my ass, pulling me closer. Now I was caught in the storm of my own conflicted emotions. Each touch, each movement brought back memories of Atticus, blurring the lines between past and present.

Panic hit, suffocation climbing up my throat as my chest tightened. I tore myself away from him. In a moment of confusion, the words spilled out. "Stop it, Atticus!"

Conan froze instantly, his expression shifting from passion to shock in the blink of an eye. When I realized my mistake, my cheeks burned with embarrassment, and I fought the urge to run out of the door and disappear.

"I'm so, so sorry," I stammered, following Conan as he stepped back. Hurt briefly crossed his face before he masked it with a guarded expression. I wanted nothing more than to take back those words, to rewind time and erase my gaffe. "I can't believe I did that. I...I don't know where that came from." My words tumbled out in a desperate attempt to mend the moment.

His initial shock gave way to a cautious understanding. He ran a hand through his hair as he processed my blunder. "Samantha, it's okay," he finally said, his voice steady but distant. "I get it. Things...they've been complicated for you."

I shook my head, struggling to find the words to explain a confusion I didn't fully understand myself. "No, Conan, it's not okay. I shouldn't have... That was unfair to you." The apology seemed inadequate, a paltry attempt to smooth over a stupid mistake.

This man was caring, thoughtful, and handsome as sin, and yet all I could see when I looked at him was Atticus. All I could feel were Atticus's hands, Atticus's lips, Atticus's body moving against mine. It made me sick to my stomach, but I couldn't deny it.

He offered me a tight smile, one that didn't quite reach his eyes, signaling a rift that had opened between us. "We should probably...take a moment," he suggested.

"Conan, I really am sorry," I whispered, knowing full well that the apology couldn't undo what I'd done.

Night Shift

Instead of responding in anger like I'd expected, Conan shook his head, then burst into a fit of laughter. It was unrestrained, genuine amusement. I stared at him in disbelief as he doubled over, clutching his sides. His mouth opened and closed as though he was attempting to speak but couldn't get any words out. My face grew hot with embarrassment. Was he laughing at me?

I stood there, dumbfounded. "Conan...why are you..."

Unable to bear the humiliation any longer, I retreated to the window, burying my face in my hands to hide my flushed cheeks and wishing the ground would swallow me whole.

Finally, after catching his breath, Conan stepped up behind me again. Still chuckling softly, he reached out and gently encircled my waist with his muscular arms, though I remained stiff and unyielding. "I'm sorry, Sammy girl," he murmured. "I didn't mean to laugh like that. It's just, when you yelled, 'Stop it, Atticus!' I didn't know whether to take it as a compliment or an insult."

I still couldn't bring myself to lower my hands.

Trying to make sense of his words, I blinked away the tears threatening to spill over.

"I mean, it would have been a whole lot worse if we were going at it hot and heavy, and you called me his name with lust in your voice." He paused. "Your reaction caught me off guard. The way you tensed up like that, I could almost swear you wanted to punch him in the face rather than anything else. Yeah, if you're going to confuse the two of us, I'd much rather it be because you're pissed off at him rather than because you're about to say something saucy to me. Either way," he went on, "I think you and I both know you have mixed emotions about Atticus. I know him way better than you and have seen how he affects all the ladies. His voice alone yanks their chain and makes women fall at his feet." Conan's grip tightened around me. "I have to tell you though, Sammy girl, I think you're not only gorgeous but so much more—intelligent, hardworking, and a skilled nurse."

He paused, taking a deep breath. "For now, though, I think it's best for us to only be friends. How about we just chill out and order some room service?"

The tension dissolved, and I finally lowered my hands and faced him. "Room service sounds perfect," I said, a smile tugging at the corners of my mouth. "You're not mad? You don't want to leave and never speak to me again?"

His response was immediate. "Oh God no. I'd never do that," he assured me, giving me a chaste kiss on the forehead.

A giggle escaped me, breaking through the remnants of my embarrassment. "Hmph, well that's already better than your older brother. He would've gone ballistic or something."

"Seriously, let's just hang out tonight, nothing more," he said. "I've got a pair of sweatpants and a T-shirt you can wear if you want to get out of that dress."

"Oh my God, that sounds awesome."

He gave me a squeeze and stepped back. Then he rummaged through his bag that sat on the dresser and laid a pair of gray sweatpants and a navy blue T-shirt on the corner of the bed.

"How about you go change, and I'll order us up something good to eat. Are you drinking?"

"I'd better not or else I'll fall asleep on you." I laughed as I picked up his clothes and headed for the bathroom.

My body relaxed as soon as I changed into the comfortable clothes. They were huge. The collar of the T-shirt hung off my shoulder, and I had to roll up the sleeves and the legs of the pants—and even flip the waistband—just to manage. I went from fairy princess to hobo real quick—but oh, I was all kinds of comfy now.

Night Shift

The vibe really shifted for the better when I returned to the room and we started grubbing down on what room service had brought. I'd never stayed in a suite and had no idea they came with a gaming console. I couldn't get over how cool it was along with everything else in this room. And gaming? Turned out, it was my jam—or maybe he just let me win sometimes. Either way, we had a blast. Our easy laughter and playful teasing made the earlier tension seem like a distant memory.

At one point, I commented on his seemingly insatiable appetite. "Do you always eat this much?" I asked when he reached for yet another snack, half-amused, half-impressed by his continuous munching.

He paused the game and turned to me with a grin. "I have to eat a lot to keep up my size. I work out every day," he explained, flexing an arm in a mock show of strength.

Curious, I ventured a question that had been on my mind since we met. "Is Conan really your name though?"

He gave a deep, hearty laugh. "No, my real name is Constantine."

The revelation sent me into a fit of laughter. "You definitely don't look like a Constantine," I managed to say between giggles.

"Yeah, I got the nickname Conan in high school when I first started bulking up, and it's just stuck ever since."

We continued playing for a few minutes, and then he turned to me again with a mischievous glint in his eye. "Braxton and I call Atticus 'Atti' because we know he hates it so much. We tease him about it being his feminine alter ego. We joke that he never gets into relationships with women because he actually swings the other way," Conan said, trying to keep a straight face.

The image of Atticus, who saw himself as a sexual connoisseur, the answer to every woman's wildest fantasy, being sensitive about a slightly girly nickname, was too much. I laughed so hard my sides ached. "I've called him 'Atti' a bunch of times, thinking it was just a shortened version of his name. He never seemed to mind."

"Oh, he minds. Trust me. The thought of him having to control his reactions and not get mad over the nickname with you must drive him crazy."

We turned back to the game, and for a few hours, the incident at the gala, the tension with Atticus, and the earlier awkwardness with Conan faded into the background.

At 3:07 a.m., the shrill ring of my phone cut through the noise of the game, instantly drawing my attention. I fumbled for the device. I hardly ever received calls at such an ungodly hour, since most people were asleep and I was often at work. Alex's name appeared on the screen.

"What on earth could he want? I only gave him my number when I first moved in and needed help to receive a delivery," I murmured, more to myself than to Conan, who had paused the game and turned his attention to me.

"Alex?" I answered, placing the phone on speaker so Conan could hear.

"Sam! Shit, I'm glad you're okay," Alex blurted out. "Listen, I just called the cops—some thugs are tearing up your apartment!"

The words hit me like a physical blow. "What? My apartment?" My voice shook slightly as I struggled to process what he had just said.

"Yeah, they're beating the shit out of everything. Those bastards don't give a damn about waking up the whole building. Sounds like mobsters doing a full-on shakedown or something. Your place is getting destroyed." I could make out the faint wail of sirens in the background, and it sent a shiver down my spine.

Panic fluttered in my chest. "I'm on my way," I managed to say. "Thanks for calling the cops, Alex. Really, thank you."

After I hung up, I stared at the phone for a moment, stunned.

"Let's go," Conan said firmly, grabbing his keys and stuffing his feet into a pair of tennis shoes. I jerked on my heels—because they were the only shoes I had—as Conan handed me a hoodie. We dashed out of the hotel room, through the lobby, and out to his car.

I wondered how much of my life would be left intact when we arrived. The drive to my apartment was tense, the silence filled with unspoken worries about what we'd find.

The thought of someone invading my personal space and destroying my belongings sent waves of anger and fear through me. First the kidnapping attempt and now this. What in the world was going on?

Chapter Fifteen

I returned home just after midnight. The silence of my kitchen hummed in my ears after the festivities at the St. John's holiday gala. The event, meant to celebrate employees and benefactors alike, had left a sour taste in my mouth, not because of the event itself but because of the fuckery of my brother Conan. The memory of him and Sam together gnawed at me like a persistent itch. Unable to find rest, I paced the length of my kitchen, my discontent escalating with each step.

Seeing Conan's hands on Sam had ignited an unexpected firestorm of jealousy within my gut. The image replayed in my mind, a relentless loop that fueled my agitation. Why did her choice to attend the gala with Conan distress me so? How could she just ignore me after our weekend together? The trip had been a revelation, an intense connection...or so I'd thought.

Night Shift

I recalled her soft skin pressed against mine, the wetness of her folds, the taste of her. She was a perfect partner, designed for me—naive, submissive, responsive, and beautiful. I'd not been able to stop thinking about her fiery mane tangled in my fingers, those captivating stormy blue eyes, and those goddamn freckles. We had fit together so perfectly, and yet it seemed as if she'd slammed the door on any future possibilities without a second thought.

That weekend, she'd shared everything with me—not just her body but her deepest secrets, her fears. The way she had responded to me was intoxicating. Her trust, her eagerness—they were unlike anything I'd ever experienced. She had matched every move and reciprocated every touch with innocence and enthusiasm that had affirmed everything I'd guided her to feel.

Why hadn't she called or texted? Was it my age? Sure, she was quite a bit younger than I was, but I still had the grit and the grip. Was it fear that our coworkers would find out about us? Conan and Braxton barging in? Or was she simply curious about the rumors of my sexual prowess? The cold dismissal stung like a slap to the face. I'd never experienced such rejection before.

I stopped pacing and leaned against the cold marble of the kitchen counter, the chill seeping into my palms. The thought that she might have regretted our time together, that perhaps it really had been only an experiment for her, a curiosity, pricked at my pride and sent a wave of frustration through me. I'd never been one to lack confidence, especially when it came to women. Yet, here I was, second-guessing every moment, every touch.

With a huff, I pushed off from the counter. "Atticus," I muttered to myself, "get a grip. Stop being such a damn fool." I took a deep breath, trying to calm the rage within me. But just as I began to regain some semblance of control, my phone buzzed with an incoming text.

Conan's name flashed onto the screen, accompanied by a message that sent a jolt of adrenaline through my veins.

Sam's place got hit by...I'm guessing the thugs who tried to kidnap her. Neighbor saw it all. Place is trashed. Cops headed there now. Get here ASAP.

Anger and fear gripped me simultaneously, a potent cocktail that had my heart pounding. I couldn't make sense of these feelings. I'd never been one to get involved with other people's personal baggage, yet the thought of her being harmed ignited a fierce protectiveness within me. Thumbs flying over the screen, I shot back a message:

Heading there now. Telling Braxton to meet us.

I couldn't get out of here fast enough, not with Sam in danger, her world turned upside down by violence. The idea of her feeling scared or hurt twisted in my gut like a knife.

After texting Braxton, I grabbed my keys and bolted out the door. The cool night air did nothing to temper the heat of my fury. I jumped into my car, and soon the engine roared to life. My mind raced as I navigated the empty streets. The drive to Sam's apartment had never felt longer.

It was true that I'd never been one for relationships, always keeping a safe distance from anything that resembled emotional entanglements. But Sam...she was different. She'd slipped past my defenses, awakening a fierce desire to protect, to claim, to cherish. What kind of monsters would do this to her? And why? I had my suspicions. The attempted kidnapping, the ransacking of her apartment—this sounded like the work of a drug lord. The thought of her in danger, possibly at the hands of the Russian mafia, who ran those sorts of operations around here, had me spiraling.

The streets blurred past me as I pushed the car to its limits and ignored every traffic law.

Night Shift

Within minutes, I was screeching to a halt outside her building. The place was already swarming with police cars, lights flashing. I leaped out of the car, barely registering Braxton's arrival behind me. With laser focus, I scanned the scene, searching for any sign of her.

"We need to find her and make sure she's safe," I said to Braxton.

He nodded, his usual jovial demeanor absent. "I'll check with the officers and see what they know."

The chaos of the scene, the police tape, the shattered windows of her apartment—all of it felt surreal.

I hurried up to Sam's apartment and found the door hanging off its hinges. The scene within made my blood run cold. Everything was overturned, smashed, or broken. It was a horrifying mess. A raw, pulsating anger surged through me at the sight of her violated home.

Braxton walked in then. His expression was grim as he took in the scene. Together, we approached the officers on duty. "Hey, guys," I said, "what are you doing to find out who did this?"

The officers, who were familiar with me from countless hospital emergencies, gave me a nod of recognition.

"Dr. Thorin, we're doing everything we can," one of them said. "We're collecting evidence, sir, taking statements from neighbors and assessing the damage. We'll do everything we can to investigate and get to the bottom of this."

"This wasn't just a random break-in," I said, clenching my hands at my sides. "She was attacked just a few days ago in the hospital parking lot after her night shift! You need to connect the dots. Someone powerful is after her."

Braxton placed a hand on my shoulder, a silent plea for me to control my temper. I shook him off, keeping my focus solely on the officers. "You need to protect her. Do more. Can't you see she's being targeted?"

The officers exchanged glances, and one of them jotted down some notes. "We'll follow up on the hospital parking lot incident and see if there's a link. Can you provide more details about that attack and why you think they might be connected?"

I recounted the event and then told them about Sam's altercation with her father back in October. "Fucking drug addicts. They're capable of doing just about anything," I muttered, mostly to myself. The frustration of feeling helpless, of not being able to shield Sam from harm, was nearly suffocating.

Sam's world had been turned upside down, her safety shattered. The police would do their job, but I resolved then and there to do whatever it took to protect her, to ensure no more harm would come her way. Whoever was behind this had just declared war, and I was more than ready to fight back. For Sam.

Just as I was wrapping things up with the police, Conan walked through the doorway, followed closely by Sam. Her eyes widened at the sight of her ruined home, and the color drained from her face. Immediately her breaths became shallow and quick.

The moment her knees buckled, Conan was there, wrapping his arms around her in a steady embrace. "I've got you," he said softly, guiding her gently to the ground as a panic attack seized her.

"Sam!" I shouted, rushing to her side. My anger was momentarily quelled by concern for her well-being. "Just breathe, okay? You're safe." I kneeled beside them, my professional instincts taking over.

Conan looked up at me, a silent plea in his eyes, and I nodded, understanding the immediate need to focus on Sam. The police officers stepped back, giving us space.

Night Shift

Taking Sam by the arm, I guided her to a kitchen chair, the only one that seemed to have not been destroyed. "Sam, I need you to sit here." Still shaking, she complied, and I crouched in front of her. "Now, lean forward, head between your knees. It'll help; trust me."

While she did that, I scanned the kitchen and spotted a bag on the counter. Grabbing it, I returned to her side and held the bag open. "Breathe into this, slow breaths," I said, demonstrating the pace. "In and out, nice and steady."

As she followed my instructions, I placed a hand on her back, tenderly rubbing small, soothing circles.

"Everyone, out!" I ordered. "She needs a minute to recover."

"We'll step outside, give you some privacy," one officer quickly offered.

Everyone, including my brothers, filed out of the apartment, leaving just the two of us. I laid my hand on her shoulder and gave her a reassuring squeeze.

"Atticus," she choked out between breaths. "Why would anyone do this? I don't understand."

"Shh, Sam," I murmured, trying to calm her down. "We'll figure it out; I promise. But right now, you need to focus on your breathing, okay?"

She nodded, her chest heaving as she continued to struggle for air. My heart ached for her, and the fire inside me burned hotter. Whoever was responsible for this would pay.

Within a few minutes, her shoulders began to relax, the initial panic subsiding under the rhythm of controlled breathing. "Keep going, Sam. You're doing great," I encouraged.

Gradually, the sharp rise and fall of her chest evened out, the bag crinkling less frequently. Her face, previously drawn tight with distress, softened as the waves of panic began to recede.

"Better?" I asked.

"Y-yes, thank you," she whispered.

She rose from the kitchen chair, and her movements were slow, almost mechanical, as she stepped through the wreckage. Her gaze fell on the remnants of her modest possessions. With tears in her eyes, she took in the aftermath of the violence that had invaded her space.

"I don't get it," she muttered, swallowing hard. "I've got nothing, Atticus. I worked so hard just to become a nurse... worked for everything I have. Why would anyone do this?"

Glass crunched under her feet, and her eyes caught on the shattered frames on the living room floor. "Those Ansel Adams pictures...they were the one luxury I allowed myself," she said, her voice cracking. She bent to pick up a piece of broken glass, only to let it drop again.

"Sam," I began, but she stepped further into the apartment before I could finish, moving into the kitchen. Every cabinet had been emptied, its contents strewn across the floor, a jumbled mess of broken dishes and unrecognizable debris. The devastation was overwhelming, even for someone who hadn't had much to begin with.

"Everything's gone," she said softly, her voice trembling. She made her way to her bedroom, and I followed closely behind, unsure of what else to say or do.

The bedroom was in no better shape than the rest of the apartment. Her bed was flipped over, and the dresser and nightstand drawers had been strewn about, their contents scattered everywhere. And then, amid the chaos, Sam's focus narrowed on a small, intricately carved music box—or what was left of it. Her hand trembled as she picked up a fragment. All at once, her knees buckled, and she collapsed to the floor.

"This was my mother's," she whispered, her voice barely audible. Tears streamed down her face. "You know, she died when I was eight... This and a few pictures were all I had left of her."

For a few minutes, we sat there in silence in the midst of all her memories that now lay in ruins. Sobs wracked her body.

The sight of her grief tore at me. I kneeled beside her, pulling her into my arms. She cried against my chest. "Shh, Sam," I murmured, rubbing her back gently. "It's going to be okay; I promise. We'll find who did this, and we'll make sure they pay for it."

She lifted her tear-streaked face from my chest, searching my eyes for reassurance. "How, Atticus?" she asked. "How can anything ever be okay again after this?"

"Because you're stronger than you think," I told her firmly, wiping away her tears with my thumb. "And you have people who care about you, who will do whatever it takes to help you through this. You're not alone, Sam."

I scooped her up into my arms. Her slender frame trembled as she wept into my shoulder. My chest tightened, but I swallowed the lump in my throat and reassured her, "You'll be okay, Samantha. I promise you, I'll protect you and make everything right."

Still holding her, I navigated through the wreckage and carried her down the stairs to my car. Gently, I placed her in the passenger seat.

A few seconds later, Conan and Braxton approached. As soon as she caught sight of them, Sam jumped out of the seat, throwing her arms around Conan. Something deep inside me twisted, but I clenched my jaw and forced down the jealousy. Now wasn't the time for that; now was the time to focus on keeping Sam safe.

Conan's voice was soft, comforting as he reassured her, his hand steady on her back. "We're here for you, Sam. You're not alone in this."

With a gentle touch, he helped her back into the seat, securing the seat belt around her carefully. Each action was a silent declaration of his intent to protect and support her, a role I now realized I had to step back from, given the circumstances.

For a while, no one said anything, and my brothers and I stood there in the dimly lit parking lot, the open door of my Mercedes casting a pool of light on the asphalt. Sam, still visibly shaken, glanced at us uneasily.

"Who do you think did this?" Braxton finally asked.

"Looks like a professional shakedown," I said in a low, gravelly voice, giving each of my brothers a knowing scowl.

"Yeah, this wasn't just any break-in," Conan said, crossing his arms. "The way they trashed her place, it's not random. It's a message."

Braxton nodded, his brow furrowed. "And I'd bet the Russian mafia's behind it. This smells like their kind of intimidation tactic."

The pieces clicked into place with a chilling clarity, pointing back to the suspicion that had been nagging at the back of my mind. "I'd be willing to bet her father has something to do with all this," I said, the words tasting like bile. "He's mixed up in some bad stuff, drugs mostly. What if he's in over his head and now they're coming after his daughter—targeting Sam?"

Sam's eyes widened with terror, and she wrapped her arms around herself.

"We can't let her go back to that apartment. It's not safe," I said.

Sam said nothing, just stared ahead into space, so my brothers and I discussed where she should stay. After we'd considered the options, I submitted to the fact that the logical choice was my place. It had extra bedrooms, plenty of space, and a state-of-the-art security system.

Braxton looked at me, then at Conan, and finally, back to Sam. "I agree. Atticus's place is the best option."

Conan met my gaze, a silent question in his eyes. After a moment, he nodded. "Yeah, it makes sense. Sam will be safe there."

I hesitated, acutely aware of the tension and unresolved issues between Sam and me. But despite everything, the protective instinct that had driven me here tonight overrode any personal reservations. "Okay, sounds like a plan," I agreed, turning to Sam and leaning against the car. "You'll stay with me until we figure this out."

Slowly she turned to me, anger flaring in her eyes. Until now, she'd been silent, a spectator to our hurried plans to keep her safe, but now she could no longer contain herself.

She burst from the car. "You can all go fuck yourselves!" she yelled. "I'm not some damsel in distress. I'll stay with Bethany."

Conan immediately stepped forward, raising his hands in a gesture of peace. "Sam, I'm sorry. We didn't mean to—"

Braxton echoed the sentiment. "Yeah, Sam, we're just worried about you."

"Samantha," I began, attempting to approach things logically instead of emotionally, "Bethany's couch isn't a solution. She doesn't have the security you need right now. You being there would only put her in danger too. It makes sense for you to stay at my place."

"Stop treating me like a child!" she snapped. "I should be in my apartment, cleaning up the mess they made!"

"Your safety is more important right now," I argued gently, trying not to provoke her. "You can't go back there."

Backing me up, Conan and Braxton nodded.

"Fine," she agreed reluctantly, sliding back into the passenger seat of the car. Although she'd conceded, her anger visibly simmered beneath the surface. "Just get me somewhere safe so I can figure out what to do next."

With that, the fight in her seemed to deflate, and she sank back into the passenger seat.

"Let us grab some of your things from your apartment," Conan offered, and he and Braxton hurried off. While Sam and I waited, I tried to offer her words of comfort, but she would have none of it. She crossed her arms and turned her face away, refusing to engage with me.

Soon enough, Conan and Braxton returned with bags full of her belongings. Sam's stony silence persisted as we piled them into the trunk of the car.

"How about you guys take care of securing her apartment after the police leave?" I suggested. "I'll send a crew out to clean up the mess as soon as I can."

"Sure, no problem," Braxton said. "The chief of police is a good friend. I'll check in with him and see if he can help us out."

"Let's get out of here," I said to Sam, closing the car door with finality. We drove away from the wreckage of her life and toward an uncertain future.

Her silence continued as I navigated the dark streets, only the soft purr of the engine and occasional sweep of the tires on the pavement cutting through the stillness. She wouldn't even turn to look at me.

I needed her to know that I cared about her safety and well-being, despite our unresolved feelings toward each other.

"Look, Sam," I began, trying to break through her silent anger, "I know this is far from ideal, but I promise you'll be safe at my place. And I'll do everything in my power to find out who did this and bring them to justice."

"Stop treating me like a baby!" she shouted. "I should be cleaning up my apartment, not running away from it!"

"Your safety is more important than your apartment," I said, keeping my eyes on the road. "You don't need to worry about it, okay? I'll take care of everything."

Samantha huffed. She seemed to be caught between anger and sadness. "Well, maybe I want to go home and deal with it myself."

It seemed that the more I tried to offer protection, the more it made her cling to her independence, the distance she wanted to maintain between us.

"Home?" I asked, glancing over at her. "You don't have a home. Sam, that place isn't safe anymore, and you're all out of options."

Tears welled up in her eyes. Though she tried to blink them away, her frustration was obvious. Maybe I'd been too blunt, but I couldn't let her put herself in danger.

She lashed out, her words like daggers. "Why do you even care, Atticus? Aren't I just a one-night stand to you? Just a meaningless fuck? A young, plain nurse in the shadows of the almighty Dr. Thorin?"

Her accusations stung, but I didn't want to get into the complexities of what had transpired between us.

"Did you have to climb out from under the perfectly beautiful Dr. Vanessa Sinclair to rescue poor, pathetic Sam? Is that why you came rushing to help me tonight? Out of pity?" she bit out.

"Enough!" I roared, my patience at its limit. "You have no idea what you're talking about, Samantha. We can discuss this later, but not now."

With those words, a heavy silence fell over us once more.

She crossed her arms and turned her head away, staring out the window.

The tension in the car was thick, an invisible force that seemed to push against the leather seats and fog the windows. It was as if the air itself was charged with all the words we weren't saying, with every emotion we'd kept buried since that weekend at the cabin.

The drive continued, each mile stretching longer than the last.

Finally the car pulled into the driveway of my townhouse, the security lights illuminating our arrival. The quiet was now a temporary truce.

Tonight was about ensuring her safety, but the road to understanding each other had become precarious at best.

As the garage door closed behind us, Samantha remained seated in the passenger seat, her arms crossed over her chest and her gaze fixed on the floor. We needed to address the unresolved issues between us, but for now, she needed rest.

"Come on, let's go inside," I said.

She huffed, opened the door, and stepped out.

I led her through the door connecting the garage to the first floor.

"This is it," I said, attempting a tone of casual hospitality as we stepped into the foyer. "I know it's late, but let me give you a quick tour. Since I work odd hours, I've invested in a sophisticated security system." I gestured toward the control panel by the door. "There are discreet cameras and motion sensors placed throughout the house. You'll be safe here; I can tell you that."

We moved through the kitchen, its sleek lines and stainless-steel appliances catching the dim light filtering in from the rest of the house. Not lingering, I guided her through the living and entertainment area. The house suddenly seemed too large, its cool tones and minimal design too impersonal.

"There's a screened-in porch out back, an office, and a home gym down here," I mentioned in passing as I gestured to my left. At this point I was talking more to fill the silence than to give her information as she walked along behind me. The tour was brisk—a deliberate choice to avoid any more unwanted discussions or questions.

We ascended the stairs, and I steered clear of indicating where my room was located, taking her straight to one of my guest bedroom suites. Setting her things down, I faced her. "Here you go. If you need anything, just let me know."

"Thanks," she said, avoiding eye contact.

"Try to get some rest," I suggested gently. "It's nearly daybreak."

With that, I made a swift exit and retreated to my room, leaving Samantha standing in the doorway of the guest bedroom. Her face was unreadable. We both had a lot to process after everything that had been said in the car. The tough conversations could come later.

How had everything become so twisted between us? The question lingered, unanswered, as I paced the length of my room. Did I still stand a chance with her? Did I want to be with her after...Conan?

The way he and Sam had kissed on the dance floor, their lips locked together with such passion, had stunned me. An image of them flashed in my mind, reigniting a sense of betrayal. I had stood there at the gala, invisible to her, while she was completely absorbed in the moment with my brother. The memory burned like acid in my chest. When Conan had broken off the kiss, the look of sheer ecstasy on her face had stung worse than any physical blow ever could.

Anger surged through me again as I remembered how they'd hurried away from the ballroom, rushing toward the elevator that led to the hotel guest rooms. I'd assumed they were going to his room to fuck all night, and the thought made me sick to my stomach.

"Conan," I growled, clenching my fists so tight that my knuckles turned white. He'd given me such a hard time about taking Sam to my cabin, accusing me of taking advantage of a naive young nurse who worked for me. Yet, there he'd been, seducing her at the gala just after she'd been attacked in the hospital's parking lot. Hypocrisy at its finest.

Unable to contain my frustration any longer, I slammed my fist against the wall. The pain succeeded in momentarily distracting me. I forced myself to undress, lie down in bed, and try to sleep. I fumed over the fact that Sam had been invading even my dreams for months now, dreams where I'd willingly handed over all control to her. The thought made me shudder. I was a man who never gave anyone control. It was a trait that had served me well in my career and personal life.

"Dammit, Samantha," I muttered into the darkness, running a hand through my hair in exasperation. "How are you affecting me like this?"

Throughout my life, I had prided myself on knowing exactly what women wanted and needed, never once feeling out of my depth or unsure of where I stood. But with Sam, everything was different—this was uncharted territory. She was a temptation, and I was drawn to her despite the chaos she'd brought into my life.

As the night gave way to the faintest hints of dawn, sleep remained elusive. *I'll confront her in a few hours*, I told myself. *Set things straight. Demand answers.*

Night Shift

The complexity of our situation, compounded by my brother's involvement, left me adrift in a sea of emotions, and I had no compass to navigate it.

In the silence of my room, the only certainty was the turmoil that was nagging at me. My long-held restraint was teetering on its breaking point.

Chapter Sixteen

I bolted upright, my heart pounding and my eyes blinking rapidly. Crisp white sheets were tangled around my legs. Disoriented and groggy, I rubbed my eyes and tried to make sense of my surroundings. My gaze darted around the room, taking in the high ceilings, the unfamiliar decor, and the plush king-size bed enveloping me in its soft embrace. The luxury of the linens and the way the sunlight played on the walls made everything seem alien. It took me a moment to piece together where I was—Atticus's home.

My mind raced as I thought about the events that had led me here. The horror of the previous night crashed over me. My apartment had been turned upside down, ransacked by men with who knew what kind of bad intentions. The memory of finding my belongings, my life, scattered and destroyed, flashed vividly in my mind, igniting a fresh wave of despair.

I recalled the attack in the parking lot that had happened just days earlier. The cut from the knife, the bruising from their rough treatment…it was all like a nightmare I couldn't wake up from. Presumably, those were the same men who had torn through my personal space with violent abandon. The mere mention of them being associated with the Russian mafia had sent a cold wave of dread creeping over me and induced a suffocating fear that threatened to swallow me whole. I brought my hands to my face. Tears were streaming down my cheeks before I'd even realized I'd started crying.

I wiped at the tears, drawing in a shaky breath. My body was still a little sore from the attack, and the ugly stitches in my arm served as a painful reminder of the horrifying ordeal. The knowledge that those men were hunting me, possibly wanting to hurt, kill, or kidnap me, weighed heavily on my mind.

"God," I whispered, flopping back down onto the pillow. "Why is this happening to me?"

My life was a complete mess. And even though Atticus had come to help me and insisted that I stay with him, I was frustrated and downright pissed off at him. My anger bubbled up to the surface. "Dammit, Atticus," I whispered, wiping away more tears with the back of my hand. "Why did you ignore me after our hike and our night at your cabin?" I'd bared more than my soul, only to have him ignore me.

"Was a one-night fling all you wanted?" I hissed, thinking about how he'd kept his promise of keeping our sexual encounter as a mere experiment. But had it really been just an experiment? The connection we'd shared seemed like more than that, more than a night of sex to be disregarded so easily.

As I stared blankly at the ceiling, I recalled opening up my heart to him during our hike. I had shared my darkest secrets, my deepest pain—the death of my mother, caused by my father when he'd driven drunk, his abuse, his addiction to alcohol and drugs, my lack of trust in men...everything. And he had shared some of his past with me too, telling me about how his mother had died when he was fifteen.

I didn't get it. Why would he want to know so much about me if his intention had only been to have sex? Why waste his time? It made no sense.

When we'd gone to his cabin, I'd trusted him completely, and he'd made me feel things I hadn't known I was capable of feeling. It had been the most incredible experience of my life. Sure, I'd been the one to make him promise it would be a one-time thing, that we would never talk about it or tell anyone, but I hadn't expected him to actually keep that promise, and it had crushed me when he'd never called or texted after that night.

Did he really not care?

Had I been so wrong about him?

Was he just another man who would let me down?

Maybe I wasn't good enough for him. The pain of rejection twisted inside me like a knife. The age gap between us was significant, but it hadn't seemed to matter that day...that night. Maybe it was all my baggage, what had happened with my father. Who would want to deal with that? Now I was becoming more certain I had simply been naive.

Tears continued to fall as my misery assailed me. Vicious thugs lurked in the shadows of my mind. Everything I owned had been lost. Atticus's rejection...it was all a testament to how quickly things had spiraled out of control, beyond recognition. And here I was, trying to find my footing when the ground itself seemed to be shifting beneath me. I clenched my fists, willing myself to be strong despite it all.

"Get a grip, Samantha," I scolded myself. "You need to figure this out; you can't rely on Atticus or anyone else." My resolve hardened, fueled by anger. I had trusted him with everything, only to have him ignore me—that is, until now, when circumstances had forced him back into my orbit. That had not been by choice but by necessity. The thought of relying on him, of being in his space, chafed against my desire for independence, for control over my life—a control that seemed laughably out of reach now.

But even as I tried to convince myself that I didn't need him, a part of me still craved the safety and comfort I had found in his arms. The truth was undeniable: I wanted Atticus, but it seemed he didn't want me. Unfortunately, I had to stay here and impose on him, and that was a bitter pill to swallow.

I pulled the covers tighter around me, a futile attempt at bringing myself some comfort. The safety of this place, and Atticus's protection, was a double-edged sword. The room, with all its comfort and security, was like a gilded cage, a temporary reprieve in a world that had shown me its darkest face. And in this moment of overwhelming vulnerability, I realized just how much had been taken from me—not just possessions but pieces of myself I feared I would never get back.

"Enough!" I screamed. "No more self-pity. You're stronger than this, Samantha."

Pushing myself upright, I reluctantly dragged my weary body out of bed, deciding that a cup of coffee might at least put a dent in my gloomy thoughts. My foggy mind craved the sharp clarity only a strong cup of coffee could provide.

Barefoot, I stumbled down the stairs and caught a glimpse of my disheveled reflection in the hallway mirror. The state of my appearance was the least of my concerns, but I really did look dreadful. My hair, which had been a cascade of controlled curls at the gala, had kinked up into a wild, tangled mess. Last night's makeup—what little was left of it—was now smeared under my eyes. Tears had carved paths down my cheeks, leaving salty trails on my skin, giving me the look of a scruffy raccoon. Conan's sweatshirt and pants hung off me, the fabric swallowing my frame. I heaved a sigh.

The kitchen, with its sleek lines and state-of-the-art appliances, felt cold and unwelcoming. I moved automatically, searching a couple of cabinets before finding a mug. Thank God there was already some coffee made. I doubted I'd be able to figure the science fiction-looking coffee machine out. The fridge hummed softly as I opened it to grab the creamer, the chill of the air briefly jolting me.

It wasn't until I turned around, cup in hand, that I realized I wasn't alone. Atticus sat at the table, sipping his coffee and scrolling through his phone. Dressed in a black three-quarter zip-up, gray T-shirt, and joggers, he looked as if he'd just stepped out of a magazine. He was clean, composed, and devastatingly handsome, his short, perfectly trimmed beard and curly brown hair effortlessly casual as always. And here I stood, a total hot mess. The contrast between us couldn't have been more stark.

I paused, the cup halfway to my lips, and he turned his attention to me. There was a moment, brief and charged, when the air between us seemed to crackle. Then, his lips twitched into a smirk, the kind that had always infuriated me.

"Good morning," I said, trying not to make eye contact as I took a sip.

"Planning to audition for a role in a zombie apocalypse movie?" His voice was light, teasing, but it cut through me like a knife.

Night Shift

I blinked, taken aback by the jab at my appearance. A part of me wanted to snap back, to hurl a witty retort that would wipe that smug look off his face. But my weariness held me back.

Instead, I managed a weak smile and tightened my grip around the ceramic mug. "Didn't realize I had to be camera-ready to get coffee in your house."

Atticus's smile widened, and a gleam of amusement appeared in his eyes. "It's not the camera-readiness that's in question," he said, setting his phone aside. "It's whether you survived the night or if I should start calling you a *walker*."

Atticus always knew how to push my buttons and draw a reaction out of me. I let out a huff, a sound that was half-laughter, half-sigh. "Very funny," I said, taking another sip of my coffee. The warmth of the liquid did little to thaw the chill that had settled inside me, but it was a start.

"Are those Conan's clothes?" he asked, raising a brow and folding his arms across his chest. He eyed me critically from top to bottom.

A surge of wicked satisfaction coursed through me at his realization. "Oh, this?" I gestured to the attire and gave him a nonchalant shrug. "Yeah, it's Conan's. We went back to his hotel room after the gala. Which reminds me, my dress is still there, and I need to run and pick it up. Or maybe he can drop it by later today." Each word had been deliberately dropped like a match, intended to ignite his discomfort, and it worked. He wasn't pleased about it. A shadow crossed his features, the corners of his eyes tightening while his jaw clenched slightly. It was subtle, but it was there—a flash of something unmistakably akin to jealousy.

"Is that so?" He set his coffee cup down. It clinked lightly on the table. He cleared his throat, and his professional doctor's mask returned. "I'll be out on business for most of the day, Samantha.

But when I return tonight, we need to have a serious discussion. I expect you to be available."

"Sure," I snapped, annoyed by his condescending tone.

Atticus rose from the table, rinsed his cup, and placed it in the dishwasher with precise movements. "I've just texted you a document containing my house rules. You're staying in my home, and I expect you to adhere to them." He paused, then added, "And no guests without my prior approval."

"Okay, whatever," I muttered, taking a long sip of my coffee, hiding behind its rim. Boy, had he woken up on the wrong side of the bed.

"Also," he said, heading toward the door, "you might want to consider a brush and some face wash before the fashion police come knocking." Before I could muster a response, before the irritation boiling inside me could spill over into words, he was out the door, leaving me standing there, fuming in his immaculate kitchen.

The silence that filled the house in his absence was deafening. His words, his rules, the way he had looked at me—everything seemed specifically designed to infuriate me. I was left to stew in my thoughts until his return.

I shook my head. How dare he talk down to me? After everything I've been through—the attack, the fear, the loss—his concern was for his precious house rules? He'd made it clear I wasn't his guest; I was just an aggravation.

My stomach rumbled loudly. I needed to calm down and get something to eat, because I was *haangry*. Fine, if I were to be a prisoner in this modern fortress, I might as well explore the amenities.

Atticus's kitchen really showed off his taste for the finer things. It was a culinary haven equipped with gadgets and appliances that most chefs would envy. Despite my anger at him, I had to stand back for a second and admire the gleaming stainless-steel refrigerator, professional-grade stove, and array of devices whose purposes I could only guess at.

Instead of grabbing something quick, I decided to make a real breakfast, something to distract me from my swirling thoughts. Atticus's penchant for healthy eating was evident from the contents of the fridge—organic vegetables, free-range eggs, grass-fed beef, an assortment of fruits, and various dairy alternatives. Impressive yet intimidating. I settled on making an omelet and started chopping vegetables with zeal. The process was therapeutic in its monotony, a healthy outlet for my frustration.

As the omelet cooked, my curiosity got the better of me, and I began to open cabinets. Each one revealed more about Atticus's lifestyle. I found quinoa, a variety of nuts and seeds, exotic spices, an impressive collection of teas and coffees, and even a hidden stash of dark chocolate. Each item spoke of a man who valued quality and took care of himself.

I was impressed—not just because of the cost of these things but because of the care he had taken in their selection. Atticus lived a life of intentional choices. I'd witnessed that at the hospital as well. But did that meticulousness extend to his relationships? Did he compartmentalize his emotions as neatly as he did his kitchen utensils?

As I plated the omelet, a pang of sadness pierced my anger. Here I was, standing in the kitchen of a man who could orchestrate harmony among ingredients, appliances, and aesthetics, yet we couldn't find a way to communicate without irritating each other.

Settling into the chair with my omelet, I pulled out my phone to open the document Atticus had texted me. As I scrolled through, my annoyance from earlier found new fuel. Each rule was more ridiculous than the last.

House Rules

1. *Curfew:* You must be inside the house by 10:00 PM every night. No exceptions. The doors will be locked at 10:01 PM. (This shouldn't be a problem since the hospital gave you extra days off.)

2. *Guests:* No guests are allowed in the house without my prior approval, which I may withhold at my discretion.

3. *Dress Code:* Please dress modestly in common areas.

4. *Kitchen Use:* You may use the kitchen only if you agree to clean it up immediately after use.

6. *Internet Use:* No illegal downloads or inappropriate browsing. Internet password: FidelisMD1967.

7. *Alcohol Consumption:* Alcohol is permitted in moderation.

9. *No Snooping:* Personal spaces not explicitly shared are off-limits. This includes my office and storage room.

10. *Security System:* The security system will be armed at 10:30 PM. Do not attempt to disable or tamper with it.

11. *Communication:* If you need to discuss something with me, please text me or leave a note on the fridge. I prefer to keep our interactions documented for clarity.

12. *Bedroom Privacy:* My bedroom is my sanctuary. Under no circumstances is entry or even lingering near the doorway permitted.

13. *Firebird Protocol:* The '67 Firebird Convertible, 326 in the garage is off-limits. Do not touch, do not go near, and certainly do not entertain thoughts of driving it.

14. *Hot Tub Hours:* The hot tub is available for use between 8:00 PM and 10:00 PM, but not without prior notification. Excessive noise or disturbance will not be tolerated by the neighbors.

15. *Neighbor's Dog Warning:* Be wary of the neighbor's "vicious" dog, Newton. Do not interact with him without the neighbor's presence. He's small but mighty and has a keen sense of who strangers are and will take your hand off.

Night Shift

Disclaimer: *While the rules seem stringent, they're designed with your safety in mind.*

"Curfew at 10:00 PM? Dress modestly? Bedroom privacy? What the actual fuck?" I muttered under my breath. "What is this, a boarding school for prim and proper young ladies?"

The kitchen clean-up policy had me looking around at what was left of my breakfast-making. I half-expected some alarm was about to go off for me not having it cleaned up already. And the internet password—FidelisMD1967—only he would come with something pretentious like that. It painted a picture of Atticus that was both fastidious and infuriating, or perhaps he was just a douchebag.

"Don't touch the Firebird. Watch out for Newton, the vicious dog," I said mockingly. I couldn't help but laugh. The absurdity of it all was overwhelming.

"Fine," I said under my breath, taking another bite of my omelet. "Let's see how many of your precious rules I can break before you get back tonight." A wicked smile spread across my face as I imagined all the ways I could get under Atticus's skin. This little game might be just what I needed.

I'd call Bethany, I decided. She would jump at the chance to cause a little chaos. Imagining her reaction, and her likely enthusiasm for the challenge, gave me courage. It wasn't just about breaking rules for the sake of it; this would be a statement, a declaration that I wasn't going to simply roll over and accept Atticus's dictatorial terms without pushing back.

When I'd finished my meal, I took the dirty dishes to the sink and rinsed them off, not bothering to put them in the dishwasher as Atticus had done earlier. Let him find them when he returned home. With a renewed sense of purpose, I made my way upstairs.

The thought of a harmless little revolt brought a spark of light into my life, a reminder that I still had some fight left in me.

The decision to start my mini rebellion by snooping through Atticus's bedroom might have seemed petty to some, but at that moment, it seemed like the perfect first act of defiance. I walked down the long hallway, checking each door, my determination growing with every step. When I finally reached the last door, it was, unsurprisingly, locked. I chuckled, not out of frustration but amusement. Atticus really didn't know who he was dealing with.

One thing about growing up where I had—I'd picked up a few tricks.

I headed back to the kitchen and rummaged through the drawers until I found a thin icing spatula. It wasn't the ideal tool for the job, but it would have to do. Returning to Atticus's bedroom door, I slid the spatula between the doorframe and the latch, angling it slightly downward while mentally thanking every dodgy lock I'd encountered in my childhood home.

I pressed firmly against the lock mechanism, anticipation and a tiny bit of guilt making my hands clammy. But the thrill of the challenge, of doing something I knew Atticus would disapprove of, pushed any hesitation to the back of my mind.

With a steady hand, I wiggled and nudged the spatula forward, applying pressure until the latch gave way with a satisfying click. The door swung open, revealing his inner sanctum.

I let out a little whoop of triumph and stepped inside, pausing for a moment, struck by how different it was from the rest of the house. The personal touches made this room distinctly his. As I stood there, surrounded by his private world, I was hit by a strange blend of curiosity and guilt. I'd crossed an invisible line.

Yet, the act of breaking in, of defying one of Atticus's explicit rules, felt like reclaiming a piece of myself. It was a reminder that I wasn't a passive participant in the events that had upended my life.

Night Shift

For better or worse, I was still capable of making my own choices, of stirring the pot just enough to remind both Atticus and myself that I wasn't one to be underestimated.

The room was surprisingly elegant, warm and homey, with dark hardwood floors and tasteful artwork hanging on the walls. A large king-sized bed covered in luxurious linens took up most of the space. I couldn't help but imagine how comfortable it would be to sleep in such a bed.

Large windows framed by formal drapes let in plenty of natural light, which cast a soft glow over everything. A big side table with a giant bouquet of fresh flowers caught my eye. A subtle, pleasant fragrance filled the room. I'd never pictured Atticus to be the type to keep fresh flowers in his home, much less his bedroom. I surmised that he must have some sort of maid or personal assistant. Turning, I found an ornate mirror standing against the wall. It added a touch of depth to the room. The furnishings—from the big comfy armchair to the headboard and nightstands—spoke of his penchant for luxury. What surprised me more, however, was the absence of a TV. It was an interesting omission that gave me another hint about Atticus's personality.

Curiosity propelled me forward, into the massive adjoining bathroom, which was expansive enough to rival the size of my entire apartment. It was the epitome of modern elegance, with beautiful marble finishes that gleamed under the soft lighting. My eyes wandered until they landed on Atticus's grooming products, which were neatly lined up in rows on the countertop near the sink. Intrigued, I stepped closer and brushed my fingers against the sleek bottles until one caught my attention—a bottle of Acqua di Gio by Giorgio Armani. I couldn't resist; I picked it up, uncapped it, and sprayed a little into the air. The rich aroma enveloped me. It was a scent that I couldn't help but love. After a moment of indulgence, I gently set the bottle back down. Only then did my gaze drift to the shower. It immediately captured my full attention. Talk about modern technology—it was equipped with multiple jets, a digital temperature display, and an array of settings that promised an experience more akin to a spa treatment than a simple wash.

Beyond the bathroom was Atticus's closet—a carefully organized space with clothes arranged by type and color in a display that bordered on the obsessive. Even the dresser drawers dedicated to socks adhered to his strict organizational scheme. Everything was sorted by color and style in a manner that was both impressive and slightly bewildering. And, wow, was his collection of watches impressive. I'd noticed he wore watches outside of the hospital but had never paid close enough attention to realize he had different ones.

I continued to snoop, my exploration leading me to discover a small chest hidden in the back of the closet. The lock on it only piqued my interest further, a tangible mystery amidst the ordered world of Atticus Thorin. Without a moment's hesitation, I decided to take it back to my room.

With the chest carefully tucked under my arm, I left Atticus's bedroom. I made sure to lock the door behind me, erasing any evidence of my intrusion. As I moved back to the room I'd been staying in, my mind raced with the possibilities of what the chest might contain. I hid it away, a plan forming in my mind to try to open it later. For now, it was enough to know I had something of his, a key to understanding the man who had suddenly become so central to my life.

I grabbed my phone and dialed Bethany, eager to share everything that had happened since I'd seen her at the gala.

"Hey, Bethany," I said slowly once she answered. "You won't believe what happened. My apartment—it's been trashed, destroyed, and I'm a mess. I got a call around three in the morning, and Conan rushed me over. Bethany, my life is so out of control. You're not going to believe—"

"Oh my God, Sam! Are you okay?"

After reassuring her I was safe now, I sighed and recounted the events. Somehow, saying them out loud was more terrifying than living through them.

"That's horrible, Sam. Why didn't you call me sooner? Where are you staying now? Are you with Conan?"

I hesitated for a moment, knowing how bizarre my next statement would sound. "Well, Atticus insisted I stay with him. Evidently, his townhouse is the only place with enough room and a sophisticated security system—or at least that's what the Thorin brothers decided last night. Not that I had any say in the matter."

Her chuckle rang through the speaker. "That sounds just like Atticus. Always the fixer...has to be the one in control, huh?"

"Yeah, exactly," I admitted, a small smile tugging at my lips despite everything. "I actually wanted to stay with you, but Atticus wouldn't hear of it."

There was a pause, and then Bethany's voice took on an edge of excitement. "Wait, you're at Atticus's place now? I've never been there. You know how he is...so private."

Her interest didn't surprise me. Bethany had always been curious about the parts of Atticus's life he kept shielded from everyone else. "Yeah, I'm here. It's...a lot to take in."

"Say no more. I'm on my way, and I'll bring all of your things. Give me an hour," she said eagerly.

The thought of Bethany coming over, of seeing her and having a piece of normalcy, lifted my spirits a little. "Thanks, Beth. I really appreciate it. And, um, brace yourself. His place is going to blow your mind."

Chapter Seventeen

Knowing that Bethany would soon be here made me feel a lot better. I desperately needed a friend to talk to. In anticipation, I decided to take advantage of the guest bathroom's niceties. I was surprised and slightly awed by the array of products Atticus had on hand—shampoos and conditioners with names I barely recognized, luxury soaps that smelled of lavender and jasmine, plush towels that felt like clouds against my skin, and a Dyson hair dryer, if you can believe that.

I indulged in a long, soothing bath, letting the warm water and bath salts wash away some of the stress and dirt that had accumulated over the past few days. Afterward, I showered, appreciating the way the fancy shampoos and conditioners made my hair feel silky and smell heavenly. I wrapped myself in one of the plush towels and dried my hair, feeling a bit more human with each passing minute.

With a sense of trepidation, I went to look through the things that Conan and Braxton had managed to salvage from my apartment. I wasn't sure what to expect—so much of my life had been turned upside down in such a short time. Rummaging through the bags, I found clothes and shoes but nothing else. Surprisingly, the discovery didn't upset me. Most of my makeup and other personal items were at Bethany's condo anyway, and I'd never been one to wear much makeup in the first place.

I chose a pair of jeans with holes in the knees, a cute, comfy sweater, and a pair of boots I was surprised to find among my salvaged items. By the time I was dressed and feeling somewhat like myself again, the doorbell rang.

Rushing to the front door, I swung it open to find Bethany standing there, her arms loaded with my bags. "Beth!" I exclaimed. I stepped forward to squeeze her in a big hug, awkwardly wrapping my arms around her despite the bulky stuff she carried. "I can't tell you how good it is to see you."

She stepped inside, and her brows shot up as she took in her surroundings. "Sam, this place is incredible. I can't wait to check it all out. But forget about that for now. How are you holding up?"

"Oh my gosh, I can't tell you how awful it's been," I said.

She grunted, maneuvering through the entryway. "Let's get all this stuff out of the way first," she suggested. She walked into the living room and dropped my belongings onto an armchair.

"Can I get you something to drink?" I offered, leading the way to Atticus's kitchen.

"Sure, let's see what he has to offer!"

Her eyes widened as soon as we stepped into the kitchen. It was the Jura GIGA X8 Professional Espresso Machine that caught her attention first. "Wow, would you look at that?!" she exclaimed, poking around with the machine's settings. "Leave it to Atticus to have the Ferrari of coffee machines. Oooh, let's make a cup of espresso!"

I hovered nearby, watching her as she got to work. "I swear, that thing probably costs more than everything I own, car included. I'm just glad one of us knows how to use it."

With a laugh, I searched the cabinets, finding a couple of cups and setting them next to her.

"Yeah, well, all those early mornings working as a barista in college are finally paying off," Bethany said. We watched the espresso pour smoothly into the cups. "There's something almost sensual about how it brews, don't you think?"

The rich aroma of freshly made espresso filled the air, and soon we carried our cups over to the bar overlooking the living room. We settled down on the stools and sipped the delicious coffee. Our conversation flowed easily, but the mood turned serious when we started talking about the horrific incident at my apartment.

"Atticus and his brothers think it might be the Russian mafia and that it might tie back to my dad's...issues," I confessed.

"Sam, that's terrifying." Bethany shook her head, her brow tight with concern. "But you're safe now, okay? Atticus will make sure to take care of you. You know he has a compulsion to always be Dr. Fixer. The man has a serious savior complex, especially when it comes to women."

"Oh God, tell me about it," I said, rolling my eyes.

Bethany leaned in, raising one brow and giving me an expectant shrug.

"Sam...you've got that look in your eye. The one that says you've been keeping secrets. Now spill the beans!"

"Um, well—" I sucked in a deep breath. It was time I told her about my dirty little fling at Atticus's cabin. "Bethany, promise me you won't hate me when I tell you this, but I sort of hooked up with Atticus. I'm so, so sorry. Really, it wasn't—It didn't mean anything. I...I was curious, and well—"

Bethany erupted in hysterical laughter. "I already knew it, Sam! Everyone does! Sweetheart, your face tells it all. Hope you never play poker, cause you're the worst liar I've ever known."

I was stunned. My mouth fell open, and my cheeks blazed with heat. She laughed so hard that tears streaked down her cheeks. Wiping them away, she squeezed my cheeks between her hands and pulled me to her face, kissing me playfully. "Now you know what great sex is...am I right or am I right?"

"Yeah, well. I... But...how did you know? And by everyone... do you mean *everyone*, everyone?" I stumbled over my words, my voice coming out in a high-pitched whine I didn't recognize.

"Oh, honey, don't get yourself all worked up. My first inkling that there was something up with you two was when he gave you that ridiculous nickname. Then, at Friendsgiving, you practically crawled under the table when I told you he was taking Dr. Sinclair to the gala. No one can mention his name without your face flashing with a hundred different expressions."

"Oh God, please just kill me now. I can't believe I'm that obvious."

"It's no big deal. Seriously. Besides, that's why I liked you right away when you started your first shift. The face you made when you smelled that drunk... I thought you were about to pass out. Instead of denying it, you were honest and said that it was hitting a little too close to home. That's when I knew we'd be friends. You aren't one of those fake little prima donnas who think they know everything."

I pulled Bethany into a hug. "I'm really sorry. I never wanted to lie to you... I just didn't want you to hate me."

Pulling back, she clutched the sides of my arms and chuckled. "Sam, there's no way I or anyone who knows Dr. Atticus Thorin would ever judge you for fucking that man. Trust me, he's undeniably a forbidden fruit...an addictive substance. He lures women in, and with each encounter, we're left craving more, making him even more irresistible. You don't have to explain. Remember, I've been there, done that. If anyone gets it, it's me." She sighed and frowned a little, dipping her head. "I just hate to see him hurt your feelings. I tried to warn you, but some mistakes you just have to make on your own." Giving me one last squeeze, she leaned back and took a sip of her coffee.

I mumbled, "Yeah, the only problem is...I don't hate him."

She gave me an understanding smile. "Don't worry, I get it."

Wanting to change the subject, I opened the "House Rules" document Atticus had sent over and handed my phone to Bethany. "You've got to see this. It's like living in a boarding school," I said, only half-joking.

Bethany scanned the document, her eyebrows arching higher the more she read. "Wow, seriously?" She handed the phone back, shaking her head in disbelief.

"He obviously wrote the rules this morning before I woke up specifically for me. Don't you think that seems like next level OCD?" I stuck my phone back in my pocket. "So of course my first impulse was to figure out how many I could break before he gets back tonight."

Bethany burst out laughing. "Count me in as your partner in crime. He'll be lucky if we don't set this place on fire."

"Deal!" I declared, and we clinked our espresso cups together in celebration. Then, when we were finished, we left the dirty

Night Shift

cups in the sink without a second thought, knowing that would irk Atticus.

"Hey, you're not supposed to have guests without prior approval, right?" Bethany asked. "So, having me here is breaking another rule!"

I laughed as we started on a tour of his house. "You're right! Can you imagine what Atticus would do if he knew we were snooping around? He'd die."

The thought of his reaction, coupled with the absurdity of the situation, had us giggling as we looked in every drawer and cabinet we came across.

"All right, let's get down to some rule-breaking," Bethany said once we'd thoroughly perused his space. "What's next?"

I shrugged.

All of a sudden, her eyes sparkled. "I've got it! Let's throw a party. Imagine the look on Atticus's face. It's the perfect way to break every rule in the book and then some."

The idea was so daring that it sent a thrill of excitement and apprehension through me. The rebellious part of me, the part that Bethany seemed to bring out, found it irresistible. "A party? Here? Do we really have the guts?" I hesitated, the images of possible outcomes flashing through my mind.

"Yes! It's settled then. We're doing this," she said, clapping her hands. She pulled out her phone and started firing off texts, inviting people over with the promise of an evening to remember.

Caught up in the moment, I grabbed the entertainment system remote and, within minutes, figured out how to sync my Spotify account. The house was soon filled with the rhythms of our favorite playlist, the bass reverberating through the walls.

Bethany finished texting and turned her attention to me, excitement written all over her face. "We need supplies. Lots of them. Food, drinks, you name it."

I nodded, a plan forming in my mind. "Let's do it. And I know just the way to get there." I couldn't suppress a smirk as I led her to the garage, directly to the forbidden fruit of Atticus's possessions—the Firebird convertible.

Bethany's mouth fell open. "No way. Sam, that's like...rule number one on the do-not-do list."

"Exactly," I said, sliding into the driver's seat with a sense of defiance that was both exhilarating and terrifying. "No holds barred. Let's gooo!"

Predictably, Atticus had left the keys in the glove box. With the top down and the heater blasting to combat the chill in the air, Bethany and I sped off to the grocery store. The wind whipped through our hair, laughter escaping us in bursts as we jammed out and sang to some old-school rock classics. What could be better than some Springsteen in a candy apple red convertible? It was a moment of pure freedom, of joyous rebellion against the constraints that had been tightening around me since my world had turned upside down.

We zipped down the streets like wild maniacs and quickly arrived at the store. Here we were, about to throw a party in Atticus's meticulously maintained home, and driving his prized Firebird, no less. With Bethany by my side, this rule-breaking escapade was exactly what I needed. It was a chance to reclaim a bit of control, to laugh in the face of the nightmare that had become my life.

Two hours later, Bethany and I returned home, the Firebird none the worse for wear. The news of my ordeal had spread among our friend group, and soon the house was full of people. Their kindness and support were both overwhelming and heartening. People I knew, and some I didn't, were going out of their way to offer support. But the atmosphere was far from somber. Laughter and music filled the air, and everyone seemed determined to lift my spirits. It wasn't a wild party by any means, but it was a good distraction from my plight.

"Sam, we're all here for you!" Marissa called out from the living room, raising her glass in a toast. Kristen wrapped an arm around her waist, and they swayed to the music.

"Thanks, guys!" I shouted.

Since it was a Sunday night, people began to leave around nine, until it was only Bethany, Marissa, Kristen, and me left standing amidst the disarray. Empty cups and plates littered every surface, and a few tipsy dancers had reconfigured the furniture in the living room. We looked at each other and burst into laughter at the chaos we'd created.

"Should we clean up?" Marissa asked, surveying the mess with a raised eyebrow.

"Maybe later," I said, feeling the buzz from all the wine I'd consumed throughout the evening. "Right now, I could go for a dip in the hot tub."

"Ooh, that sounds amazing," Kristen agreed. "But I don't have a swimsuit."

"Me neither," chimed Bethany and Marissa together.

"Who needs swimsuits?" I said, grinning. "Let's just go in au naturel!"

I ran to my bathroom and returned with a stack of towels. With giggles and excited whispers, we stripped down and dashed outside to the hot tub, making quick work of removing the cover. We sank into the warm water with sighs of contentment.

The hot steam surrounded us while the jets massaged away the remnants of stress and fear that had clung to me since the attack and the break-in. Marissa and Kristen quickly became lost in their own world, sharing kisses and gentle touches, their affection for each other clear and unapologetic.

Bethany and I exchanged amused looks. "Find a room, you two," I joked, splashing water at them. They splashed me back and sank deeper in the water.

We sat there serenely, the stars overhead the only witnesses to our naughty girls' dip, and our conversation meandered from the trivial to the profound. It was a rare bubble of peace, a much-needed respite from what had become my daily existence. In the sanctuary of the hot tub, I couldn't help but feel grateful for the love and support of my friends. They had my back through thick and thin.

Bam! The door to the back porch crashed open and shattered our bubble of tranquility. I turned, my heart skipping a beat. Atticus's silhouette loomed in the doorway, his body tense with fury.

The air seemed to freeze around us. I'd pushed him over the edge.

"Get out!" he roared at the top of his lungs, a command that brooked no argument.

Bethany, Marissa, and Kristen scrambled out of the hot tub, water dripping from their bodies. They grabbed towels and swiftly wrapped themselves, whispering hasty apologies and promising to call me tomorrow. They fled into the house, shouting to me that they'd get an Uber.

I remained in the hot tub, meeting Atticus's furious gaze with a defiance I hadn't known I possessed. My heart pounded—not just from the shock of his sudden appearance, but also from the realization that I was about to confront him head-on.

The silence that followed was charged. This was a standoff between his outrage and my refusal to cower. I could see him

Night Shift

more clearly now, my eyes having adjusted. His chest heaved with each breath, and his posture was rigid with anger.

"Why?" His voice was lower now but no less intense.

"Why not?" I countered, calmly unapologetic despite the adrenaline coursing through me. "You were gone, the rules were suffocating, and I...we needed some normalcy."

Atticus tensed, and for a moment, I wondered if I had pushed him too far. But there was something in his posture, a flicker of something behind the anger, that made me hold my ground.

The standoff continued, a silent battle of wills under the starlit sky. In that moment, everything that had transpired between us—all the tension, the unspoken grievances—seemed to crystalize. This was more than just a breach of his precious rules; it was a clash of our very natures, a collision course that had been set in motion from the moment our lives had become entangled.

Atticus broke the silence. "Sam, get out and come inside. Now." His voice rumbled with irritation, but I wasn't sure I was ready to back down.

After considering his demand for a moment, I complied, albeit with a deliberate slowness that I knew would challenge his patience further. As I rose from the water, it cascaded down my skin. I stood there for a moment, making a silent statement of defiance, and let him get a good look at me, allowing the tension to stretch between us.

Finally I stepped out of the hot tub and walked directly into the living room without grabbing a towel, leaving a trail of water behind me. Atticus, driven by rage at what he perceived as my blatant disrespect, followed, towel in hand.

He caught up to me just as I got to the stairway. "Damn it, Sam!" he growled. Yanking me around by the arm, he threw the towel at me. "You're not going anywhere until this mess is cleaned up."

Holding the towel in one hand, I found myself being pulled into the kitchen. Atticus's grip was firm and unyielding. The surreal nature of the situation was not lost on me. Moments ago, I'd been enjoying the freedom of the night, and now, I was ensnared by a man enraged.

In the kitchen, the party's aftermath awaited—spilled drinks, scattered food, and the other tangible evidence of the night's festivities. It all lay there mocking the usual order of Atticus's house.

The tension between us escalated. Atticus's reaction to my deliberate provocation—my lack of attire, the water dripping from my body onto the floor—was swift. In a moment of unchecked impulse, he shoved me against the island. His lips crushed against mine with a desperate hunger as his hips pinned me against the cabinet in a moment of raw, unfiltered lust.

Abruptly, he pulled away, a storm of confusion and frustration playing across his features. He took several deep breaths, trying to regain control.

In a dark voice laced with a hint of something more carnal, Atticus stepped back. "You've got two hours, and then we're gonna have that talk. This place had better shine, and you'd better be dressed."

His face was flushed with anger, and there was a visible twitch in his eye that betrayed the effort it took for him to contain his emotions. It made me feel powerful to know I had that effect on him.

"Fine," I spat out, glaring at him.

"Two hours to clean this place up," he repeated, his face red with rage. His eye twitched again. "Then we're going to have that talk."

From out of nowhere, an unexpected distraction came in the form of a small, black-and-white furball that bounded up to me

Night Shift

with uncontained energy. The little shih tzu, with its tail wagging furiously, jumped up, placing its paws on my knee, breaking the tense atmosphere for a brief moment.

Leaning over, I scooped up the dog and cradled him against my bare chest. Its soft fur was warm against my chilled skin. The pup, seemingly oblivious to the hostility in the room, licked my chin affectionately. I smiled and scratched behind his ears while murmuring, "Aren't you just the sweetest boy?"

Atticus, however, was not amused. "What the honest hell?" he spat out, barely able to contain his anger. "What have you done to the neighbor's dog? Did you give him alcohol?"

"What are you talking about?" I replied, genuinely confused. "This sweet boy showed up a couple of hours ago and was the hit of the party. He's so sweet. Aren't you, honey?" I cooed at the pup, nuzzling my face into his fur.

Atticus took a step closer, and the dog's demeanor shifted dramatically. In my arms, he transformed from a cuddly creature into a ferocious little beast, growling and barking aggressively at Atticus. I couldn't resist the urge to needle Atticus further. "You know, dogs are good judges of a person's character."

At that, his face contorted with rage. He opened his mouth to speak, but no words came out. Instead, he stormed up the stairs, screaming, "You'd better be ready in two hours, or else I'll come find you, and trust me, that won't be a pretty scene!"

As I stood there alone, wet, cold, and naked, guilt washed over me for what I had done to Atticus and his home.

I gave him time to make it to his bedroom before I sprinted upstairs and dashed to my temporary room, the little shih tzu scampering along behind me. Then, I sprang into action. Quickly, I slipped into a pair of shorts and a comfy T-shirt. I grabbed the pup and headed back downstairs, determined to tackle the horrendous mess. The temporary high from my little rebellion was gone, and now regret sat in my stomach like a stone.

Thankfully, cleaning was second nature to me. It was a skill I'd honed through years of living with an abusive father. I'd been the one who'd had to manage the household. It had, in fact, been a coping mechanism, a way to bring order to a life that had often felt out of control. Tonight, it served as a means to rectify the evening's transgressions.

Armed with a couple of large trash bags, I moved from room to room, picking up all the garbage. I wiped every surface down and returned every misplaced item to its rightful place. The rhythm of the work was familiar, almost comforting, and I was glad to have a task to focus on. The pup followed me around with curious eyes.

The kitchen required the most attention, so I dedicated myself to it with exacting care, cleaning every nook and cranny until it gleamed under the soft lights. It was a cathartic process. Each swipe of the cloth was a step toward redemption, toward making amends for what I'd done.

With the house nearing its former state of pristine order, I took the dog outside for a brief walk, hoping to reunite him with his owner. The night air was cool on my skin, a welcome relief after the hard work of cleaning. As if on cue, the pup darted toward a woman who greeted him with open arms and relief in her voice. "There you are, little man. I was getting worried about you."

I introduced myself as a friend of Atticus, apologizing for any concern Newton's unexpected adventure might have caused her. She was gracious, dismissing my apology with a wave of her hand and a kind smile. "Not a problem at all," she assured me before bidding me good night.

Night Shift

When I returned to the house, I surveyed my handiwork one last time, proud that Atticus's home had not only been restored to its former state but was perhaps even better than before. With ten minutes to spare, I flopped down into one of the living room armchairs, my heart pounding as I nervously awaited Atticus and his all-important *big talk*.

Chapter Eighteen

I charged up the stairs, the pounding rage in my chest nearly drowning out the sound of my footsteps. When I reached my bedroom door, I went to turn the knob, only to be met with resistance. Right, I'd locked it. God, I was glad no one had access to this room. Securing it had been a rare but necessary measure, considering the current situation. My personal space was sacred, not a place for just anyone to wander into, least of all Sam.

Hastily, I searched for the small key I'd hidden at the top of the doorframe, cursing my paranoia that had led me to lock it in the first place. The door was meant to be a barrier between Sam and my most personal space, but now it stood as a barricade against my fury as I fumbled for the key.

Night Shift

It wasn't so much about hiding it from others as it was about setting boundaries, especially for Sam. I expected her to understand without explanation.

Finally grabbing hold of the key, I slid it into the hole. The lock gave a *click*, and I pushed the door open and stepped into the sanctuary of my bedroom. Nothing seemed out of place... until I walked a bit further into the room. There was no disarray, nothing that would seem out of place to the casual observer, but I sensed it—Samantha had been here. It was an inexplicable sensation but undeniably there. I clenched my fists and tried to focus on anything else—the king-sized bed with its crisp white linens, the artwork decorating the walls, the clean scent of the room that spoke of order and control.

I tossed my wallet on the side table and walked across the room, scanning the entire suite. Yep, she'd been here. Even though there were no obvious signs of her intrusion, I could somehow tell she'd ventured into my closet and bathroom. The doors to the closet were slightly ajar. Inside, the items in my meticulously arranged wardrobe, from bespoke suits to casual wear, all hung in perfect order. Yet, something seemed off. Maybe it was the shift in the position of a leather belt, or perhaps it was the way the light caught on a watch I hadn't worn in weeks, which now lay slightly askew. It was a subtle disturbance, a whisper of intrusion.

Next, I rambled into the bathroom. The marble countertops were pristine, the chrome fittings gleaming under the recessed lighting. My grooming products were still lined up in precise rows. At a glance, they appeared to have been undisturbed—except the bottle of cologne that now sat on the wrong side.

My hands shook from the anger coursing through my veins as I wandered back into the bedroom. She'd invaded my personal space. I rarely invited people into my home. The women I brought here never expected to stay long. Their presence here was temporary and transactional. I invited them here with only one purpose—my gratification. Nothing more, nothing less. But Sam...she defied those unspoken rules. Her presence here was a challenge to the order I'd so carefully maintained.

I'd erected barriers, physical and emotional, to keep women out and to protect my privacy. Yet, as I stood at the corner of my bed, toeing off my shoes and shucking off my clothes, I couldn't escape the realization that perhaps I was the one who was trapped. Walking to the closet, I carefully placed my shoes in their rightful spot and tossed my clothes in the basket. This room, with all its order, suddenly seemed less like a sanctuary and more like a cell. Why did her defiance, her curiosity, stir something within me?

"Control," I whispered, trying to regain some semblance of it amid my frustration. I had given Sam two hours to clean up the mess from her little rebellion, and I needed to find something to occupy my mind with until then—anything to keep me from exploding at her.

"All right, a shower. Just take a damn shower and relax," I told myself, making my way back into the bathroom. The tile floor was cold beneath my feet. I stepped into the shower and turned it on, adjusting the water temperature. Steam quickly filled the room. I stepped under the spray, allowing the hot water to soothe my tense muscles. With each minute that passed, my anger seemed to lessen, albeit only slightly. By the time I turned off the water, toweled off, and pulled on a pair of gray sweatpants and an old fraternity T-shirt, I felt somewhat calmer. *Two hours*, I thought. *Just two hours to kill, and then I can deal with her*.

As if on cue, the neighbor's dog barked downstairs, bringing me back to the moment that Sam had held the mangy mutt in her arms and told me that dogs were good judges of character. The nerve of her! My anger resurfaced with full force.

"Music," I decided, shoving earbuds into my ears in an attempt to calm myself. Once I'd started my favorite playlist, I kicked back on my bed and picked up a medical journal. The latest research on emergency medicine stared back at me, but despite my attempts to focus on the words, my thoughts were consumed by Sam. The image of my brother kissing her at the gala played on repeat in my mind, fueling my fury even further. Had they slept together? The mere idea of it made my blood boil, but I tried to remind myself of the unspoken bro code: none of us would ever fuck another brother's ex. Not that she was an ex, but still, she and I had hooked up, and he had caught us at the cabin.

Who was I angrier at—Sam or Conan? Did I even have a right to be pissed off?

After precisely two hours, I stomped down the stairs, barefoot and on edge, and entered the living room, where I found Sam lounging in one of my oversized armchairs. As soon as she caught sight of me, she leaped up with a smug look on her face, clearly proud of her cleanup efforts.

"Impressive work," I grudgingly admitted, surveying the spotless room. "The place looks decent."

"Oh, it's more than decent," she said, settling her hands on her hips and screwing up her face in defiance. "Trust me, it's spotless, just the way you demanded."

As we stood there, both seething and sizing each other up, I couldn't respond, distracted by the way her thin T-shirt clung to her curves and showed the peaks of her hardened nipples. She wasn't wearing a bra. In spite of my blinding anger, my body reacted to her. It was maddening how badly I wanted to fuck the smart-ass attitude right out of her until she wasn't able to walk.

"Is that so?" I grumbled. "Well, maybe next time you'll think twice before breaking my rules."

"Maybe," she replied flippantly. "Or maybe you'll learn to loosen up a little. Try it sometime. You might like it."

All I could do was glare at her, dumbstruck by her blatant obstinance. Sam, with her fiery hair and equally fiery spirit, had become an unexpected variable in the equation of my life. And as much as I wanted to maintain my usual dominance, I found myself intrigued, challenged, and inexplicably drawn to her sass.

Taking a slow, deep breath, I silently prepared for the confrontation that was bound to unfold. I took a couple of steps toward Sam, and she stood her ground, placing one hand on her hip as she cocked it to the side defiantly.

"Explain."

"Explain what?" she shot back, her blue eyes glaring at me as her lip raised in a snarl.

"Dammit, Samantha! You know exactly what! You threw a fucking party at my house! How could you violate my trust like this after everything I've done for you?"

"Trust? What trust? You sent me your ridiculous *house rules* as if I was more of a prisoner than a guest! Obviously, I'm not a guest; I'm just an annoyance. Could you have been any more rude?" She crossed her arms over her chest and let out a frustrated huff. "It's not like I had any other choice. You and your brothers made the decision for me to come here like I was a child."

We scowled at each other.

"At least I invited you to stay when you needed it. Hell, you wouldn't even let me into your apartment for a cup of coffee."

"That was different," she snapped.

"Was it? Or is it just a matter of being polite?" I moved another step forward, smirking. "Did you forget what they taught you in Manners 101 in nursing school, or is that not part of your *Common Sense for Doctors* handbook?"

"Please, like you know anything about manners."

"Maybe I don't, but I rarely have unexpected guests, and I sure as hell have never left anyone in my home alone before. I can't believe you'd go so far out of your way to piss me off by throwing a party while I was gone. I'm disappointed in you, Samantha."

Her face contorted into an expression of guilt and anger. "Well, it's not like there's a *Dr. Thorin the Control Freak Handbook* lying around!"

I tightly pinched the bridge of my nose, forcing myself to take deep breaths and focus on the pain instead of the irritation that threatened to consume me.

That was when Sam's cell phone buzzed on the end table next to me. I stared at the text notification on her phone for a long time, clenching my fists. My gut twisted with jealousy, and all I wanted to do was toss her damn phone across the room. Instead, I held it up so she could see it too. "Who the fuck is 'Derek—Your future husband'?" I asked, my palm twitching with the desire to spank her for even daring to talk to a guy who thought he had a claim on her.

"None of your business! Give me my phone back." Her expression twisted with rage. "Stop being so damn possessive, Atticus!" she exclaimed, finally grabbing her phone.

"So tell me, how many guys have you fucked since we were at my cabin, Samantha? Derek, my brother—how many more?!" I was screaming now, my control slipping away.

Her face flushed red with anger, and her eyes blazed. "Screw you, Atticus. You have no right to be jealous or judge me."

"Jealous? No, I'm just curious."

Sam crossed her arms defensively and stomped her foot. "Why do you care?! You don't own me!"

I opened my mouth to respond, but she cut me off.

"Since we're throwing accusations around, how many women have you fucked in this house, Atticus?" she hissed. "I bet you can't even count the number of women you've fucked in your big ole king-size bed, or how about the number you've fucked right here on this sofa, or kitchen counter, or office, or hot tub... I bet, as old as you are, it's been hundreds!"

"Enough!" I shouted, silencing her for a moment. I hesitated, unsure of whether or not to answer. This only seemed to fuel Sam's anger. She tossed her hair and began to stomp away, but I caught her by the arm and spun her around. "Oh, no. You're not going anywhere until I say so."

"Let go of me!" she demanded, trying to pull her arm free. "This is ridiculous!"

"Ridiculous? You're the one who started this by throwing a damn party in my house!"

"Maybe if you weren't such a controlling asshole, I wouldn't have felt the need to do it!"

"Fine!" I snapped, letting go of her and throwing my hands in the air. "Maybe I was a bit overbearing with the house rules. But I didn't expect you to throw a fucking party as payback!"

"Payback?" Sam's eyes flashed with indignation. "You think this is about payback? No, Atticus, this is about me asserting my independence!"

"Independence, huh?" I scoffed. Frustration coursed through me, and I began to pace around the living room like a caged animal, every step a futile attempt to quell my temper.

"Damn right," she retorted, her voice trembling ever so slightly. "I'm not your little plaything, and I will not sit here and let you dictate my life."

Night Shift

"Nobody said you were," I said, returning to stand in front of her. She was seething at me now, her lips pressed into a tight line and her cheeks flushed. Despite myself, I found it hard not to admire her fiery spirit. "But this is my home, Sam. I have a right to set boundaries."

"Get out of my face, Atticus," she hissed, and I knew I had pushed her too far. She turned and started to walk away.

Before she had made it more than a few steps, I moved in front of her, blocking her path to the hallway that led to the staircase. Then I slowly edged forward, crowding her until she started stepping back. Soon her back bumped against the wall, and she jumped, startled to find herself caged between the hard surface at her back and the hard-faced man standing in front of her.

"Why do you care who I fucked in MY house? You haven't given two shits about me since you bolted from my cabin, reminding me multiple times that night was purely an experiment, nothing more. 'It will be as if it never happened, remember?'" I said, mimicking her earlier words. "No strings, no feelings, right? Then to smear my nose in your brush-off, you told my brother right in front of my face that our time together was a mistake, right before you batted your adoring eyelashes at him and called him your knight in shining armor. Then, also right in front of my face, you agreed to go to the gala with him. So what in the god-honest-fucking truth did you expect me to think?"

"I figured if that night meant anything to you, you'd at least text or call me, that I would see you at work and we'd banter and tease like before, that you would pursue me if you were interested, but nooo. Talk about nothing... I was completely invisible to you. I didn't lay eyes on you until Conan carried me into the emergency department after I was attacked. And you could barely stand to look at me." She rolled her eyes, swallowed hard, and poked an accusing finger directly into my chest.

"Don't roll your eyes at me," I warned through gritted teeth. Widening her eyes, she jabbed her finger into my chest again.

"How do you think I felt, finding out in front of all my friends at Friendsgiving that you were taking the fabulous Dr. Vanessa Sinclair to the gala?" She jabbed her finger in my chest a third time. "I hadn't even planned on going until I saw your reaction to Conan taking care of me in the emergency department," she said, followed by another poke.

"Enough!" I roared, the last of my self-control slipping away. I had to find a way to rein it in before I went ham on her ass. This wasn't the time or place for me to unleash the darker side of my desires. Her repeated jabs had ignited a fire within me, pushing me closer to the edge. With the tension building, her actions stirred up something wicked inside me. And the angrier I became, the more agitated she seemed to get. The hostility between us was only growing. Samantha was testing my limits, forcing me to spiral into a malevolent place.

"Fuck you, Atticus! All of your assumptions about me are ridiculous! Why don't you get your fucking facts straight? You're the one who treated me like you didn't even know me after that night in the cabin. You looked down your nose at me at the gala like I was some street urchin!"

"Jesus fucking Christ, that's bullshit, and you know it. I did exactly as you asked and kept your secrets. And don't you worry; I wouldn't *want* anyone to know, so stop acting like a fucking child."

Without warning, she hauled back to slap me across the face.

I caught her by the wrist and slammed it against the wall behind her. Samantha gasped, her eyes wide, her pupils blown.

"Raise your hand to me again, *Samantha*, and I'll show you how it feels to get smacked."

Night Shift

She heaved a gulp of air. "I might be naive, I might be hunted, I might even have panic attacks that claw their way up my throat, but one thing I'm not...is someone's dirty little secret."

The raw emotion in her voice stunned me. I let go of her arm, cocking my head to the side in an attempt to figure out what could possibly be going on in that big brain of hers. All her accusations about me had been wrong. Hundreds of women, humph! I'd just assumed she didn't want to be with me and moved on.

Before I could process what was happening, she lunged forward and smacked the shit out of me, leaving a hot, throbbing handprint on the side of my jaw.

The pain sent a shockwave through me, igniting something wild and animalistic inside. My eyes locked onto hers, and I registered the moment she realized there was a darker side to me. The fear in her eyes gave me a sadistic thrill.

"Are you done?" I growled.

"Maybe I am," she scoffed, her chest heaving. "But now you know how it feels to be slapped in the face with the truth."

"Truth?" I snarled. "You don't know anything about the truth, Samantha. You have no idea what I've been through or how far I can take things."

"Then show me!" she challenged, her eyes flashing with defiance and something else—a hint of delight? Was she getting off on this shit?

"Be careful what you wish for," I warned, my voice barely more than a whisper. It was clear our anger, pain, and desire were threatening to consume us both.

My hand shot out, grasping her throat. I shoved her against the wall, and her skull hit it with a thud.

"Did you fuck my brother?!"

Her eyes were giant and blinking rapidly. She shook her head, barely able to move within my hold.

"Realize now there's a darker side to me?" I growled, my voice dripping with menace. Sam merely stared at me, her eyes glassy, her chest heaving as she fought for breath. My heart hammered in my chest, adrenaline pumping through my veins as we stood there, locked in a battle of wills.

And then I snapped.

I heaved her forward, shouldering her weight, and dragged her ass to the armchair in the living room where she'd been sitting when I'd first come downstairs to talk. I slung her, butt-side-up, over the arm of the chair, pinning both of her wrists in one hand above her head.

"This isn't about your pleasure; it's about mine," I hissed in her ear. "Tonight, you're gonna need a safe word. Say it now!"

Samantha's legs were shaking, but even so, she turned her head and gave me a coy little smile, daring me to unleash my worst. That was when I realized I'd been a pawn to her queen in this game of hers since the moment I'd given her unfettered access to my world—fuuuck!

"Say it now, Samantha!" I threatened.

She inhaled deeply, wincing in pain, and hissed out, "As you wish." Those three tantalizing words hung in the air between us, causing my dick to jerk to attention. A red haze fell over my vision, and I lost all control.

I jerked down her little cotton shorts, baring her lily-white ass to me. Still holding her wrists in one hand, I smacked her with brutal force. She cried out and tried to move away, but I denied her escape. A raised red handprint appeared on her ass, and I couldn't resist giving her a matching one on the other cheek. She jerked against the cushion of the chair—as if that would somehow get her away from the pain—and whimpered softly.

Before either of us could take a breath, I struck her three more times.

"Please, Atticus," she gasped, but whether it was a plea for more or a plea for mercy, I didn't know. And in that moment, I didn't care. All that mattered was the heat of her body, the feel of her beneath me, and the intoxicating power coursing through my veins.

"Shut up," I growled, yanking down my sweatpants just enough to free my throbbing cock.

I slammed into her pussy in one merciless thrust, and a guttural moan escaped her lips. "Don't you fucking dare move your hands," I ordered, my voice strained with lust and fury.

She shuddered beneath me but complied, so I released her wrists. The sass I'd grown to love was momentarily gone. As much as I hated to admit it, I liked her rattled like this—but I wanted some fight still left in her.

With my hands finally free, I wasted no time yanking off her shirt and mine, tearing the fabric in my haste. I kicked away my pants, which had tangled around my ankles, desperate to rid myself of any hindrances, leaving us both naked, panting, and heated. Nothing else mattered except getting closer to her. I leaned over her back and pounded into her savagely. My fingers dug into her hips, and I pulled her closer to me, then shoved her back again as our bodies became slick with sweat. Each thrust drove her hard against the side of the armchair and into the soft cushions. The sound of our flesh colliding filled the room, echoing off the walls like a primal drumbeat.

"Atticus...please..." she whimpered, her voice barely audible over our ragged breathing. A part of my subconscious knew I'd probably regret this later, but for some reason, that potential for regret didn't concern me right now.

All at once, I noticed that Samantha wasn't only taking my harsh strokes—she was returning them, meeting my brutality with her own fierce energy. Her moans grew louder, turning into desperate cries, until finally, she screamed out, her orgasm ripping through her body like wildfire.

The sensation of her walls clenching around my cock sent me hurtling over the edge, and an explosive orgasm surged through me. At that moment, I grabbed a fistful of her gorgeous red hair, yanking her head around to force her to look at me. "Now, that's a *good girl*," I growled, my voice heavy with satisfaction as I withdrew from her.

Sam's cheeks flushed crimson, and in a flash, she turned around and leaped into my arms, straddling my waist. Her eyes, wild and stormy, locked onto mine as she begged in a hoarse cry, "Say it again...please..."

Night Shift

Chapter Nineteen

"Such a good girl," Atticus whispered, his words heavy with dark promise. I'd never seen the spark of true desire in a man's eyes directed at me before. It was almost laughable to think that the same grumpy doctor who had barely acknowledged my existence that first chaotic day in the emergency department would end up making me feel like I was his everything—body and soul. The heat of his hands wrapped around my thighs as he pressed me firmly against him, and I couldn't hold back my need for him any longer.

In a swift move, I grabbed his face between my hands, crushing my lips against his in a fierce kiss. I took control, pushing my tongue into his mouth. His full lips tasted like sin and salvation in equal measure, and his tongue danced with mine in an erotic ballet that left us both panting. Atticus groaned into my mouth, the sound vibrating straight down to my core. His grip on my thighs tightened, and I pulled him closer, the heat rising between us. I bit down on his lower lip, drawing a little bit of blood. The coppery taste sent a jolt of excitement through me.

I pulled away from him. "Consider that payback," I said, smirking at the look of surprise on his face.

"Feisty," he responded, his eyes narrowing. He stepped around to the sofa, threw me down onto it, and leaned over me. "I'm going to fuck that attitude right out of you," he growled.

Tilting my chin up impudently, I raised an eyebrow and gave him a provocative glance. With my feet on the floor and my ass in the seat, I slowly, deliberately spread my knees wide to the edges of the sofa, baring my soaked entrance to him. Biting my lip, I dared him to take what he wanted.

"Damn, that pussy looks so fucking tasty. Mmm, she's so pretty." His deep, rumbling timbre rolled over my skin as his eyes darkened. He winked at me, a wicked grin spreading across his face. "Don't move an inch," he commanded before striding into the kitchen.

My heart pounded in anticipation as I listened to him rummaging through drawers. Moments later, he returned carrying a jar of coconut oil and a wooden spoon with a stainless steel head—one I recognized from his collection of flatware.

"Interesting choice." I laughed, watching as he placed the items on the coffee table and lit a trio of pillar candles. Then he dropped to his knees directly between my legs, his eyes never leaving mine.

"Are you ready to play?"

"Hmmm," I replied, breathy with anticipation.

He wasted no time sliding his hands up my thighs and bringing his mouth to my folds. His tongue flicked out, teasing my swollen cleft before dipping lower to taste my wetness. His

Night Shift

fingers trailed over my inner thighs, lightly brushing against my sensitive skin. I shuddered when he slid two fingers inside me, pumping them in and out—in and out—in and out.

Lifting his mouth away from me, he watched me closely, taking in my reactions and adjusting his movements accordingly. His fingers dove inside my soaking core and curled upward, pressing against my inner wall, finding the rough texture of that special spot within. A sudden pressure on my abdomen made me gasp. My eyes shot open to see his palm pressing down on my lower belly, intensifying the sensations within me.

"You like that, don't you? Your wetness is filling my palm. Mmm, fuuck, if you only knew how badly I want to sink my thick girth into your tightness."

Without stopping or slowing down, he returned his mouth to me and expertly worked over my tight bundle of nerves while his fingers filled and stretched me. I could feel every ridge and pad of them massaging the inside of me while his palm exerted a delicious pressure from the outside. He lapped up my wetness, drawing moan after breathy moan from deep within me. He swept his tongue around my clitoris like an artist with a brush, painting strokes of pleasure that drew shivers down my spine before he sucked it into his mouth, sending shocks of pure ecstasy coursing through my veins.

The sharp nip of teeth against sensitive flesh sent a jolt through me, causing me to buck into his touch. His laugh vibrated against me, adding another layer to the multitude of sensations.

"Mmm, tastes so good." He hummed against my skin before continuing his assault.

Then he did something unexpected. He picked up the wooden spoon and dipped it into the jar of coconut oil. His smirk returned when he caught my curious stare.

"Relax," he commanded, spreading my lips wide with his other hand.

My breath hitched as he pressed the cold metal of the spoon against my ultra-sensitive nub. My body arched desperately into him, craving more contact. Then, I watched, mesmerized, as he turned the spoon around and slowly pushed the handle inside me, swirling it across my sweet spot and bringing me to the edge of orgasm.

His mouth returned to my clitoris—and he continued sucking, licking, and nipping until I was writhing under his touch. He knew exactly how to play my body.

"Oh God...Atticus," I whimpered, feeling my climax on the edge.

His lips curled into a devious smirk against my skin. But just as I teetered on the brink of coming, he pulled away, leaving me panting and desperate for release.

"What?" I huffed, my legs trembling from the unfulfilled desire coursing through me. "Why did you stop?"

A wicked grin spread across his face. He leaned forward, brushing his lips against my ear. "Because we're just getting started, Sammich," he whispered, his breath hot on my skin. "We're going to explore depths of pleasure you've never imagined."

I couldn't stop the gasp that escaped me. "But...but I was right there—"

He bit sharply into my shoulder.

"Ow!"

"Hush. Tonight, I'm in control. You, my little midnight snack, don't get to have an opinion. Be happy that tonight isn't about letting you dangle on the edge."

I took a deep breath and steadied my pent-up need by studying the shadows that danced across the walls from the flickering candlelight. The scent of coconut oil hung heavy in the air, mingling with that of my arousal.

"Watch me," Atticus growled. "Let me show you a secret indulgence." I did as I was told, intently tracking his hand as he reached for the jar of coconut oil on the coffee table and scooped out a generous fistful. I shuddered at the devilish look in his eyes. He licked his lips like a predator about to devour its prey and dropped a dollop of the creamy white paste on my mound. Expertly, he massaged it down my clitoris and around all my folds. My breath hitched when he smeared some more of the oil onto his middle finger and began rubbing slow circles around my puckered hole.

Instinctively, my knees jerked together. "Atticus, I don't know if—" But he silenced me by putting a finger to my lips.

"Try that again, and I'll turn you over my knee and give you another spanking, more harsh than the last one," he threatened, tracing his fingers around the edges of my still tender bottom. I swallowed hard, embarrassed at the thought of him exerting such domination over me. It was both terrifying and thrilling.

"Trust me, Samantha."

I swallowed hard and had to bite my tongue to avoid reminding him that I didn't trust anyone.

"Keep your eyes open, Samantha," he demanded in a low and dangerous tone. Reluctantly, I complied, locking my gaze on his fingers as they continued their agonizing journey. What he was doing was entirely new and forbidden, and I was both mortified and intrigued by the pleasure it brought. As he slipped the tip of his finger in and out and circled the inner edge, I imagined how it would feel to be filled and invaded *there* and clenched my opening tight.

"Relax," he urged. "Watch what I'm doing to you." I tried my best to comply and enjoy his ministrations, earning praise from him as I submitted. "Mmm, aren't you the good girl," he said, giving my inner thigh a quick kiss. He pulled his fingertip out and added more coconut oil. My nerves were on edge, and I was unsure about what was coming next. Then, with a smoldering gaze, Atticus pushed his finger fully inside me, holding me in place with his palm on my belly and his fingers curled around my mound. Taking his time, he slid in and out and round and round. I would have never guessed that the nerves there would elicit such fiery tingles from the depths of my spine to where his palm held me. The sensation was strange, unlike anything I'd ever experienced.

"Atticus...!" I let out a breathy exhale, my body tensing as apprehension took hold.

"Shhh...just trust me," he whispered, pulling his finger out and adding even more coconut oil. This time, he was more aggressive, plunging two fingers into my tight hole. I pushed back against the sudden intrusion, my breath hitching in my throat. He chuckled darkly and moved his fingers back and forth, slowly at first but gradually increasing in speed.

Unable to help myself, I shut my eyes and let my head fall back while he continued to explore my body. Then, without warning, he smacked me hard across my folds. The jolt of pain made me yelp.

"Eyes open," he demanded as his thumb slid into my wet entrance, and he stroked my clitoris with his other fingers, driving me wild. It wasn't long before my moans turned into a high-pitched whine. Within moments, I reached my climax, shuddering in pure bliss. Atticus grinned at me, his eyes filled with triumph as he released me.

"See? I knew you just needed the right man to pleasure you," he said confidently. "And I'll make sure to give you plenty of

Night Shift

orgasms. You'll see. Don't question me. Do as I say, and you'll never be left wanting."

Feeling brave and wanting to challenge his controlling nature, I sat up and pressed a brief kiss to his lips before standing and pulling him up with me. I turned him around so he could take my place on the sofa. He smirked as he sat down, running his hand over the wet spot where my arousal had dampened the fabric.

"Looks like someone made a mess," he taunted, raising an eyebrow.

I leaned over and gave his hard shaft a couple of slow strokes. "I'm sure you won't mind a little more *untidiness*." I winked. "Turnabout is fair play, after all." Slowly, I ran my nails up the tender skin of his inner thighs, and then I sank between his knees, keeping my eyes locked on his. Scooping out some coconut oil, I coated my hands and began massaging it onto his cock. His eyes became hooded with pleasure as I slid oiled fingers over the tip, down the shaft, and around his balls. Firmly, I drew one finger up and down the sensitive skin beyond his balls, eventually teasing his puckered hole. A low groan escaped him. "Remember, you have to watch," I reminded him, wrapping my slick hand around his throbbing length and licking my lips.

"Trust me, watching you suck my dick is no hardship," he said with a chuckle as his eyes darkened.

I giggled, then moved closer and opened my mouth, taking in his glistening cock. My tongue swirled around the head and over his meatus, tasting him and savoring him before moving slowly down the shaft. I sucked gently, increasing the pressure as I worked toward the base while the veins throbbed beneath my eager lips. The coconut oil made it easier for me to take more of him into my mouth with each stroke.

When I sensed him nearing climax, I stopped abruptly, pulled away, and blew cool air across his sensitive skin. His chest heaved, and he glared at me. "Don't fuck with me, Samantha," he growled, "or you'll get more than you bargained for."

"Big talk from a man with—" He brusquely grabbed my hair and yanked me toward his cock.

"Finish. You're not leaving me like this," he said firmly, and I obliged but took my time, softly teasing his taut frenulum with my tongue before flicking it back and forth across the sensitive band, eliciting a soft groan from him. A bead of pre-cum emerged from the tip of his cock, and I carefully allowed the drop to roll onto the tip of my tongue. Meeting his eyes, I smeared the slick drop across my lips like sinful lip gloss. His dick twitched in response.

"God, you're so fucking hot," he praised as I moved down to lavish attention on his balls, licking and sucking on them while rubbing my thumb around the sensitive skin of his tight hole. Atticus squirmed, tangling his fingers in my hair and growling. His rumble ignited the heat between my thighs.

Taking a deep breath, I rose up on my knees and guided his cock back into my mouth, pressing the head against the back of my throat. Atticus moaned, further twisting his fingers in my curls as he began pumping in and out of my mouth. I grabbed his firm, round cheeks in each of my hands to steady myself against the force. Although I tried to accommodate him, swallowing around his thickness, I struggled to breathe and suppress my gag reflex. His grip on my hair became almost painful, and he forced himself deeper. He began to control the rhythm and depth, pushing me past my comfort zone as his cock filled my throat. The coconut oil helped, but only so much.

Atticus's thrusts grew more aggressive. Suddenly, he shoved his dick down my throat. Panic set in when I realized I couldn't breathe any longer. Desperate, I looked up at him with pleading eyes and tried to blink away the tears streaming down my cheeks. In response, he offered a dark smile, pulling out just long enough for me to gasp before plunging back in and pounding my throat mercilessly.

In a last-ditch effort to regain some control, I slipped my lubed-up finger into his tight little asshole, surprising him. He let out a guttural groan and released his load down my throat in waves, finally letting go of my hair. Gulping for air, I slid off of him, licked my lips, and swallowed hard, drinking down his cum.

Still reeling from the intensity, I collapsed against his hip, panting. I didn't move for a long time, lightheaded from all that we'd done.

Breathing heavily, he glided his fingers through my hair while we took a moment to gather ourselves. He cleared his throat and let out a cleansing breath, then reached down to grip my waist and pull me up and onto his lap so I was straddling him.

Heat rose in my cheeks when his finger traced over one of my breasts. Even though we'd just been as intimate as we possibly could be, his intense gaze made me a little shy. It was as if he could see right through me. His brow furrowed.

"Hey, what's wrong?" he asked softly.

I dipped my head, unsure of how to put my thoughts into words. "I...I really believed that you weren't interested in me. That you didn't want me because I wasn't experienced enough or on your professional level...or any of another million reasons."

"Look at me," he said softly, hooking a finger under my chin and lifting my face. "Does this *not feel* like I want you?" He glanced down at his growing hardness that was pressed against my core.

"You acted as if I didn't exist. You never considered inviting me to the gala. And before the cabin, you flirted with me at work and even pushed me to go hiking, of all things. Then nothing. I just don't get it. I guess I fell under your spell. Hearing so many women, especially Bethany, talk about what an amazing lover you are...I was curious, and you knew that. You knew exactly what I wanted...what I needed."

"I get it, but *you* made me promise never to bring it up again, and I was respecting your wishes. I wanted to earn your trust. Since you were adamant that I not acknowledge anything between us...not even use the nickname I gave you, I figured you thought I was too old or something and moved on."

"Well...you are awfully old," I teased, poking him in the ribs. "But you're in pretty good shape and still seem pretty sharp."

Laughter rumbled from deep within his belly, sending vibrations to my most intimate places, causing me to laugh too. Pulling me closer, he pressed his lips to mine in a tender kiss before pulling back and studying my face, taking in every detail. He brushed his thumb over the tattoo beneath my left breast, curiously tracing the arrow design.

"What's the story behind this?" he asked.

"Unbroken, Still I Rise," I whispered, repeating the phrase inked into my skin. "It's inspired by Maya Angelou's poem. It represents resilience, triumph over adversity, self-love, and self-acceptance. I got it after graduating from college with my nursing degree. You know, with everything I've been through—my dad's addictions, losing my mom when I was eight—this tattoo is... well, it's my badge of courage, a reminder of my strength."

His expression softened, and he cupped my face in his hands. "You're so strong, Sammich. You have no idea how lucky I feel to have you in my life. You're unique. I've never wanted to share my life with a woman before—" He kissed me tenderly, making my heart race. "But I have to be honest with you—you gutted me when you accused me of fucking women all over this house.

Night Shift

I'm not the man-whore Bethany makes me out to be. Yes, I've had my share of lovers, but few have come into my home."

Playfully, I pressed my forehead against his. I couldn't resist asking, "So how many women have you been with? Have you fucked other women on this very sofa?"

Heaving an exasperated sigh, he caressed my arms and shoulders, gathering my hair into a ponytail behind my back. "Samantha, let's not talk about past lovers, okay? You can't change the past, and it only causes problems. It doesn't matter how many there were before; the only one who matters is the last."

The implication of his words sank right into my soul. In that moment, the connection between us seemed to strengthen, and the storm of anger and passion that had been raging between us quieted. It allowed me to consider what truly mattered.

Atticus broke the silence. "I need to understand what happened between you and Conan. I know you said you didn't... you know, fuck my brother, but I've got to know where you stand with him. The way you kissed him at the gala, the look in your eyes, Samantha...it was...God, the way I'd want any woman to look at me."

His words, almost an accusation, stung. I took a deep breath. "No, I swear, I haven't been with anyone since we were together in your cabin. Yes, Conan kissed me at the party, but I was only into it because I was sad and angry, perhaps vulnerable..."

He blinked, appearing surprised by my answer.

I pushed forward, needing him to understand. "So when Conan tried to kiss me again in his room, all I could see was you...and he knew. Conan knew I wasn't into him. He figured out right away why I couldn't let him touch me. And like a gentleman, he backed off. We played video games until I got the call about my apartment being ransacked by those thugs."

Atticus stared at me, realization—or maybe it was guilt—swirling in his gray eyes. "How the fuck did we end up here? How did things get so confusing between us?" he asked.

"I don't know." I sighed. "I'm sorry for all the mixed signals. But I'm telling you the truth. There was nothing other than friendship between Conan and me. You know...you're a hard man to follow."

He stroked my back softly. "I'm sorry for assuming the worst about you. From now on, there can't be any secrets between us. We can't hide our relationship, or whatever this is, not even at work."

"Relationship?" I asked, surprised and a bit nervous. "I didn't think you ever did relationships."

Atticus gave me a small, thoughtful smile. "I haven't...but there's always a first time for everything." He leaned in to kiss me sweetly. "You're special, Samantha. I'm willing to try an exclusive situation on a trial basis."

"An experiment, huh?" I teased, laughing softly. It wasn't what I'd hoped for when he'd mentioned the word *relationship*, but it was enough for now.

"Let's go grab some snacks and a drink," he suggested, nodding toward the kitchen. "We need to stay hydrated for what's coming next. I'm not finished with you tonight."

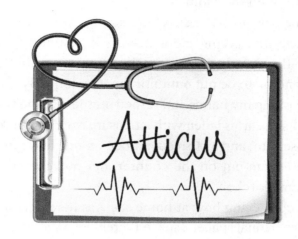

Chapter Twenty

"Very funny," she said, crawling off my lap. I stood up and pulled my sweatpants on in one quick motion while she slid my T-shirt over her head.

"You think I'm jesting? I told you at Swan Creek I was in prime condition," I said, smacking her on the ass and steering her toward the kitchen.

"Let's see what kind of good food you can come up with in this fancy kitchen of yours," she teased, her hand finding mine. With an eager tug, she pulled me from the room.

In the kitchen I flipped on the pendant lights. The stainless-steel appliances gleamed, and the marble countertops practically sparkled—she really had done a good job cleaning up. The scent of sex still lingered in the air around us, and I couldn't help but admire Samantha's lithe, sweat-slicked body as she moved gracefully around the room.

I stepped over to the sink to wash up, and Sam was right there beside me, giving me a cheeky hip bump. She hogged the water, flashing that grin that always meant trouble. I had to wait, pretending to be put out until she was done. By the time I'd finished washing my hands and turned off the tap, she was already back at my side, arms laden with a treasure trove of snacks: cheese cubes, prosciutto, and a crisp cucumber, among other fridge finds. She placed them out on the counter, her movements easy and familiar in my kitchen.

It was odd seeing how at home she was here, seeing her so at ease in my personal space, a space I rarely let anyone invade. And even more odd was the fact that I liked having her here. Normally, I was eager to usher women out the door, making empty promises of future calls. But with Sam, it was different. I wanted her to know me, to reveal myself to her, to let her see the true me, with all my complexities and vulnerabilities laid bare.

I shook my head, forcing those thoughts aside. No, there were plenty of reasons to keep my guard up, to resist catching feelings for her. What everyone said about me was true—I didn't become involved in romantic relationships. That ship had sailed ages ago. This was just an infatuation, most likely triggered by my instinct to protect and fix the world around me...to fix *her* world.

"I guess we're going for a gourmet snack platter tonight," I said, turning to the pantry to grab a box of crackers. Digging around, I found the artisanal kind I'd been saving for an occasion just like this.

"I don't know about you, but I'm starving," she replied, giving me a playful wink and setting out a couple of bottles of water next to our burgeoning spread. Hydration, it seemed, was as much a priority as satiation.

"All right, let's get some food in that sexy little body of yours,"

Night Shift

I said, pulling a cutting board out from the cabinet and selecting a bunch of grapes from the bowl on the counter. Bottle of water in hand, Samantha sauntered over to the entertainment system and grabbed the remote.

"Mind if I put on some tunes?" she asked, wiggling the remote at me. After downing nearly half her bottle of water, she set it down next to where I was working.

"Go ahead," I replied, focused on slicing grapes and arranging them on the board. She scrolled through her playlist, and before long, the first notes of a romantic jazz melody filled the room—Chet Baker's "I Fall In Love Too Easily."

I raised an eyebrow. "Didn't peg you for a jazz enthusiast."

"Don't act so surprised. I love all sorts of music. Sometimes a girl needs a little romance in her life," she replied, sliding her arms around my waist from behind and resting her head on my back. We swayed together to the sultry rhythm of the trumpet and bass, the music adding a layer of intimacy as I cut the cucumber and arranged our spread on the board.

"Seems you're full of surprises tonight," I murmured.

Sam's hand dropped a little lower, brushing against my growing erection. "Jesus, Atticus, I didn't know men your age could recover so fast."

"You make it sound like I'm eighty. Hell, I haven't yet hit forty and you make it seem like I'm older than dirt. Besides, I've always been big on fitness," I said, unable to hide my pride. "And if memory serves me correctly, you were the one who fell asleep after our not-so-long hike. Trust me, I can more than keep up with a sassy spitfire like you. Better eat and drink up, Sammich; we're not sleeping tonight."

"Is that a promise or a threat?" she purred with a naughtiness that had my dick twitching again. I couldn't believe the effect this woman had on me.

"Both," I replied, dropping my knife, turning, and grabbing her by the waist. I swung her around and lifted her onto the cold marble countertop. She yelped when her vulnerable flesh made contact with the chilly surface.

"Damn, that's cold on my girlie bits!" she exclaimed, squirming to get off the counter, but I held her firmly in place, taking her mouth and swallowing her protests in a demanding kiss.

Pulling away slightly, I whispered against her lips, "Trust me, my pretty lady, I'll warm you up soon enough."

Sam's pupils widened with arousal, and she reached up to cup my cheek. The stitches on her arm reminded me of those bastards who had attacked her. At some point, I needed to tell her about the meeting I'd had today with the private detective I'd hired, but now wasn't the time.

I had also put together a crew to clean up her apartment and salvage whatever they could. Tomorrow, they would bring her things over, but seeing all of it would probably upset her all over again. That, along with what the PI and I suspected, was going to be a lot for her to deal with. Right now, she was in my hands, and I knew exactly how to keep her mind off her situation.

I took her hand and placed a chaste kiss on her palm. Then I stepped back and reached for her bottle of water and handed it to her, gesturing toward the mini charcuterie board. "Now eat. I've got plenty of ideas of how I want to take you before the morning's light."

As if on cue, Samantha's stomach growled loudly, and we both laughed.

"Guess I'm hungrier than I thought," she admitted, blushing a little as she picked up a cracker and topped it with some cheese.

I grabbed a few cheese cubes, popping them into my mouth and scarfing them down. Then I snagged a handful of grapes, enjoying the taste of sweetness as they burst open in my mouth.

Night Shift

Cracking open my water bottle, I took a long, refreshing sip before setting it down next to her. Sam was making quick work of her cracker, effortlessly devouring it along with several grapes in just a few bites. Her appetite matched mine, and soon we had devoured almost everything on the board.

"And here I was thinking you had only one kind of appetite," I said, laughing in a low rumble.

"Well...I can multitask." She shot me a cheeky grin, picking up another grape and popping it into her mouth. "You know, Atticus, your age really does look good on you. I would've never guessed you were knocking on forty if Bethany hadn't told me. It's good to know I don't have to worry about wearing you out." She reached down to run her hand up my length.

"Keep talking like that and I'll show you just how much stamina this old man has."

"You've got quite the appetite, don't you?" After popping several more grapes into her mouth, she bit down, and juice dribbled out of the corner of her mouth. My cock stirred at the sight.

"Careful there. Wouldn't want to waste any," I murmured, stepping closer and wiping the juice away with my thumb. Her tongue darted out to lick her lips, and I couldn't resist leaning in to taste her, our mouths melding together in a heated kiss.

I reached for my bottle again, taking a long, satisfying gulp. Out of the corner of my eye, I noticed Sam watching me with a mischievous glint sparking in her eyes. I should've known better, should've anticipated her next move, but I was too caught up in the moment. Just as I was lowering the bottle, she pounced, squeezing it and sending a stream of water over my face and down my chest. I jumped back, sputtering and dripping, while she erupted into peals of laughter.

"Oh, you're going to regret that," I said in mock warning.

I wiped my face with the back of my hand, water still running down my neck.

My eyes darted to the drawer by my hand, and in a flash, I pulled out a large stainless steel spatula. Holding it up, I smacked it against my palm menacingly. "I think someone's earned herself a spanking," I declared, trying to sound stern, but the grin breaking through gave away my true amusement.

Samantha's laughter only increased, her hands flying up in a defensive gesture as she leaned back. "Oh, you wouldn't dare!"

Brandishing the spatula, I advanced, a salacious grin on my face. "Wouldn't I?" I teased, closing the distance between us. She tried to scoot backward on the island, squealing when I caged her between my arms and planted my hips against the edge of the counter between her legs.

The chase was short-lived, her laughter fueling my desire. "You're a handful, you know that?"

"And you love it," she said, resting her hands on my waist.

"I do," I admitted, kissing her forehead. "Your shenanigans trigger both my temper and my thirst."

With the spatula still in my hand, I traced her round bottom.

Her eyes widened when she realized my intentions. "You wouldn't—" she began.

"Oh, I would," I said with a wicked grin, giving the side of her ass a sharp swat.

Her lips turned up in a saucy smile. "I'm not one for good behavior, Doctor Thorin."

"Do I need to remind you that you're currently sitting on my kitchen counter and the only thing you're wearing is my shirt?"

I leaned back and tapped the spatula on her thigh. "Hmm, maybe I should spank you with this for all of your transgressions?" Playfully, I slid it under Sam's leg. Her gaze followed the spatula as I brought it around to the front and tapped it on her other leg.

Night Shift

A hint of curiosity gleamed in her eyes. "Spank me? No, I don't think I deserve a spanking," she replied brazenly.

"But it doesn't matter what you think now, does it? You threw a fucking party in my house while I was gone. Yeah, I think you've earned quite a number of spankings—pretty much any time I want to—for that."

Samantha lazily arched an eyebrow, clearly not intimidated. "No, I disagree. Your rude list of house rules, which were ridiculous by the way, means you asked—yes, practically *forced*—me to retaliate."

"Is that so?" I growled, trying to suppress a grin at her audacity. Looking down, I caught sight of her naked pussy peeking out from beneath my T-shirt and couldn't resist running the cool edge of the spatula along her exposed skin, making her shiver and giggle.

"Besides, you need to lighten up and have more fun," she added, pulling the hem of the T-shirt up even further and fully exposing her glistening folds. My resolve crumbled, and I growled again, sliding the edge of the spatula between her legs in quick little flicks, tickling her and making her squirm.

"Okay, okay!" She laughed, trying to catch her breath. "But seriously, that Firebird shouldn't just sit in your garage growing dust. I loved driving it. You know, it's got some kick to it."

My eyes widened in disbelief. "You what?! No one is allowed to touch that car—"

Before I could finish my sentence, Samantha silenced me with a hard, unyielding kiss. Our lips locked, and my anger melted as I gave in to her irresistible charm. Damn, what was happening to me?

I growled and slid my hand between her thighs, finding her clitoris swollen and begging for attention. She shuddered beneath my touch, her breath coming in short, desperate gasps as I teased her mercilessly.

"Tell me, Samantha," I whispered huskily in her ear, my fingers working their magic on her tight bundle of nerves, "do you think this old man can make you come again?"

All she could do was let out a whimper that turned into a groan.

"Fuck, Samantha!" I snarled, then pulled her heels up onto the marble countertop, spreading her legs to reveal her fully to me. I leaned in, breathing in her enticing scent before running my tongue along her slick folds. She tasted like heaven—sweet and tangy—and it drove me fucking insane.

Tossing the spatula aside, I dropped to my knees, burying my face between her thighs and feasting on her like I'd been dying of hunger my entire life. She was intoxicating, like the sweetest nectar, and I couldn't get enough. For a while, I lapped at her folds, teasing her swollen clitoris. Then I slid two fingers inside her, groaning when she clenched around me. I could feel her pulse racing beneath my lips as I sucked and licked at her sensitive flesh.

"Atticus, oh God," she moaned, her fingers gripping my hair as I continued my assault on her pussy. Her body trembled, and I could tell she was close.

"Atticus," she begged, arching her back and grabbing the edge of the countertop. "Oh God, don't stop."

As if I could've stopped even if I wanted to. I was lost in her, drowning in her. I wanted to make her feel good, make her forget the ghosts of her past. Furiously, I tongued her clitoris, twisting my fingers inside her, and listened to her moans turn into whimpers.

"Oh... Oh... I'm going to... I'm..." She panted, unable to get out a complete thought.

"Come for me, Sam," I coaxed, increasing the pace of my tongue, wanting to push her over the edge. "I want to feel you clench around my fingers." I didn't relent until her entire body tensed and she cried out my name, her walls contracting as she shattered. My fingers held her through her orgasm. I only withdrew them when her trembling subsided.

While her breathing slowly returned to normal, I rose from my knees, wiping my lips with the back of my hand. "Still think I'm just a grumpy old doctor, Nurse Sheridan?"

She panted, her eyes heavy with lust. "Oh, you're grumpy, Dr. Thorin, but God are you skilled."

"You'd better get used to this feeling, my little midnight snack," I whispered. "I hope you've got good stamina. After tonight, you might not be able to walk in the morning."

Pulling the board of snacks closer, I grabbed a couple of grapes and placed them in her mouth, grinning wickedly. "You need to hurry up and eat, Samantha. Because I need to fuck you soon, or I'm going to end up with a case of blue balls."

While Samantha munched on the grapes, she kept her playful eyes locked on mine. We devoured the last of the snacks and continued to tease each other about our age difference, debating who had more stamina. She tried to hold her own in our sexually charged conversation, but my years of experience allowed me to fire back with wild threats that made her cheeks turn crimson.

"All right, old man," she teased, wiping her mouth with a kitchen towel. "Let's see if you really have what it takes."

"Ah, but don't forget that I've got extensive expertise on my side," I said, deliberately running my hand up her thigh and brushing my thumb up her folds. "Besides, age has its advantages, darling. Like knowing exactly how to make a woman scream my name."

"Is that so? Well, maybe I'll just have to put your claims to the test."

"Absolutely," I replied.

With that, Samantha sprang off the counter and darted up the stairs. I chucked the cutting board in the sink and followed close behind her.

By the time I got to the staircase, she had reached the top. I paused on the first step, my eyes drawn to the curve of her perfect ass that led down to her slick slit. A primal hunger surged through me; I couldn't wait another moment to devour her again. Tonight, we'd push each other, and I was more than ready for the challenge.

The rest of the night was a blur of steamy encounters, with Samantha and I taking turns exploring each other's bodies. We were insatiable, like starving animals, our moans and cries bouncing off the walls of my bedroom. It was sinful, erotic, and everything we'd ever needed.

Hours later, as the sun rose over the horizon, we surfaced from our passion-fueled haze, drenched in sweat and panting for air. I couldn't remember the last time I'd felt so alive, so free. My world, which had once been black and white, was now full of vibrant hues of red, yellow, and blue, thanks to her.

"I want more," I rumbled, running my fingers down her spine and then tracing the delicate tattoo beneath her breast. "I need more of you, Sammich."

The sun peeked through the blinds, casting its soft golden light on Sam's creamy skin. For a moment, I just lay there and admired her. Our bodies were entwined, exhausted from the hours of powerful physical intimacy we'd just shared. Her red hair was splayed across the pillow, a gorgeous contrast to the white sheets. How had this exquisite, intelligent, trusting—yes, even though she claimed to have never trusted anyone—woman come into my life? I wanted to earn—no, I wanted to *deserve*—her trust.

I squeezed her tightly, drawing her to me and inhaling her unique scent. I didn't want this night to end, but we had to emerge into the real world and deal with things. She was being stalked by what appeared to be the Russian mafia. The injustice of it wrapped around my mind like a suffocating shroud. Sam lay peacefully against me, breathing softly, unaware of the turmoil raging within me. How could I keep her safe when danger lurked in the shadows, threatening to tear her from me?

My thoughts drifted back to the meeting I'd had yesterday with my friend, Colton Davidson, a private detective who lived up in Laurelhurst. The evidence of the attacks, the attempted kidnapping, and the ransacking of her apartment painted a chilling picture of the danger Sam faced, and Colton's grim warnings echoed in my ears. I hadn't found the right moment yet to share any of this with her. How could I burden her with the weight of such terror?

But the truth gnawed at me like a ruthless beast. Ignoring the danger wouldn't make it go away. If anything, it only heightened the peril she was in. The Russian mafia was not to be trifled with, and their continued pursuit of Sam filled me with a paralyzing fear.

I tightened my embrace around her, as if by sheer willpower alone I could shield her from the looming threat. But deep down, I knew it wasn't enough. We were both caught in the crosshairs of forces beyond our control. And as the silence pressed down upon me, I couldn't help but wonder—how long until our luck ran out?

I'd gotten myself all wound up again. Worrying wouldn't help either of us. We both needed a shower and a couple of hours of sleep so we could figure out our next steps.

"Hey, Sam," I whispered, pressing a gentle kiss to her freckled shoulder. "What do you say we go shower? We could both use it."

Her blue eyes fluttered open, and she turned her head to look at me. A tired but satisfied smile graced her full lips. "That sounds lovely, Atticus."

We untangled ourselves and made our way to the bathroom.

Soon, steam billowed out from the showerhead, and we stepped in, the hot water soaking into our spent, sated bodies.

"Here, let me wash your back," Samantha offered, taking the loofah from my hand. I turned around, allowing her access, and relaxed under her tender scrubbing. It was a simple gesture, but it spoke volumes about the connection we were building.

"Thank you, Sammich," I whispered.

After rinsing off, I took the loofah back and lathered it up with her body wash. "Your turn."

Starting with her shoulders and working my way down, I gently cleaned her. When I got to her breasts, I couldn't resist teasing her nipples. This caused her to let out a soft moan, and she shot me a playful glare.

"Atticus, you're incorrigible," she scolded, but a slight grin betrayed her amusement.

"Guilty as charged, beautiful," I replied, taking her in my arms and giving her a chaste kiss. We stayed in the shower for a few more minutes, rinsing off and enjoying the closeness.

Once we were both clean, we turned off the water and stepped out, grabbing towels to dry ourselves. I wrapped my arms around Samantha's waist, pulling her close and stealing another kiss.

"Let's get back to bed," I suggested, the exhaustion finally catching up to me. "We need to grab a catnap if we have any hope of functioning." She nodded, and we made our way back to the bedroom.

I closed the blinds to block out the morning sunlight as best as I could. We both needed rest. Climbing into bed, I pulled Samantha close. Her body fit perfectly against mine. Our breathing synchronized, and before long, we drifted off to sleep.

Chapter Twenty-one

After a night of marathon sex that left every inch of my skin humming, Atticus and I barely managed to rinse off the evidence of our lust before collapsing back into bed. He was out like a light the second his head hit the pillow, snoring softly. Me? Not so much. I lay wide awake, tracing the lines and ridges of his face with the tip of my finger, marveling at the unexpected peacefulness written across his features.

"God, you're something else, Atticus," I whispered. He didn't stir, lost in whatever dreams caught up with a man like him after a night like ours.

He looked different asleep—younger. All the hard edges softened, and the usual furrow between his brows smoothed out. I trailed my fingers over his strong jawline, his slightly crooked nose, and those lips that had left me breathless all night. I had a hard time believing that this was the same man I was so eager to annoy with my rule-breaking. Yesterday, I'd thought I had him pegged, but I hadn't known anything about him really.

Our fight and subsequent hours of passion-fueled sex had given me insight into who the real man was. Yes, there were still some deeply emotional secrets locked away, but I was beginning to understand his *love language*. Most women who knew him probably assumed it was an *acts of physical touch* type. But no, much more than that defined his heart. He was an *acts of service* kind of man. To him, actions spoke louder than words, especially when it came to protecting those he cared about. And as hard as it was for me to fathom, he seemed to care for *me*. Why else would he have sprinted over to my apartment in the middle of the night when I was sure he could have been in the arms of one beautiful OB-GYN?

My hand wandered lower, exploring the contours of his body that had become so familiar yet remained endlessly fascinating. This was new, this feeling of tenderness that welled up inside me as I watched him sleep. For the first time, we were sharing a bed for more than just sex, and it felt…right.

It hit me then how deep I was falling into…whatever this was between us. I'd given myself over to him in ways I'd once sworn I never would, and it scared the crap out of me. This wasn't supposed to have happened. He'd made it clear that relationships weren't his thing, and yet, here we were, tangled up in each other's arms. It was dangerous territory for both of us, given our pasts and our trust issues.

Letting someone hold your heart? That was risky business, and in my experience, it didn't usually turn out well. And yet, here I was, contemplating doing just that with a man who'd never trusted his heart to a woman and had no intention of ever doing so. Except, there had been that slip-up—that "We can't hide our relationship" comment. And he'd mentioned wanting to try an exclusive situation on a trial basis. It sounded a lot like a relationship to me. Something told me Dr. Atticus Thorin didn't throw around those kinds of words often. And dammit, I wanted it just as much as I feared it.

My gaze lingered on his face, taking in the softness that sleep brought to his rugged features. "You make it hard to keep up my walls, Dr. Thorin," I whispered.

Atticus and I were cut from the same cloth. We were survivors of childhoods that had taught us we could be hurt by those we loved. Yet here I was, watching him sleep, feeling a pull towards him that went beyond physical attraction.

I lay back down, resting my head on the pillow and keeping my attention focused on his peaceful face. This was a man who'd seen me at my most vulnerable, who'd held me as I came apart and then put me back together again, piece by piece.

My thoughts drifted to the little box I'd sneakily taken from his closet earlier. Guilt gnawed at me. I shouldn't have taken it, but curiosity had gotten the better of me. Opening it would be crossing a line, and I realized that was a line I didn't want to cross anymore. The last thing I wanted was to shatter the fragile trust we were building.

As I lay there curled up beside him, I allowed myself to imagine what it would be like to wake up like this every day. No fears, no walls, just the two of us. The more time I spent with him, the more I wanted to stay—not only in his bed but in his life.

Lost in my thoughts, I didn't notice Atticus stir until he wrapped his arm around me and pulled me against his chest. His warmth enveloped me, his heartbeat thumping steadily under my ear. We breathed quietly for a few moments until a soft snore came from him, and I realized he hadn't fully awoken. "Sam," he mumbled in his sleep, his hold on me tightening. That one word, my name on his lips, even in sleep, was enough to make my heart do a stupid little flip. The truth was, this man was getting to me, breaking down walls I hadn't ever thought I wanted to be torn down.

And just like that, with his steady heartbeat as my lullaby, I drifted off to sleep, a happy smile curving my lips. For the first time in a long time, I felt safe, truly safe.

"Rise and shine, sleepyhead," Atticus whispered in my ear. Slowly, I woke up, finding myself still wrapped tightly in his arms. His fingers glided up and down my back and shoulder in tender lines.

"Ugh," I groaned, feeling the soreness between my legs from our untamed, passionate night. "Feels like my girlie bits are on fire."

Atticus chuckled. "Well, you are young and tender. But don't worry, I'll take care of you."

"I might be sore, but you're the one who passed out the moment your head hit the pillow."

"Can you blame me?" he asked, grinning. "You wore me out." He pushed up onto his side and turned to look at me. The furrow between his brows deepened. "How about a long soak in the tub to ease those sore muscles and other—what did you call them—girlie bits?"

Huffing a laugh, I reflexively squeezed my legs together, thinking about all we'd done. "Yes, girlie bits and places I didn't even know could ache. Oh, and a hot bath sounds heavenly." I started to pull the sheet off but then hesitated. I glanced down at my naked body, exposed to the light of day, and was suddenly overcome with shyness. "I'm not exactly dressed for company," I mumbled self-consciously.

"There's no need to be embarrassed, Sam. It's just me, and I've seen everything you've got. I probably know your body better than you do."

Placing a hand over my face, I grinned and shook my head. He was right. After everything he'd done to me, he owned my body, and there would be no going back from that.

When I finally got out of bed, every muscle in my body protested. I still hadn't fully recovered from the attack in the parking lot, and now I had a fresh set of marks. Of course, I had to admit that I'd fully enjoyed getting these.

Together, we made our way to the bathroom. He started filling the tub for me.

His unexpected tenderness caught me off guard, and I leaned in and kissed him sweetly, whispering, "Thank you" against his lips.

Gingerly I sat on the edge of the tub and watched the water rise. My cautious movements caused Atticus to chuckle. "We may have to wait a day or two before we go at it again."

He turned to his vanity, picked up a bottle, and held it out. "Did you like my cologne?"

"Ooo, yes..." I replied, remembering the scent but forgetting when I'd smelled it until it was too late and my words were already out.

"Strange," he mused, raising a suspicious eyebrow. "Because I've never worn it around you. How do you know what it smells like?"

"Uh, well..."

"Sam, you'd make a terrible spy. You can't even cover your tracks," he said half-jokingly.

"Hey, at least I didn't touch anything else or let anyone else into your bedroom!" I protested, although that wasn't entirely true. But now was not the time to mention the little chest I'd taken.

He gave a gentle chuckle, but it wasn't done in a mocking way. It was more like he found the whole situation amusing. "Out of habit, I always put things in the same place. There aren't any little chaos creators toddling about, so everything always stays exactly as I left it." He placed the bottle back on the counter and added, "I noticed it wasn't in its usual spot. Look, I don't mind that you were curious, but honesty is important to me. Why did you feel you had to go into my room when I specifically asked you not to and had gone to the trouble of locking my door?"

Desperate to change the subject, I added bubble bath to the tub and turned on the jets, creating a foamy, bubbling commotion. But Atticus wasn't distracted. Reaching over, he turned my face toward him and prompted me to tell the truth.

"I was curious about you," I said. "I wanted to know more about the man behind the doctor's facade. And well, there was a part of me that just wanted to do it because you told me not to. Childish, I guess."

"Thank you for being honest, but remember, that's just one more reason for me to spank you." He winked at me and gave me a quick kiss on the top of my head.

I slipped into the bubble-filled sanctuary, submerging my body in the almost-too-hot water. "Promises, promises," I shot back, trying to keep the mood light despite the guilt that was churning inside of me for not confessing about the chest. "Hey, can you hand me the loofah?" I asked, stretching my arm out. Atticus reached into the shower and turned to hand it to me but then stopped, taking my arm in his hand.

"Those stitches are more than ready to be removed. How about I take care of that today?" All at once, his features shifted into his doctor's mask, and he started examining my arm. His brows pulled together, and a strange darkness descended over his face. It was the same expression he'd had when putting in the sutures after the attack. He gently ran his thumb along the skin next to them, lost in thought. Then, squeezing his eyes shut, he leaned over, took my cheek in his hand, and kissed my forehead, lingering against it as he took a deep breath. When he pulled away, I could have sworn his skin had turned ashen.

"I'll go make us some coffee and breakfast," he offered quietly, even though it was probably closer to lunchtime. "You soak. Relax. Let me take care of you."

With a nod, I sank deeper into the bubbles and let out a contented sigh, not wanting to reveal the worry that had crawled up my chest. I wondered if he'd ever be able to trust me enough to share the memory my arm evoked. Whatever was happening between us, I was here for it, prepared to wait patiently for him to open his heart to me.

epping out of the shower, I wrapped a towel around my body and another around my head. It had taken me forever to figure out how to work his shower on my own, but eventually I'd been able to wash and condition my hair. The steam curled around me as I wiped away the condensation on the mirror. My hair was a tangled mess, and my face had that just-bathed flush. After a bit of work blow-drying and a touch of makeup, I almost looked like my world hadn't been turned upside down. Dressed in a towel, I headed to the guest room, still marveling at how quickly my life had shifted since I'd moved to Tacoma.

When I stepped into the room, I noticed a box wrapped in a bow sitting on the bed. Curious, I picked it up and opened it to find a lululemon outfit—a dark heather long-sleeve top and black leggings. The size was spot on. I was stunned. The thoughtfulness, the extravagance—it was unlike anything I'd ever experienced. Eagerly I slipped into the outfit, admiring the way it fit me like a glove. The leggings sculpted my legs and, yes, made my butt look amazing.

I headed downstairs, following the mouthwatering scent wafting through the air. My stomach growled as I walked into the kitchen to find Atticus hovering over a beautifully prepared breakfast of waffles, homemade whipped cream, strawberries, scrambled eggs, and bacon.

"You went all out," I said.

He shrugged. "Gotta make sure you start the day right, even if it is two in the afternoon."

"Atticus, this is...wow." I crossed the distance and wrapped my arms around him, pulling him in for a big, grateful kiss. "Thank you."

He grinned, clearly charmed by my enthusiasm.

"Oh, and thank you for the outfit," I said, spinning around. "It's perfect. You didn't need to do this."

He chuckled, giving me a playful once-over. "I got it for you yesterday while I was out. I knew it would make your ass look fantastic." Playfully, he smacked my backside.

"Hey!" I laughed, swatting his hand away but secretly loving the compliment. "You're terrible." My lips twisted into a teasing frown, but I wasn't able to hide my delight.

We sat down to eat. The food tasted even more delicious than it smelled. Between mouthfuls, we chatted casually, but I could tell there was something on Atticus's mind.

When we had both finished, he grew serious. I could tell by the deep furrow between his brows that he was concerned about something. We were about to tread into deeper waters. I braced myself.

"So, while you were busy throwing a rave in my house," he began, raising a brow and shooting me a *you know exactly what you did* look, "I was actually out trying to help you." Guilt pinched at me, but before I could let it get to me, he waved it off with a chuckle, moving on to the meat of the conversation.

"I met with an old college buddy of mine, Colton Davidson, who lives up in Laurelhurst. He's a big deal in the private investigator world and owns a security firm. Colton agreed with me that it must be the Russian mafia who's after you. They're the only organized crime in this area who'd think they could kidnap a nurse right out front of a hospital. He thinks they're a serious threat to you. Honestly, he was surprised you survived the kidnapping attempt and believes the attack on your apartment was a message."

"A message? Why?"

"The Russian mafia doesn't fuck around." Atticus's face tightened with worry as he drew his thumb across his lower lip. "He thinks your dad is the reason they're after you because of his connections to drug trafficking, which was my first thought too."

"My dad? But that doesn't make any sense. Why would they come after me for something *he* did?"

For a minute, he seemed lost in thought, then said, "Most likely to force Mac to bend to their will or to settle a score. Who knows, but I saw the desperation for money in your dad's eyes when he confronted you outside your apartment. Colton's pretty sure that now that they've made a move and tipped off the cops, they'll try to take you out...and maybe even go after anyone close to you too."

My hand flew to my mouth as I gasped. It was one thing to be some bad guy's target, but it was a wholly different one for Atticus and my friends to be put in the crosshairs of mafia thugs.

"Hey," he said, reaching across the table and taking my hands in his, "I swear on my life, I will protect you."

The reality of how serious and dangerous my situation was hit me full force, and tears blurred my vision. "So what do I do? I just...I can't go back to my normal life, but I can't stay here knowing I'm putting you in danger too."

"You're not going anywhere. Not until we figure out how to get them off your back. You still have a week before the hospital expects you back, so you're going to sit tight right here. If Mac owes them money, then I might be able to negotiate a deal. At the end of the day, I don't think they want to draw that kind of attention to themselves."

"But Atticus, you know I don't have any money, and there's no way I'm letting you waste your money on something like this."

"Samantha, trust me, I can handle this."

"You know I don't trust anyone!" I shouted, even though it was a lie. I'd already given him not only my trust but also my heart. But under the circumstances, it was better for him to not know that. It would be better for him to not have anything to do with me at all. This thing with my father reminded me that I had too much baggage.

He squeezed my hands, his gaze unwavering. "There's one more thing I need to tell you. To put your mind a little more at ease, I had a crew clean up your apartment. It's back to how it was when you moved in. I also had a conversation with the leasing manager and pointed out several violations with the building, and he was more than happy to let you out of your lease. Don't be mad, Sammich, but you know you can't go back there. I want you to stay with me until we can sort all of this out. I can help keep you safe, and you know that."

I blinked, trying to process everything. "What about all my stuff?"

"Anything salvageable will be here tonight or be put in storage. You haven't lost everything."

I was overwhelmed by the great lengths he was going to in order to protect me. My life had become such a mess in such a short time. It made my head spin.

"How can I ever thank you?" My hands began to tremble, and he pulled one to his mouth, placing a soft kiss on my knuckles. "I'll never be able to repay you. This isn't fair to you. Maybe I should leave and go somewhere far away."

I was spiraling, and if I didn't pull myself together, a full-blown panic attack would ensue.

"You don't have to thank me. I'm doing this because I care about you. We're in this together, okay?"

"God, my life's gone completely off the rails," I muttered.

My breathing hitched, and I couldn't stop shaking. The information overload and the reality of my situation hit me like a truck. Mafia? My dad? It was too much to process. Atticus, noticing my distress, stood up, pulling me into a hug.

"Just breathe," he said softly. "I'm here. I promise you, Samantha, everything's going to be okay. I've got you and will keep you safe."

"Okay," I whispered, trying to believe him.

Shifting the conversation, he suggested, "Let's get those stitches out, huh? They've got to be bothering you, and it's time they came out. It won't take but a minute, and then we'll chill the rest of the day and maybe binge-watch something on Netflix."

He took his plate to the sink, and I followed suit.

After placing a soft kiss on the top of my head, he said, "How about you start rinsing off the dishes and putting them in the dishwasher while I go find what I need to take care of that arm?"

"Sure," I agreed, welcoming anything—even the removal of my stitches—that would help me to take my mind off the Russian mafia and my dad's potential involvement.

He retrieved a medical kit from a room down the hallway and returned, laying out sterile scissors, antiseptic wipes, tweezers, sterile pads, and tape with practiced ease. "Let's do this on the island. There's better light there," he said, slipping into his role as a doctor.

As I settled onto a barstool, I watched Atticus carefully and again noticed a shift in his demeanor. Each time he had to deal with my arm, he would become this quiet, almost withdrawn version of himself. It was like he was somewhere else, lost in a memory that caused him pain. What tragic secrets was he hiding?

"Atticus," I said softly as he began removing the stitches, "you don't have to keep everything bottled up. You can trust me, you know. Whatever it is that makes you react this way to my injury, I want to help."

He didn't look up, focusing on the task at hand, but the tension in his shoulders relaxed a fraction. "I know, Sam. Just old memories."

He paused for a moment, his winter gray eyes searching mine. Then he resumed his work, his fingers steady as they removed the last of the stitches. After cleaning the area with an antiseptic wipe, he applied a fresh bandage and secured it with tape. When he finished, he looked up at me, his expression unreadable.

I remained seated on the stool while he poured us both coffee and added a little cream to mine. He picked up the remote sitting on the counter and turned the TV on. We moved to the sofa, a comfortable silence settling between us. While we sat there, cups in hand, I realized how much I wanted to break through his walls. I hoped someday he would trust me with his past as much as I had come to trust him with my future.

For the dozenth time, I thought back to how he had reacted when he'd seen the cut on my arm after the attack in the hospital parking lot. Why was he struggling with this? I was certain he'd seen this type of thing often and so much worse.

The room was quiet, and it was the kind of silence that wrapped around you, thick and almost tangible. For several minutes I sat and watched him, scrutinizing the lines of his face. Would he open up to me and tell me about the demons that haunted him? Earlier, I thought I'd seen a crack in his armor, but now I wasn't so sure.

After a long while, he set his cup on the table and stretched his arms out along the back of the sofa.

"Talk to me," I urged, gently snuggling up inside the crook of his arm. "Tell me why this...why it upsets you so much." I rubbed a hand over the fresh bandage he'd applied.

Atticus released a slow exhale that seemed to carry the weight of years within it. He looked away and then moved to sit forward, resting his elbows on his knees and dropping his head. "My mother," he began, and his voice was different now—more open, raw even. "She became an alcoholic, probably before I was born, likely because of my father. He was...a cold, unemotional bastard who always made work his priority—not us, not her. He wasn't the type to play catch in the backyard, leaving all parental duties to her."

I remained silent, giving him the space to continue, to share the story that pained him so much to tell.

"I was thirteen... Braxton was ten, Conan just six." He took another long breath. "I remember that day as if it were yesterday. Every detail is carved into my very soul with a clarity that time has failed to dull. I was just a kid coming home from school, tossing my backpack aside without a care in the world. The house was too quiet, eerily so. I called out for my mother, expecting to hear her call down from upstairs in return, but there was nothing. That silence...it was the first sign that something was horribly wrong.

"After searching the house, I found her in the bathroom. The scene before me unfolded in a series of snapshots that I wish...I wish I could erase from my memory."

At this point, Atticus struggled to continue but finally said, "Water filled the tub, but it wasn't clear; it was tainted with blood—a deep, dark red that swirled on the bottom like dark clouds on the verge of a storm, while vivid red rivulets flowed through the clearer water like puffs of smoke. My mother's body was limp, her skin pale in contrast to her blood. She was nude, exposed, and so very still. Her wrists... God, her wrists were like a nightmare come to life." He sank his hands into his hair and shook his head as he relived the graphic memory.

"Time seemed to stop, to stretch into infinity as I stared at her, my mind refusing to accept what my eyes were seeing. It was as if I was outside of my body, watching someone else's horror story unfold. But the cold, hard truth crashed into me, dragging me back to my sickening reality.

"I remember the sheer panic, the primal instinct to save her. Dragging her out of the tub was like trying to move a mountain. She was my mom, but in that moment, she was dead weight. Her body slipped from my grasp as I tried desperately to pull her to safety. Water splashed onto the floor, mixing with her blood. It was everywhere.

"My pants were soaked by the time I managed to get her out, the blood staining the fabric—marking me. I ran to the phone, and my hands were shaking so violently I could barely dial nine-one-one. My voice shook as I begged for help, for someone to come and save my mom.

"The operator's instructions were a lifeline in the chaos, forcing me to focus—to be in control. I grabbed towels, wrapping them around her wrists, pressing down with all my strength, trying to stem the tide of blood that seemed determined to take her from me. It was all I could do, all that was within my power, and it was so woefully inadequate.

"When the EMTs arrived, they pushed me aside. They were so professional and calm, and unlike me, they knew just what to do. I watched, helpless, as they worked on her, as they loaded her onto the gurney and wheeled her away. I was left standing at the open door.

"I didn't know if I'd ever see her again. That uncertainty was like a crushing weight that threatened to suffocate me. I was alone, utterly alone, standing on the front porch, my hands still stained with her blood. And when I looked down, when I really saw the evidence of what had just happened, my stomach revolted. I vomited, my body purging the terror and the helplessness that had consumed me.

"I was thankful, in a way, that Braxton and Conan weren't home." He swallowed hard, the words barely making it past the lump in his throat. "The last thing I wanted was for them to see... that. After the ambulance took my mother, I was desperate to erase any trace of what had happened. I scrubbed the bathroom until my hands were raw, trying to wash away the horror, and threw away my clothes, not wanting any physical reminder of the day. But then, the dread of having to explain it all to Braxton and Conan loomed over me. I knew our father, with his hard-ass nature, wouldn't offer the sensitivity they needed. They were just kids, and I...I felt this overwhelming need to protect them, to shield them from the worst of it. It's funny, looking back... I guess that was the moment I started down the path to becoming a doctor. I just wanted to care for them, to make sure they never felt as helpless and scared as I did when I found her."

The pain in Atticus's voice carved a hollow in my chest, and the way his hands clenched as he spoke was heart-wrenching. I rubbed my hand over his back in a silent gesture of support.

"It was awful, the worst thing I've ever experienced," he whispered. "Finding her like that—I can't fully describe it."

My heart broke for him, for the boy who had faced such a traumatic scene, for the family that had been shattered by a moment's desperation, and for the man who carried that burden with him still.

"There's more," he said after a pause, his gaze drifting away as if he was peering into the dark corridors of time where those painful memories lurked. "She survived, but...she was never the same. My father became even more distant—if that was possible. And my mother, she just...drank herself into oblivion and isolated herself from us even more after the attempt. Two years later, she died from alcohol poisoning."

The sorrow in his voice, the loss he had experienced at such a young age tore at me.

"My father..." he added, "he didn't even act like he cared that she was gone."

Sitting there, witnessing the unraveling of Atticus's soul, tears pricked at the corners of my eyes—not only because of the tragedy of his mother's life and death but because of the profound effect her actions had on Atticus and his brothers. The man before me, always so in control, the man who always had all the answers, had been shaped by these events, wounded by them in profound ways.

Night Shift

After listening to his story, I understood so much more about who he was, about the walls he had built and the reasons he'd built them. This was a pivotal moment because I finally understood the depth of Atticus's emotional scars and now realized why the bond that had formed between us was so strong. It had been forged in the crucible of shared pain.

While he continued to stare at the space between his feet, he took a steadying breath, the kind that heralds the continuation of a story.

"A little more than a year after my mother passed, my father died from a widow-maker heart attack," he said with an undercurrent of unresolved grief. "I'd just turned sixteen and suddenly found myself thrust into the role of parent for Braxton and Conan. Technically, my grandmother was our guardian and tried to help as much as she could, but she was old and frail. So it all fell on my shoulders."

My heart ached for the young Atticus. He'd had to grow up too quickly to shoulder burdens no child should have to bear. Tears welled up in my eyes.

"Taking care of my brothers, I did the best I could. I love them more than anything, you know?" There was pride and an undeniable love in his voice. "After college, I joined the navy and trained to become a doctor. I felt guilty for leaving, but I knew I needed to make a decent living to support them."

He scraped a hand through his hair. Although the choice he had made was an act of profound love and sacrifice, it was clear he harbored quite a lot of guilt because of it. His words painted a picture of a man who had been shaped by trauma yet was determined to forge a path of healing not only for himself but for his brothers.

I leaned back on the sofa a little, sweeping away the tears with the back of my hand before he could notice them.

"Being helpless...it terrified me. I became a doctor because I never wanted to feel that way again and wanted to make things better. I thought if I couldn't save my mom, at least I might have a chance of saving someone else.

"I've never wanted to let someone in before. I guess I've been afraid of experiencing that abandonment all over again," he admitted.

While he shared the pain of feeling unwanted and unloved by his own parents, it became heartbreakingly clear why he feared getting close to anyone or forming lasting attachments.

He sat back and turned to look at me. Unable to stop my tears, I kept my head down; he wasn't the kind of man who wanted anyone's pity. But hiding my emotions had never been my strong suit. He hooked a finger under my chin and lifted it so that I would meet his gaze.

"But you...you're different, Samantha. You understand my pain and loss in a way no other woman ever has."

After Atticus said this, he bit back the tears welling in his eyes, a silent testament to the years of pain he'd kept bottled up. Guilt gnawed at me for crying so profusely when he couldn't allow himself to do so at all.

But, truth be told, he was right. I could understand him, maybe more than anyone else ever would. The parallels between our lives, the shared traumas of parental loss and neglect, connected us, gave us an unspoken understanding that went beyond words or tears.

He knew of my past, of the shadows that followed me from my own family's history of violence and addiction. I was glad now that I'd chosen to open up to him and share my life story during our hike.

Night Shift

As his story had unfolded, the walls he'd meticulously built around himself began to crumble, revealing the raw, unguarded heart of a man who had carried too much for too long.

And then something shifted. Atticus, the man who had always held himself with such rigid control, broke.

In that moment, he took a leap of faith I felt certain he'd never taken before—he laid bare the full extent of his anguish, trusting me with it completely. He moved closer, wrapping me in a tight embrace, and pressed his face into the crook of my neck. His chest shook with suppressed sobs, a single sniff breaking through as he clung to the last threads of his composure. We stayed locked in that embrace for what seemed like an eternity until he finally took a deep, shaky breath. Then, with a tenderness that spoke volumes, he turned and planted a soft kiss on the tender spot beneath my ear.

He trusted me.

There on that sofa as I held him, an overwhelming sense of protectiveness overcame me. My tears flowed freely. This was about more than just sharing our past sufferings; it was a time of healing, a coming together of two souls who had weathered their storms and found solace in each other's arms.

It was a trust I vowed to honor, to cherish, and to never take for granted. We had found something rare—a connection forged not only in shared pain but in the hope of what could be.

Chapter Twenty-two

After Atticus's heart-wrenching revelations, we took a moment to collect ourselves, letting the intensity of our conversation settle. The news playing on the TV was an easy distraction, so we sat in silence, sipping on our coffee and watching. We couldn't dwell in that emotional space all day. So we decided we needed a change of scenery and got up from the sofa to go for a walk around the neighborhood park.

Atticus and I were running on empty as we dragged ourselves through the door. The last couple of days had been an emotional rollercoaster. I was sure I actually did look like a member of *The Walking Dead* at this point. When I caught a glimpse of myself in the hallway mirror, I almost didn't recognize the zombie staring back. Meanwhile, Atticus annoyingly still looked like he'd stepped out of a magazine.

We walked for a while, chatting and making our way around the corner of the park where there was a playground. There were a couple of little kids at the swingset, getting pushed by their moms while an older man tossed a frisbee for his dog. It was all so normal...except for the feeling I was being watched. I studied the edges of the park but didn't notice anyone who was behaving unusually. Maybe I was overly tired and being paranoid.

"You know," Atticus said, catching yet another yawn of mine, "you just need to give it a few years in the ED, and you'll be as tough as me." He flashed a cocky little grin that was equal parts teasing and proud.

He'd been on a roll for our entire walk, making snarky comments about the fragility of people my age.

"Oh, please." I rolled my eyes. "As if that has anything to do with it. Nooo, it wouldn't have anything to do with you fucking me six ways to Sunday."

At that, he burst into genuine laughter, his eyes heating as they swept over me.

He'd been in a strangely good mood since we started our walk. Our heart-to-heart had been cathartic, like hitting a reset button. And when he had suggested we take a walk through the neighborhood park, it felt like we were finally breathing easier, finding a slice of normalcy in the whirlwind of the last few days.

"Need I remind you again to never roll your eyes at me? There are consequences for that, you know." The smirk on his face sent warmth to my most intimate places, reminding me how sore I was from the sexy doctor who now stood at the center of my life.

While we continued to walk, he held my hand. We meandered along the path, chatting about everything and nothing. It was the most uneventful yet oddly comforting time we'd shared. It was a much-needed reprieve we both needed.

On our way back, Newton, the neighbor's black-and-white shih tzu, bounded up to us, wagging his tail like he was trying to take off. Amused, I scooped him up, and his little body vibrated with excitement as I scratched behind his ears and waved to the neighbor lady.

When Atticus reached out to pet him, Newton responded with enthusiastic licks, prompting me to tease, "Looks like he's decided you've worked through your demons and you're friend material now."

In return, Atticus shot me a look that screamed, "Really?" but the corner of his mouth twitched up in a smile. Clearly, Newton's seal of approval meant more to him than he wanted to admit.

Once we got back to his place, we both sank into the couch, exhausted and content.

"Why don't you pick something for us to watch?" Atticus suggested, handing me the remote with a gentle nudge. "Anything you want."

I scrolled through Netflix, landing on the holiday section. "How about a Christmas movie marathon? It's the perfect time for it, right?"

He chuckled, nodding in agreement. "Sounds like a plan to me."

While I cued up the first movie, Atticus got on his phone to order us some food. "Hope you're in the mood for sushi. I went all out—salmon nigiri, a rainbow roll, some spicy tuna. I even got us some tempura veggies."

My stomach immediately responded with a rumble. "That sounds amazing. Can't wait."

With the movie playing and our food on the way, a cozy silence enveloped us. It was comfortable and easy. But there was one thing that I'd been curious about. "So, why don't you have a TV in your bedroom? Any reason for that?"

Night Shift

He paused the movie, then turned to me with a thoughtful expression. "You know how you told me you didn't want to use your phone during our hike? Wanting to be in the moment? I feel the same about having a TV in the bedroom. It's about making those moments count, not getting distracted by screens."

I smiled, appreciating our similarity. It was one of the things I admired about him—his ability to be present, especially in the bedroom.

The conversation naturally drifted to Christmas, inspired by the festive movies we were watching. "I've been meaning to ask, why haven't you put up any Christmas decorations?" I said.

Atticus sighed. "I haven't celebrated Christmas in years. It just...hasn't been the same since I was a kid, and even then, it wasn't a huge thing."

"Christmas used to be everything to me. My mom and I would decorate the tree and bake cookies. Our house was always full of music—that is, up until she passed... After that, it just wasn't the same. My dad couldn't stand the sight of decorations, and of course, everything changed."

He turned to face me, eyebrows arched, his head slightly tilted in silent curiosity about where this was leading.

"Well, so, this year, I was super excited to decorate and fix up my place for the holidays, since I'd just moved to Tacoma and all. Especially since it's my first Christmas away from Aberdeen. I had all these plans for a fresh start, you know? Then my apartment got ransacked, and now that I'm your...guest, I was curious if you were going to decorate or anything."

Atticus reached over, took my foot in his hand, and began massaging it. "I don't have any Christmas decorations, but I got a call from the cleanup crew. They'll be bringing your stuff home tomorrow. They just need a bit more time. Maybe some of your decorations survived."

Hearing him say they were bringing my things "home"—like it was *my* home too—sparked something hopeful inside me. It felt like a promise, a beginning.

"But I'll be honest with you, Sammich. I haven't celebrated holidays in years, nor have I given it any thought. Not sure how I feel about you decorating this place," he admitted, frowning slightly.

I let out a sigh and slumped my shoulders, not hiding my disappointment. "But decorating could be fun. It's about making the place festive. It's about making it feel homey."

For a few minutes we went back and forth debating it. I tried to convince him how fun celebrating Christmas could be, but he continued to express his doubts. "I'll think about it," he finally conceded. "Let's not worry about it tonight."

Our food arrived, and we feasted on it, not letting a bite go to waste. We laughed so hard at the fried pussycat scene in *Christmas Vacation* that I almost peed myself. As the evening wore on, with Christmas movies playing in the background, we found ourselves relaxing and drifting off. With the movies still running, we nestled closer on the couch, eventually falling asleep snug and warm, fitting perfectly together. It was all we needed for the moment.

Over the next four days, life at Atticus's place took on a rhythm that was both comforting and surreal. Atticus had decided to take some time off work. It would allow him to stick close by my side and help me work through the tangled mess I'd been thrust into.

Turned out, life in lockdown with Atticus wasn't half bad. When we weren't all over each other's bodies, having sex on practically every surface, we spent our time digging for answers

Night Shift

about the Russians, piecing together what little we knew and trying to understand why they were after me. Here in his townhouse, we were in our own safe little bubble, away from the danger lurking outside. It was a brief respite, a chance to breathe before facing whatever came next.

The cleanup crew had finally brought over what was left of my belongings. It felt good to have my things nearby. Among the boxes, I found my Christmas decorations intact—a small victory. But Atticus's holiday spirit was still lacking, so I couldn't bring myself to break out the ornaments and lights. It didn't seem right, not with everything else we were dealing with. Despite my longing to get a tree and fill the house with holiday cheer, I kept the decorations packed away, trying to be mindful of his aversion to celebrating. The last thing I wanted was to stir up any more turmoil.

Atticus was all about ramping up the security, his concern for my safety morphing into action as he bolstered his home's already impressive security system. There was something in the way he went about it—double-checking locks, installing new cameras—that was all very *Mission: Impossible*. He made me feel safe, and I believed his promise that I'd be okay when he returned to work tomorrow.

But as much as I trusted him, the thought of him walking out that door, leaving me alone, cast a dark shadow over my mood. I'd enjoyed us being glued to each other's side night and day, and I didn't want to return to reality.

When the day finally arrived for him to go back on shift, I woke up with a heavy heart. The morning light filtered softly through the blinds, casting a gentle glow across the bed that did nothing to lift my dark mood.

Atticus leaned in, his lips meeting my forehead in a tender kiss that lingered longer than usual. "I'll be back before you know it," he murmured, his voice wrapping around me like a warm blanket.

He pulled back, and the familiar worry over him leaving settled in my chest even before he'd gotten out of bed. Despite the layers of protection he'd put into place, I couldn't shake the feeling that something bad was going to happen.

Atticus must have noticed my worried expression because he cupped my chin gently, turning my face toward him. "Hey," he whispered, giving me that lopsided smile that always seemed to reach right through me, "this place is Fort Knox. The security system is top-notch. You're safe here." Though his words were meant to reassure me, to ease my anxiety, they didn't.

"But if anything—anything at all—feels off, give me a call at the hospital, okay? I mean it, Samantha."

I nodded, managing a smile that I hoped would convince him I wasn't falling apart on the inside. "I will. Don't worry about me; I'll be fine," I promised. I kept my voice steady, even as a whirlwind of unease churned inside me.

Atticus studied me for a moment and then leaned over, sliding his fingers through my hair to the back of my head. "God, you're gorgeous first thing in the morning. Fuck," he growled, twisting his fingers in my hair. He crushed his lips against mine in a searing kiss. It was the type of kiss I'd learned meant he didn't allow for any other thoughts than what he was doing to my body. It was the type of kiss that instantly got my juices flowing. As his tongue commanded my attention, he took my hand and placed it against my heated core. Then he guided my fingers over my clitoris, capturing my moans in his mouth as together we stroked the tight bundle of nerves. Slowly he pulled his lips away from mine and gave me a cocky grin while together we continued to move over my drenched folds. His fingers guided mine within. "Now you be my good girl and finish yourself off. I've gotta get a shower and get out of here." With that, he chuckled and pulled his hand away. "I expect to hear your satisfaction over the running water. You wouldn't want to disappoint me first thing in the morning, now would you?" A quick kiss later, he slid out of bed and walked away whistling.

Pleasing the man had become my addiction. I swear he could ask me to walk through fire and I would. But right now, the fire I needed to stoke was under my hand. Now that I was completely distracted from my earlier gloom, I had a feisty idea. Reaching over for my phone, I took a video of what he was missing. Yes, that would come in handy. I would send it to him when he was driving to work. I made sure to put on a show and that he heard exactly what he'd asked for.

Not long after, as I lingered under the warm covers, the front door closed with a thud and a click, sealing me inside, and I was alone.

Chapter Twenty-three

The morning started off better than I'd hoped. I made coffee and something to eat before showering and putting on a bright blue workout set. It was one of my favorites because it didn't clash with my hair and it brought out my blue eyes. It wasn't posh like the one Atticus had given me—because on my budget I was lucky to buy dupes—but I still loved it nonetheless. I had no plans for working out but needed something cheerful and comfortable to wear if I was going to be stuck here all day, bored out of my mind.

The silence in Atticus's house grated on my last nerve. For a while I tried to lose myself in one of the many books that lined the shelves of his living room, but the words seemed to blur together, my thoughts constantly drifting to the events of the past few weeks. Regardless of the difficulty I was having concentrating, I kept trying to read, if only to pass the time, but ended up scrolling through TikTok on my phone while it perched in the center of the book.

It was nearing midmorning when the first stirrings of unease began to take root. A faint, almost imperceptible noise from outside disrupted the stillness, pulling my attention away from the pages in front of me. I strained my ears, trying to identify the sound, telling myself it was only the wind, or perhaps a neighbor going about their day.

Then a scraping noise cut through the silence. It was coming from the back porch. I grabbed my phone, dropped the book, and sprinted to the tablet on the kitchen counter, tapping furiously on the security app. "Come on, come on," I murmured, paranoia bubbling up as I flicked through the camera feeds—front yard, side alley, back patio.

Nothing but the calm, undisturbed exterior of Atticus's home filled the screen.

"Seriously? I must be losing it," I whispered to myself. The tranquility of the scene outside clashed with the adrenaline pumping through my veins. In an attempt to slow my racing heart, I took a deep breath. All of a sudden, a *thud*—louder and closer this time—jolted me.

"No way that was just the wind," I muttered, abandoning the tablet. Quickly I scanned the kitchen, my eyes landing on the sturdy cast iron frying pan. It was better than nothing, I decided, picking it up and gripping it with both hands.

I tiptoed toward the back door, attempting to be stealthy. With each step, the floor beneath me creaked, the noise amplified in the silence. When I reached the door, I pressed my ear against it and tried to catch any hint of sound from the other side.

Silence.

Then, I detected the faintest scrape, like metal against concrete. It sent an icy wave down my spine, and I backed away, my heart thumping against my ribs like it wanted out. This was definitely not good. Keeping my eyes locked on the back door, I inched toward the kitchen and soon reached the island. The tablet lit up with a notification. A motion had been detected at the back perimeter. "Great," I huffed, taking a closer look at the screen. The camera feed showed the edge of the garden, but whoever, or whatever, had caused the noise remained just out of view.

I was just about to dismiss it, chalk it up to nerves, when a shadow darted across the screen. My breath caught. This was really happening.

Grabbing the tablet and the pan, I retreated to the safest room I could think of—Atticus's office. It had a lock and a window I could escape from if needed. I darted inside and locked the door behind me, my hands shaking as I dialed Atticus's number, praying he'd pick up.

"Come on, Atticus," I begged into the phone, waiting for him to answer. Each ring was unbearably loud in the quiet room, stabbing into my ears and amplifying my fear. Then his voicemail picked up. His hands were most likely tied up with who knew what kind of chaos in the ED. My fingers fumbling, I quickly typed out a message, telling him that I was hiding in his office while someone was trying to break into his house. Ignoring all the typos I'd made in my haste, I sent the text and shared my location, hoping that might help if these people ended up taking me. I shoved my phone into the pocket on my leg and zipped it closed.

Crack! Glass shattered near the back of the house, and the splintering of wood made my heart skip a beat. They were breaking in. The back door gave way with a thunderous crash

Night Shift

that echoed down the hallway. Boots hit the floor, heavy and fast, spreading throughout the house.

More invaders poured in. Their movements sounded purposeful, like a well-oiled machine. More crashes and bangs of destruction followed—things breaking, furniture being overturned. They tore through Atticus's home with ruthless efficiency. The neighbor's dog started barking frantically, adding to the chaos of the moment.

It was time for me to try to escape through the window. I carefully peeked outside, only to find there was a guy dressed in black just to the right. There was nowhere for me to go. The sounds grew closer, louder. They were storming through the house in a wave of violence. My breath caught, and every muscle tensed for the inevitable.

All I could do was wait, trapped, while they moved closer and closer to my hiding place. The office door loomed as my last barrier.

As I stood there frozen, indecisive, and scared, my heart pounded to the beat of the advancing footfalls—a rhythm of impending doom. Clutching the tablet like a lifeline, I edged away from the office door.

In a moment of reckless courage, fueled by my escalating fear and the urgent need to assert some control over the rapidly deteriorating situation, I used the tablet to access the security camera mics and shouted, "Who's there?!" The words sliced through the house. For just a moment, all movement in the house stopped. Then the intruders resumed their search with a fury. My breathing became uneven as the familiar panic crawled up my throat.

I grabbed the phone attached to Atticus's ancient-looking fax machine, hoping there would be a signal. Hearing the tone, I dialed nine-one-one.

Despite the obvious danger, my need to confront the unknown and demand answers overpowered my instinct to remain hidden. "I called the police! They're on the way," I shouted at the tablet. My voice was laced with a bravado I didn't feel. Perhaps this would make the intruders hesitate. My feeble threat hung in the air, a last desperate attempt to wield the prospect of law enforcement against these intruders, even though I knew it wouldn't do any good.

Suddenly the lights flickered and died, plunging the room into darkness. "Great. Just great," I hissed. They'd cut the power. That meant the fax machine was dead too. Atticus had mentioned that he had a backup generator. For a few breaths, I waited for the power to shift over and the lights to come back on, but they never did. When I checked the tablet, the camera feed had gone black.

The full weight of the situation crashed down on me like a tidal wave. This was no random break-in. They were here for *me*. My father's dealings, his shadowy connections, had finally caught up to him, and I was the price for his sins.

The footsteps paused, and the intruders started talking in low voices, speaking in a language that was both familiar and foreign.

As I listened, I was struck by a chilling familiarity. The harsh, barked commands and the gruff exchanges... These weren't just any intruders. The accent haunted my mind, taking me back in time. It was unmistakably Russian. I recognized the tone and cadence all too well—not from crime dramas or any fictional world of espionage but from something far more mundane and yet profoundly ingrained in my memory. My hometown. My neighbors, the Ivanovs, had spoken this familiar language, and they were from Russia. Atticus had been right—it was the Russian mafia that was after me.

Night Shift

It was only a matter of time before they found me. My thoughts turned to Atticus, to the promise of safety that had been so cruelly snatched away. I wondered if he would ever forgive himself if he knew that, in these final moments, his fortress had become my trap.

Each breath I took threatened to give me away. They would surely find me any minute now.

The quietness of the room shattered in an instant as the door was kicked open with violent force. The door exploded inward, sending splinters flying. The sound reverberated ominously through the hallway, heralding the nightmare that was about to descend upon me. Standing before me were two shadowy figures. The light filtering through the window allowed me to discern the moment they zeroed in on me. For a second, they stood there scowling at me, their eyes cold and unyielding.

As the men advanced, I stumbled back, my heart pounding in my ears. I barely had time to react, to brace myself, before the first of them was upon me. He clamped a rough hand around my arm and yanked me out from behind the desk.

In the whirlwind of terror and confusion, my head snapped to the side as a sharp sting blasted my cheek—a brutal introduction to who these men were. The back of the man's hand snapped back, his knuckle striking my lip. My mouth was flooded with the taste of iron. The blunt pain reminded me of my drunken father's fists.

"Who the fuck are you?" I gasped out.

In response, one of the men, his face a mask of cold indifference, grabbed my chin, forcing me to look at him. With his other hand, he casually patted the emblem on his jacket—a stylized trio of snarling wolves. The emblem spoke louder than any words could. That symbol branded my assailants perfectly.

Atticus and I had come across information and news articles about them during our research about the illegal drug trade that operated out of Tacoma and Aberdeen.

The realization hit me like a physical blow. These men were Volkovi Nochi.

Out of pure desperation, I kicked out at the guy who was holding my face, hitting him in the knee, and then started struggling to get away.

Grunting in pain, he bent over to grab his knee as the other man seized me by the scruff of my neck.

"Enough, you little bitch!" he barked, his voice laced with cruel amusement. Then, without warning, he punched me in the kidney. "We don't have all day for this." I sank to my knees as the pain tore through my back.

My arms were roughly wrenched behind me, my wrists bound with a zip tie. I fought against it, but the plastic bit into my skin with every futile twist and pull.

The Russian assholes dragged me through the house. By now, I'd stopped struggling, my body limp from the shock and the realization of my helplessness. There was a clear path of destruction in every room we passed through, a demonstration of the ruthless message they wanted to send.

The place was unrecognizable, a shell of the home it had been mere minutes ago. Pictures had been torn off the wall, furniture upturned. Atticus's precious memories and possessions lay in ruins. Unbidden, a flashback of my apartment assaulted my mind.

When they finally dragged me through the door, I blinked against the bright daylight. They shoved me into the back of a van, and the door slammed shut, echoing like a death knell.

As the van pulled away, I lay on the floor reeling from the pain of their punches and trembling from the terror. The ties that bound me were a cruel, painful reminder that I was now a captive to the whims of those who had torn through my life, leaving nothing but devastation in their wake.

After a few minutes, the van came to a stop, and I attempted one last flight for freedom, lunging for the back door handle. Then there was a sharp *crack* at the base of my skull before darkness claimed me.

I was slipping in and out of consciousness. It was to a world unmoored, a reality where time and space seemed fluid, indistinct. One thing I was certain of—I was still in a moving vehicle. The hum of the engine was a constant undertone to the throbbing pain in my head.

The interior was cramped and dimly lit, the only illumination coming from a flickering overhead light that cast eerie shadows on the faces of my captors. Occasionally I could make out a muffled conversation in Russian, coming from the front seats, before I fell back into darkness once more.

I had just come to again when the van came to an abrupt stop and the back door was yanked open, flooding the space with harsh daylight. Rough hands grabbed me, pulling me out of the vehicle and onto my feet. The dramatic change in environment made my head spin. I squinted against the brightness, my eyes slowly adjusting to take in my surroundings.

We were beside a warehouse, the kind frequently found on the outskirts of cities, forgotten and rarely visited. Unceremoniously, I was led inside, our footsteps echoing eerily in the vast open space. My captors—the two men from the van and one who'd met us when we arrived—all had stern faces and unemotional eyes. None of them cared about my fear or the swelling of my face.

In the center of the warehouse stood a man who seemed distinctly out of place in the dilapidated surroundings. He was dressed in a tailored suit that spoke of power and control. He scrutinized me with eyes as black as night. His icy stare sliced through the air and right into my soul, chilling me to the bone. The air around him practically crackled with authority, and it was clear that he was the epicenter of power within this grim setting.

As I was brought before him, one of his companions, a man who had a particularly cruel glint in his eye, leaned in and said maliciously, "Perhaps we should teach her a lesson before we send her off, Pakhan. Make sure she knows her place."

"It would appear that Igor already has," the leader whispered in an unnervingly calm voice just before he fired his gun—a gun I hadn't even noticed he was holding, so transfixed was I by his cruel gaze. My ears rang, and I suddenly felt the moisture of the man's blood on my face. The man who'd held a death grip on my arm was now lifeless on the ground next to me.

The other man beside me stood still, unwavering in his stoicism. I, on the other hand, began shaking uncontrollably.

"We are not barbarians," the leader said. "She is valuable, and I had given you explicit orders not to harm her. Now look at that face... Are we clear on this now?"

"Yes, sir," the other man said as he shifted behind me.

The leader then turned his attention back to me. "You are Samantha, yes?" I nodded. "Your father has caused me trouble, the kind of trouble that has unfortunately brought you here." Although his English was good, it was tinged with a heavy Russian accent that made his words all the more intimidating.

My fear rendered me unable to speak. The boss seemed to consider my silence for a moment before continuing. "You will come with us, Samantha. It is not personal, you understand. Simply business."

The dismissive tone he used as he spoke about my fate, treating me as if I were just a piece of property, was demeaning. However, his order for my protection provided me with a sliver of hope that I might survive this.

I couldn't keep my thoughts to myself any longer. "Who are you people? And why have you taken me?!" I demanded to know, my voice wavering from exhaustion and fright.

"*Milen'kaya devochka*...my sweet girl, you are in the presence of *The Wolf*." He paused, and a grin that was menacing yet enthralling appeared on his face. "And *we* are the Volkovi Nochi."

He dragged his thumb across his lips, scanning me from head to toe, appraising my worth as though I were a prized pig on display at the fair.

He signaled his men, tilting his head subtly in my direction. One of them gently grasped my elbow and guided me toward a dark SUV parked within the warehouse's dim interior, while another strode ahead to swing open the door to the backseat. Just as I was about to step in, The Wolf issued another command.

"Ensure she's comfortable," he ordered, his tone leaving no room for challenge. "And remember, any harm to her will see you sharing Igor's fate."

The directive seemed to be more for my benefit than that of his men, signaling I was, for now, shielded from physical violence. Yet, the underlying threat lingered; my safety hinged on the whims of a man who didn't think twice about killing his own.

A surge of self-preservation hit me. The thought of never seeing Atticus again, of the life we might have had together being snuffed out by these horrible men, sparked a fierce will to survive within me. The fear of losing him dwarfed my fear of enduring the Volkovi Nochi's wrath.

My hands remained bound behind my back, the zip ties biting into my wrists with each movement. The car pulled away from the warehouse, and our industrial surroundings soon gave way to urban sprawl. A chilling realization settled over me. Each passing second might be leading me further away from ever returning to Atticus.

As the SUV slid into the shadowy confines of a warehouse along a waterway within the Port of Tacoma, my heart jumped. I vaguely recognized where they had taken me. I wasn't exactly sure where I was, but the looming cranes and the scent of saltwater were unmistakable markers of the port's industrial heart. The men yanked me out, gripping me with a caution that was almost laughable. They were unyielding yet careful not to hurt me, a contradiction born from fear of their leader's wrath. They didn't want to end up like Igor, who had learned the hard way what happens when you disobey. He had made the mistake of punching me in the mouth and slapping me across the face earlier, and let's just say he wouldn't be making that mistake again. The Wolf's command had given me a bizarre form of protection, but it was also clear that my safety hung by a thread.

Inside the grim portside warehouse, the air was thick, smelling of oil and chemicals. The goons were in the process of dragging me toward the back, but then, like a gift from the gods, they slipped up.

One of them got a call, and for a second—just a second—their attention faltered. That was all I needed. With a twist and a shove, I broke free from the guy on my right. The sheer audacity of my maneuver was apparently so surprising to them that they paused, stunned, giving me a heartbeat's lead.

Night Shift

I bolted, a cocktail of terror and desperation fueling my legs. The warehouse was a labyrinth, crates and containers casting long shadows. It was perfect for a game of hide-and-seek—a game I couldn't afford to lose.

"Shit, she's getting away!" one of them yelled.

I didn't look back. Dodging between crates, I pushed my body to its limits. Each breath was a sharp dagger in my side. Their boots slapped heavily against the concrete behind me, a reminder that they were hot on my heels.

Up ahead, I spotted an open container. The darkness inside it promised concealment, so without slowing, I dove in, tucking myself behind a stack of boxes. My heart hammered against my ribs.

The shuffle of footsteps grew closer, and then my pursuers split up, their cursing painting a vivid picture of their frustration. I dared not move. As they continued to search, I barely breathed.

For a moment, the world narrowed down to the sound of my heartbeat and the distant murmur of the port. Then, as suddenly as it had all started, silence fell. Had they given up? Or was it a trap? Were they baiting me so I would reveal myself?

I waited, counting each second.

And then, a voice cut through the silence. "Find her, or answer to The Wolf."

The game was far from over.

Peeking out from the edge of the container, I spotted a door. It wasn't that far away, so I ran for it. I weaved through the obstacles as best I could with my hands tied behind my back. In the struggle for survival, I ignored the pain from the zip ties cutting into my wrists.

I burst through an emergency exit, the sudden brightness of the outside world momentarily blinding me. The noises of the port's daily hustle, the screeching of seagulls, and the cranes groaning under the weight of cargo became an unnerving backdrop to my frantic escape.

Behind me were my captors, and ahead was a pier leading to the murky waters of the bay. The ladder hanging off the edge of the pier offered a daunting escape route to walkways on the water's surface. Desperation lent me courage. The shouts of my pursuers grew louder and closer, urging my tired legs to carry me faster.

Without a moment's hesitation, I ran straight to the edge of the pier. In my haste, I hadn't thought about how I would manage the ladder with my hands behind my back. The height was dizzying, the water below a menacing promise of both salvation and peril. I'd always been a good swimmer—and had participated in Aberdeen's annual polar plunge—so I was mentally prepared for the shock of cold water. But this would be so different.

As I teetered on the edge of indecision, a shout from behind made me glance back. The men had drawn their weapons. Their deadly intent was clear in their stance. But even as my heart leaped to my throat, a flicker of hope ignited within me. The Wolf had given them a strict command not to harm me.

With a final, desperate breath, I pushed off from the railing. My body hurtled toward the icy embrace of the water. Air rushed past me, time seeming to slow as I dropped.

The impact was a shock I'd expected, so I didn't freak out. I even kept my composure as the cold water enveloped me in its freezing grasp, muffling the sounds of the world above. But then I started to quickly sink, the weight of my clothes pulling me down into the murky depths. Panic squeezed at my throat. It was nearly impossible for me to swim with my wrists tied. But surrender wasn't in my vocabulary—not today, not ever. With a burst of energy, I forced my bound hands to move, sweeping them from behind my back, under my bottom, and up to the back of my knees. It was a clumsy, desperate move of survival. Thank God I was flexible.

The zip ties bit into my skin, but the sting was a reminder that I was still alive to fight. I maneuvered my legs, one at a time, through the tight circle of my arms. Although my movements were hampered somewhat by the biting cold that sought to seize my muscles, I finally succeeded.

Finally, with my hands now in front of me, I kicked hard, swimming like a dolphin and using every ounce of strength to propel myself upwards. The water around me became brighter, a sign that the surface was near. My lungs screamed for air, but finally my head broke through the surface, and I gasped, the sweet, life-giving oxygen flooding my body.

The relief was instantaneous, the frigid water forgotten for a moment as I gulped down breath after desperate breath. I was alive, free from the immediate clutches of death, and although I was freezing and far from safe, I had given myself a chance. Now, with my hands in front of me, I could swim.

I swam and swam and swam until I was sure I had put some good distance between myself and my captors. I was alone, in the freezing bay, with no clear plan of what to do next.

Finally, I risked a look back. The men stood at the railing of the pier, their weapons still drawn, their faces contorted in anger. But they held their fire. I could only assume that their leader's order to keep me alive was restraining their trigger fingers.

As I drifted with the current, the cold seeping into my bones, I watched the men scatter from the dock. This respite would be brief. They would not give up their pursuit easily.

The icy water seemed to pull at me, each wave like a cold hand dragging me under the surface. The salt stung my eyes while the stiff wind buffeted me, blurring the line between the water and the sky.

Just when the darkness began to close in at the edges of my vision, a distant hum pierced through the fog of my desperation. A boat, its outline hazy through the spray and mist, was moving toward me. Voices, rough and urgent, cut through the roar of the engine and the slap of the waves.

"Hold on! We're coming!" one of the men called out, the words barely reaching me over the tumult of the water.

I tried to shout, to signal them, but my strength was waning, each kick and stroke becoming weaker as the cold numbed my body.

The boat was close now, its hull a dark shadow against the water. Strong hands reached out and pulled me from the bay. I was hoisted up and dropped onto the rough floor of the boat.

"Gotcha, girl. You're safe now," a man said, his grizzled face peering down at me. His beard was matted with sea spray, his eyes kind but wary. After scrutinizing me, he jerked a knife out of his pocket and squatted beside me. "What's a pretty little thing like you doing in the bay with your hands bound?" With a swift yank, he sliced through the zip ties, freeing me.

Unable to respond, I lay there, shivering and gasping. The relief of being out of the water was quickly being replaced with uncontrollable shaking from the bone-deep cold that had taken hold. "We need to get her warm, and fast," someone said. The tugboat's men moved around me with purpose and soon they had me wrapped in one of their long oilskin coats to stave off the hypothermia that threatened. The older man who'd cut the zip ties rubbed his hand down his beard, eyeing me contemplatively. After a moment, he gave a nod of understanding. I was sure he'd put two and two together.

Night Shift

Slowly I began to thaw and relax a bit. I listened to the boat's engine humming with the promise of safety, but then all of a sudden, a salvo of gunfire shattered the fragile hope I had. Bullets sliced through the air, thudding into the hull with terrifying precision.

"Get down!" one of the men on the boat bellowed. But it was too late; the barrage of gunshots from the Russian thugs was unyielding. The men around me, my saviors mere moments ago, had become targets in the blink of an eye.

I huddled low alongside them. Screams of pain and shouts of desperation filled the air.

We were sitting ducks, and these men, who had only sought to rescue a stranger, were now paying the price for their kindness with their lives. The low sides of the tugboat didn't provide much shelter from the gunfire. One by one, the men went down, their bodies slumping onto the deck, their sacrifice a testament to the cruelty of my pursuers.

Soon, only one remained—a young man whose wide eyes mirrored my own terror. Blood from a superficial wound on his arm trickled down his skin, but he was alive. His gaze met mine, a silent understanding passing between us.

The gunfire abruptly ceased, and we lay still, listening to the waves lapping against the boat and the Volkovi Nochi shouting distantly. With labored movements, the young crewman crawled over to me and pulled me toward an open storage cabinet in the center of the tugboat.

"We have to hide," he whispered, his voice shaking. "They're going to come looking for you."

"You're right, but I can't go with you. They'll find me and kill anyone with me."

"No, I can't let you stay here alone to face them," he said.

"It's the fucking Russian mafia," I said. "Do me a favor and live. Call St. John's hospital and ask for Dr. Atticus Thorin. Tell him everything." I shoved him away when I heard the speedboat pulling up behind us. I crawled to the front of the tugboat, wishing I could jump back in the water. But it would just be a matter of time before the Russians apprehended me again. Slowly I stood up, raising my hands in the air. Looking back, I saw the guy nod, mouthing "*Dr. Thorin*" before closing himself in the cabinet.

I shivered—not just from the cold but from the horror of this situation, the loss of life, and the ever-looming presence of the Volkovi Nochi. I was trapped. The shore was so close yet impossibly far.

I could only watch, numb and shaking, as the shadowy figures boarded the boat and approached me with a chilling precision. My body was rigid with fear, every shout and command from them tightening the noose of terror that choked my breath.

Seconds later, their savage hands were on me, dragging me back to the place I had so desperately hoped to escape.

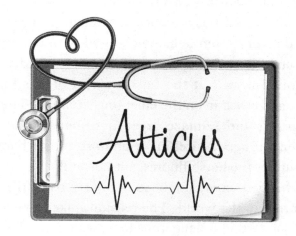

Chapter Twenty-four

I couldn't shake off the nagging worry about Samantha being alone at home as I clocked into my shift. It chewed at the back of my mind, relentless and distracting, even as the emergency department ran its usual marathon of chaos. The fact that I'd left her there didn't sit well with me, but duty called—loudly.

The intensity of my routine was notched up when a pregnant woman, in the throes of full-blown labor, burst through the doors. Her screams of "The baby is coming!" sliced through everything else with razor-sharp urgency. It was like a slap to the face, snapping all my senses to high alert. All of my previous concerns were immediately shelved. "Atticus! We need you!" a nurse yelled over the commotion. Together, we rushed the laboring mother into the nearest room.

"No time to wait for an OB or midwife. This baby's on a fast track out!" I said as we got the woman positioned on the bed. The delivery room became charged with energy, and we prepared ourselves to bring a new life into the world.

I stationed myself at the business end of this high-stakes operation and zeroed in on the emerging situation. The mother's strained grunts and Lamaze breathing filled the air. "Almost there," I encouraged, catching a glimpse of the baby's head, crowning under the harsh fluorescent hospital lights.

Sweat beaded on my forehead as my hands worked to guide the newborn into the world. The tension spiked when I spotted the umbilical cord in a dangerous loop around the baby's neck. My heart raced—not from panic but from a controlled rush of adrenaline. "Easy does it," I said calmly to the mother, working to free the newborn from its entanglement. In a delicate dance of fingers and forceps, I gently unwrapped the cord without causing harm to either mother or child.

The moment the cord was clear and the baby slid free, the room shifted into a new kind of excitement—cries of relief from the mother, soft coos from the nurses, and the most important noise of all, the hearty wailing of a baby. It was the sound of victory, a cry that punched through the tension and signaled success.

Sweat cooled on my brow as I took a moment to marvel at the life we'd just ushered in under less than ideal circumstances. It was a moment of humanity in the sterile confines of the ED, a reminder of why I did this job.

My phone had buzzed over and over again in my pocket while I'd been elbows deep in the delivery. I'd been forced to ignore it until now. I yanked it out, and the screen lit up with a barrage of notifications—Samantha's missed call, alerts from the security company, and a discombobulated text that hit me like

Night Shift

a punch to the gut: *Im hidig in you office A bnch guys breaking in Help!* Following the text was a notification that she had started sharing her location with me.

It floored me that Samantha had had the presence of mind to share her location amidst the break-in. That was sharp—exactly the kind of quick thinking you'd hope for in a tight spot. It hammered home just how tenacious and smart she really was.

My blood boiled at the thought of her alone, cornered by thugs. My usual calm was nowhere in sight, replaced by a new surge of adrenaline, readying me for action.

The baby's cries and the mother's thankful sobs faded into the background. I now had a singular focus. Samantha was in danger, and I would stop at nothing to ensure her safety. My mind raced through the fastest routes home and the tools I had at my disposal. It hit me then with cold, hard clarity—I would, without hesitation, do whatever it took to protect her.

I flew out of the delivery room and quickly arranged coverage for the rest of my shift. Then I texted my brothers the basic details of the situation, telling them to meet me at my house. As I slid into my car, I called Colton. I had to gather my troops, make a plan, and go find those bastards and rip their heads off.

Within seconds, I was tearing through the streets, barely noticing the blare of horns and the flashes of red lights I left in my wake. As my Mercedes roared toward home, the phone auto-connected to the speakers. "Colton, my house, they've hit it," I spat out the moment he answered.

"Atticus, I know. Got the alert and sent my guys straight over. They're on it," he calmly explained.

"Fuck, Colton, what happened with the security? We beefed it up for a reason. How did they get through?" My grip on the steering wheel tightened, and the tires screeched as I took another corner at a speed that flirted with disaster.

"They cut the power, Atticus. Not just to your place, but the whole damn neighborhood. Even hit your backup generator. This wasn't amateur hour; it was professional, costly. Only someone with deep pockets and serious motivation could pull a stunt like this. This is high-level shit, man. Russian mob's signature is all over it."

"Christ, Colton. My place...what's the destruction like?" I demanded, weaving through traffic like a madman, the roar of my anger drowning out the rational part of my brain that screamed for caution.

"My guys are there now, assessing and documenting the damage. This was a pro job. They knew exactly what they were doing. They weren't just there to take Samantha. It's a warning for you not to interfere."

"Hmph, they don't know me very well. I'm minutes away. Look for Braxton and Conan. They should be there soon. She shared her location with me, and it looks like they're on the move. We've got to get going before they find her phone—or worse, get her on a plane!"

When I pulled up, Colton was waiting, his expression grim. The front door hung open. I stepped through the gaping hole and into my violated home. It lay in ruins. With every step I took, shattered glass crunched beneath my feet, and I had a flashback of Samantha's apartment.

Colton led the way to my office. "I had my people hold off on calling the cops," he said, scanning the wreckage. "Wanted you to see it first. The neighbors might've dialed nine-one-one though. So, I'm guessing we don't have much time."

The office was a disaster zone. The doorframe was splintered, and the fax machine's handset dangled by its cord. "Look," he said, nodding toward small blood spots on the wall. "We think it's Samantha's. I wanted you to see it first, but we gotta keep moving."

A red haze descended. "I'll kill them," I seethed in a low growl.

Colton grabbed my arm, pulling me toward the back door. "This way, before the cops show and take over."

Every broken and mangled piece of my home put more fuel on the inferno inside me. The back door, ripped from its frame, lay in pieces at my feet.

"This is where they came in," Colton said, his voice cutting through the fog of my rage. "Professional job. No doubt about it."

I barely heard him over the blood pounding in my ears. This attack had been personal, a declaration of war. And as I stood there, amidst the ruins of my life, I made a vow that I would not stop until I found her.

I descended from the back porch, and my attention was immediately drawn to a whirling ball of fur. The last thing I'd expected was to find Newton here, yapping like the place was on fire. "Not now, Newton," I grumbled, trying to shoo him away with a nudge of my foot, but the dog was on a mission, persistent as hell, and kept jumping up on my legs.

He dashed around the corner, then back again, barking louder, practically doing backflips to get us to follow him. "What's gotten into him?" I muttered, going after him out of sheer frustration.

We rounded the corner of the house, and he led us straight to the generator, which lay silent and dark. Then he started digging furiously at something behind it. Colton leaned over and pulled out a man's wallet. "Guess they weren't so slick after all," he said with a snort, flipping it open.

I gave Newton a quick pat on the head. "Not bad for a little furball," I told him. He seemed pleased with himself and trotted off with his tail wagging—mission accomplished.

Inside the wallet, Colton found an ID and tossed it to me. "Well, this confirms it—Russians," he said, then resumed flipping through the wallet for more clues.

He pulled out a business card from some shipping outfit based out of the Port of Tacoma. "Bet this is where they're heading," he said, snapping a picture of it as I checked Samantha's location on my phone. Sure enough, she was moving toward the port.

"Shit, let's move," I said, already turning back toward the front of the house.

"Let's go! Let's go!" Colton yelled into his phone. He had already dialed up his team and was barking orders like a general. "Wrap it up here, leave guards, and get our best on this. We're heading to the port!" He ordered his men to secure the house and call in his private SWAT team. "And get the cops to the port, ASAP. We'll update them on the way."

When we rounded the house, Braxton and Conan were there, looking like they were ready to tear into someone. "In the SUV, now," Colton said, gesturing with his thumb and hopping into the driver's seat. "We'll brief you en route."

We piled into Colton's SUV. As the engine roared to life, he started to lay out a plan. "Since we've got a lead on their location, and they appear to be heading for the port, I've called in the big guns, and we're coordinating with the police. Time's not on our side." The vehicle peeled out down the street before anyone could even buckle up. "After twenty-four hours, the chances of successfully recovering a person who has been kidnapped decrease significantly."

The drive was a blur of motion and tension as we barreled toward the port. Now that I had a moment to sit still and think, the gravity of the situation began to settle in. Samantha was out there, in the hands of the Russian mafia, and every second counted.

"We're going to get her back," I said through clenched teeth, my resolve hardening. "And God help anyone who stands in my way."

As we veered off I-5 onto Port of Tacoma Road, adrenaline surged through me, and I mentally prepared myself for whatever hell awaited us. The roar of the SUV's engine became background noise to the calm, cold focus taking over.

Glancing at my phone, I realized Samantha's location hadn't been updated in over fifteen minutes. "Shit, her phone's gone dead," I muttered, my panic starting to rise. "Last ping was midway up the waterway."

Colton didn't miss a beat. He started jabbing at his phone. "We'll find her, Atticus. Trust me." He dialed one of his top guys. When the man on the other end picked up, Colton said, "Listen up. Samantha's last known location is at the intersection of Port of Tacoma and Ashton Way. Head to the address we found in the wallet. Fan out, look for anything odd, and move fast!"

The SUV's tires screamed against the pavement as we took a sharp turn, everyone inside bracing against the shift in momentum. The SUV was now a pressure cooker, and the taste of uneasiness and retribution mingled in my mouth.

"Check every warehouse, every boat, every goddamn container if you have to!" Colton barked into the phone. The port loomed ahead, a sprawling maze of possible danger.

Soon we approached Samantha's last known location. This was the moment of truth. The port's vast, industrial landscape stretched out before us, hiding who knew what secrets within its shadows.

When we rolled into an area along the Blair Waterway, a pang of uncertainty hit me. There were a thousand places where they could have stashed Samantha before stealing her away on a container ship. Warehouses, small structures, and containers littered the vast expanse. Colton steered us into the shadows behind a towering stack of metal giants. Moments later, two of Colton's cars slid in behind us, silent as ghosts.

"We're close," Colton said, his voice a low growl of focus and fury. The SUV skidded to a halt, and we all leaped out, ready for anything. We gathered behind the SUV.

With a click, the back door popped open, revealing an arsenal fit for a small army. Colton lifted an eyebrow in a silent question, sweeping his gaze over us. "Ready for a real fight?" he asked.

"We've got this," Braxton and Conan stated flatly, their eyes gleaming with fury.

I couldn't help but add, "The navy didn't just teach me how to patch people up. I can hold my own."

Armed with guns and strapped into Kevlar, we moved like shadows along the foreign landscape. The port loomed around us, a giant sleeping beast we were about to poke.

And there, against the backdrop of towering cranes and stacked containers, I spotted it—a flicker of shimmering red movement, a shadow that didn't belong, the unmistakable bounce of auburn curls I'd grown to know so well. My heart skipped a beat. They were dragging Sam into a sprawling warehouse.

"Over there!" I whispered, pointing toward the anomaly.

Immediately, we all took off running. After what felt like an eternity we came to a halt outside of the building. Sam was nowhere to be seen. Then we crept forward until the distinctive sound of a safety clicking off shattered the silence.

We froze, the realization hitting us all at once.

We weren't alone.

Night Shift

Chapter Twenty-five

The ride back to the pier was torturous. The frigid breeze bit at my skin while the water slapped against the hull tauntingly, mocking my failed attempt at escape. When the warehouse came into view, a hollow feeling settled in my stomach.

As soon as the boat bumped up against the dock, two of the thugs hooked their hands under my shoulders and dragged me into the warehouse. The door slammed behind us, making me jump.

The Wolf was there, waiting, his face twisted into an expression of fury as I was thrown at his feet. "Impressive, Samantha," he spat out, the anger in his voice as frosty as the chill in the air. "You have spirit, but it's as foolish as it is futile!"

I could barely lift my head to throw him a pathetic, defiant glare before falling back down, my body shaking from the cold and fear.

"You think you can run from the Volkovi Nochi? From me?" He paced like a caged animal, his voice rising with each step he took. "There is no escape! You belong to us now, *to me*. Your little swim has cost me time and resources. And pissed me off."

His men watched on, a silent audience to the spectacle of his anger. In that instant, I realized any further attempts to flee would be pointless; his control was absolute, his reach far and wide. The cold, hard floor of the warehouse pressed against my cheek, and as I lay there, it became clear to me that I was utterly, entirely trapped—not just by the walls of the warehouse or the waters of the bay, but by the will of a man who considered me nothing more than a piece of property at his disposal.

His eyes burned with an intensity that seemed to ignite the very air between us. We stared at each other in silence for a few heartbeats. Then he gave a nod to his men, and they lifted me by the arms, shoving me into a chair in the center of the warehouse. I knew not to fight against them. My best hope now was simple self-preservation. I had to use my mind, not my body, to stay alive. These types of men demanded subservience, so I would give The Wolf exactly what he wanted.

He pulled at each finger of his glove until he freed it from his hand. Then with careful precision he repeated the same with the other hand, shoving the gloves into a pocket of his black overcoat. Shucking off his coat, he tossed it to one of his men, never breaking eye contact with me. No longer able to take the ferocity of his glare, I dropped my face, focusing on the red welts crisscrossing my wrists from the zip ties that had bound them for so long. The Wolf was upon me then, the tips of his black leather shoes stepping between my feet, knocking my legs apart. "Look at me!" he shouted.

"Yes, sir," I said softly as I slowly raised my eyes to meet his, keeping my chin down and taking a passive posture.

He made three menacing *tsks*. With one quick movement, he grasped my chin and tilted it upward, positioning me to allow his palm to deliver a swift, stinging slap across my cheek.

"Today, you will learn your place and that your Pakhan will not tolerate insolence from anyone." He squeezed my cheeks between his thumb and fingers. "You will show me respect at all times. You will address me as sir unless we are in public, and then you will use Mr. Volkovi." Running his thumb across my lips, he leaned closer. "And if you were ever to win my favor, then perhaps one day you could call me Viktor." He chuckled ominously, releasing my chin.

Taking a step away, he began to pace back and forth, his hands clenched into fists at his sides. I dropped my eyes back to my lap, not daring to meet his gaze.

"Try as you might, you will not escape," Viktor hissed. "Look at me, goddammit!" His anger was a force that filled the room, suffocating and dark. I snapped my head up. *Smack*! The back of his hand struck the other cheek. "You must understand, Samantha," he continued in a more controlled tone, "you are not here by mere chance. It was your father who placed you in this... predicament." *Smack*! Another hit, this time splitting my lip in a new place. Blood trickled down my chin, but I didn't move.

"Mac made his choices," Viktor continued, pacing slowly once more. "He made promises he couldn't keep, racked up debts he could not repay. And when we came to collect, he offered up the only thing he had left of any value to us—his own flesh and blood."

My mind reeled. My father had traded my life to save his own. It was a truth that should have been too horrifying for me to accept, a betrayal too deep to fathom. But I knew my father. His addictions had claimed his soul long ago.

"You see," he said, leaning down so his face was level with mine, "in this world, everything has a price. Your father understood that. And now, here you are, a payment for his sins. You bring to the Volkovi Nochi certain useful skills. I'm sure you understand your value." His breath was a mix of mint and something foul. It was a scent I would never forget.

He loomed over me. "You and I are going on a little journey, Samantha," he said in a smooth, almost casual voice. "Back to Russia, on that container ship out there." He gestured toward the pier. "We will leave shortly. You be a *khoroshaya devochka*...a good girl, and no more harm will come your way."

The finality in his tone, the promise that this was not up for negotiation, made my heart sink, but I had to play his game and try to stall our departure as long as possible. I raised my face to look him in the eye and licked the blood off my lip. "Yes, sir," I said, giving him a soft smile.

His pupils shot wide open. That lick had stirred something within him.

Once again, he grabbed my jaw in his hand and yanked me out of the chair, pulling me to him. With only a breath of distance between us, his other hand found the back of my head. Twisting his fingers in my hair, he crushed his mouth against mine and ran his tongue along my split lips, demanding entrance.

Just play along, Samantha, and give the monster what he wants! I screamed in my mind. Forcing myself to relax, I leaned into the kiss. All I had to do was pretend it was Benji from back in college. Lord knew I'd faked my enthusiasm with him enough times.

Night Shift

As our tongues jousted, I gently cupped Viktor's cheek and moaned softly. The hand not holding me captive by my hair snaked around my waist, forcing my belly against a burgeoning erection. A hand crept up and around to my breast, causing me to gasp.

Then suddenly, he released me. Chuckling, he said, "Yes, you will do just fine."

Turning to the man holding his coat, he ordered him, "Go clean up her face and bring her to my office. I have unfinished business I need to attend to before we depart."

Returning his attention to me, he looked me up and down like a lion sizing up its kill. "And I may have time for a brief distraction as well."

Damn, maybe I'd overdone it.

The man with the black coat draped over his arm pointed at me and then toward the back of the warehouse. I turned and walked to where he indicated.

I stepped into the shadows and soon found myself in a hallway lined with closed doors. When we reached the end, the man pushed one open and shoved me forward. "Go clean yourself up and make it quick."

It was a dingy bathroom with a couple of stalls and a sink. I took my time, trying to delay the inevitable. My reflection reaffirmed what I already knew—I was a disaster. Searching under the sink, I found a small box containing various toiletries. Among the items was a hairbrush. God, how it grossed me out thinking about having to use it, but what choice did I have? I quickly washed my face and did the best I could with my hair. I tried to sponge off some of the filthy smell of the bay water from my skin, but it was no use.

All too soon, the man slung open the door. "Let's go," he said, standing there looking annoyed as hell.

I followed him back down the hallway a little ways until we came to another one of the closed doors. He knocked three times. "Enter," Viktor said from within. The man opened it and shoved me inside. Stumbling, I fell against the desk. He leaned back and smirked, clasping his hands behind his head. "Have a seat."

I started to sit in the chair across from him, but before my ass hit the wood, he shot a hand out, wagging his finger at me. "No, not there. Here." He hammered his index finger on the center of the desk.

Resisting the urge to frown, I scooted the small desk lamp to the side and perched my hip on the edge of his desk.

"Don't start playing shy now," he said. "Your reaction to my kiss told me everything I need to know."

He got up, removed his jacket, folded it in half, and placed it carefully on the back of his chair. Next, he rolled up his sleeves.

Shit, shit, shit, this was getting all too real—too fast. My heart hammered in my chest. But I could do this. I could do whatever it took to stay alive. The oh-too-familiar claws of panic threatened to choke me. Swallowing hard, I focused on my breathing—breathe in, one, two, three—breathe out, one, two, three.

With a swift scrape of his arm over the surface of his desk, everything went flying, hitting the ground with a loud clatter. Before I could blink, his hands were around my waist, dragging me across the desk and flipping me around to face him.

He clutched the hem of my shirt and then, in one powerful motion, jerked it up and off me, tossing it aside. Then he smiled broadly, bouncing his brows. "Yes, this trade will work out quite well after all." Leaning in, he gave me a quick, hard kiss and pulled me off the desk in front of him. Slowly he ran his hands down along my sides to the band of my pants. Hooking his thumbs under the edge, he yanked them down to my knees,

Night Shift

leaving me bare to his gaze. "Mmm, what a pretty little pussy you have," he growled. Without warning, he lifted me up and slammed me back down on his desk, causing me to fall back, nearly knocking the breath out of me.

He leaned forward on one hand while the fingers of the other traced a line from the notch between my collarbones and down over the valley of my bra, then moved lower to my belly button. As his middle finger dipped in, he drew little circles around its edge. My body shuddered violently in panic. I wanted nothing more than to punch him in the face, but that would only result in him punishing me in ways I couldn't allow myself to think about. Squeezing my eyes shut, I clenched my fist against the surface of the desk. He laughed darkly and then dragged a fingernail down, lower and lower, to my cleft.

BAM! BAM! BAM!

Shots rang out distantly, somewhere near the pier.

Viktor reached into the top desk drawer and pulled out a sleek, dark steel handgun. The weapon had a long barrel topped with a silencer, which meant it would be as quiet as it was deadly. "Stay here!" he shouted before darting out the door, closing it firmly behind him.

I jumped off the desk, jerked up my pants, and scrambled to find my top and throw it on. Frantically, I tried the doorknob, but to no avail. Of course, it was locked from the outside. This was my chance. I'd never get an opportunity like this again, and I had to figure out how to get out of this damn room.

I punched the door. "Think Sam, think!" I screamed.

That was when I saw them—the door hinges. They were on *my* side of the door. Now, if I could just find something to pry the pins out, maybe I could escape. Whirling around, I scanned the office. It was fairly barren.

A frantic search through the desk drawers yielded nothing but a few old pens and stacks of neglected paperwork, but then I spotted it—a toolbox tucked away under the desk, almost hidden in the shadows. *Finally*, I thought, a spark of hope igniting within me. *Maybe my luck's about to change.*

I dove for the toolbox, my fingers nervously trembling as I flipped the clasp and threw it open. Inside it, I discovered a hammer, a screwdriver, and pliers. It was like finding treasure. I couldn't suppress a grin—I had gotten lucky.

Wasting no time, I grabbed the screwdriver and positioned its pointed shank at the bottom of the first hinge. With the hammer, I tapped the screwdriver firmly, nudging the pin upwards. It took a few solid hits before the pin gave way, but finally it emerged, clinking softly as it hit the floor. "One down," I whispered to myself as adrenaline coursed through me.

The second hinge proved trickier, the pin stubbornly resisting my efforts. Sweat beaded on my forehead, but I persisted, hammering away until, at last, with a gratifying slide, the pin popped free. Repeating the same procedure, I swiftly freed the pin from the third hinge.

Heaving a quick sigh, I wiped my clammy hands on my pants. More and more gunfire rang out, reverberating against the door. I had to ignore what was happening and focus on what I needed to do—open the door itself. Carefully I wedged the head of the screwdriver between the floor and the door's bottom edge. It was a tight fit, but after a bit of wiggling, the screwdriver caught the bottom edge securely. The pliers were next—I clamped them around the screwdriver's shank for a better grip.

I hammered against the pliers, but the door wouldn't budge. In frustration, I gave one last knock with all my strength. With a *crack*, the door popped open just enough for me to peek out.

Night Shift

Peering through the gap, I held my breath, searching for any sign of movement. The coast seemed clear. This was it. I pulled the door open, my pulse racing as I made a silent vow not to look back.

My feet slapped against the concrete as I darted down the hallway. Every second was a gamble, but I was all in. There was no turning back now.

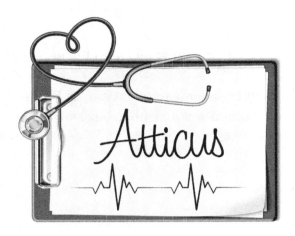

Chapter Twenty-six

Colton and the rest of us slowly turned to locate the source of the disengaging safety. There, not ten feet away, stood a man with a large black rifle aimed squarely at us. My heart skipped—not from fear, but from a surge of recognition and disgust. It was Mac Sheridan, Samantha's sorry excuse for a father, the asshole who'd sold her out to these Russian thugs.

"Son of a bitch," I spat, my anger boiling over as I locked eyes with him. "That's Mac, Samantha's father—the fucker who traded his own daughter to these animals." Glaring at Mac, I raised my weapon and pointed it at him. "If you've hurt her, if one damn hair on her head has been harmed, you're a dead man."

Colton, ever the strategist, edged closer and calmly began to negotiate. "Mac, put the gun down. You're outnumbered, and this won't end well for you."

Mac's eyes darted around among us, realization dawning that he was outgunned and outmatched. His features morphed from an expression of animosity into one of unease. The rifle wavered, and his resolve seemed to evaporate. After a tense moment, he lowered the weapon.

"I'll help you if you help me," he grumbled. "These Volkovi Nochi are sick bastards. I know where she is." He took a deep breath, a flicker of something akin to concern crossing his features. "But you need to know, there's at least a dozen of them in there. Armed and dangerous."

For a beat, we all stood there wordlessly, listening to the distant waves crashing against the dock. This was it, just us and the looming battle. My grip tightened around my weapon, the taste of revenge sharp on my tongue.

"Lead the way, Mac. And remember, if this is a trap, it'll be the last mistake you ever make," Colton warned in a low growl.

We moved as one, a unit bound by a singular purpose, following Mac's shaky lead. The warehouse loomed ahead, a Russian mafia stronghold hiding Samantha. My senses were on high alert. Every shadow was a potential threat.

We rounded a corner, flanked by towering stacks of containers, and crashed straight into a world of chaos. Two of the Russian lookouts spotted us before we could even blink, their guns up and firing before a single word was exchanged. This was a "shoot first and ask questions later" kind of scenario.

"Shit!" I yelled, diving behind a container as the first volley of bullets flew. Colton, Braxton, Conan, and the rest of our makeshift squad scrambled for cover, seeking protection behind anything we could find. The air cracked with the continuous gunfire. Bullets zipped past us, ricocheting off the metal containers with deafening cracks.

Without hesitation, we returned fire. My gun kicked in my hands, the sharp smell of gunpowder filling the air as we took down the two lookouts. They hit the ground hard, their weapons clattering onto the concrete.

Colton's voice cut through the resulting silence like a knife: "Move, move, move! They know we're here now!" The danger was obvious; our element of surprise had been blown to hell.

With no need to be stealthy, we sprinted toward the warehouse. One of the guys, without breaking stride, took aim and shot the wheels of the SUV and sedan parked inside the garage door, ensuring no one could make a quick getaway.

Pandemonium reigned when we breached the interior, gunfire ricocheting off the walls. The Volkovi were quick to respond. We were hit with a deadly hailstorm of bullets as we maneuvered through. We ducked, weaved, and fired, moving with a singular focus—to find Sam.

Mac, that treacherous snake, was surprisingly true to his word, leading me toward the office hallway where he suspected Sam was being held. With my heart racing and my gun ready, I remained wary. Every step was a gamble. A potential ambush waited around every corner.

Just as we neared the back area, the most unexpected thing happened. Sam, like a vision from heaven amidst the madness, came running out of the hallway, straight into the heart of the fray.

"Sam, get down!" I shouted, my voice barely audible over the discord of the battle. Every instinct screamed at me to run to her, to shield her with my body, to get her out of this hell.

The warehouse was a frenzy of bullets and chaos as Colton's team pushed forward. They moved with lethal precision, each man a shadow darting from cover to cover, systematically taking

Night Shift

down the Volkovi who dared to stand in their way. The smell of gunpowder and blood choked the air.

Mac and I made a beeline for Sam, whose auburn curls were a beacon in the madness. But then, out of the corner of my eye, I spotted two Volkovi approaching. They raised their guns and took aim directly at her.

"Fuck!" I cursed, my instincts kicking in. Without a second thought, Mac and I leaped forward, hurling ourselves into the line of fire. Time seemed to slow as we flew, guns blazing, returning fire in midair. The sounds of the warehouse—the shouts, the gunfire, the clattering of spent shells—all faded into a distant whirr as my entire focus narrowed down to stopping those bullets.

Conan, spotting the imminent threat, let loose a volley from his rifle, his aim true as ever. The bullet hit one of the Volkovi and sent him staggering back like a lifeless marionette cut from its strings.

I was almost on top of Samantha when a shot hit me. The force of the impact, even blunted by my Kevlar, was like a sledgehammer propelling me backward into her. We hit the ground hard. Samantha's head made a sickening *crack* against the concrete, and she went limp beneath me—unconscious.

For a moment, I was disoriented, the world tilting dangerously. But then adrenaline surged, snapping me back to reality. Glancing around, I spotted the lifeless body of the second Russian. My return fire had found its mark even as I'd fallen.

Conan and I had stopped the immediate threat, but Sam and I were down. She was out cold, and I was dazed, my chest screaming in protest.

The fight raged around us, Colton's men pushing the advantage. But, with Sam lying in a heap on the cold ground,

I couldn't focus on any of that. I trusted Colton's team to finish this while I stayed by her side.

The stench of blood was thick in the air. As the last sounds of gunfire faded, I noticed Mac slumped against a container, a dark stain spreading across his chest. "Shit," I muttered under my breath.

Conan scrambled over to us, quickly assessing Mac's wound.

Sirens wailed in the distance. The cavalry was finally on its way. The remaining Volkovi didn't stick around, vanishing into the shadows as they made their escape.

Conan kneeled beside Mac, his hands moving with practiced competence, but the grim set of his mouth told me all I needed to know. "It's bad," he mouthed.

Mac coughed, blood flecking his lips. "Tell Samantha...I'm sorry," he rasped, each word a struggle. "She deserved...better."

Conan nodded solemnly. "We'll tell her, Mac. We promise."

At that moment, I was overcome with a grudging respect for Mac. For all his faults, in the end, he'd shown a glimmer of decency. "You did one thing right," I said to him, shifting my attention to Sam, who still lay unconscious beside me and was breathing shallowly. "She's the best damn legacy you could ever have had."

Braxton was already on his phone. "We need an evac, fast," he barked into the receiver, clearly speaking to one of his EMT buddies. While Conan tended to Mac, Braxton and I sat on either side of Sam, keeping an eye on her vitals and ensuring her safety. All we could do was wait.

The police arrived in a whirlwind of sirens and flashing lights, securing the scene as Colton debriefed them on the events of the last few hours. Somehow the Volkovi had managed to run off and take their injured with them. Through it all, Colton kept a close watch over us, ensuring the police knew we were the good

Night Shift

guys in this mess. Braxton's friend, Chief Ayers, knew us all and didn't hassle us with a lot of police procedures. There would be time for that later and I'd already given him my statement.

Soon, I got the news that all of Colton's men were accounted for. A couple of them were banged up, but nothing life-threatening. That was a slight relief in the night's chaos.

The ambulance crew arrived, moving swiftly to stabilize Sam while being mindful of the potential for spinal or brain injuries. They loaded her onto a gurney with the utmost care, their professionalism a small comfort in the turmoil.

Because the police were well acquainted with me from the emergency department, they allowed me to stay with Sam. I climbed into the ambulance without a second thought. My place was by her side. Colton, Conan, and Braxton each gave me a curt nod.

"We've got this," Braxton said. "You go take care of her."

As the ambulance doors closed, cutting off my view of the chaotic scene outside, my focus narrowed in on the woman lying before me. There was no way to know what trauma her brain had suffered. The ride to the hospital was a blur—every wail of the siren and every bump in the road heightening the urgency of getting Sam the help she needed.

As soon as we pulled into the trauma bay at St. John's, the back doors of the ambulance were flung open to reveal a team of nurses, some of whom recognized Sam immediately.

"We need a CT scan, stat!" I said, finding myself barking orders, slipping into the role I knew best.

Dr. Rosemary Medina, my colleague and tonight's attending physician, was quick to meet us. With a calmness that only years in the ED could bring, she said, "Atticus, you're too close to this. Let me handle it." Her eyes flickered with concern—not just for Sam but for me as well. "And you look like hell. By the way you're holding those ribs, it's obvious you took a hard hit. Let's get you checked out too."

"I'm fine," I snapped back, more harshly than I'd intended. I kept pace with the EMTs as they wheeled Sam towards the CT room. The pain in my side was a distant second to the worry gnawing at me. When we got inside the triage area, I stepped back, allowing Dr. Medina to take over, trusting her expertise. But I was unable to move far from Sam's side.

After the CT scan finished and the results were processed, Dr. Medina approached me, her expression unreadable. "She's fortunate," she began, and my world came to a standstill while I waited for her to continue. "There are no signs of brain bleed or swelling. However, she's not out of the woods yet. We're admitting her for intensive monitoring since she has yet to regain consciousness. Try not to worry excessively at this point. As you're aware, recovering from brain and emotional trauma can be a slow process."

"Thank you," I murmured, relief flooding my veins. Although the results were reassuring, the uncertainty of when she would wake up bothered me. We both knew Sam's recovery would be unpredictable.

Soon, they settled Sam into her room, and I followed to sit as a silent sentinel at her bedside. The hospital's night shift moved around us, a flurry of activity, but for me, the world had narrowed down to the steady beeping of Sam's heart monitor and the rising and falling of her chest. Anxiously, I waited for her eyes to open.

The dim light from the hallway barely illuminated her face, casting shadows that made her appear fragile. I leaned forward, the chair creaking under my weight, and took her hand in mine. It was cold, so I rubbed it between my palms, trying to infuse some warmth into her. "Samantha," I whispered, my voice rough with emotions I couldn't fully hold back. "I love you. More than I've ever thought possible."

The words were hard to get out. "And I swear, I'll spend the rest of my life making sure you're safe, being the man you deserve." My throat tightened, choking on the promises and the fear that I might not get a chance to keep them.

I'd always wanted more than what life offered me, more than the transient shallow connections I chose to make. I'd yearned for someone to see me, really see me, and not turn away when they learned about the demons that lingered in my past. But I'd never thought I deserved that kind of love, that kind of devotion. My friends had all moved on from casual relationships, found their soulmates, and started families, while I focused on work and other things, a mere observer of their happiness, convinced that kind of joy wasn't meant for me.

But then Samantha had come along. She'd burst into my life like a fiery, freckled spitfire, igniting a hope I'd long since buried. With her, the possibility of a future I'd never dared to dream of suddenly seemed within reach. I wanted her heart, her trust, everything she was willing to give, and even the things she wasn't sure she could. I wanted her completely.

Wrapping my fingers around one of her long red locks, I let the words that would have been impossible for me to fathom just a few months ago come tumbling out. "I never thought I could be someone's...someone's everything. I never allowed myself to believe that I could be the person you lean on, that we could... maybe...have a future, a family." Uttering this confession of my deepest fears and hopes lifted a weight off my shoulders.

While I studied her face, which appeared peaceful despite the bruising, a surge of protectiveness fired through me. "You changed everything, Samantha. You showed me what it means to truly care for someone, to want to protect them with every fiber of your being."

I bowed my head, tears blurring my vision. "Just come back to me, Sam. Please."

In the room's silence, with only the soft hum of medical equipment for company, I poured out my heart to her unconscious form, clinging to the fragile thread of hope that she would somehow hear me, feel my love, and find her way back.

Night Shift

Chapter Twenty-seven

The first thing I noticed when my eyes fluttered open was that there was a head of disheveled brown hair resting near my hand, our fingers locked together. It was Atticus, fast asleep. While I slowly returned to my senses, I watched him, taking in the stubble on his jaw, the steady rise and fall of his chest, and the way his brow occasionally furrowed even in sleep. The fragments I recalled from the nightmare at the warehouse began to piece themselves back together in my mind.

Carefully, not wanting to startle him, I lifted his hand to my lips, pressing a kiss to the rough skin of his knuckles. His eyes slowly opened, confusion giving way to a flood of relief as he focused on me. "Sam, oh God, you're awake," he breathed out.

He sat up straight and roamed his gaze over me, his eyes clouded with worry. "How are you feeling? Tell me everything, and don't leave anything out, because you've been unconscious for fourteen hours. Does your head hurt? Are you dizzy? Can you see okay?"

I offered him a weak smile despite the dull throb in my head and the ache that seemed to permeate every inch of my body. "I'm okay, really. Just a bit battered, and yeah, my head's pounding like I've got my own personal drummer in there."

Reaching up, I rubbed the back of it.

"And I remember everything," I said, "right up to the moment my head decided to intimately acquaint itself with the concrete." I gave a small laugh, hoping to ease the worry that was so evident in his eyes. "Turns out, having a hard head can be a real lifesaver."

Atticus responded with a soft chuckle, followed by a tender kiss on my forehead.

Leaning over and placing one hand on the bed, he looked down, then up, bracing himself to say something that clearly didn't come easy. The hard lines of his face eased, revealing a glimpse of some emotion I hadn't seen before. His other hand fidgeted slightly at his side, betraying his nervousness. Coming closer until his lips were mere inches from mine, he said, "I love you, Samantha. More than anything. And I'm going to spend the rest of my life making sure you're safe, making sure you never doubt that you are mine, now and forever. This isn't just some fleeting moment. This is the real deal." He wasn't good at this—revealing his feelings—and it showed. He seemed to be struggling with his words.

His eyes burned into mine, fierce and unyielding, a storm of emotions swirling in the winter gray depths. "I'm not just here to say sweet nothings and make promises I can't keep. I'm here to stand by you, to fight for you, to protect you with everything I've got." His hand found mine and gripped it tightly.

Night Shift

"No one will ever hurt you again, not on my watch. I'll stand between you and the world if I have to. You're my heart, my soul, and I'll spend every last breath ensuring you feel loved, cherished, and safe." It was a powerful declaration, a solid vow from a man who knew exactly what he wanted and wasn't afraid to lay it all on the line.

I blinked, surprised by the rush of happiness his words unleashed within me. Tears welled up, spilling over despite my attempts to hold them back. "Atticus, I—I love you too," I managed to whisper. "I've never felt so...loved, so truly loved."

Just then, the door opened with a soft click, and a nurse stepped in. Atticus stepped back. "Good morning, Samantha. How are we feeling?" she asked.

The interruption, although necessary, sliced through our intimate bubble and jolted us back to reality. But even as the nurse went about her checks, Atticus's promise of a future filled with love made my belly flutter with excitement.

When the nurse finally left, we were alone again, surrounded by the sterile furnishings of the room and the faint hum of medical machinery. Atticus's doctor's mask had fallen over his features once more. I was disheartened that we had been so unceremoniously interrupted at such a tender moment. There were so many worries swirling inside me that I didn't know where to start to deal with them. A wave of frustration overtook me. "Atticus, can you help me sit up? I hate this—hate being stuck in a bed like a patient," I grumbled, trying to shift my position with little success.

He moved closer, raised the head of the bed, and helped adjust the pillows behind me so I could sit up more comfortably. "There, how's that?"

"It's good. Thank you." I smiled, enjoying his attentiveness.

Once I was settled, the myriad of questions swirling in my mind found their way out. "What happened after...after I got knocked out? What happened to everyone else...your brothers?" I needed to know, to understand how I'd ended up here, safe but broken. I was terrified that someone else might have ended up like Igor and the men on the tugboat.

He hesitated for a moment, as if weighing how much to tell me. "We got you out of there, Sam, and that's what matters most to me. Colton's team, my brothers, they...they took care of the Volkovi and were mostly unscathed. But Mac"—his voice softened—"he...he helped us find you."

My heart skipped at the mention of my father. "My father?" A pang of dread hit me.

Atticus took a deep breath before continuing. "He...he didn't make it, Sam. He was shot. But before he...he died, he wanted me to tell you he was sorry. That you deserved better. You need to know that he played a big part in getting you back to us in the end."

The news struck me like a physical blow, leaving me breathless. My father, despite everything, was a part of me. Tears pooled in my eyes as I grieved the man who had been my tormentor most of my life but was still my father. "So, I'm... parentless now," I said, the words tasting bitter. "All alone."

"No." He took my hand and squeezed in gently. "You're not alone, Samantha. Not now, not ever. I'm here, and I'm not going anywhere. I promised to protect you, to love you, and I intend to keep that promise for the rest of our lives."

The intensity in his gaze and the sincerity of his words wrapped around me like a warm blanket. "I love you, Atticus," I said, the words coming easier this time. "And knowing you're here...it means everything to me."

Night Shift

His thumb brushed away a tear that had escaped down my cheek, and he sat on the bed next to me.

"This whole thing is just so mind-blowing," I said. "It doesn't seem real, you know? I have all my memories about what happened, yet I still feel like I'm missing a lot of the pieces."

He watched me for a moment. "Let me see if I can fill in some of the missing details. Maybe I should start from the time I left for work."

Then he chuckled and shook his head. "Um, by the way, that little video you texted me almost made me have a wreck," he said, giving me a quick kiss.

My face instantly flushed. "Oh, God. I'd forgotten all about that naughty little video." Atticus laughed and then winced in pain.

"Did you get hurt?!" I exclaimed, sitting forward. I hadn't even considered the possibility that he might have been shot or something.

"No, no, it's not a big deal. I did take a hit, but Coton's high-end Kevlar vest saved my ass. I'm just a little bruised."

"Show me! Show me right now!" Atticus lifted his shirt to reveal a nasty, dark red welt on his lower side. I tenderly ran my fingers across his ribs. "That looks like broken ribs to me. Did you get an X-ray?"

He leaned over and gave me another kiss. This time it was sweet and heart-melting. "Yes, Nurse Sheridan, I did. One hairline fracture, but mostly just some bruises. I'll be fine."

He lowered his shirt, and I leaned back. Curiosity getting the better of me, I asked, "Why didn't you answer my call?"

He sighed. "I was in the middle of delivering a baby. I heard my phone ringing in my pocket, and then when your text came through, I felt it vibrate, but there wasn't anything I could do. There wasn't an OB in sight, just me. But as soon as I finished, I checked it and saw your message along with a bunch of notifications from the security firm, and my world...it just stopped." He shook his head as if he still couldn't believe it all had happened. "You sharing your location with me? That was quick thinking, Sam. It gave us a fighting chance to find you. It probably saved your life."

Wiggling my eyebrows, I let out a small laugh. "Well, you know, sharing locations is what us youngsters do," I teased, poking fun at our age difference.

Before he could respond, Dr. Fitzgerald, a neurologist, walked in.

"Hello, Miss Sheridan," he said in a warm greeting. "I've been reviewing your scans, and you're quite lucky not to have sustained more serious injuries." He then went over the details of the scans and treatments I'd undergone since my arrival. "We'll need to do a follow-up CT to ensure everything is as it should be. So it looks like we'll be keeping you here for a couple more nights, just to be on the safe side."

Then, Dr. Fitzgerald's expression shifted into one of concern. "Samantha, considering the ordeal you've been through—being kidnapped, traumatized by some seriously bad men, and losing your father on top of the concussion and other injuries—I strongly recommend seeing a therapist to help you navigate through this. It's a significant amount to process psychologically," he said gently.

I nodded, agreeing without hesitation. "Sure, I have no objection to that." I glanced briefly at Atticus before returning my focus to Dr. Fitzgerald. "I worked with a therapist for a long time in college to manage my panic attacks. She helped me a lot, but since moving to Tacoma, I haven't had the time to find a new one."

Dr. Fitzgerald smiled. "I have a good friend who is an excellent therapist. I'd like to recommend her to you. She's helped many of my patients through various kinds of trauma."

The room fell silent for a moment before Dr. Fitzgerald turned his attention to Atticus. "I'd suggest you consider seeing someone as well, Atticus. It's been a lot for you to handle too."

Atticus's body tensed immediately at the suggestion. I reached for his hand, squeezing it gently. "Atticus, it might be good for both of us. What we've been through, it's not something we should try to deal with alone."

After a moment, he sighed, and his posture relaxed as he looked from me to Dr. Fitzgerald. "Okay," he relented. "For you, Sam, I'll give it a try."

Dr. Fitzgerald nodded, pleased. "I'll make the arrangements and get you both the contact information. Remember, it's a sign of strength, not weakness, to ask for help," he reminded us, then looked pointedly at Atticus before leaving the room.

I giggled a little. "You know therapists don't bite."

Atticus rolled his eyes.

It was then I noticed just how drained he looked. He was still covered in dirt and grime, and his eyes were shadowed with fatigue, like he'd been in a war zone—which wasn't far from the truth. "Atticus, you need to go home and get some rest...and maybe a shower," I added with a small smile. "I'll be okay here. You've already done so much."

He started to protest, setting his jaw in that familiar, endearing way, but when he saw the look in my eye, he relented. "Okay, but I'm coming back later," he said, standing up reluctantly.

He called Conan and asked him to come pick him up. After he'd spent a few minutes updating his brother on my condition, they discussed what the police had discovered at the warehouse.

Midway through the conversation, Atticus got that wicked gleam in his eye that told me he was up to something.

But before I could ask him about it, he gave me a quick kiss and headed for the door. "Promise me you'll rest."

"I promise."

As he walked out, I settled back against my pillows, feeling a wave of love for this man who had become my everything. The silence soon enveloped me once more, but despite the circumstances, I didn't feel alone anymore. And I was at peace.

Two days slipped by in a haze of routine hospital checks and restless nights. Atticus was a constant presence, coming to be with me as often as he could, his visits punctuating the monotony of my recovery. Each time he walked through the door, it was like a breath of fresh air had swept into the room.

Today, his mood seemed noticeably lighter. And the lines of worry that had etched themselves into his face were a little less noticeable. "You seem...happy today," I commented, curious about the shift.

"Yeah," he said, giving me a genuine smile. "I've got some good news. The mess your father got you tangled up in? It actually helped the FBI make significant progress against the Volkovi Nochi's operations here."

I sat up a bit straighter, interested despite the dull ache that still lingered at the back of my head. "Really?"

"Yes," he confirmed, leaning back in the chair beside my bed with a pleasant sigh. "They've made a bunch of arrests, and it looks like they're finally getting a handle on shutting down the drug trade in Tacoma. It's a big win."

"That's...that's amazing, Atticus."

He grinned, and it was a rare, full-hearted smile that reached his eyes, transforming his entire face. "Yeah, it is. And it's all thanks to you."

"Me?" I laughed lightly, shaking my head. "All I did was get kidnapped and hit my head on a concrete floor."

"And shared your location, which led us straight to them," he reminded me. "You played a big part in this, Sam. Your life was on the line."

It was nice to see this side of Atticus. He beamed like all his burdens had been lifted, and his happiness was infectious.

"So, how's your house coming along?" I asked. "Have you been able to get it cleaned up and the doors replaced?"

Atticus's lips quirked up into a mischievous grin. "Just wait until you see it. Braxton and Conan, plus a crew of others, have worked their magic on it. You'll see. Now, how about us getting out of here? I snagged your discharge papers on the way in here."

"What, really? I thought I'd be here until the morning."

He smiled brightly again. "Nope, let's go," he said, leaning in to kiss me soundly.

Chapter Twenty-eight

The moment I stepped out of the hospital, the fresh air hit me like a wave of freedom. "Wow, it feels so good to be out of there," I said.

When we reached the car, Atticus opened the passenger side door for me, and I slid in. "Being on the patient side of things really puts it all into perspective. Makes me appreciate what our patients go through."

Atticus chuckled, dropping into the driver's seat. "I bet it does. Let's go home."

While he drove, I caught him grinning like the Cheshire Cat and instantly knew he was up to something. "Okay, what are you hiding? That grin is a dead giveaway."

"Just wait and see," he teased, keeping his eyes on the road.

Before long, we were parked next to the Firebird in his garage and heading in. From the outside, everything looked exactly like it had before the raid on his house. It was like the entire ordeal had never happened.

As soon as we walked in, the inviting scents of pine needles and cinnamon hit me, wrapping around me like a hug. My eyes widened in surprise as I took in the sight before me. A Christmas tree stood in the living room. Its lights twinkled softly in the dim light, casting a magical glow over the room.

"I thought you said you didn't do holidays," I said, stepping closer to the tree.

Atticus smiled softly and shrugged. "I wanted to make this Christmas special—for you."

Spinning in a circle, I took in the sight of all the lavish decorations. They brought Atticus's home to life. It was like stepping into a Christmas wonderland, and my heart swelled. The thought and effort he'd put into this was truly gratifying.

When I approached the tree, I noticed my childhood ornaments, the ones that had somehow survived the ransacking of my apartment, beautifully integrated with new ones. It was like a bridge between my past and our future.

Atticus handed me a small package, his eyes shining. "This isn't your main Christmas present, just a little something for now."

Tearing open the wrapping paper, I found an ornament that featured the only photo of us together—taken on our first "not-a-date" hike at Swan Creek Trail. In the photo, Atticus was smiling brightly, looking a bit caught off guard as I poked him in the ribs. I remembered him taking it but had never seen it. God did that day seem like a long time ago now.

Eagerly, I stepped forward and hung the ornament on the tree. Yet, amidst the joy, a flicker of uncertainty remained. Was this a forever thing for us, or was Atticus merely caught up in the moment?

As if sensing my hesitation, he stepped closer and said, "This is just the beginning, Sam. I want every Christmas to be like this, with you."

He pulled me into a hug, and I simply melted into him, embracing him tightly.

As soon as we were settled in, Atticus glanced at me with that determined look he sometimes got, the one that said he was about to insist on me doing something for my own good. "Why don't you head upstairs and take a nice, long bath? Let me take care of things down here."

"Atticus, I'm fine. Really, I can—"

He cut me off with a gentle firmness. "No arguments. Go relax. You've been through a lot."

I gave in. It was pointless to argue with him when he was in this mode.

The bath was soothing, the warmth seeping into my muscles, but my mind couldn't stay still. I kept thinking about the little chest I had taken from his closet on my first day here. The guilt had been eating at me, and it had only gotten worse with everything he had done for me.

After drying off and wrapping myself in a soft robe, I made my way to the guest bedroom where I'd stashed the chest. For a moment, I stood holding it in my hands. I was still curious about what was inside, but never in a million years would I peek. He probably hadn't noticed it was missing—because he hadn't said anything yet—and it occurred to me that I might be able to sneak it back into his closet. But in my heart, I knew I needed to come clean, even if it meant making him mad.

Night Shift

Taking a deep breath, I ran to place the box in the bathroom, then called down to him, "Can you come upstairs? I...I need to talk to you about something important."

Within a few seconds, he bounded up the stairs and entered the room, frowning slightly in concern. "Sam, what's wrong? You sound awfully serious."

Suddenly, I wasn't just nervous; I was terrified of his reaction. "There's something I have to tell you, and you're not going to like it," I started, my words coming out shaky.

He braced himself, his body tensing. "Sam, what is it?"

I walked into the bathroom and returned with the chest, holding it out to him. "I took this the first day I was here. I shouldn't have, and I wanted to tell you before, but the timing never seemed right. Not that you have any reason to believe me, but I swear I haven't opened it. Please don't hate me."

For a moment, he just stared at the chest. Then he looked up at me. Unexpectedly, he chuckled and rolled his eyes. My confusion must have been written all over my face because he calmly sat the chest on the bed and unlocked it with a key he pulled out from the nightstand next to him.

"It's just...I thought you were going to say something much worse based on your tone when you asked me to come up," he said, as he opened the chest to reveal its contents. Inside were photos and keepsakes from his childhood, pieces of a past he rarely spoke of. "I've always found these hard to look at," he admitted. "But now, with you it feels different."

He sat on the edge of the bed and patted the spot next to him, indicating I should join him. After shuffling through the pictures and mementos, he pulled a few out and began to tell me about them.

As he shared the stories behind the photos, the atmosphere seemed to shift. It was almost as though he was working through the memories, finally accepting these parts of his past. He talked about his parents more than he ever had before, telling me about the good times as well as the bad. By showing me these mementos, it was helping him come to grips with a childhood full of trauma he didn't deserve.

"All right," he said, tucking the last photo back into the little chest. "That's enough reminiscing for tonight." He set the chest on the floor, and his eyes darkened as they lingered on me, full of desire. Heat flooded my lower belly when he shifted closer. His lips met mine in a tender kiss that sent fiery tendrils down my spine.

"Let me take care of you," he whispered against my mouth, his strong hands slipping the robe over my shoulders and untying the knot. Licking his lips, he dragged it off my arms and growled. "Well, aren't you making it easy for me to access these beautiful breasts of yours, Samantha?"

He cupped my breasts, grazing my nipples with his thumbs before he laid me down on the bed. Then he trailed his fingers along my curves and began to slide them down, peppering kisses along my hips and the insides of my legs as he went. I could feel the heat of his breath against my skin with each kiss. When he got to my feet, he stood and slowly began removing his clothes. First, he pulled his shirt over his head and tossed it to the side. He shoved his jeans off his hips, and they fell to the floor, releasing his already hard cock.

"Wow, commando, huh?" I giggled, and he joined me on the bed, pushing my shoulders down and placing his hand on the flat of my stomach while his eyes roamed over every inch of me.

"Stay still, beautiful," he instructed, tracing his fingertips in lazy circles over the center of my body as his lips moved up to my mouth. His kisses were slow and sensual, igniting a fire deep within me. Soon, he pulled back and rested on his forearm. I reached over, wanting to touch the purple marks over his ribs, but he stopped me, grasping my wrist firmly and pressing my hand onto the mattress.

"But you're hurt. I don't want—"

"Hush. Tonight, you don't touch me," he rumbled, gliding his hand up my side and across my collarbone before wrapping it around the curve of my throat. His lips moved to my mouth, whispering, "I'm going to worship every inch of you—tenderly, thoroughly, and completely."

My heart raced as Atticus nibbled gentle kisses along that sensitive area at the corner of my jaw. The sensation made me arch my back and release a soft whimper. I craved more of him. I tried to take his face in my hands and return the affection, but he gently took hold of my wrists and placed them on either side of my head, reminding me of his rule for tonight. "You do nothing."

With that, I relinquished control, allowing him to have his way with me.

Atticus continued his exploration, lavishing attention on my breasts as he kissed and nipped at them. He rolled and pinched my nipples between his fingers, making me gasp and squirm beneath him. This man knew exactly the best balance between pleasure and pain, knew how to provoke the best response from my body. Wet heat flooded my core, and I began to pant softly. He lowered one hand, slowly tracing across my belly and hips until his fingers dipped into my slick folds.

"God, you're so wet for me already," he growled. And when his fingers glided over my most sensitive spots, my body melted, yielding to him. I had never been more willing to surrender myself completely to him, this man who, despite the darkness of our past, had managed to bring light into my life.

"Atticus," I breathed out, overwhelmed by the sheer pleasure he was giving me. He smirked, knowing full well what he was doing.

"Trust me, Samantha," he whispered before continuing our intimate entanglement.

I didn't make my usual snarky remark, because this time—I did trust him.

As his fingers continued their ministrations, rolling over my swollen clitoris, I rocked my hips up to meet him, my breath hitching and my mind reeling from the bliss.

"Remember, Samantha," he warned with a devilish grin, noticing the way my hands clutched the sheets at my sides, desperate to reach for him, "don't you dare try to touch me. If you do, I might just have to tie you up."

His words sent a shiver down my spine, but I managed to comply, keeping my hands firmly on the bed. His fingers continued their delicious torment, teasing and tantalizing until I could hardly think straight.

"Atticus, please," I begged, desperate for relief from the escalating tension that was threatening to consume me.

He responded by inserting one finger into my pussy, then a second, before curling them up to find that sensitive spot deep inside me. My body arched off the bed when he hit it, and a rush of warm liquid flooded the edges of my thighs.

He withdrew his glistening fingers from within me, licking and sucking my sweet juices off each digit while keeping his eyes locked on mine the whole time, daring me to look away. "God, you taste so good," he murmured while I watched. The sight was both carnal and enthralling, fueling the fire burning between my legs.

"More, Atticus…please…I need more friction."

Night Shift

Without a word, he shifted, positioning his face between my legs and putting his muscular hands under my ass as he pulled my pussy closer to his eager mouth. I was exposed and completely surrendered to his capable hands. The anticipation was maddening, but what came next was beyond worth it.

His tongue plunged into me, fucking my pussy in a way that made my entire body tremble. He bit and sucked on my clitoris, sending jolts of electricity rocketing through me. My breathing grew heavier with each pass of his tongue, my vision blurring while I fought to hold back my building climax. It took everything I had not to reach out and grab onto him as the sensations threatened to send me over.

"Atticus..." I gasped when I neared the edge of climax. Somehow, though, he knew exactly when to pull back, leaving me teetering on the brink but not allowing me to tumble over just yet.

"Patience, my love," he whispered against my heated skin. "I'm not done with you yet."

He trailed wet kisses up my belly, and I shivered in expectation of what was to come next. His tongue swirled around the edge of my navel before continuing its journey upward, leaving a path of tingling sensations as it went. He paused to lavish attention on my breasts, planting slow, deliberate kisses on them before moving on to my throat.

"Are you ready for more?" he murmured, a teasing smile playing at the corners of his full lips.

"Yes," I whispered.

Careful not to put too much weight on me, Atticus positioned himself over my body. I gasped when he rubbed the head of his cock against my sensitive clitoris, giving me the delicious friction I craved. With one smooth motion, he thrust himself inside of me, filling me completely. My breath hitched as I adjusted to his size, a mixture of pleasure and pain swirling within me.

"Relax, Samantha," he urged, his voice soothing. When I did, he began to move, rocking his hips back and forth rhythmically. He fucked me slowly and deeply, and with each thrust, the fiery tendrils of pleasure climbed up through my core, once again bringing me to the edge.

One of his hands traveled down my body, finally coming to rest over my mound. His thumb grazed the sensitive nub, and my arousal intensified. He quickened the pace of his hips, slamming in and out of me, his thumb expertly circling the swollen bundle of nerves.

"Atticus!" I cried out, his name morphing into a moan.

"Go ahead, my love," he encouraged, his own breathing ragged with desire. "Let go for me."

And obediently, the walls of my pussy clenched tightly around his cock, and I came, wave after wave of blazing rapture washing over me.

"Mmm, Samantha," he groaned. His thrusts grew more erratic, and I could feel him swelling inside me, preparing to fill me. He panted, and with one last thrust, he came hard, flooding me with shot after shot of his hot cum.

For a few minutes, he stayed buried deep inside me, and we lay with our bodies entwined as if they were meant to be connected always.

"You're the most incredible woman I've ever known," he whispered into my ear. "I will worship your body until I breathe my last breath."

He kissed me deeply then, and I tasted myself on his lips—an intoxicating blend of our passion. Catching his breath,

Atticus carefully pulled out of me, leaving a lingering emptiness in his wake.

"Stay right here," he instructed lovingly, and I nodded, too exhausted to protest. "I'll take care of you."

He disappeared into the bathroom, returning moments later with a warm, wet washcloth. Gently, he cleaned my folds and thighs, tenderly removing any traces of our lovemaking. All the while, his eyes never left my most private area. I relaxed into his hands, opening my knees fully and trusting him with all of me.

"Sam, I can't imagine ever spending another day waking up without you," he confessed, his eyes shining with sincerity.

He crawled up beside me on the bed, and we snuggled up together, our bodies intertwined once again. As we lay wrapped up in each other, the world outside faded away. It was just us, and for the first time, I allowed myself to truly believe in the possibility of a future together, one filled with love and understanding, no matter what the past held.

Soon sleep claimed us both.

The next morning, I awoke and stretched languidly, reveling in the familiar ache between my legs. Atticus—who had apparently already risen, showered, and gotten dressed—stood at the bottom of the bed, watching me with a smirk.

"Good morning, sleepyhead. Sleep well?" he asked.

"You have no idea! After that horrible hospital bed, this is like sleeping on clouds."

"I'm glad it pleases you so much, because you need to stay in bed today," he insisted in his doctor's professional voice, as if it were an all-powerful decree.

"Atticus, I'm fine," I argued, rolling my eyes. I sat up and threw off the covers. A grin spread across my face as I watched him try to maintain his stern expression with my nude body on display. "I can handle dinner and holiday celebrations with your brothers."

"Mmm, you rolled your eyes at me," he said with an appraising bounce of his brow and a soft chuckle. "Look, I know you're tough, but you've been through a lot, and brain injuries take time to heal. You know that. Just take today to rest, okay? You'll enjoy the evening better if you do. Doctor's orders."

"Ugh, fine," I conceded, sinking back into the pillow and pulling the covers over me. In truth, spending a lazy day in bed sounded downright heavenly.

After I'd spent a few hours lounging and dozing, my patience wore thin. I decided to get up and make myself presentable. Atticus had invited his brothers over for dinner—not only for a little holiday celebration but also to thank them for helping us through the tumultuous situation with the Volkovi. I luxuriated under the warm spray of the shower, letting the water cleanse away any lingering fatigue. Once I was dried and dressed, I slipped into a cream-colored angora sweater and dark heather leggings, wanting to be comfortable but also a bit festive. I didn't bother with shoes. I relished the cool sensation of the wooden floor beneath my bare feet.

As I descended the stairs, Conan's boisterous laughter floated up from the front door. Rushing down to greet him, I teased, "You'd better keep an eye on that brother of yours. He's turned into quite the mother hen."

Conan laughed heartily again, his emerald eyes twinkling with amusement. Moments later, Braxton joined us, his warm smile lighting up the room. We chatted idly for a while until the brothers suddenly concocted an excuse for me to go fetch an important letter from Atticus's car in the garage. With a puzzled shrug, I headed out, searching for whatever letter they claimed to need.

Night Shift

I rummaged through Atticus's car, wondering what this ruse was really all about.

After searching his entire car, I finally gave up and went back inside empty-handed. When I returned to the living room, Atticus was standing there with his signature smirk, gesturing toward the Christmas tree.

"Your Christmas present is under the tree," he announced.

"Really?" I asked, bouncing on my toes in anticipation. "Can I open it now?"

"Actually," Atticus replied, "it looks like it's opening itself."

Confused, I turned to the tree to find a tiny black-and-white furball lifting the lid off a big red box. My heart leaped, and I rushed over, scooping up the adorable shih tzu puppy from its festive prison. The puppy wriggled enthusiastically in my arms, wagging his fluffy tail furiously. A vibrant red bow was tied around his neck, making him the perfect holiday gift.

"Atticus, he's beautiful! I can't believe you did this. What a sweet little boy!" I cooed, pressing my face against the pup's soft fur, inhaling his puppy scent and embracing his unconditional love.

As I cuddled the pup, I noticed something. There was a glint of metal in the oversized bow tied around the pup's neck. Scrutinizing it a little closer, I found a ring and a key tied to the bow. When I turned back to Atticus, he was down on one knee. Tenderly, he untied the bow and retrieved a stunning princess-cut diamond set in a platinum band.

"Sammich," Atticus began, his voice choked with emotion. "From the moment you ran into me in the break room, I knew there was something special about you. You've shown me what it means to love and be loved. I want nothing more than to protect and cherish you for the rest of our lives. Will you do me the honor of becoming my wife?"

Tears welled up in my eyes as I looked down at the man who had become my rock, my confidant, and my soulmate. Without hesitation, I extended my hand, allowing him to slide the ring onto my finger.

"Of course I will marry you," I whispered, sealing the promise with a passionate, teary-eyed kiss.

Leaning back, I said teasingly, "Atticus, are you sure about this?" I raised an eyebrow as I studied his face. "I didn't think you did relationships."

His mouth opened to respond, but I silenced him with a tender kiss, cupping his face with my hand.

Braxton and Conan burst into the room, popping open a bottle of champagne. The cork flew through the air and hit the ceiling with a loud *thud*.

The puppy yelped in surprise at the sudden noise, causing us all to burst into laughter. I cuddled him closely in my arms, nuzzling my face against his soft fur.

"Wait!" I exclaimed before anyone could make a toast. "What about this key?"

Atticus grinned, his eyes shining with love. He took the key from the bow and held it out to me. "It's the key to our new home. I bought it because I never want you to wonder who else has been with me in the house we share."

He stepped closer, pressing his cheek against mine and speaking softly so only I could hear. "And I promise you, my love, I will have you on every surface and in every way imaginable, because you are mine and I am yours, completely and eternally."

The powerful commitment in his words left me breathless, and my heart swelled with love for the man who had changed my life forever.

Night Shift

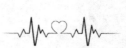

If you're curious to find out about the other Thorin brothers as they battle their own inner demons, look for them in their respective books, "Day Shift" and "Swing Shift," as the "Broken Heroes" stand-alone series continues.

Enjoy the read?
Take a couple of minutes to leave a review!

Reviews are everything to an Indie Author, and we would greatly appreciate it if you would take the time to leave one or click on the star rating. All you need to do is leave a few words.

Thank you!

Books in the Broken Heroes stand-alone series

Night Shift

Day Shift July 31, 2024

Swing Shift (Coming in 2024)

Acknowledgements

Writing this book was a journey, one that we couldn't have imagined taking alone. So, to you, our readers, we want to say a big thank you. Your decision to spend time with our words, to give this story a chance, makes all the difference. We know the world is full of distractions, and the fact that you choose to invest your time with us means more than we can express. It's a road with its ups and downs, and knowing you are there with us makes the tough parts easier and the great parts even better. Your support—whether through a message, a social media like, a recommendation to a friend, or simply by reading—is a source of motivation and encouragement. We wrote this book for you as much as for ourselves, and we're thankful you are part of this adventure.

Emily Cargile, tackling this manuscript with you at the helm has been nothing short of remarkable. Your ability to dive deep into our narrative, untangling and refining our thoughts with such precision, felt as if you were reading our minds. The dedication and professionalism you've shown, especially under the tight deadlines we faced, went far beyond what we could have asked for. Your edits didn't just polish our work; they elevated it, ensuring that every sentence sang with clarity and purpose. It's rare to find someone who commits so wholeheartedly to a project, and even rarer to see that commitment translate into action as effectively as you have managed. For your extraordinary efforts, your insightful feedback, and the late nights you've spent poring over our manuscript, we are ever so grateful. Thank you, Emily, for being more than just an editor to this book. Your touch has left an indelible mark on every page, and for that, we cannot thank you enough.

Jourdan Gandy, from day one, your support for our book has made a real difference. Your professionalism and insight have exceeded every expectation we have had. You've always been ready to share your insights, offering clear, actionable advice that has helped shape our approach every step of the way. Your willingness to dive into our concerns, to offer solutions, and to guide us through decisions both big and small has been nothing short of invaluable. We appreciate your commitment, your patience, and the genuine enthusiasm you've shown for our work. Thank you, Jourdan, for being an integral part of this adventure, for your unwavering support, and for believing in us from day one.

Vanessa Medina, we owe you a huge thank you for everything you've done. From the very beginning, you took the reins of a brand new Instagram account with a level of creativity and organizational skill that was truly exceptional. Your independent approach and in-depth knowledge of what makes content engaging and cohesive had a huge impact on the book's social media presence. It's clear you didn't just manage the account; you breathed life into it, making our book visible in ways we couldn't have imagined and connecting with our audience through genuinely engaging content.

Special dedications:
I would like to thank my mother for teaching me that anything is possible. ~ Love you, Evie

This journey has been an unexpected one, so I must be humble and recognize that I didn't get here on my own. I have everyone to thank who encouraged me to take this leap of faith in writing. I thought the pen to paper would end with my poems or maybe my short stories, but enough people believed in me. Pushed me. Reminded me that I am capable. So because of you, this book is here, and with that, thank you. ~ Craig

About Craig

   With a background rooted in compassion and care, Craig Richards brings a unique blend of empathy and creativity to the world of writing and narrating. Born and raised in the picturesque landscapes of Washington State, Craig embarked on a noble journey as a registered nurse, dedicating years to healing and supporting others through their most vulnerable moments. It was during this period of profound human connection that Craig discovered the power of voice and story.

Encouraged by the soothing and calming quality of their voice, Craig was initially drawn to the art of narrating. It wasn't long before this auditory talent, coupled with a deep-seated passion for storytelling, led to a flourishing career in narration. The transition from healthcare to the arts was further solidified when Craig's talent for weaving words into poetry and short stories came to light, earning them accolades and encouragement to delve deeper into writing.

Craig's journey from the hallways of hospitals to the realm of writing and narrating is underpinned by a lifelong pursuit of education and professional development in Washington State. This journey not only shaped his clinical skills but also honed his ability to empathize, listen, and articulate the human experience, qualities that now breathe life into his written and spoken words.

Today, Craig is a full-time writer and narrator, intertwining the threads of their nursing background with their literary and vocal skills to create works that resonate with warmth, depth, and healing. With each story told and every character brought to life, Craig continues to touch the hearts of audiences, proving that the journey from caring for the body to nourishing the soul is a path worth traversing.

About Evie

Evie James is a music industry business manager turned proud romance writer. She crafts tales of fiery passion and bold encounters, weaving stories where headstrong women meet their matches in equally dominant men. The kind of spicy, contemporary romance that sets the page on fire. James's narratives are soaked with steamy scenes, loaded with angst, and dripping with sass. Each story is a bold adventure, packed with high-stakes drama that keeps readers on the edge.

James believes that the power of love conquers all, and that if her characters can do it, so can we. Diving into her world offers an unfiltered, heart-pounding experience, where readers live every moment from both sides through a dual point of view. She welcomes you to join her on a journey where love wrestles with reality, and every story promises a raw, gritty ride to a happily ever after that'll leave you breathless.

When she's not busy writing her saucy plots, she's most likely got a camera or brush in her hand. She lives with her family, four dogs, and a cantankerous old cat in Nashville, TN.

Made in the USA
Las Vegas, NV
28 July 2024